# BRENDA NOVAK

## Stop Me

MIRA®

**MIRA®**

ISBN-13: 978-0-7783-2460-7
ISBN-10:     0-7783-2460-5

STOP ME

www.MIRABooks.com

**Printed in U.S.A.**

To Lieutenant James Hendrickson (Mr. Incredible)
of the Sacramento Police Department,
who took me to work, gave me the
grand tour and generously answered every
crime-related question I could think of.
It's comforting to know that there are
Super Heroes like you out there on
the front lines.

Dear Reader,

Welcome to The Last Stand, where victims fight back. Jasmine Stratford, the heroine of this novel, is one of three women who began The Last Stand in order to make a difference in the community—but also because she couldn't get over her own brush with evil. What happened sixteen years ago drives her to fight for every lost child, every kidnap victim, every missing person. With each new case, she's trying to "bring her sister home," hoping to achieve the closure she's never had. But when a new development in her sister's case takes her to Cajun Louisiana and a dark hero intent on nursing his own wounds, her own life hangs in the balance.

In the first book of this series (*Trust Me,* which came out in June), you met Skye Kellerman. She's still involved in The Last Stand, still fighting for the rights of the victims of violent crime. So is Jasmine's other partner, Sheridan Kohl. You'll learn more about Sheridan in *Watch Me,* which comes out in August.

Please visit www.brendanovak.com, where you can take a virtual tour of the offices of The Last Stand, read a prologue that doesn't appear anywhere else, download a free screen saver for signing up on my mailing list, read interesting interviews with police and other crime fighters in my Crimebeat blog, browse through merchandise with the "The Last Stand: Where Victims Fight Back" logo, enter my monthly draws for mystery boxes and other prizes and check out the items in my May 2009 Online Auction for Diabetes Research. The diabetes auction is my own passion, my own effort to give back. Together with my fans, author friends and publishing contacts, I've raised over $350,000 to help those, like my son, who struggle with this disease.

I love to hear from my readers, so feel free to e-mail me via my Web site. For those who don't have e-mail access, please write to P.O. Box 3781, Citrus Heights, CA 95611.

Be smart and stay safe!

Brenda Novak

# Prologue

*New Orleans*
*Four years ago...*

The man who'd murdered Romain Fornier's ten-year-old daughter didn't look like a killer. He sat slumped in the courtroom with puffy bags beneath his eyes, a halo of mousy brown hair circling his otherwise bald head and jowls that hung lower than his chin. There were moments when even Romain couldn't believe frumpy, middle-aged Francis Moreau had done something so vicious, moments when he glanced back over the days and weeks since Adele's abduction and felt as if he was living someone else's life.

The way the case had been going this morning, Romain had a feeling the nightmare was about to get worse.

The judge pounded his gavel, bringing the noise in the courtroom to an abrupt halt. It grew so quiet Romain could hear the defense counsel shuffling his papers.

"The law is very precise on this matter," the judge announced. "The police may have obtained verbal approval from the proper authority, but they didn't get the affidavit signed until *after* their search of the defendant's home, which means the evidence found in that search is not admissible in court."

Romain heard the gasps of his family. His parents sat on one side of him, his sister on the other. *Without that evidence, we don't have a case.* The D.A. had said that over and over.

Romain leaned forward to whisper to Detective Huff, who sat a row in front of him. "Is this as bad as it seems?"

"Don't worry," Huff whispered back. But his voice sounded odd, almost strangled, and his expression didn't promote much confidence. When a witness for the defense revealed that Huff had searched Moreau's house without the correct paperwork, Huff's face had flushed crimson. It was still crimson and several beads of sweat had popped out on his forehead.

Although he felt desperate to make sense of what was happening, Romain was nonetheless distracted when the prosecutor asked to approach the bench. The judge waved both him and the defense counsel forward. They kept their conversation muted, but the way the D.A. gesticulated with his hands suggested he was in the middle of a heated argument.

This case *couldn't* get away from them now, not when there was no doubt they had the right man, Romain told himself. But the D.A. didn't seem happy when he finally returned to his table. Before sitting down, he searched the crowd, singling out Huff, whom he gave a look of such contempt Romain could hardly breathe.

"They're going to let him off," Romain said to no one in particular. His sister sat like a statue; his mother was crying, his father trying to comfort her. "He's going to get off!" he repeated, and this time he gripped Huff by the shoulder to guarantee a response.

Huff twisted around to face him. A fan hummed in the corner. The air-conditioning had been out for two days and the weather had turned unseasonably warm for October. "He did it, Romain," he said, mopping his forehead with a handkerchief. "I saw the tape."

Romain had seen part of the tape, too—as much as he could bear to watch. Which was why he couldn't understand this. How could the technicalities involved in serving a search warrant take precedence over a child's life? *His* child's life?

"They can't let him walk," Romain said. But the judge pounded his gavel, curtly announced that the D.A. was dropping all charges and exited the courtroom.

Stunned, Romain stood with his mouth agape as Moreau's watery blue eyes cut to him and a victorious smile curved his lips. The sight of it made everything around Romain go black. For a few seconds, there were only the two of them, staring across the courtroom at each other.

"It's the detective's fault?" his mother was asking. "Why didn't he get the affidavit signed before he searched?"

"Moreau knew the police had been tipped off. He would've destroyed the evidence if Detective Huff had waited," his father said.

Huff must've heard them, but he kept facing forward. He was staring at Moreau, too, whose attention and "you lose" smile had shifted to the detective. Then the defense attorneys started shaking Moreau's hand, congratulating him.

The crowd surged toward the door. Romain's sister pulled on his arm, trying to get him to follow her. But he was rooted to the spot. The judge and the lawyers had to come back. This wasn't over. It *couldn't* be over. Moreau was a *killer*. He'd murdered a child. Romain's child. And he'd do it again.

Romain wasn't sure how he eventually got out of the courtroom. He didn't remember making the decision to leave, walking toward the exit or passing through to the outside. He only remembered seeing the detective remove his jacket and swing it over his arm as they descended the steps—and sensing the presence of Huff's gun in its holster as they moved side by side, jostled by the crowd and attacked by the media, who waited like a pack of wolves.

"Mr. Fornier, what do you have to say about seeing the man who allegedly killed your daughter go free?"

"Mr. Fornier! Mr. Fornier! Do you still believe Francis Moreau murdered Adele?"

"Can you tell me if you'll pursue this in a civil proceeding?"

As one reporter after another shoved a microphone into Romain's face, he saw Moreau a few feet away, pandering to the cameras—and suddenly craved the feel of a gun in his hand more than his next breath. He was an excellent marksman. At this distance, he'd scarcely have to aim. One pull of the trigger and he could fix the terrible mistake that had just been made.

And the next thing Romain knew, he heard a blast, Moreau fell to the ground and Detective Huff began forcing him to the hot, gritty concrete.

# 1

*Sacramento, California*
*The present…*

When Jasmine Stratford opened the package, she was standing in the middle of a crowded mall. Suddenly she couldn't hear a single sound. The laughing, the talking, the click-clack of shoes on the colorful floor, the Christmas music that'd been playing in the background—it all disappeared as her ears began to ring.

"What is it?" Sheridan Kohl touched her arm, eyebrows gathered in concern.

The words came to Jasmine as if from a great distance, but she couldn't speak. Her lungs worked frantically, but her chest felt so tight she couldn't expand her diaphragm. Sweat trickled down her spine, causing her crisp cotton blouse to stick to her as she stared at the silver-and-pink bracelet she'd just pulled from the small cardboard box.

"What is it, Jaz?" Still frowning, her friend took the bracelet from Jasmine's cold fingers. As she read the name spelled out in silver letters separated by pink beads, her eyes filled with tears. "Oh, God!" she murmured, pressing a hand to her chest.

Jasmine's head spun. Afraid she might pass out, she reached for Sheridan, who helped her to the center of the mall and asked a man sitting in one of the few seats to move.

He collected the shopping bags piled at his feet and jumped up, allowing Jasmine to sink onto the hard plastic chair.

"Hey, she no looking good, eh? She sick or somet'ing?" he asked.

"She's just suffered a terrible shock," Sheridan explained.

The words floated over Jasmine as if they'd been written in the air, each letter flying past her, meaningless. Her nervous system seemed to be shutting down. Overload. Rejection of current input. Inability to cope.

"Don't move," Sheridan barked and put the bracelet back in the box on her lap. "I'll get you something to drink."

Jasmine couldn't have moved even if she wanted to. Her rubbery legs refused to support her weight, or she would've walked out of the mall. People were beginning to stare.

"What's wrong?" someone murmured, pausing near the Mexican man who was still watching her curiously.

"I don't know, but she no look good, eh?" he repeated.

A teenage boy ventured closer. "Are you okay, lady?"

"Maybe someone should call the paramedics," a woman said.

*Wave them away.* But Jasmine's thoughts were so focused on what was in her lap, she couldn't even raise her hand. She'd made that bracelet as a gift for her little sister. She remembered Kimberly's delight when she'd unwrapped it on her eighth birthday, her last birthday before the tall man with the beard entered their house in Cleveland one sunny afternoon and took her away.

Jasmine's mind veered from the memories. Until she was twelve, she'd led such a safe and happy life she'd never dreamed she would encounter a threat in her own home. Strangers were people outside on the street. This man had acted like one of her father's workers, whose faces changed so often she wasn't familiar with them all. They were always coming to the house to pick up equipment for his satellite TV business, to get a check, to drop off some paperwork. Occasionally he hired vagrants to organize his warehouse or build a fence or even clean up the yard. In any event, she'd believed their visitor was a nice guy.

Heaven help her, she'd believed he was *nice*. And she'd let it happen….

"You want I should call an ambulance?" the Mexican man ventured.

Jasmine had to cover her mouth so the screams inside her didn't escape. *Breathe deeply. Get hold of yourself.* After nearly destroying each other with their bitterness and grief, her parents had given up hope. But she'd kept a candle burning deep inside. And now this…

Sheridan returned and nudged her way through the four or five people who were watching to see if Jasmine would rally. "I've got her. Everything's fine," she told them, and they began to drift off, but not without a backward glance. "Drink this," she said.

The freshly squeezed lemonade tasted reassuringly normal.

A man seated next to them stood and offered Sheridan his chair. She thanked him and perched on the edge of it.

After a few minutes, Jasmine's breathing and heart rate slowed. Still, she was damp with sweat and when she tried to talk tears slipped down her cheeks.

"It's okay." Putting an arm around her, Sheridan squeezed her shoulders. "Take all the time you need."

Jasmine appreciated her friend's empathy, but now that the shock was wearing off she had so many questions. *Who had sent the bracelet?* Why after so long? What'd happened to her sister? And the biggest question of all—was there *any* chance that Kimberly was still alive?

"I'm so sorry I brought that package with me, that you had to deal with this in a public setting." Sheridan's expression revealed her chagrin. "When I saw it sitting on the reception desk with the rest of the mail, I thought it might be something you've been waiting for. I knew you weren't planning on coming into the office today so I was…" she shrugged helplessly "…trying to be helpful."

Jasmine wiped her eyes. "It's okay. Of course you'd never expect anything like this."

"Who sent it?"

"I don't know." She studied the box. There was no return address. There wasn't even a note, just some crumpled packaging material—

Jasmine's pulse spiked. *Wait a minute…* There was something written on one of the papers that'd been wadded up.

Careful not to tear the note or get her fingerprints all over it, she flattened it out—and saw two words printed in what appeared to be blood: *Stop me.*

That night, Jasmine hovered over the phone. Should she tell her parents about the bracelet? She couldn't decide. According to the cancellation stamp, the package had been sent from New Orleans, but she didn't know if she'd ever be able to glean more information than that. She was reluctant to open old wounds—and yet, her folks had a right to the information, didn't they? Would they *want* to know?

She picked up the handset. Her father would. After the bearded man took Kimberly, Peter Stratford had become so single-minded in his quest to find his youngest daughter that he'd eventually lost everything—his business, his wife, his home. He'd searched until he'd nearly driven himself mad. Searched until everyone else in his life, including Jasmine, had become nothing more than shadows. Even then he'd given up only because he had no choice. There was nowhere else to go, nothing more he could do.

Now that Peter had moved on, he was doing better than he had in years. Would learning about Kimberly's bracelet send him into another tailspin?

Jasmine set the phone down again. It probably wasn't wise to take the chance.

And then there was her East Indian mother. Gauri was so full of bitterness and blame, toward Peter *and* Jasmine, she had difficulty being in the same room with either of them.

The phone rang. Nervous that it might be one of her parents—that she'd be confronted with a situation she hadn't figured out how to handle—she checked caller ID, then breathed a sigh of relief. It was her friend and coworker, Skye Kellerman. Actually, Skye Willis since her marriage last year.

Dropping into a seat at the kitchen table, Jasmine rubbed her fingers over her left eyebrow as she answered. "Hello?"

"I just got your message. And several from Sheridan, too." Skye's voice came across as brisk, worried. "I'm sorry it took me a few hours to get back to you. David and I were in Tahoe and didn't have phone reception."

"It's fine," Jasmine said.

"It's not fine. Are you okay?"

Jasmine wasn't sure. One minute she was filled with re-kindled hope, the next terrified that nothing could change the outcome of her sister's abduction. "I'm okay," she said, although her mind added a little "not."

"This is so…unexpected," Skye exclaimed. "Why now? Why after so many years?"

Jasmine had asked herself the same question. But it hadn't taken long to come up with the most probable answer. "It must be because of the publicity on the Polinaro case." Four weeks ago, she'd been on *America's Most Wanted,* profiling a sex offender who'd victimized nine boys. When authorities got too close, he fled. She'd been invited on the show to suggest places he might have gone, things he might be doing.

"Of course," Skye agreed. "That episode aired right before Thanksgiving."

"How else would he have known where to find me?" After her mother had remarried and left Cleveland, where Jasmine was born, Jasmine had dropped out of high school and moved away from home, starting a three-year descent into drug abuse and self-destruction. During that time, she'd drifted from one city to another, working odd jobs, even begging in the streets for enough money for one more fix. She doubted anyone could've tracked her movements back then. Her parents certainly hadn't been aware, much of the time, of where she was or what she was doing. It wasn't until Harvey Nolasco, a long-distance trucker, picked her up and insisted she get some help that she settled down. And then she'd married a white man, like her mother, and became Jasmine Nolasco for a short while.

"I'm pretty sure they posted our address at the charity," Skye said.

"They did." When dealing with the media, Jasmine always mentioned her affiliation with The Last Stand. TLS relied exclusively on donations to keep its doors open. She couldn't miss the chance to raise public awareness and support, and it'd proved to be a good move. Since the episode had aired, they'd received thousands of dollars—and more requests for help than ever before.

"The package came to the office, right?" Skye clarified.

"Sher found it with the other mail and brought it with her when we met for lunch."

"Have you had anyone inspect that note?"

"We took it directly to the police."

"And?"

"They confirmed it was written in b-blood." She stumbled over the last word because picturing the large square letters on that note sent a chill up her spine.

"Do you think it could be Kimberly's?" Skye said.

"Even if she's dead, I suppose it could've been frozen."

"But you're guessing? You don't have any psychic perception about this?"

"None. I'm too close to it." Her impressions came and went at random, anyway. Although her abilities had helped in a few heavily publicized cases, sometimes even *she* didn't know if she could trust the brief visions that occasionally intruded into normal thought.

"There's still the potential for profiling, isn't there?"

Jasmine had a GED and barely thirty credit hours of college, all of which she'd obtained in the two years she'd been married to Harvey, but she read just about everything she could find on deviant behavior and psychological profiling and had become so proficient at it that the FBI occasionally called her in as a consultant. Some people assumed it was her psychic ability that made her so good, but she knew it was primarily an instinctive understanding of human nature and the knowledge she'd gained through self-education that guided her, because she could do it even when she had no discernible psychic response.

"Yes. This is more about the shock." Half standing in order to reach it, Jasmine pulled the box across the table. The note was on top of the fridge, where it wasn't likely to get damaged, and the bracelet was in her jewelry box because she couldn't bear to look at it. "He's letting me know he's the one who took Kimberly," she said, her finger running over the deep grooves created by the ballpoint pen he'd used to address it. "Without the note, the bracelet could conceivably have come from someone peripherally connected to the abduction. Maybe someone who knows the kidnapper and what he did—a friend, relative or wife who wants to do the right thing but doesn't dare come forward for fear of reprisal. And…" she hesitated, trying to get a feel for the type of person who'd do something like this "…the blood is to upset me, to let me know he's serious."

"About what?" Skye asked.

"About stopping him."

"That makes it sound like he's playing games."

"It's not a game; it's a challenge. He doesn't have the guts or the willpower to turn himself in. But he knows he needs to be stopped." *The Last Stand* was more deeply imprinted in the cardboard than the other words. As her fingers moved over the letters, the impressions Jasmine had thought weren't there, or were repressed because of her closeness to the victim, suddenly began to flow. She could see the man with the beard—a face she'd long forgotten and despaired of ever describing accurately enough so police could track him down. Although still partially hidden in shadow, as if he stood beneath the shaded eaves of a house, the image took her breath away. "He's a killer."

"You're sure?"

She could sense the bloodlust. "Positive."

"Does he feel guilty about that?"

Jasmine was tempted to lift her fingers from the words he'd written, to break the gossamer thread of energy that'd sparked the foreign thoughts and feelings swirling through her. It was frightening, uncharted territory for someone who tolerated, rather than embraced, her psychic gifts. But she couldn't. She knew this might be her only chance to learn something about this man that would give him away. "Not guilt. That would take empathy." Closing her eyes, she experienced *his* confusion, *his* desire to be like everyone else. "It's not a cry to ease the pain he's inflicting on others. It's a cry to stop the pain he's feeling himself. It's all about him. He kills to stop the pain."

"What does he get out of hurting others?"

"A power high. He craves…" The answers were coming, but they were so dark, so frightening, Jasmine's mind balked. She pulled her hands away and went blank.

"Attention?" Skye finished.

"That and recognition, for starters." Jasmine stared at the box. He'd felt closer than he'd been in the sixteen years since he'd stood in her living room, talking to Kimberly. Too close. It made her queasy, but she retraced the individual letters he'd written, forcing her subconscious to go where it refused. For Kimberly.

"So you think there are others?" Skye asked.

The scraggly beard. The bottle-green eyes. The bladelike nose. The baggy, dirty clothes…

"Jasmine?" Skye prompted when she didn't answer.

It was no use. The vision was gone, leaving her with only the memory of it. "What?" she said.

"Do you think he's kidnapped other children?"

Covering her eyes with a shaky hand, Jasmine took a deep breath. "Don't you?"

"Killers don't kill everyone they meet. It could be that he's held Kimberly captive all these years and not taken anyone else. Maybe he wanted a daughter, someone to love him unconditionally, and she filled that need."

Gooseflesh rose on Jasmine's arms. "It had nothing to do with love." And he wasn't satisfied, probably could never be satisfied, or why would he need her or anyone else to stop him?

"He might've let her go at some point," Skye reasoned. "But that doesn't mean she would've come home."

"Of course it doesn't. She was eight when she went missing," Jasmine said. "Abducted children often begin to feel an attachment to their abductor, to relate and adjust and go on living as if they never had another life."

"Maybe he kept her with him until she grew up and now she's out there…somewhere."

*A version of her former self but not the same person,* Jasmine nearly added, but she couldn't say that aloud. If she ever had the good fortune to find her sister, that was something she'd think about when and if the time came.

"Are you going to order a DNA test to see if the blood on that note is similar to yours?" Skye asked.

"Of course. I'll use the private lab in L.A. that did so well with the evidence in the Wrigley case." She'd also have a fingerprint specialist search for latent prints. She doubted they'd get anything from the cardboard box. Too many people had touched it in the process of mailing. And, after three or four days in transit, any prints the sender might've left would've soaked in too much to be recovered even with chemicals. The tape or the paper itself might give them more....

"Why not let the police handle it via their own lab? You were living in Cleveland when Kimberly was taken. Doesn't that give them jurisdiction?"

"I don't want to turn what I have over to them."

"Why not?"

"Because the detective who was in charge of the initial investigation is still on the force." Jasmine stood and went to the window, where she gazed out at the parking lot two stories below. Old trucks, economy cars and an occasional SUV sat beneath the heavy floodlights attached to the building. Her condo wasn't located in one of the more affluent suburbs of Sacramento. She, Skye and Sheridan took only as much from the charity as they needed to survive, which didn't allow for an expensive home. But it wasn't one of the worst neighborhoods, either. She felt safe here, or as safe as she could feel, considering that her work involved opposing so many dangerous people.

"How do you know?"

"I checked earlier today."

"You don't think he's capable of handling the investigation?"

"My father almost cost the man his job over that ruined tire track evidence." Ripping a paper towel from the holder at her elbow, Jasmine dabbed at the perspiration that'd broken out on her forehead. "I don't think he'll want to reopen the case."

"Maybe you could talk his captain into assigning it to someone else."

"No, Captain Jones stood by his detective the last time. I'm sure he'll do it again. And I refuse to work with Castillo." Jasmine couldn't abide the thought of relinquishing key evidence to someone she didn't consider competent. It wasn't as if the Cleveland police would be open and forthcoming with her. They knew her father's reputation, the trouble he'd caused. Besides, after working in several capacities on numerous criminal investigations, she felt she was better equipped to do justice by her sister than anyone else. She was more motivated to resolve the kidnapping than an outsider could ever be.

"What about a private investigator? What about getting Jonathan involved? You know how good he is."

"I'll handle this one myself."

"How?"

"I'm going to Louisiana."

These words were met with shocked silence. Then Skye said, "But all you have to go on is a cancellation stamp!"

No, she had more than that. She had his image in her mind, the one she'd conjured out of nowhere when she touched the package. She'd meet with a sketch artist, start circulating a flyer, promise a reward—anything she had to do. Maybe once the shock wore off and she was stronger, she could even plumb the chilling connection she'd felt so briefly.

That strange vision had convinced her of one thing. The man with the beard knew she could stop him. And that was exactly what she intended to do.

Even if it was too late for Kimberly.

# 2

Jasmine had never been to Louisiana. She'd donated money to the recovery effort after Hurricane Katrina and felt terrible about the damage that remained, but only in a general sense. She couldn't mourn specific losses like someone who'd been familiar with the area as it was before. It was too dark outside to see much, anyway.

She sat in the backseat of the taxi she'd hired to shuttle her from the airport to the hotel, fidgeting with her purse and wondering if she'd been crazy to come here. She knew next to nothing about New Orleans, had no contacts in this part of the country. How would she ever find the man she was looking for?

A steady pounding behind her eyes warned of an escalating headache. The plane had been cramped and overheated and the flight had cost her a full day, dumping her halfway across the country after dinnertime. While in the air, she'd been offered only a drink and a small bag of peanuts. She was famished and exhausted. She'd been up all night carefully packaging the box, bracelet and note, and making travel plans that included a stop in Los Angeles so she could hand-deliver those items to the lab, but she hadn't been able to sleep on the long flight. Far too restless, she'd kept going over the day Kimberly had gone missing, hoping to remember something new or different that might help her now.

As if she hadn't done it a million times during the past sixteen years, she replayed those few moments yet again, resting her head on the back of the seat.

Jasmine hadn't heard the knock. She'd been lying on the floor in the living room when a man's slightly scratchy voice overrode the sound of her TV show. Kimberly was talking to him. The comfortable, almost familiar way he behaved signaled that this was just another of her father's workers or soon-to-be workers, so Jasmine hadn't bothered to move.

*Where's your daddy?*

*At work.*

*When will he be back?*

*Not till later. Do you want me to call him?*

*No, I can call him from the car.*

The fact that he'd acted as though he knew her father, as though he had Peter's phone number, had fit with day-to-day life in the Stratford household, so Jasmine had thought nothing of it. But it'd played a major role in the subsequent investigation. Her parents believed Peter had met the man somewhere, that he'd invited him into their sphere of existence. That was part of the reason her mother blamed her father so much. Prior to the incident, Gauri had often complained about so many people coming to the house, but Peter had always teased her out of her concern by calling her Chicken Little. He'd swing her around the kitchen, saying, "The sky is falling, the sky is falling," in a high-pitched voice as he laughed.

And then the sky fell....

Refusing to get caught up in unhappy memories of the arguments that occasionally bordered on violence, and the tears that followed, Jasmine directed her thoughts back to the bearded man at the door, speaking to Kimberly.

*How old are you?*

*Eight.*

*You're sure a pretty little girl.*

Jealousy had momentarily flared inside Jasmine at the compliment. She wanted to be told she was pretty, too. Although their father was Caucasian, their mother was from India and both sisters had her thick black hair and golden-brown skin. But Jasmine had wide almond-shaped eyes, which were so startlingly blue that she normally attracted more attention than her younger sister. She would've gotten up to bask in the praise Kimberly was receiving, but Kevin Arnold was about to have his first kiss with Winnie in *The Wonder Years,* and she couldn't pull herself away.

*I can do a cartwheel. Want to watch?* Her sister's voice carried in from the entry hall.

"Not in the house," Jasmine had yelled, and that was when the man leaned around the corner to take a look at her, and she'd seen his face.

*You're babysitting?*

*Yep.*

Kimberly had peered into the room, too, but only long enough to stick out her tongue. "She's being *so* bossy," she said. Then she told the man she'd show him her cartwheel on the lawn, and they'd gone out. Pleased that she'd done her duty by making sure her sister didn't kick over a lamp, Jasmine soon forgot all about the interruption and simply enjoyed the rest of her show. But when the episode ended, the front door was still standing open and Kimberly was nowhere to be seen. Neither was the man.

Jasmine knew that even if she lived to be a hundred, she'd never forget having to call her parents to tell them her little sister had gone missing.

On her watch.

"Your hotel is on St. Philip Street?" The taxi driver seemed to find that odd.

Jasmine met his eyes, with their caterpillar-like brows, in the rearview mirror. "That's what it said on the Web site."

"And the name is Maison du Soleil?"

His accent was French, but not the kind of formal French Jasmine had heard on television. His *r*'s weren't spoken in his throat; they were rolled. "That's right."

"Not Maison Dupuy on Bourbon Street."

"No."

Those bushy eyebrows met. "I have never heard of this hotel, but I am fairly new to the city. Are you certain of the address, my friend?"

"I'm positive."

His gaze moved back to the road. "*Mais* we will find it then. No problem. No worries."

No problem? Was *he* certain? Jasmine knew she hadn't reserved a luxurious room. She didn't know how long she'd be in town, and she had to be careful about the expenses she incurred. Her credit cards would bear only so much. But now she was afraid she might end up in a broom closet. The Internet hadn't shown any pictures of the hotel itself, just the interior of a room. It was the location—"right in the heart of New Orleans where the city began"—and the reasonable price that had convinced her to stay there. She'd figured it couldn't be too bad if it was in the Quarter.

Another Web site had warned her not to stay in the *Vieux Carré* unless she could tolerate the noise of constant revelry, but that strange feeling, that creepy sense of being inside the skin of whoever had written that note, spooked her so much she wanted to be around people. If she could open her window late at night, hear jazz playing in the street and see a crowd laughing, talking and enjoying the holiday season, she thought she'd feel safer.

"Will you be staying through Christmas?" the driver asked, his tone more conversational.

Christmas was just six days away. Could she accomplish what she needed to do in time to return to California? She doubted it. But maybe that was for the best. She usually spent the major holidays with Skye. Sheridan had family in Wyoming and often went home for Thanksgiving, Christmas and Easter. Skye's only living family was a stepfather and two stepsisters, all of whom lived in L.A., which generally left her available. Until this year. Now she was married and had a family of her own, and Jasmine didn't want to interfere with their first Christmas.

Which left her as alone in Sacramento as she'd be in New Orleans. "I'm staying through New Year's."

"Not *Mardi Gras?*"

"When does it start?"

"In February. I cannot say exactly when. It is always a different day, you know? On Fat Tuesday." He said "Tuesday" like "Chooseday." "Forty-six days before Easter," he clarified.

She certainly hoped she wouldn't be in New Orleans until February. "Probably not," she said.

"Are you here on business *peut-être?*"

The question momentarily threw Jasmine. She was in

town on a personal matter—as personal as a matter could get. And yet the work she'd be doing would be no different from the investigations she spearheaded while trying to help other victims of violent crime. Maybe it'd be easier if she considered the investigation that lay ahead in a more professional manner. Maybe that would counteract the disquiet that hugged her like a sweater.

"Yes," she murmured.

"You must be a very busy lady to travel on business over Christmas."

"Some things can't wait." This was one of them. She planned to do all the research she could while waiting for the lab results—build this case from square one, like she would any case.

But as they turned into the French Quarter, she realized again just how foreign New Orleans was to her. The city had a distinctly European feel, one she would've loved had she been on vacation. As it was, the narrow streets, wrought-iron balconies and center courtyards, more reminiscent of Spanish influence than French, made her feel out of place. And the crowds and clichéd but famous *Laissez les bon temps rouler* atmosphere of the many bars, jazz clubs, hotels, restaurants, "gentlemen's clubs" and boutiques contrasted a little *too* sharply with her purpose and mood.

"What is the address of your hotel, madam?"

The driver turned on the cabin light as Jasmine fished the receipt she'd printed out on the computer at home from her purse and rattled it off.

"That should be *ici*," he said, pointing out the window.

They both stared at the front of a bar named The Moody Blues. Painted completely in purple, it had a throng of revelers, an abundance of Christmas lights and a lot of loud music, which sounded more like rock than jazz.

Putting the taxi in Park, the driver got out and went in to speak to the bartender. When he came back, his squat legs carried him with a quicker gait, and he swept his arm out for her to exit as he opened the door. "You can get down." He gave her a slight bow. "This is it."

"This is…what?" she asked in confusion.

"The hotel. It is above the bar." He stopped on his way to the trunk and motioned toward the entrance. "Once inside, you will see. Turn to your right and go up the stairs."

No wonder there hadn't been any pictures of the hotel posted online….

Swallowing a sigh, Jasmine paid him and stepped into the damp, fifty-something weather to accept her bags. He hesitated as if he was tempted to carry them up for her, but she could tell he was reluctant to leave his cab. "I've got it," she said.

Wishing her a pleasant stay in town, he drove off, leaving her to thread her way through the crush of bodies partying in the bar to the bead-covered entrance of a narrow staircase that led, according to a glittery sign posted above, to the Maison du Soleil.

When Jasmine woke up, she was fully clothed and lying on the covers of her narrow bed. The dim lightbulb hanging from the ceiling was still on; the psychology journal she'd been reading had fallen to the floor. She wasn't sure how late it was. It was still dark outside but the music that'd drifted through the floorboards when she first arrived had stopped and she could no longer hear the television of the guest next to her. She would've opened the window to see what was going on down in the street, except the only window in the room was part of the door leading to the fire escape, which overlooked the redbrick wall of the adjacent building.

So much for location…

Blinking to clear her vision, she checked her watch and worked out the two-hour time change. It was five-thirty in the morning. She didn't know what had awakened her but she had vague memories of disquieting dreams, the kind of nightmares that'd plagued her as a girl after Kimberly's disappearance. There were many different versions, but mostly she dreamed that her sister was crying out to her as she was being pulled into a large dark room. When Jasmine followed, the room always changed into a labyrinth of corridors. Her sister seemed to be right around the next corner and yet Jasmine could never reach her. She usually woke up drenched in sweat, and this morning was no exception. But she was pretty sure that was partially due to the wall heater she'd cranked up before lying down. It had to be close to eighty degrees.

Feeling rumpled and more exhausted than before she'd fallen asleep, she got up, switched off the rattling heater and stumbled toward the shower. Afterward she'd go downstairs to speak with the manager. Before reserving her room, she'd called to make sure the hotel had Internet service. She had to retrieve her e-mail and, depending on what she found in New Orleans, would need access to the usual search engines. But she hadn't been able to connect when she got in last night.

The shower consisted of a small cubicle with barely enough room to turn around, but it was clean and the water pumped out forcefully enough to massage the stiff muscles in her shoulders and back. She supposed it was the quality of the shower that convinced her not to hunt for a better hotel—the shower and the fact that it seemed pointless to waste the time. She had too many other things to worry about.

Feeling almost human after she'd dressed, she grabbed her hotel key and took the rickety elevator down to the second floor. She found a slight young woman at the front desk and asked for the manager.

"Mr. Cabanis owns the hotel and the bar. He should be downstairs." Because she was dressed in gothic black and looked barely nineteen, Jasmine got the impression she was somehow related to Cabanis, possibly his daughter.

"Thank you." Jasmine descended the final flight of stairs to ground level, where a wiry, energetic man with dark hair was restocking the beverage glasses in The Moody Blues.

"Mr. Cabanis?"

His eyes flicked her way, but his hands continued to transfer glasses in a smooth, well-practiced motion. "Yes?" Thanks to his muscular forearms, which were covered in tattoos, he reminded her of Popeye.

"I'm one of your hotel guests. I called before I left home to confirm that you have Internet service, but I haven't been able to connect."

"It's not in the rooms yet." News played on the television bolted to the ceiling in the corner. He glanced at it every now and then as if he resented being interrupted during his morning ritual. "We just opened the hotel and are still making improvements. This building used to be apartments," he added.

Somehow that came as no surprise. "So how do I gain access to the Internet? Can I move to a different room or something?"

The television showed highlights of the latest Hornets game. "The ten rooms that are finished are full. For now, Internet is only available in the lobby, anyway."

"That isn't what I was told over the phone."

He finally gave her his full attention. "Someone told you we have Internet service in the rooms?"

She couldn't exactly make that claim. She'd said, "Do you have Internet service?" and the person on the other end had said, "Yes." It wasn't a lie, but it would've helped had that person expanded on his answer.

"Maybe not. So, can I use what you've got in the lobby?"

"Of course. There's a dedicated line opposite the reception desk. Just plug in and away you go."

She imagined herself trying to concentrate amid the activity she'd witnessed last night—and the noise that rumbled through the whole place—and decided she'd get on the Internet in the early morning. "Thank you." She started toward the stairs, then hesitated. "Do you watch the news every morning?" she asked, turning back.

"For the most part." He'd finished the first rack of glasses and was halfway through the second.

"I was wondering if you've heard any reports recently about young girls being abducted."

This got his attention. "Why do you want to know?"

"Someone took my sister a long time ago. I think he might've moved here, that he's still active."

He pursed his lips as he thought it over. Most kidnappings ended within twenty-four hours so they rarely hit the news. But there were instances where the child couldn't be located—or was found dead.

"Nothing that I can remember," he said at length. "Not

since the uproar over the Fornier girl, which was…what…
four years ago? It was definitely before the hurricane."

"The Fornier girl?"

"You didn't hear about that?"

"I'm from California. If it made the national news, it
doesn't sound familiar."

"A pervert named Moreau kidnapped her while she was
riding her bike. She was only ten."

According to estimates provided by the U.S. Department
of Justice, 354,100 children were abducted by a family
member each year. Strangers, or nonfamily members, attempted to abduct another 114,600 children but were successful in kidnapping only 3,200 to 4,600. Of those cases, 100
ended in murder. Jasmine could've recited the statistics in her
sleep. Most victims of nonfamily abductions were average
children leading normal lives. Seventy-six percent were girls,
with a median age slightly over eleven. In eight percent of the
cases, initial contact occurred within a quarter mile of the
victim's home, and in the majority of cases—nearly sixty
percent—the abduction was a matter of opportunity. But
Jasmine knew that anyone out there looking for an opportunity would eventually find it.

In any event, it sounded as if this little girl fit the profile.
"Was she ever found?"

"Not before Moreau killed her."

Almost half the victims abducted by a stranger were
murdered. Of those, the vast majority—seventy-four percent—were dead within three hours. Considering the fact
that most parents or caregivers spent two hours searching
before notifying police, authorities typically didn't have
much chance of saving the child. "How sad."

He grimaced. "You don't want to know what he did to that little girl."

No, she didn't. She could guess easily enough. "The primary motivation in any child-abduction murder is generally sexual assault."

"Yeah, well, he did that and more." Mr. Cabanis straightened. "He'd still be out there, victimizing other children, if it wasn't for Adele Fornier's father."

*Adele.* That personalized the story too much for Jasmine. She pushed the name away, refused to connect emotionally with the poor victim, choosing to focus instead on other, more positive aspects of the story. Like the father's success. Jasmine had become invisible because of her own father's complete absorption. At least in this case, Mr. Fornier's dedication seemed to have made a difference. "What did the little girl's father do?"

"Helped hunt him down. My own daughter was fourteen at the time, so I followed the story pretty closely."

"Moreau's in prison, then?"

"Nope. Got off on a technicality." With a sigh, the hotel owner shook his head. "Damnedest thing you ever heard of."

Even if Jasmine found whoever had sent her sister's bracelet, she'd face other challenges. If the prosecutors didn't build a solid case, if they made a single misstep, Kimberly's kidnapper could walk, just as Adele's had. It was one of those harsh realities that often burned out the sympathetic souls who gravitated to her line of work. "What sort of technicality?"

"The detective in charge messed up the way he gathered the evidence or something."

"How?"

"I forget. The case went to trial. Seemed like a slam dunk. Then everything went to hell."

Sometimes it all seemed so futile, and stories like this one, where a case should've come together but didn't, made it worse. "If he didn't go to prison, where is he?"

The man's eyes lit with a sense of justice and the joy of telling of a good story. "Romain shot him."

Jasmine felt her jaw drop. "You're kidding. Moreau's *dead?*"

"As dead as a man can get. When he walked out of the courthouse…*pow.*" Cabanis made a gun with his finger and thumb, pulling the trigger as he imitated the sound.

It took a moment for the finality of Fornier's action to sink in, but certain questions soon pushed to the forefront of Jasmine's brain. "Did Fornier go to prison?"

His work forgotten, Cabanis rested his elbows on the bar. "Of course. Didn't even bother to resist. He dropped the gun on the courthouse steps and let them arrest him. I saw it on TV. The networks were there. They got it on tape."

"Really. How long was his sentence?"

"Due to the situation, the judge went easy on him. He got two years and served about—" Cabanis's whiskers rasped as he rubbed his chin "—eighteen months or so. I saw a news piece on his release a couple years back."

Jasmine wondered if her father would've shot Kimberly's kidnapper if he'd had the chance and thought it was a definite possibility. Then she put *herself* in Fornier's place.

Would she ever take the law into her own hands? Demand justice at any cost? What kind of person would she be after something like that? She was no advocate of vigilantism, but if she was sure—as sure as Fornier seemed to be—that she had the man who'd brutally murdered her sister, and that man was about to walk…

"Fornier's not your average fellow," the hotel owner was saying. "Used to be Special Forces."

"I wonder if he regretted firing that shot." She was asking herself more than him, but Cabanis answered.

"I don't think so. Prison made him even tougher than he already was. He appealed to the public for help when his daughter was first missing. But he didn't want anything to do with publicity after he got out. In the clip I saw, he kept turning away from the camera, refusing to comment, until a reporter cornered him as he was getting into a car. Then he looked right into the camera and said, 'I'd do it again.'"

Jasmine rubbed away the goose bumps that rose on her skin. "Do you know how Fornier managed to track down Moreau?"

"I couldn't give you the details, no."

"Thanks." She smiled as if Fornier's story was merely one of those horrific tales that fascinated the casual listener, but there was nothing casual about the impact it'd had on her. She'd once feared her father would follow a similar path; now she felt her own thirst for vengeance.

*Stop me.* How far would she go in order to accomplish that?

# 3

There was a sketch artist listed in the Yellow Pages under Forensic Consultants, but Jasmine wasn't convinced she could rely on the talents of a woman named Rayne Gulley. She was pretty sure the listing had to be a misprint or maybe a joke—until she called. Then she spoke with Ms. Gulley, who sounded surprisingly capable and experienced.

"I've been drawing for nearly forty years," she said. "Completed more than two thousand composite sketches and, boy, have I met a lot of interesting people during that time."

"I'd be describing a man I haven't seen for sixteen years," Jasmine admitted.

"So we're talking about age progression."

"Yes. And you should probably know that I was only twelve when he came to the door."

"I'm sure you'll do fine."

"I think I will." It was a relief just to be able to say that, to feel confident that she could finally describe the bearded man's features in enough detail to walk away with a good likeness. In the first few years after Kimberly's abduction, her parents and the police had her meet with several sketch artists. But no matter how hard she tried, each session

resulted in a picture that didn't resemble him in the least.
The constant failure created so much frustration and stress
that, at sixteen, Jasmine had been hospitalized for anxiety
disorders. At that point, her doctor forbade her parents to
speak about the abduction in front of her. He told them to
accept what had happened and go on with their lives, and
to take better care of the daughter they had left. It was as if
they'd all but forgotten her. But nothing he said made any
difference. Her parents were mere shells of the people
they'd once been. Her mother had started sniping that she
should never have married outside her race and religion. Her
father had started suggesting she go back to "her people."

After her stint in the hospital, Jasmine couldn't picture
her sister's kidnapper anymore. He'd become an out-of-
focus face with a beard. That was all. And the drugs she took
in her late teens made the image even fuzzier. She'd thought
she'd lost those details—until three days ago, when she'd
seen him in her mind's eye.

"I have company for the holidays," Ms. Gulley said,
"but I'd be happy to set up an appointment with you for
after they leave."

The holidays. Jasmine felt none of the festivity or excitement. Christmas had become an irritant to her, an obstacle that
made what she was trying to accomplish more difficult.
"When will that be?" she asked, unable to conceal her disappointment.

"Tuesday?"

That was a whole week away! "Is there anyone else in
the area who could help me sooner?"

"Frank West might be available. He just moved here, but
he's done a lot of work for various police departments in
Tennessee."

She spoke politely, but Jasmine sensed an underlying vein of annoyance. Ms. Gulley felt she had the right to enjoy Christmas without interruption, and she did—but Jasmine couldn't sit and do nothing until the world was ready to turn again. "Is he any good?"

"I'm better. Especially if you want age progression. That requires a certain knack."

Jasmine wished she didn't believe Ms. Gulley's frank appraisal of her own ability, but the woman's confident manner and decades of experience had convinced her. Torn and impatient, she hesitated, but ultimately conceded. "Fine. Where's your office?"

"I work out of my house. In Kenner. Where are you staying?"

"The Quarter."

"I'm about fifteen miles away. Do you have a car?"

"Not yet, but I can get one."

"Shall we say two o'clock?"

Jasmine swallowed a sigh. "That's fine. I'll see you after Christmas."

"Ms. Stratford?"

"Yes?"

"Don't let this get the best of you," she said and hung up.

Jasmine sat in her small chair at her small desk in her small room and slowly set the phone in its cradle. Ms. Gulley's advice came far too late. The abduction had gotten the best of her sixteen years ago. She'd lived beneath the crushing weight of it ever since.

Suddenly yearning for the Christmases that once were, *before* Kimberly was taken, she picked up the phone and dialed her father. These days he lived with a woman and her two kids whom she'd met only once in Mobile, Alabama, which wasn't far from New Orleans. But imagining how the call might go—the stiff formal reception, the underlying current that led her to believe her father would rather not hear from her, even during the holidays—she hung up before it could ring. Then she went to the library.

The New Orleans Public Library, located only a mile from Maison du Soleil, was *too* quiet. Like the call to Rayne Gulley, it reminded Jasmine that it was Christmastime and everyone else was out shopping, trimming trees, baking, celebrating. But at least the solitude meant she probably wouldn't be interrupted.

She sat on the third floor in the microfilm section, with only the male librarian at the desk for company, poring over past issues of the *Times Picayune,* New Orleans' biggest paper. She was searching for anything that stood out or brought to mind the man who'd taken Kimberly. Mr. Cabanis didn't recall hearing about any stranger abductions since the Fornier case, but that didn't mean there hadn't been any. Hurricane Katrina had dominated the news for so long, a case involving a young girl or early teen found murdered could have turned into one more statistic, especially if there were no leads in the case, no parents screaming for action. If the man with the beard had begun targeting easier victims, victims whose absence wasn't so quickly noticed, he could be here, indulging his sick impulses just as his note suggested.

But Jasmine had already put in six hours and had yet to spot anything remotely useful.

Leaning back, she pressed her palms to her eyes to give them a much-needed rest. Her back ached and she was hungry. All she'd eaten for breakfast was a muffin, which she'd purchased on the walk from her hotel. But the library closed in another fifty minutes. She figured she might as well make good use of the remaining time. If she was careful, and lucky, she could come across something important, something that might seem at first glance to be unrelated but would make sense to her.

After stretching her neck and rolling her shoulders, Jasmine returned to the microfilm. She'd worked her way back to September 2005. Because that was immediately after the hurricane, the headlines resurrected the horror the entire nation had felt at seeing people stranded on rooftops or swimming for their lives. Jasmine doubted she'd find anything related to her search here—one child who'd mysteriously disappeared wasn't going to make the news when thousands were dying—and began to skim faster: another day, week, month, year.

When she reached October 2004, the name she'd heard from Mr. Cabanis just that morning jumped out at her: Romain Fornier.

The article, which reported on Mr. Fornier's sentencing, showed a picture of him. Somewhere in his early thirties, he had light-colored hair that fell across his forehead as if he'd forgotten about regular haircuts—which he probably had—high cheekbones that made the contours of his face more pronounced, a slight cleft at the chin. He wasn't unhandsome. As a matter of fact, he would've been gorgeous, except for the furrow between his eyebrows, the determined set to his mouth and the stormy expression in his eyes.

Jasmine stared at him for several seconds. She could identify with the rage he carried in every line of his face….

In another section of the same paper, she saw a few letters to the editor. Some condemned what he'd done;

others applauded. A Lee James said Moreau got what he deserved, that any father would do the same and rightfully so. A "Concerned Citizen" maintained that society cannot foster vigilantism, even in such a heartbreaking case.

*What if victims took the law into their own hands and killed the wrong person? We can't allow any tolerance for this kind of behavior regardless of the situation. We have laws, which must be upheld.*

Jasmine didn't want to consider the issue. She felt too sympathetic to Romain Fornier, although she understood the dangers, both legal and moral, involved in what he'd done.

Skipping farther back, she saw an article that gave more information on the shooting, which had occurred pretty much as Mr. Cabanis had described. As they were leaving the courthouse, Fornier had grabbed a gun from the hip holster of an accompanying detective—Alvin Huff. Fornier fired, then immediately dropped the gun.

From there, it was easy to find information on Fornier because the trial had been covered so extensively. The case made the front-page headlines the day it was dismissed. There was another picture with that article, this one in color, showing Fornier from the waist up.

A muscular, rugged-looking man dressed in a denim shirt, he had a golden tan and streaky blond hair. Although the accompanying article lacked some details Jasmine would've liked, it mentioned Alvin Huff as the detective who'd headed up the investigation into Fornier's daughter's disappearance and explained the reason the case had been dismissed. Apparently, an informant called Detective Huff late one night to say she saw Moreau, who was already a suspect because he'd been spotted at Adele's school, carry something wrapped in a blanket into his house the night Adele was kidnapped. Understandably, Huff moved to get a search warrant as fast as possible. He called the judge and obtained verbal permission, but he had to wait until morning before he could get the affidavit signed and he didn't do that.

Afraid the suspect would destroy any evidence that remained, Huff performed the search and, instead of leaving a copy of the warrant on the premises as he was supposed to do, he dropped it by later that morning. The suspect didn't know there was anything wrong with the late receipt so it went unnoticed until his mother brought up the fact that the detective had returned to the house. Then the defense team demanded the evidence collected from the illegal search be thrown out, the prosecution didn't have a strong enough case without it, and the judge was forced to dismiss.

There was also an article the day following the discovery of Adele's body. The child was discovered by a picnicker nearly four weeks after her abduction. Prior to that article, there were several others that chronicled the search. In the earliest mention of Fornier, Jasmine learned he was originally from a town called Mamou, which she assumed was in Louisiana because the journalist didn't specify another state. She also learned that he'd been a Reconnaissance Marine, and that he'd moved to New Orleans after being released from the military; he'd opened a custom motorcycle business where he built high-end machines by hand. As if his story wasn't sad enough, he was a widower. He'd lost his wife, Pamela, to breast cancer only two years before his daughter went missing.

Considering Fornier's extensive military training, Moreau was stupid to provoke him. But he probably hadn't understood what kind of man he was dealing with.

Sexual predators rarely thought beyond their own cravings. Chances were that Moreau had simply seen Adele, wanted her and didn't think about anything other than fulfilling that desire. Jasmine knew most children who fell prey to a kidnapper had had some previous contact with their abductor, usually a brief visual observation that takes place while the perpetrator has a legitimate reason for being in the area.

In Kimberly's case, their own father had most likely jotted their address on a business card and given it to the bearded man, telling him to stop by if he wanted work. Jasmine had seen Peter do that when they were out and about. In those days, her father had no concept of danger—from what Jasmine could tell, he'd never even considered the possibility—and he'd possessed a friendly, generous heart.

A heart that'd subsequently been broken and was now filled with guilt, bitterness and remorse.

The hushed voice of the librarian, speaking directly over her, made Jasmine jump. "We're closing in ten minutes."

Twisting around, she glanced up at him. With her thoughts so mired in death and evil, his narrow shoulders and pasty face reminded her of the vampire librarian in a novel she'd read, *The Historian,* which did nothing to calm her.

After a deep breath, she managed an acknowledging nod. "I'm going," she said. There was nothing here, anyway, except the depressing story of a man who, like her, had lost most of the things that made life good.

Before getting up, however, she took a final look through the films she'd just perused. And then she saw it. An article she'd somehow missed while scanning headlines for references to Romain Fornier: *Man Writes Victim's Name in Blood.*

She read it quickly, with an overwhelming sense of urgency.

Most people know the name of Adele Fornier. We've seen her picture on TV. Searched for her. Loved her, even as strangers. And now we mourn her. When she was taken from her own street more than three weeks ago and disappeared without a trace, we had hopes of seeing her safely returned to her father. Instead her body was found March 2nd in a park restroom.

There was more, but it was a recap of what she'd read. She skimmed over the text until she reached the last paragraph:

There is much about the crime we don't know. The police are keeping a tight lid on the case so that they have a better chance of apprehending the murderer. The father has begged for our discretion, as well. But, according to the man who found her, there is one chilling detail he will never forget: her name written on the wall above her—in her own blood.

The hair on the back of Jasmine's neck rose as she stared at that last sentence, but her mind rejected what she read. Writing in blood was what forensic psychologists called a signature—some unnecessary or added flourish while committing a crime—and it was as unique to the perpetrator as choice of victim or method of murder. Was it possible that

Kimberly's kidnapper and this man, this Francis Moreau, had the same signature?

It *had* to be possible. Francis Moreau was dead by Fornier's hand. But the man who'd sent her that package was alive as of four or five days ago....

"Ma'am, we're closed. You'll have to come back tomorrow."

It was the vampire librarian again, and this time his voice was impatient.

Jasmine stood and edged away from him. In her current state of mind, she was unwilling to let a stranger get too close. But she knew her imagination was running away with her. He only wanted her to leave so he could go home. He didn't realize that, for some kids, Christmas might not be all about Santa this year.


The more Jasmine thought about it, the more she wanted to speak to Romain Fornier.

After returning from the library, she spent three hours in the lobby of her hotel—before the bar downstairs got too busy—searching the Internet for information on him, but came up empty. A few of the articles she'd seen in past issues of the *Times Picayune* showed up. And there were other Romain Forniers—a musician and a Jet-Skier and someone who appeared to be a fairly famous French painter. But that was it. Even LexisNexis, to which she had paid access, yielded no clue as to Romain's current whereabouts.

But she doubted he'd left southern Louisiana. He'd been born here, grown up here, married here, and he'd come back here after his service in the military.

She tried directory assistance for Mamou, but there were no Forniers. That didn't necessarily mean anything, though.

With all the publicity surrounding the trial, it was very likely he had an unlisted number. Or maybe he was living with someone else. Even if he wasn't there, maybe he had family in the area who could tell her more….

When she Googled the town, she found a summary that estimated the population in June of 2005 to be 3,400. Numbers had probably dropped since then, unless a lot of hurricane refugees had chosen Mamou as a place to relocate. But it had a significantly higher unemployment rate than the state average, so she'd be surprised if it had been appealing to displaced families. Regardless, in such a small town someone would know Romain Fornier. Given the news coverage, there probably wasn't a single citizen who *hadn't* heard of him.

It was nearly ten o'clock and the music and voices from downstairs were getting loud. Doing her best to tune out the noise, Jasmine finished the half-eaten sandwich at her elbow and switched over to MapQuest for driving directions. Mamou was three hours and eighteen minutes west of New Orleans.

Her father was actually closer, although he lived in the opposite direction….

Frustrated by that random thought, she pushed it from her mind and decided to rent a car and drive to Mamou first thing in the morning. She couldn't meet with the sketch artist until next Tuesday, anyway. And she had to learn more about the man who killed Fornier's daughter, more about the investigation and how it had unfolded. Moreau's method of operation might help her figure out the psyche of the man she was dealing with, or maybe something Fornier knew might prove valuable.

But Hurricane Rita had struck after Hurricane Katrina

and completely destroyed some of the coastal communities to the west. She wasn't sure how much of Fornier's hometown remained. Nothing on the Web site gave her any indication.

Waiting until the person at the front desk had finished dealing with another patron, she raised her voice above the music coming from below so she could be heard. "Excuse me."

"Yes?"

Vaguely reminiscent of the girl Jasmine had seen there earlier, this woman was older and heavier. "Do you know anything about the town of Mamou?"

"Not much. I've never been there."

"You're married to Mr. Cabanis, right?"

"Yep. This is a family affair." Folding her arms, she leaned against the counter. "Are you planning to visit Mamou?"

"If it wasn't too terribly damaged by the hurricanes."

She walked over to study the computer screen, which showed a map of the state. "I don't think it was. It's farther north than the towns that were hardest hit."

That was hopeful. "Do you know where I can rent a car?"

"Sure, come on over to the desk and I'll make a reservation. When do you want to pick it up?"

"Tomorrow morning."

"If you're hoping to see Cajun country, you don't have to drive that far. They offer swamp tours from right here in New Orleans. Although I'm not sure what's available this time of year."

"No thanks. The idea of heading into a swamp makes me uneasy." Even Skye's home, located in the San Joaquin River Delta, was too isolated for Jasmine's tastes.

"Think an alligator might getcha?" Mrs. Cabanis asked, chuckling.

"Maybe." Or something worse. Especially since a vast, largely uninhabited swamp would be an ideal place to dump a body. Although Jasmine knew that wasn't something most people would consider, for her, it was an automatic reaction, one of the negatives of her job.

"They won't bother you if you don't bother them," Mrs. Cabanis said, preoccupied with running a finger down the listings in the Yellow Pages.

Jasmine wished she could say the same for human predators. "I *can't* bother them if I keep my distance, right?"

"True. But a swamp tour would be better than going to Mamou. Other than Fred's Lounge, I doubt there's much to see."

Jasmine had stumbled on a Web site for Fred's Lounge—the famous bar that'd sparked renewed interest in Cajun music, language and culture after World War II—while searching for information on Fornier's hometown, so she recognized the reference. "I'm actually not interested in going to the lounge."

"What's the attraction, then?"

"Do you know anything about Romain Fornier?" she asked.

Mrs. Cabanis was already reaching for the phone, but she hesitated. "Oh, I wondered if you were the one. My husband told me why you're visiting New Orleans." She frowned sympathetically. "I'm sorry about your sister."

"Thank you. About Mr. Fornier—"

"You don't think there's any connection between his daughter and what happened to your sister, do you?"

"That's what I'm trying to find out."

"Well, you don't want to bother him."

"Why not?"

"He might be handsome as the devil, but he's also angry…and dangerous."

"What makes you think so?"

"I saw him on TV, too." She brought the phone to her ear and started to dial the car rental place. "Bothering him would be like baiting that alligator you're so afraid of."

Jasmine thought it might be smart to pay the New Orleans police a visit the next morning. She wanted to tell them her sister had been abducted sixteen years ago and that Kimberly's kidnapper might've brought her to Louisiana. She also wanted to ask about their cold cases. Maybe they were working on something that would provide a connection between the man who'd sent Kimberly's bracelet and an incident in New Orleans.

The station on Loyola was farther from the hotel than the car rental place, so Jasmine picked up the compact car Mrs. Cabanis had reserved, then stopped by the homicide division on her way out of town. But her visit didn't go as well as she'd hoped. Huff had quit the department and moved away only a few months after Fornier went to prison. And because there was no indication that the man who'd sent that package had committed a crime here, the other detectives weren't particularly interested in talking to her.

The two detectives who did take a few minutes to chat assured her that there'd been no stranger abductions in recent months and that they couldn't remember any cases, cold or otherwise, similar to Kimberly's. They promised to ask around and contact her if they found anything of potential value, but as she was leaving, one suggested, for the third time, that she get in touch with the Cleveland police and turn over the evidence in her possession. When she finally admitted she wasn't willing to do that, he shrugged and said, "You either want police help or you don't." Then they both walked away, and Jasmine was fairly sure they wouldn't trouble themselves further. They didn't care about a cold case in Cleveland. Her sister's disappearance wasn't their problem.

But if the bearded man was indeed living in New Orleans, and the note she'd received meant anything at all, that could easily change.

Her cell phone rang as she got into her rental car. "Hello?"

"Jaz? How's it going?"

It was Sheridan. "Fine, I guess," she said.

"You find anything yet?"

Jasmine frowned as she put on her seat belt and started the car. "Not really."

"So what are you going to do?"

She turned down the radio when "Silent Night," sung by Natalie Cole and her father, blasted through the speakers. "Keep looking."

"You won't stay in New Orleans for Christmas, will you?"

For a moment, Jasmine longed to fly back to Sacramento and pretend her sister had never been abducted. She'd built a good life in the West. It felt as though she was making a difference in the lives of other victims, she had close friends, a home. She didn't need to risk unraveling all the progress she'd made.

But she couldn't ignore that bracelet, couldn't forget her

sister. Her only hope of peace was through finding the bearded man. And then…

She didn't want to consider what she might do then. She kept having visions of pulling a gun as Fornier had done.

"I think I'll stay," she said.

"But you don't know a soul there. Who will you spend Christmas Day with?"

Jasmine wondered about all the holidays Kimberly had spent away from home. Somewhere. At the mercy of a dangerous man. Or in a cold grave. What'd her life been like? Had it lasted longer than eight years? "This is more important to me than anything else."

After checking the directions she'd printed out at the hotel, she turned onto South Broad, which quickly became Perdido Street. Then she made a quick right on South White. She had to find I-10 West, which she'd take for seventy-seven miles toward Lafayette. "I want to bring my sister home for Christmas." Even if it was only Kimberly's body or the knowledge of where she'd gone and what had happened to her.

The following pause was filled with sadness. "I wish I could be there with you."

"You already have your plane ticket to Wyoming. Your little sister's bringing her fiancé for the family to meet. You've got to go."

"But I hate what you're going through, especially at Christmas. That makes it so much worse."

"Would you be doing anything different if you'd received some note or trinket from the man who shot Jazon?" she asked, referring to the incident that'd sent Sheridan to the victims' support group where they'd met each other and Skye.

Sheridan's voice dropped. "No. I'd give anything for the

chance to go back and make things right. Or as right as I can."

"Then you understand."

"That's why I'm worried. I understand too well. I'm going to cancel my trip home and come there instead," Sheridan announced in an abrupt reversal. "Do you have a rental car? Can you pick me up from the airport on the twenty-fourth?"

"Sheridan, stop," Jasmine said with a laugh. "Your sister will be heartbroken. Go meet her new man. Enjoy your family. I may not even be in New Orleans on the twenty-fourth."

"What does that mean? Are you going to your father's?"

Jasmine winced at the hope in her friend's response. Sheridan constantly tried to talk Jasmine into pulling her family back together, couldn't stand the thought of everything that'd been left unspoken and unforgiven between them. But that was because Sheridan didn't understand that they were better off this way. Although Sheridan had her own pain to deal with, that pain didn't involve her family. They could rally around her and help her forget; Jasmine's parents only made her remember. "No, I'm going to Mamou."

*"Where?"*

"The Cajun music capital of the world."

"Sounds like a metropolis."

Jasmine smiled at the sarcasm. "Compared to some of the nearby towns, it is."

"At least it's not hurricane season right now."

"See? There you go, looking on the bright side."

"Have you heard from Skye?"

"Not today, but I talked to her when my plane landed the

night before last. I called to let you both know I arrived safely."

"She mentioned it. She also told me she wants you home for Christmas."

"She knows I have to do this. And she has David. She'll be fine."

"Do I have your hotel number?"

"You have my cell."

"Just in case."

"I don't have it with me. But you can get it online if you need it." Jasmine reached I-10 West as she gave her friend the name of the hotel.

"Thanks. I'll be on a plane to Wyoming tomorrow, but I'll call you when I get in."

"Sounds good. Have a nice Christmas."

"This sucks," she said and hung up.

Jasmine recalled her brief conversation with the detectives at the NOPD and, for now, had to agree with the sentiment. She was basically on her own. Like she'd been at seventeen, when she'd started rambling around the country. Only this time she wasn't running from the past—she was racing toward it.

# 4

The town of Mamou made real the kinds of places Jasmine had imagined when she read novels set in the South. Built on relatively flat land in a traditional grid, it was small and, judging by appearances, the buildings hadn't changed by more than a coat of paint in the past forty or fifty years.

According to the Web site Jasmine had accessed the night before, there were only about 1600 homes here. Half were owner-occupied, the other half renter. Not too many of the ones she saw from the road looked impressive, but she hadn't expected mansions. The median rent in this town was $218 a month—a figure she could scarcely believe. You couldn't even rent a doghouse for that amount in California.

"Wow," she muttered, dropping her speed to match the posted limit. Mamou wasn't much like Cleveland, where she'd grown up—and yet a nostalgic similarity existed between the wooden frame homes and her old neighborhood. The simplicity of the early-twentieth-century architecture evoked childhood memories of weekends spent at her grandparents' house, before they passed on. That throwback to American roots was notably absent in her adopted state, where most cities seemed prosperous, shiny and new.

Slowing even more, she turned into the first gas station she came across.

Before she could unbuckle her seat belt, a man close to her own age walked out of the garage. She rolled down her window to ask about Romain Fornier, but the way the attendant ducked his head and mumbled when he spoke made him seem a bit odd. That encounter reminded her of another statistic she'd read online: At last count, Mamou had 152 people in mental hospitals, a significantly higher number than the state average.

She wondered if this man had been recently released. "Excuse me?" she said, hoping he'd clarify what he wanted.

He motioned to the gas pumps but didn't speak again. Evidently, he was planning to help her and needed some direction.

She hadn't expected any assistance. In most parts of the country, full service had become a casualty of cost savings nearly two decades before.

Getting out, she told him to fill up the tank with regular, then wandered through the snack shop attached to the garage, where she selected a bottle of juice and a doughnut and brought them to the register. She wanted to talk to someone about Romain Fornier, but she could tell that this man wasn't a good option and already had her eye on the fiftyish woman behind the counter.

"Hello." Jasmine smiled as she set down her items.

Dressed in jeans, a turtleneck sweater and an oversize coat—the inside of the store wasn't much warmer than the forty-degree weather outside—the clerk barely glanced at her. "Hi."

"Nice town you have here."

"That'll be $1.85. Plus the gas."

Jasmine handed her fifty bucks. "How long have you lived in the area?"

"Most my life," the woman responded, but her attention was on the till and making change.

"It's nice to have someone pump my gas."

The woman's eyes darted to the window. The man Jasmine had encountered earlier was now checking her oil. "Lonnie does what he can."

Jasmine wasn't sure, but she thought she saw some resemblance between this woman and the man outside. "Are you two related?"

"I'm his mama—all he's got in this life and likely all he'll ever have."

She sounded weary, overwhelmed and, for the first time, Jasmine noticed the dust that covered so many products on the shelves. "You own the place?"

"Since his daddy died last year. Now it's just the two of us."

Guilt about being so caught up in her own troubles made Jasmine realize how single-minded she'd been the past few days. "I'm sorry for your loss."

The woman gave her a tired smile. "So am I. Half the time when he was alive, I wanted to kick him out. He was always going off fishing and leaving me with the station and the store. But at least I had him, you know? At least he came home to me." She gauged the progress of her son, who'd finished with the oil and was washing Jasmine's windshield. "And Lonnie did better when his daddy was alive."

Jasmine thought of her own father. She'd been so busy shielding herself from the pain of their relationship she'd seen him only once in four years. "It's that way for some kids."

"Not you, though, huh?"

Jasmine instantly regretted divulging so much of her personal history. "My father's still living. I'm just not close to him."

"Don't waste the time you got left, beb. That's the best advice I can offer."

Jasmine didn't want any advice. She was managing, wasn't she? She'd gotten off drugs, made something of her life. That was progress.

After accepting her change, she turned to go. She didn't feel comfortable asking this woman about Fornier; although they were strangers, they'd revealed too much about themselves in their brief exchange. There were other people in town, she told herself. But Lonnie's mother was finally interested enough to stop her with the question Jasmine had been expecting from the beginning.

"Where ya from?"

"California."

"You come to see Fred's Lounge?"

"No, I'm not a tourist. I'm looking for someone."

*"Here?"*

"I don't know if he's still around, but he was born and raised in Mamou."

"Who we talkin' about?"

Jasmine's reluctance to push her own agenda burned away beneath the hot glare of opportunity. "Romain Fornier."

Her eyes narrowed, the tentative connection they'd established already at risk. "What you want with him?"

"I'm hoping he can help me."

"Help you what?"

"My sister went missing sixteen years ago." A lump rose

in Jasmine's throat. After almost two decades, the hurt and loss still surfaced at unexpected moments. She swallowed hard and attempted to continue. "She was only eight."

The deep groves in the woman's face indicated that she'd lived a hard life. Money had probably been scarce even when her husband was alive. But there was genuine kindness in her, despite her apparent loyalty to Fornier. "I'm sorry."

Jasmine blinked back the tears that threatened. "It's fine. I—I don't know why I'm crying like this."

She came around the counter. "You're cryin' 'cause you care, beb. Ain't no stoppin' that. But you don't want to bother T-Bone. He's been to hell and back, fuh shore."

"T-Bone?"

"That's what we call him. Used to be T-*Boy,* which is an old Cajun tradition, but when he was eight, he got in a fight with a bully who was three years older and took a good lickin'. His *mamère* was a superstitious old lady who told him to bury a steak and his black eye would heal, so he took his papa's T-bone off the grill and did exactly that—and got another whippin'." Her laugh settled into a wistful smile. "Ever since, he's been T-Bone. He used to be a good boy, the best. But now…it's better to leave him alone."

"I'm not trying to hurt him."

"How could you hurt him? He's lost everything he cares about. He's not the same person anymore. He's so *en colère*—angry, you understand?—he works real hard to keep his distance from everyone. There's no need to make him the *misère.*"

Between her accent and the French words, this woman's English was difficult to follow, but *misère* obviously meant miserable or something close. "So he lives here?" She felt sudden hope, despite her new friend's warning.

"No, he lives near Portsville, out on the bayou."

"How far away is that?"

"'Bout five hours southeast, down near Grand Isle and Leeville, give or take twenty minutes. *Mais,* like I said, I think it'd be a waste of your time to drive down there. He barely speaks to his own kin."

Somehow, Jasmine didn't quite believe that Romain was as unfriendly to his relatives as this woman said. If the local gas station owner knew him well enough to tell a story about his childhood, the community was a close one and chances were good he maintained some ties to it. "I'm willing to do whatever it takes," she said.

Lonnie had finished with the car. He stepped inside, grinning like an eager dog after fetching a stick, and his mother put a hand on his shoulder to give him the approval he craved. "Thanks, Lonnie," she said gently. "Some things should be left as they are," she told Jasmine.

"This isn't one of them." Her tears had dried—gone as quickly as they'd come. Now she felt only a fierce determination. "Fornier might be able to help me catch a killer."

The woman's eyebrows knitted. "He's already shot one. What more can he do?"

"Stop another."

"How?"

"By providing information."

The woman's lips pursed stubbornly. "I'd rather he didn't get involved. I don't want him to go back to prison."

Jasmine spread out her hands, palms up. "If anyone gets in trouble, it'll be me. I *have* to stop the man who kidnapped my sister."

The woman reached up to smooth the hair on the back of her son's head, as if he were ten years old. Mentally, he probably was. "It's always the innocent who suffer," she said. Then she sighed. "I can't give you an address. T-Bone doesn't have one. From what I hear, he lives alone in the swamp somewheres, without mail service or utilities."

Jasmine's heart sank. "How will I find him?"

"Portsville's very small, beb. If you go there, someone will take you to him. And when you see him, tell him Ya-Ya Collins sent you. That might help." She frowned. "Then again, it might not."

"Thank you," Jasmine said and meant it.

"Good luck findin' your sister."

Jasmine nodded, got back in her car and turned around. It seemed she was going into the swamps, after all.

Now to avoid the alligators…

The headstones were a bad omen.

After passing several waterside towns with docks that disappeared into an inky morass, which grew inkier as night fell, Jasmine entered Portsville. It was located on Bayou Lafourche at nearly the southernmost tip of Louisiana. The cemetery was right there beside the road, but it was unlike any she'd ever seen. The aboveground tombs, all painted white, glowed eerily in a foot of water—the same marshy water that lapped gently at the telephone poles running parallel to the highway.

She wondered how people down here weathered each new hurricane, each storm. It'd take a certain stubbornness to hold out, people who loved this land more than she'd ever loved a particular location. She'd always felt a bit restless. There was no mystery as to the reason, of course, but she was envious of the devotion required to fight for existence in such a place. To say, "This is my home and I'm staying put."

Judging by the small group of frame houses, most of them built on pilings, plus a single two-story hotel, two gas stations, a bait shop and a coffee shop, she guessed there were maybe fifty people taking such a stand. And she was willing to bet almost all of them were fishermen. Someone had to own the motley collection of boats bumping against the dock. With only a sliver of moon in the sky, she couldn't see them very well, but they obviously didn't belong to the rich and famous.

What now? She turned in to one of the gas stations, but like the other, it was closed. Should she have gone back to her hotel and set out tomorrow morning, when she could've gotten an earlier start?

Now that it was dark, she had no idea how she'd find Fornier out on the bayou "somewheres." And she wasn't sure she wanted to stay in the tin-roofed hotel that hung over the water. Although there was nothing wrong with the hotel, except that it looked deserted.

She checked her watch. Seven-thirty. New Orleans was only an hour and a half to the northeast. She could drive back there tonight and arrive at a reasonable time. But she was hungry and exhausted, and she hated to waste another day on this search, especially if it turned out that Fornier couldn't or wouldn't help her.

After parking in a lot that was mostly crushed shells, she went into the hotel, where she found a big man who looked as weathered as the rickety dock she'd just passed.

"Wanna room?" The buttons on his flannel shirt strained with the effort of covering his barrel chest, and he was missing two fingers on his left hand, but he gave her a welcoming, gap-toothed smile.

"Yes, I do. But first I was hoping you could help me find someone."

"Who d' at?"

"T-Bone." Figuring there couldn't be more than one T-Bone in a town of four dozen people, even in Cajun country, she didn't mention the last name, hoping to sound more familiar with Fornier than she really was.

"T-Bone's down de bayou near Port Fourchon."

Down was good. She didn't know how she could go much farther south without running into the Gulf of Mexico, which meant he couldn't be far. "Can you tell me how to get there?"

He studied her for a moment. "Is T-Bone expectin' you?"

She considered telling the truth, but rejected the idea. She couldn't risk being stonewalled. She needed this man's help, and she was willing to twist reality a little in order to get it. It was what any private investigator would do, but she still felt guilty.

"Actually, I'm here as a surprise." She manufactured a coquettish smile. "A friend of his from Mamou sent me to meet him. Do you know…Poppo?" she invented quickly.

"No."

"Well, he thinks we'd be perfect for each other," she gushed. "Since my husband walked out on me, I'm hoping to meet someone new, and Poppo says T-Bone needs a woman even if he won't admit it."

The old man's thick eyebrows slid up, but he hooked his thumbs into the bib of his overalls and grinned. No doubt he saw her as a harmless young lady, and that lowered his guard. "Lord, am I glad to see you. D' at poor boy need somet'ing, I tell ya. He on'y come to town meybe every udder week. I don't t'ink he has a speck o' company in between."

"And here it is Christmas."

"What a nice surprise."

"So…can you give me some directions?"

"I can't see no harm in d'at. Go six, seven mile down de highway—" he pointed one of his gnarled fingers at the door behind her "—d'en turn right on Rappelet Road. After another half mile or so, d'ere'll be a road d'at goes toward Bay Champagne. He's back d'ere in de swamp."

*Swamp. Ugh.* "Is that a left or a right turn?" She needed to clarify as much as possible. There was no way she wanted to get lost in a place that frightened her as much as the bayou.

Taking a piece of paper from somewhere under the front desk, he drew her a crude map. "D'is will get you d'ere."

She could barely read the writing. "There isn't any chance of getting lost, is there?" she asked apprehensively. And that was all it took. With a motion quicker than she expected for a man of his age, he reached under the desk again. This time he produced a sign that said, *Gone fishin'. Be back soon.*

Within ten minutes the grizzled fisherman had led Jasmine to a large shack, which stood on a spot of dry ground tucked into a thicket of cypress and pecan trees interspersed with marsh grass. Spanish moss hung from the trees, blocking what little moonlight might've filtered through the branches, making it seem far later than it really was.

As she drove closer, she could see the flicker of a lantern or candle burning inside the shack. Someone was home, but her guide didn't proceed to the house. He pulled over, his right-side tires practically in the water, and waved her up even with him.

She rolled down her window.

"D'at's it," he shouted, half hanging out of his truck.

She tightened her grip on the steering wheel. "You're turning around?"

"I gotta get back to de hotel."

"Right." She studied Fornier's place again, feeling uncertain about coming here after sundown. The man in this house had shot another man in cold blood. There were extenuating circumstances, of course, but still… "You'll hold a room for me, won't you?" she said. "I'll be back tonight. If you don't see me in an hour or so you might come looking for me."

He laughed and slapped his door, making enough noise to bring a large man to the entrance of the shack, even though they were fifty yards away. Silhouetted by the light behind him, he stood with the door open, legs apart, hands on hips—as if he were king of the whole swamp and was none too happy at the intrusion.

Not only had Fornier killed a man, he'd lost his wife and daughter. And he'd served time in prison. Was he still sane?

Jasmine cleared her throat. "Or…you don't suppose you could spare another couple of minutes to wait for me?"

Throwing back his head, the Cajun laughed again. "He won't hurt you, podnah. I'd trust my own daughda wit' him."

"Right. You wouldn't leave me if it wasn't safe."

"'Course not. He a good man."

*A good man*… He'd suffered a great deal, and he'd avenged his daughter's death. That didn't prove he was a good man. But it'd been her idea to come out here, and she decided she might have better luck getting Fornier to open up if they didn't have an audience. What they'd both suffered wasn't easy to talk about.

After waiting for her to pass, the old man turned around.

She watched his taillights disappear in her rearview mirror before concentrating all her attention on that broad figure in the doorway.

*Quit being a baby.* It was only eight o'clock. She might as well get what she'd come for.

Fornier didn't move toward her even after she parked and got out. He crossed his arms and leaned against the lintel, watching her skeptically. At least she thought he was watching skeptically. It was difficult to be sure. She could only make out his general characteristics. Tall, maybe six-two or six-three—a full ten inches taller than she was— he had a lean, muscular build and the hyperfocus of an animal who stalks its prey. His hair was on the long side, making him look a bit careless or perhaps reckless, but the rest of him seemed very…together. Right down to his clothes.

Once she reached him, she could tell his faded jeans and long-sleeved T-shirt were clean and smelled of woodsmoke. She could also tell she'd interrupted him while he was relaxing, because he wasn't wearing any shoes.

"I suppose you have a reason for being here." His lazy Southern drawl was almost as deceptive as his stance was casual.

"Ya-Ya Collins sent me." She clasped her hands together to get control of her nerves. "From Mamou," she added.

"I know where Ya-Ya lives." His voice was as rough as tree bark, but now that Jasmine was close enough to see him better, she could tell that those pictures in the newspaper didn't do him justice. He was much more attractive in person. "How'd you get past her?" he asked.

"I told her the truth about why I want to speak with you." With the shadows on his face, she couldn't be sure but she thought his eyes wandered over her, sizing her up, drawing Lord knows what kinds of conclusions. "Which is?"

"I'm not a reporter or a journalist."

He didn't seem particularly relieved. "The process of elimination could take a while. Maybe we should start with what you *are*."

She ignored the sarcasm. "You're as friendly as I expected."

"I don't remember inviting you here."

"I came because I'm hoping you'll answer a few questions."

He lifted one shoulder in a careless shrug. "If it has anything to do with the last decade, I have nothing to say. I've put the past behind me."

Obviously, he'd done no such thing, or he wouldn't be living like a hermit. "It's about the man who killed your daughter."

"Of course it is." With a grimace, he rubbed his neck. "You should've left your engine running," he said at length, then he shoved away from the lintel as if he planned to go back inside and leave her right where she was. He probably would have, if she hadn't stopped the door.

His gaze traveled from her hand to her face, but he didn't force her to move.

"A man took my sister from our house while I was baby-sitting sixteen years ago," she said.

"I'm sorry that happened, but it has nothing to do with me." Removing her hand, he closed the door with a click.

"She's never been found," she said, raising her voice so it'd carry through the wood panel. "But I received a package three days ago. It contained the bracelet she was wearing the day she disappeared."

No response.

"That package came from New Orleans, Mr. Fornier. I think he's here…somewhere."

Still nothing.

"Mr. Fornier?" Beginning to lose her nerve, Jasmine wondered what she was doing standing in the middle of a swamp bothering a man who'd already suffered enough. But that strange coincidence, the similarity between her sister's case and his daughter's, meant *something*. She knew it did.

"There was a note with it—a note written in blood." She waited a few seconds to let that sink in before continuing. "Just like your daughter's name on the wall. That kind of behavior is called a signature. It's an unnecessary act driven by a perpetrator's own compulsion or desires and it varies from criminal to criminal. So it's highly unusual that two killers would do the same thing within the same time frame, and that they'd both have a tie to this area."

When Mr. Fornier still didn't respond, she rested her forehead against the lintel. Ya-Ya Collins had warned her, but she'd believed she could get through to him. "Are you listening, Mr. Fornier?"

A frog croaked somewhere off in the distance—and something much closer splashed into the water.

Chilled by the foreboding suggested by that sound, Jasmine glanced back at her rental car. She had a lot more to say—everything she'd been thinking about since reading those articles in the New Orleans paper—but it was no use. Fornier wouldn't help her.

"Right. Thanks for nothing," she muttered and trudged back to her car. She'd opened the door and was about to get in when he stepped out of the shack. He didn't speak—just stood there watching her—which made it impossible to tell what he was thinking.

She gripped the window frame of her car door as she looked back at him. "I'm staying at the hotel in town if you change your mind."

"Let's do it here," he said, and left the door open for her.

# 5

Fornier's shack was much nicer than Jasmine had anticipated. Though basic, it was clean and well-maintained. And he lived simply, but not as simply as she'd assumed. The light she'd noticed in the window wasn't a candle. It was a television powered by a generator, judging by the rumble coming from somewhere behind the house.

Once she stepped into the living room, she could see a small kitchen off to one side and a short hall off to the other. A door that stood open at the end of the hall probably led to Fornier's bedroom. With only the television for light, it was too dark to see much detail, but the neatness of the living room gave her the impression "T-Bone" made his bed each and every day with military precision.

The way he lived so comfortably with so little impressed her—no doubt because she'd half expected to find him drowning in booze. She knew what it was like to crave relief from the whys, to use whatever she could to block out the memories. But it appeared that he spent his time hunting and fishing instead of drinking. A stuffed alligator held pride of place in one corner, and pictures of Fornier and others, holding this catch or that, adorned the walls. Not one thing in the room looked as if it'd belonged to a woman or child. There wasn't even a framed photograph of his family. He'd rid himself of all reminders of the past.

"It's warm in here," she said.

He let that comment hang without response, which made her wonder if he thought she was looking down her nose at him and his potbellied stove. But she didn't follow it with anything more. She waited as he lowered the volume of the movie he'd been watching and motioned for her to sit across from him.

Inching as far away from the stuffed alligator as she could without being too obvious about it, she perched on the edge of an armless chair that must have hailed from the 1960s. "Thanks for giving me an audience."

He nodded, but his silent perusal, and the suspicion in his eyes, made her nervous. She wondered if his face always looked as though it was hewn from stone or only when he was confronted with a stranger intent on probing his darkest moments.

"I wouldn't have come here if I didn't think it was important," she explained. "I want you to know that. I understand what you've been through—" she thought of the shooting and his subsequent incarceration and backed away from that statement a little "—to a point."

"Are you a cop?" he asked.

"No."

"You talk like a cop."

He was probably referring to her explanation of a killer's signature. "Together with two of my friends, I run a charity that helps victims, and I have some experience in criminal profiling."

"But you're here for personal reasons."

"That's right. I'm here because of my sister and that package I mentioned."

"So what do you want from me?"

His brisk manner was insulting enough that she stopped trying to tiptoe so carefully around *his* feelings. "I want to know if you're sure you killed the right man."

A muscle flexed in his jaw, but he raised a hand as if to acknowledge that he preferred the direct approach. "I'm positive."

"How do you know?"

"They found my daughter's blood on some of his clothing."

"Was she sexually assaulted?"

He swallowed visibly, telling Jasmine the emotion he struggled to control hovered just beneath the surface—like the alligators swimming barely submerged in the bayou outside. "Yes."

"Did you find anything else in the house?"

"A video of their time together."

She winced, knowing how difficult that must've been for a father to see. "Did he keep any souvenirs—a piece of clothing or jewelry?"

"Like the bracelet someone mailed to you? Even if he did, it doesn't mean the man who sent you that package has any connection to Moreau. A lot of sick bastards keep trophies."

"There's a connection," she insisted.

"How do you know?"

The name had leapt out at her while she was reading the microfilm, made her heart beat faster. "Intuition."

He laughed, but it was a cynical laugh. "*Intuition.* God, I should've let you leave." Standing, he started for the door; their interview was over. "There's nothing I can do for you, Ms.—"

"Stratford. Jasmine Stratford."

"Ms. Stratford. You're just another person grasping at straws to ease the ache in your chest. But take it from me. You're wasting your time, and mine. Adele is dead. Moreau is, too. You need to search elsewhere for the man who took your sister."

"We could be talking about a copycat killer."

"Or a coincidence."

He couldn't deal with it. As tough as he tried to appear, he couldn't handle the memories. Jasmine understood, even sympathized because she used to be the same way. And yet his stubborn denial frustrated her. "I'm only looking for a few facts."

"It's not my problem."

"I thought you were a soldier," she said softly.

He turned on her so fast she put out her hands to stop him and encountered a hard, solid chest. Her fingers burned from the warmth of his body, a warmth that didn't reach the icy cold of his eyes. But he seemed to realize he'd frightened her. Abruptly stepping back, he opened the door as if he hadn't reacted at all.

Jasmine didn't walk through it. A photograph had caught her attention—and held her riveted. It was tucked into the glass doors of a bookcase shoved full of books and magazines. The dim lighting made it hard to see much detail, but she knew without drawing closer that it was Adele. That picture had been used in the newspaper and in the police flyers.

Fornier had kept one concession to the past.

He was still waiting for her to go, but she moved toward the picture instead—and an image crystallized in her mind.

"We're finished here," he bit out.

Jasmine barely heard him. She was having one of her visions, a random impression that came to her—a man's hand, reaching into a locker somewhere to pick up a child's pendant. She'd had enough experience with her abilities to know what it was, but that kind of sudden knowledge—of another place, another time—always unnerved her.

"Ms. Stratford?"

Straightening, she confronted Fornier. "It wasn't a crime of opportunity."

"Your sister?"

"Your daughter."

His chin jutted out. "You don't know that. You don't know anything about my daughter."

"I'm only telling you in case you've been beating yourself up for letting her ride her bike home alone."

The blood drained from his face, making him almost ghostlike in the dark room. "It was only around the block," he said, his voice a mere whisper.

She tried not to experience his pain—but that was impossible. "He stole her necklace from somewhere before that. I don't know when, but it was at a—a gym or a dance class or maybe a swimming pool. Someplace that has lockers."

"No, she lost it. I remember her crying when she couldn't find it."

"She didn't lose it. He took it."

"How do you know?" Cautious hope touched his voice. But Jasmine didn't answer. He wouldn't believe her even if she told him.

"I'm sure that's why he went to the school. He was

already fixated and he would've found her eventually," she said instead, hoping it'd make a difference in Fornier's recovery. Then, brushing past him, she headed to her car.

"What'd the necklace look like?" he called after her.

"You know what it looked like."

"I'm wondering if you do."

"It was the plastic Belle you bought at Disney World."

Romain hadn't bought it at Disney World. He'd bought it at the Disney store. But that seemed a minor difference when there were so many other types of necklaces she could've named. She hadn't said it was a gold locket or a silver heart or a pink ribbon. She'd correctly identified Adele's necklace as the Disney character Belle....

*How?*

He paced his living room, too keyed up to sit down. He'd moved to the bayou to gain some distance from the rest of the world. He'd needed breathing room, the peace of nature, a chance to achieve a better perspective on a society he no longer trusted. And he'd been doing that.

Until tonight. Who *was* this woman who'd appeared seemingly out of nowhere?

He had only her name and a few sentences about her sister being abducted sixteen years ago. But she'd understood, immediately, the regret that corroded his soul. Not for shooting the man who'd killed Adele. He felt no remorse for that—couldn't even remember actually pulling the trigger. It was the fact that he'd allowed such a despicable human being to get control of his daughter in the first place that hurt. As Adele's father, he should've protected her, should've refused to let her ride her bicycle to Elizabeth's house that day or any day.

He hadn't realized that a block—a *block*—could pose such risk. They'd lived in a good neighborhood. But it'd happened anyway, and now it was too late. He'd lost his little girl in the worst possible way and every time he closed his eyes, he saw her being whisked off her bike and forced into Moreau's rusty van, imagined the unspeakable torture she'd suffered. Torture that wouldn't have happened if he'd said *no*....

Suddenly, he was standing in front of the bookcase, where her sweet face smiled back at him. "I'm sorry," he muttered, struggling against a familiar tightening in his throat. "I'm so sorry."

As usual, there was no answer. Only the generator running in the background as Adele stared back, always with him and yet gone forever.

What did Jasmine Stratford really know about her and the man who'd killed her? If this woman could describe the necklace, she had to possess other information. But he wasn't sure that information would be as comforting as the tidbit she'd given him. It was equally possible that her answers would only lead to more questions. Or tempt him to doubt what he already knew to be true.

*Leave it alone,* he told himself, and went back to his movie. But he didn't comprehend a single word and, after an hour, he finally gave up. By telling him he couldn't have saved his little girl even if he'd been more vigilant, Ms. Stratford had offered him absolution. And absolution was irresistible.

Striding across the living room, he retrieved the keys to the motorcycle he'd built for himself and hurried outside. She'd said she was staying at the hotel in Portsville, but he had no idea for how long.

If he waited until the sun came up, she could be gone.

\* \* \*

The engine of the motorcycle rattled the walls of Jasmine's hotel room. She'd just put on the chemise and shorts set she liked to sleep in, but the moment she heard the racket, she wondered if it was Fornier. At eleven o'clock, the rest of the town was asleep; there was virtually no traffic.

She waited. If it was Fornier, and he wanted to see her, she'd receive a call from the front desk.

Instead, a heavy knock made her jump.

"Tell me the old guy didn't send him up," she muttered and grabbed the silky robe that matched her sleepwear. "Yes?" she said through the panel as she shrugged it on.

"It's me."

Fornier. Just as she'd guessed. The lies she'd told the old Cajun had come back to haunt her. He'd assumed she'd want him to send Fornier up and hadn't bothered to call first.

Taking a deep breath, she cracked the door open. There wasn't a chain or she might've used it because this man was so unsettled—and unsettling.

"What can I do for you?" she asked, unable to resist turning the tables on him.

"For starters, you can let me in."

She hesitated briefly. "Why don't we meet for breakfast in the morning?"

"Because I'm here *now.*"

She didn't usually allow strange men into her hotel room, especially out in the middle of nowhere. But she didn't sense any danger from Fornier. If he wanted to harm her, he could've done it out in the swamp where he had a convenient place to toss her body and plenty of alligators to eat it.

Stepping back, she permitted him to open the door the rest of the way.

"You've had a change of heart?" she asked as he came in.

He closed the door behind him. "Maybe you could call it that if I had a heart to begin with."

He did have a heart. That was the problem. His emotions ran so deep, he couldn't cope with the pain they caused him so he tried to shut them off.

Uncomfortably aware of her skimpy attire, she tightened the belt on her robe. "So you're here because…"

A subtle shift in his body language told her Romain hadn't missed the fact that she wasn't wearing a bra. But he wasn't obvious enough to let his eyes dip. "You know why. I want to hear how you knew about the necklace."

"It doesn't matter."

"It does to me."

"What matters is that you understand this—even if Moreau hadn't taken that particular opportunity, he would've kidnapped your daughter some other time. There's no way you could've stood guard over her every minute of every day, not when you couldn't possibly recognize the danger."

"I *should've* recognized it."

The passion in his voice confirmed the depth of his remorse. "Not if you were busy living a normal life. Not when there was nothing to alert you."

"There was the nightly news."

"But it's human nature to believe tragedies only happen to other people." She watched him carefully, hoping he'd be able to forgive himself, to trust her to some degree, but she couldn't tell what he was thinking.

He crossed to the window. "You seem to know a lot about this sort of thing."

"I've spent my life researching it."

He shoved large hands into the pockets of a brown leather bomber jacket. "Yet you haven't been able to find your own sister."

She knew he'd taken that jab simply because she'd dared bring up the past after he'd gone to such elaborate lengths to escape it. But his words still stung. Although they'd never made any accusations, her parents blamed her, too—for not being a more vigilant babysitter that day, for being unable to provide a clear description afterward, maybe even for being incapable of filling the hole in their hearts after their cherished "baby" went missing. "I haven't given up."

"It's nearly Christmas. What are you doing in Cajun country?" he asked gruffly. "Where's your husband?"

"I don't have one."

His gaze flicked to her braless chest as if he was so pre-occupied by it he could scarcely think of anything else. "Do you have any identification?"

She took her purse from the nightstand, flashed him her driver's license and handed him a business card.

"Jasmine Stratford, The Last Stand, Victims' Support and Assistance Nonprofit Organization," he read.

She smiled. "That's me."

"Why do you think I can help you?" he asked as he slipped her card in his jacket pocket.

"I told you. This kidnapper has the same signature as the man who killed your daughter. I want to see if there are other similarities."

"But you're ignoring the most salient point. Moreau's *dead*. I shot him myself, in cold blood, and if you think that makes me as much a murderer as he was, you're taking an incredible risk by bothering me."

She raised one eyebrow. "You don't want to kill me."

"And you know this because…"

"You have something far less painful in mind."

The sexual energy emanating from him was so strong Jasmine could feel it lapping around her. His wife had been dead for six years. It was possible—considering everything he'd gone through—that he hadn't been with a woman since. Jasmine definitely got the impression it'd been a while. But she didn't take his interest personally. He was living on the bayou, alone for days, even weeks at a stretch, and she was standing within arm's reach in her bedclothes, reminding him of what he'd lost. Or some of it, anyway…

But his heightened awareness didn't frighten her. There was an unpredictable, even dark quality about Fornier, but it seemed more erotic than threatening.

"You don't miss much," he said, challenging her in return by letting his gaze slide more pointedly over her body.

Jasmine's breath caught in her throat, but she didn't cover herself. She wanted to appear unaffected, indifferent, as if the way he looked at her evoked no response whatsoever—but she knew she'd failed when her nipples puckered, displaying proof of the opposite.

His eyes latched onto that proof and a knowing smile curved his lips.

"Neither do you," she said.

"You're a beautiful woman. There isn't a straight man alive who wouldn't want to touch you." His voice dropped meaningfully at the end, making it feel like a caress.

"Especially one who's been living in a swamp for two

years," she said tartly, fighting to retain hold of logic and objectivity.

"So...what do you say we make a deal?"

It was pretty easy to guess what his offer would be. "A deal?"

"I give you what you want, and you give me what I want."

Jasmine had never been propositioned quite so bluntly. Neither had she ever been with anyone who stirred her in such an instant and primal way. Was she having this reaction because she identified so deeply with Fornier's background? Because she admired his courage and resourcefulness, sympathized with the regret he dragged around like a ball and chain? She'd married Harvey out of obligation, overwhelming gratitude and the desire for companionship. The two relationships she'd had after her brief marriage had afforded the same benefits. But never raw desire. Nothing half as potent as this sudden and confusing attraction to a troubled stranger.

Curling her fingers into her palms, she fought his effect on her. "Sorry, I don't use sex as a bargaining chip."

That cynical grin returned. "Somehow I thought you were going to say that."

"I like things simple."

"No, you like them safe."

"No safer than you."

"How do you know?"

"Because you don't really want what you just asked for."

A scowl creased his forehead. "Wanna bet?"

"If you did, you wouldn't have asked for it in that way."

"You don't even know me."

"What are the odds of a woman agreeing to what you suggested?"

"There's always a chance."

"But you provided yourself with an escape hatch."

He leaned against the wall. "What the hell is that supposed to mean?"

"Just in case I surprised you and happened to agree, you set up the encounter to be so mechanical it wouldn't be any different than carrying on as you've probably carried on so far." She gestured with her hand so that he got her point, which provoked a genuine-sounding laugh.

"It'd be *a lot* different. I promise."

As far as she was concerned, Satan himself couldn't have been more alluring. She was actually beginning to wonder if one night really mattered. The desire to soothe a soul even more damaged than her own was strangely appealing.

But indulging in that kind of intimacy would be a mistake. She doubted he'd let her comfort him, anyway. He was too busy proving he didn't need anyone.

She shook her head. "It wouldn't be good."

His grin slanted to one side. "Try me."

She wanted to do just that. But it was too reckless, too irresponsible to give in to that urge. "Tempting but not tempting enough."

Releasing a dramatic sigh, he rubbed a hand over his stubble-covered jaw. "So we're back to your sister, right?"

"Right."

She knew he wasn't really disappointed. He'd been testing her, using sex to create a diversion, at the least, an escape at the most.

"What is it you want to know?" he asked.

"Tell me about Moreau."

"His house was a couple of miles from ours in the Garden

District. He lived alone, kept to himself." His monotone suggested he was attempting to distance himself from the subject. "He had a prior arrest record for molesting a little girl when he was about twenty and a young teen when he was twenty-five, but no convictions. He was as twisted as they come and, although I'm the first to admit I was wrong for doing what I did, society should thank me for the favor. That's it."

"Any other suspects?"

"A few. But there was no physical proof that any of them had my daughter in his house."

Jasmine sat on the bed. "Are you angry at Huff for bungling the search?"

"No. Huff took a calculated risk—and lost."

"Which meant you lost, too."

"Without the physical proof he discovered, there wouldn't have been enough evidence to charge Moreau in the first place."

"The cops couldn't have got what they needed in the morning, after the judge signed the affidavit?"

"Moreau had seen Huff watching his place earlier in the day. He was already spooked and would've burned it or gotten rid of it somehow." A muscle twitched in Fornier's cheek. "It was the system that failed me, not Huff. A proven predator's rights turned out to be more important to the state than an innocent child's."

She heard that sentiment often in her line of work. "Was anyone else privy to all the details of the case?"

"Like who?"

"I don't know. Someone who followed Huff's progress, who acted as if he was trying to help. Someone who kept inserting himself into the investigation, maybe even confessed?"

"Because the media took hold of it, we had all kinds of crazies calling in. One guy wasn't in New Orleans when she went missing, and there were at least half a dozen people who could prove it."

"Anyone else stand out?"

"There was a guy Huff worked with on the force, a street cop who was trying to work his way up to detective. He wasn't officially on the case but he took a real interest. Huff believed he might've been the one who tipped off the defense to the illegal search."

"Why would he do that?"

"Huff and Black never got along, and he wanted Huff's job."

"The newspaper reported Moreau's mother as the whistle-blower."

"That was just the attorney trying to protect Pearson Black. Black's the one who provided the information. Huff insists he didn't see anyone besides Moreau at the house when he returned that morning, but Black had helped with the search so, of course, he knew what happened."

"Do you have regular contact with either of them?"

"I don't have regular contact with *anyone.* And I like it that way."

"Yet you came here."

He faced her again, doing exactly what she'd thought him incapable of doing—revealing his most vulnerable self. "I want to believe you about the necklace."

"It's still missing, isn't it?"

"Can you tell me where it is?"

"No. I only know that whoever took Adele kept it in his pocket so he could fondle it when he wanted to remember her." Jasmine hadn't realized she knew that detail.

Romain's eyes grew watery, but he didn't look weak, he looked dangerous. "If you're lying, if you're telling me this to manipulate me, thinking you'll enlist my help…"

"I'm not lying."

He stepped closer. *"Then how do you know?"*

She hated admitting she had psychic abilities. She preferred to hang her reputation on her profiling skills, which was what she played up with the media and the police departments she helped, even though it was really some of both. But she couldn't say that in this instance. For one thing, she would've had no way of ascertaining the information. "I have certain…intuitive abilities."

"Intuitive?" Skepticism etched deep grooves around his mouth. "Like the crazy old woman who lives a mile from me and claims to be a witch?"

"I don't claim to be anything," she said. "Occasionally I get…impressions. Some are clear. Some are not. There's no rhyme or reason to them. I can attempt to invite them by studying a particular case and touching something that belonged to the victim or the perpetrator. Once in a while I have an uncanny amount of success. More often, I get random, fleeting, confusing signals, and I wonder if I'm losing my mind."

Her honesty seemed to deflect the criticism she felt sure would've come in the absence of her own doubt. "But we're talking about a crime that took place years ago," he said.

"It doesn't matter. I pick up on random fragments of actions, thoughts or feelings. They can be in the past, present and sometimes even the future."

"How long have you had this…*ability?*"

"Since I was fifteen or sixteen, maybe earlier, but I didn't have anything to compare it to. I chalked it up to coincidence or a good guess or whatever. I didn't talk about it until I started getting involved in criminal investigations." If she'd had the ability when Kimberly went missing, she hadn't known it or known how to use it, but she'd often wondered if it would've made a difference. Maybe she would've been able to sense the danger that summer day. Or been more help with the search.

"And then?"

"Then I realized I was more intuitive than most people. Sometimes it went beyond that, and I could foretell what was going to happen. Or I could sense where someone had died, or what a particular perpetrator had been thinking. Once I began focusing on these feelings, I got better and better at separating outside input from my own thoughts. But it's still a very rudimentary and inexact science. I just do what I can."

"Can you tell me what I'm thinking right now?"

He was being a smart-ass. "I'm not a trick pony," she said, giving him a dirty look. "And I'm not sure I *want* to know what you're thinking."

"I'm thinking there are stranger things on this earth," he said, surprising her by backing off.

"I'm not asking you to believe me," she said.

Again, she got the impression that he wanted to touch her, but it no longer came across in a sexual way. He understood her defensiveness, wanted to reassure and calm her.

At that point, she probably would've let him pull her into his arms. But he didn't try. He moved past her to the door.

Jasmine felt she should stop him. He hadn't given her very many details on Moreau. But he *had* mentioned the name of someone else who might be able to help her—Pearson Black—and that was a start. If she needed more information, she knew where to find Fornier.

"This note you received, the one written in blood," he said, turning back at the last second.

"Yes?"

"What'd it say?"

"Stop me."

"Stop me," he repeated under his breath. For a moment, he seemed miles away but his focus quickly returned. "Can I see it?"

"It's at a forensics lab in California."

"Can you show me how it was written?"

This question made Jasmine's heart race. "Of course." Walking to the desk in the corner of the room, she picked up a piece of paper and wrote the words exactly as she'd seen them on the note, complete with the strange assortment of capitals and an *e* that looked a little like an ampersand.

*S-T-o-P M-e*

The flash of awareness in Romain's eyes told her he recognized some aspect of what he saw. But he didn't reveal what. "You've got your work cut out for you," he said simply.

"That's it?" she asked, overwhelmed by disappointment. "That's all you've got to say?"

"This has nothing to do with me," he said again, and without another word, he left.

Jasmine stared down at the note. Something about the writing told him otherwise. Or he wouldn't have gone so pale under that tanned skin.

# 6

His helmet strapped to the seat behind him, Romain raced down the highway, embracing the cold wind as it numbed his cheeks, stole his breath, whipped his hair. *Had he killed the wrong man?*

No. It wasn't possible. Moreau was a pedophile with two prior arrests. Maybe those arrests hadn't resulted in convictions, but Adele's blood had been on Moreau's work pants, her barrettes in his house. And if those items had left any question, there was that revolting video.

Every muscle in Romain's body tensed when he thought about Moreau touching his daughter the way he had on that tape. Recklessly he gave the bike more gas. He was flying over the highway, going too fast for the wet roads and the darkness. But he didn't care. He needed the adrenaline rush to combat everything else he was feeling.

He hadn't been able to watch much of the video. He couldn't stand it. Huff said Moreau never showed his face on tape, but Huff also said the man in that video had the same build as Moreau and wore the same clothes. What were the chances Adele's killer could be anyone else?

None. This sister of Jasmine Stratford's who'd been missing for so long had to be irrelevant to Adele's case. Or maybe Moreau was responsible for what'd happened to her, and someone else had sent the bracelet. Someone sick enough to find enjoyment in the knowledge of what it'd do to Jasmine.

But Adele's name had been written with the same mix of capitals and that funny *e*—and those details hadn't been printed in any of the papers. Huff had kept that part quiet. So how come whoever mailed Jasmine that bracelet had also sent her a note written in blood, from New Orleans and using the same *e?*

He wasn't sure, but it made him angry. Angry that it wasn't over. Angry that someone else was out there terrorizing the innocent. Angry that Jasmine had brought this back to his doorstep.

The sound of his bike blocked out everything except the mad rush of wind. And that was exactly what Romain wanted. Jasmine had accused him of playing it safe, but he wasn't asking for much. Just peace—peace at last.

And he'd have it. He'd go back to hunting, shrimping, wood carving and tinkering with his bike, and maybe he'd eventually be able to push her and her story from his mind. She'd said she was psychic, for crying out loud. People who claimed to have extrasensory perception weren't completely sane or else they made their living out of lying.

But he still couldn't explain how she knew about Adele's necklace.

Jasmine had remained in her hotel room when Romain left. She'd listened as the roar of his motorcycle dimmed. So, how was it that she was suddenly in his bedroom?

She couldn't answer that question, didn't remember driving down the bayou. And yet, in the light of a flickering fire, she could see his nightstand. It supported a lantern-style light and a battery-powered alarm clock. His dresser held his watch and some change. Then there was the closet, where his shoes were perfectly aligned and his pants and shirts hung so that they didn't touch and wouldn't wrinkle.

Only his bedding was out of order. And, at the moment, he didn't seem to mind. His muscles flexed as he rolled her beneath him, then lowered his head to kiss her, open-mouthed and hungry. His tongue moved over hers as he coaxed her to abandon all reservation, to trust him enough to let him finish taking off her clothes.

Surprisingly, she was only too willing to accommodate him. Everything he did tore at her crumbling defenses like wind threatening to carry away a boat tied to a dock. She could feel her resistance slipping, the rush of her own blood in her ears as she welcomed each new sensation far more brazenly than she knew she should.

He pulled back, gazing down at her. His eyelids were half-closed and heavy with desire, his expression intense, his lips still wet from their kissing. She knew she was being foolish. She didn't even know how she'd come to be here. But logic wasn't enough to make her stop what was happening. Apparently, she wanted him as badly as he wanted her.

"What?" she murmured, questioning his hesitation.

*"Tu es belle."*

Jasmine liked the sound of it. He said other things, too, as he bent his head and ran his lips down the side of her throat. Some of it was in English: *So soft…*

Closing her eyes, she gave herself up to his talented ministrations. They didn't even have birth control, yet seconds later she was the one urging him on. She supposed it was the common grief that bound them that dulled her conscience, that stopped her from acting with any thought for the future. But suddenly she didn't care about "later," only here and now, renouncing those hours when she was most alone.

Then she was straddling his hips. His hands gripped her thighs, helping and encouraging her until the waves of pleasure grew so intense she shuddered and cried out, and he moaned as he reached the same release.

Breathless, she slumped onto his bare chest, and he smoothed the hair from her forehead, muttering something in French: *C'était le meilleur.*

Before she could ask him what it meant, she woke up, sweating and panting and sated—but alone in her hotel room.

She stared at the ceiling, wondering what'd just happened. How could she be in her own bed? She was still tingling from Romain's touch, could still smell the woodsmoke in his house....

Confused but relieved, she sat up. They hadn't really made love. They couldn't have. She'd never left the hotel. And yet it was too real to be a dream. She could describe Romain's body in explicit detail, although he'd been wearing long pants and long sleeves during both of their prior encounters.

And then Jasmine realized it wasn't her dream she'd just experienced. It was his.

"What are you doing here?"

Forty-year-old Casey Lynn Konitz owned The Breakfast Joint, where the locals, mostly older fishermen, came to have their coffee and *la grue*—what Anglo-Americans called grits. She also owned one of the town's only computers with Internet access.

"I need to go online," Romain responded, their voices adding to the babble of both French and English that surrounded them.

"You don't look so good this morning, T-Bone," she said.

He'd spent a restless night. He'd made love to Jasmine Stratford again and again in his dreams, each time more aggressively than the last. But dreams weren't enough to satisfy the very real hunger he'd felt since seeing her in those silky pajamas. He was frustrated and edgy and worried that the woman who'd come into his life yesterday would irrevocably disturb the delicate equilibrium he'd established since prison.

*"Soyez gentil,"* he said, grinning.

"I *am* being nice. You're still handsome as the devil, that's fuh shore. But you're *fatigué, non?"*

"I'm fine."

"Really?"

"Really. Let me use your computer."

"What for?"

Romain knew she didn't mind sharing it with him. Like most everyone around here, she was just nosy. Gossip was Portsville's main source of entertainment, especially through the winter months. "I need to do some shopping."

Her eyebrows went up. "For Christmas presents?"

"Maybe." Actually, he hadn't bought one thing and probably wouldn't. His parents were expecting him for dinner at their place in Mamou, but they'd be happy with the shrimp he'd caught in his trawling nets a few days ago, before the season ended. It'd fill their freezer and provide enough for their traditional New Year's dinner of *boulettes des chevrettes:* ground fresh shrimp mixed with peppers, garlic, onions and spices, formed into patties and deep-fried. But he wasn't excited about going home, because his older sister and her husband would be there. Susan had gone to Harvard, married an attorney and relocated in Boston. She'd done well, and Romain was proud of her, but she refused to forgive him for not fighting to stay out of prison after he shot Moreau.

"Or maybe you're looking for a woman," Casey teased. "Are you signing up for one of those online dating services, T-Bone?"

"Nah," he said. "I've decided on a mail-order bride."

She laughed. "Why would a man like you need to pay for a woman?"

"Because then I can order her just the way I want— meek and submissive, always willing to scratch my back and cook me dinner." He stretched, getting as much mileage out of needling Casey as possible.

"Right." She slugged him in the arm. "You'd be bored within a month. You need a woman with some fight in her."

"*Mais,* someone like that would be too hard for me to handle," he said, grinning. "I'm a mama's boy, remember?"

She rolled her eyes. "You're a wolf in sheep's clothing, that's what you are."

The bell sounded over the door, announcing the arrival of another patron. Distracted by it, Casey waved him toward the back room, where the computer was, and grabbed a menu for the newcomer. "I'll bring you some biscuits and gravy. You want anything else today?" she called over her shoulder.

"That's it." He was too eager to get online to worry about

changing the menu. Jasmine Stratford pretended to need his help to find her long-lost sister, but she probably didn't even have a sister. More likely she was a criminal rights attorney, bent on advancing her political agenda by convincing everyone he'd killed the wrong person. Or a journalist chasing her next "big" story. Or maybe a writer with a contract for a new book—*When Fathers Turn into Killers.* Regardless, Black had to be involved. Black was the only one, besides Huff, who could've described the peculiarities of the writing on that bathroom wall.

But that still brought him back to the necklace. Neither Huff nor Black knew it'd gone missing. It'd disappeared almost a week before Adele was taken. Even Romain hadn't connected the two incidents.

Maybe after he'd had the chance to dig a little, he'd be able to explain how Jasmine knew so damn much, he thought. But what he found only added to his confusion. Google cited a whole list of articles that featured Jasmine's name, all of which proved her to be exactly what she claimed.

…Sacramento victims rights activist Jasmine Stratford developed the psychological profile that eventually led to Bellamy's arrest…

…Jasmine Stratford, from the nonprofit victims' charity The Last Stand, spoke with officials earlier today…

…Mrs. Purdue insists her daughter would not have been found had it not been for the assistance of local victims' advocate Jasmine Stratford, who lost her own sister in a kidnapping incident fourteen years ago…

Criminal Minds: Profiling the Profiler. After the

widely publicized Robbins case, Jasmine Stratford has been called one of the best psychological profilers in the country. And yet she has no official degree in any of the sciences. With only a high school GED, the talented profiler credits her own personal crisis with spurring her interest in deviant behavior and motivating her to educate herself. According to Stratford, killers act to fulfill certain needs. Determining what those needs are provides understanding and, to a point, the ability to predict certain behavior—

"Here you go."

Fornier pulled his eyes away from the screen long enough to acknowledge Casey, who'd arrived with his breakfast. She had to shove a mountain of papers aside, but she managed to fit his coffee and his plate on the desk at his elbow.

"It doesn't look as if you're buying anything too expensive," she said, frowning at the article displayed on her monitor.

"No," he said. But what he'd read could still cost him a great deal. He was beginning to believe Jasmine was for real—and that, some way, somehow, he might've killed the wrong man.

Jasmine hadn't expected to run into Romain at the diner. She hadn't heard the roar of his motorcycle go past the hotel this morning, hadn't seen it parked in the lot when she walked over. But in order to bring water and supplies to his house, he had to have a pickup or some other form of transportation, which he must've driven. Because there was no mistaking the identity of the tall blond man who emerged from the back area of the restaurant. She would've known him simply by the way he carried himself, even if she hadn't been able to see his face.

Ducking behind her menu, she hoped he'd leave without noticing her. She knew she hadn't really slept with him last night, but it sure felt like she had. Her body burned at the memory of his hands moving *everywhere*—because the way he'd imagined the encounter was exactly as she would've liked it to be.

Unfortunately, luck wasn't with her today. When she didn't hear the bell above the door, she peeked over the corner of her menu to see where he was and found him at the cash register, slipping his wallet into his pocket and staring straight at her.

As their eyes met and held, Jasmine cursed silently for looking up too soon. Then she lowered her menu and smiled politely, trying to backtrack to where they'd been before imagination had become more honest than reality.

*We're just two strangers who aren't all that friendly to each other,* she reminded herself. Yet erotic images kept intruding—his bare arms and chest as he poised above her, the pressure of his thigh sliding confidently between hers, the play of emotions on his face when he was too far gone to hold back.

Such a heady fantasy wasn't easy to forget.

He didn't return her smile, but he made his way through the other tables and sat down across from her.

"Would you like to join me?" she asked.

He tilted his head. "You're the one who came to find *me,* remember?"

"I'm leaving soon," she said. "So I won't be around to bother you much longer."

"Are you planning to talk to Officer Black when you reach New Orleans?"

"If he hasn't taken off for the holidays."

"And if he has?"

"I'll wait till he comes back."

"You're spending Christmas in Louisiana?"

"It looks that way."

"Your family doesn't mind?"

Her family… She nearly chuckled at the thought of her parents caring where she spent Christmas but knew if she did she'd have to explain her odd reaction. "I'm determined to get what I came for," she said.

Pulling a napkin from the dispenser on the table, Romain asked her for a pen, which she took out of her purse. He wrote something, then pushed the napkin toward her.

a-D-e-L-e

A shiver went through Jasmine as she studied the mix of capitals and the strange *e*'s. *This* was what Romain had seen last night, what he'd tried to walk away from.

Setting down the spoon she'd been using to stir her coffee, she leaned back. "What made you change your mind about telling me?"

"If I could've ignored it, I would have."

"And you couldn't because…"

"It wouldn't be right."

In other words, the truth was the truth, and he wouldn't hide from it even if it meant he'd have to face some painful realities. Jasmine had to respect that. "So you'll help me?"

"I just did." He stood up and drew a set of keys from his pocket. He was finished. But Jasmine had one more question.

"Do you have a tattoo on your arm?"

One eyebrow slid up, giving his expression a sardonic cast. "I have a couple of them."

"Is one a heart, with a ribbon bearing your daughter's name?" Part of her hoped he'd say no, that this was one little test she'd fail. It happened occasionally. And when it did, she was able to convince herself that she wasn't so different from everyone else.

Obviously baffled, he hesitated but then nodded. "Why?"

Such incontrovertible evidence that she'd "done it again" always unsettled her. It made her feel that she was using only a small part of her gift. But she wasn't sure she wanted to develop her perception any further. She was convinced that she'd been able to experience Romain's fantasy because, in a sense, he'd invited her into his dream through his desire and she'd reciprocated through her own. She'd certainly never experienced anything similar with anyone else. "Just checking," she said, trying to sound nonchalant.

He watched her carefully. "What's my other tattoo?"

She told herself to give him the wrong answer. Then maybe he'd assume someone who'd seen him swimming or fishing without his shirt had mentioned it to her. But she didn't understand how he figured into Kimberly's case—and thought there might come a day when she'd need him to trust her intuition. "A rose, with your late wife's name."

He stared at her, his face a mask. "Where is it?"

"Her name? Along the stem."

"I'm asking about the tattoo."

She put her hand behind her, to the flat part of her shoulder blade, flushing because the memory of kissing him there flashed through her as she did. "Right here."

He swung the keys on his ring around and around as he considered her answer. "Do you want to tell me how you know that?"

"Not really."

He hesitated but ultimately seemed to understand that he'd be better off if he didn't allow himself to be drawn in any further. "Fine. Good luck finding your sister."

Unable to resist provoking him a little more, Jasmine lowered her voice. "Take care of that cut on your thigh."

"Sorry, Pearson Black is no longer on the force." The stocky, bald sergeant behind the bulletproof glass at the front desk of the NOPD hadn't bothered to check any employment records before dispensing this information. He'd known Black by name.

"You're sure?" Jasmine asked.

"Positive."

The badge on the sergeant's uniform identified him as P. Kozlowski. "When did he quit?"

"Didn't quit. Got fired a year ago."

Jasmine struggled against the disappointment of running into yet another roadblock. "How well did you know him?"

"I worked with him now and then."

His clipped tone indicated he had strong feelings about Black. Jasmine guessed they were negative. "But you didn't like him."

Kozlowski focused on the business card she'd passed through the slot. "What'd you say your interest in Black is?"

"He might have some information on a case that's related to one I'm looking into."

"And which case would that be?"

He was skeptical; evidently, he didn't trust outside investigators. "Adele Fornier."

At this, he turned around to see who might be listening to the conversation. When no one in the busy station seemed to be paying attention, he cleared his throat. "We've heard enough about that one to last a lifetime."

"Detective Huff's mistake cost everyone, I know."

"If you want to call it a mistake."

"What would *you* call it?"

His mouth worked as he swept his teeth with his tongue. "It's in the past. I don't have a comment."

She'd given him a card, but that didn't prove anything to him. It didn't make her who she said she was. Neither did it offer any guarantees as to her goals and motivations. He was playing it safe. "Were you involved in the case?"

"Not really."

"Do you know much about it?"

"Just the basics. Killer's dead."

"That's what I've heard."

"So what do you want with Black? He didn't work that case, either."

"Someone told me he kept close track of it. And there are a few…similarities between Moreau and the man who took my little sister in Cleveland sixteen years ago."

His eyes widened in sudden recognition. "Wait a minute…you're that profiler I saw on *America's Most Wanted*, right? What was it…last month?"

"A few days before Thanksgiving."

"I thought you looked familiar. It was your card that threw me. Victims' Support and Assistance. I only saw part of the show and I assumed you were FBI."

"I work for the FBI occasionally, as a consultant."

"That must be what I heard." Now that he had some frame of reference, Kozlowski grew noticeably friendlier. "What was it like? Going on TV?"

Jasmine hid a smile, although she found his enthusiasm

amusing. "It's great to have the media on our side for a change," she said, searching for common ground between them.

"No kidding."

"You probably already know, but they caught the guy I profiled."

"The week after it aired, right?"

"Within twenty-four hours."

"I go on their Web site every few days," he explained. "About Black—"

He grimaced and lifted a hand to stop her. "Don't waste your time with him. He followed all the sensational cases. But he was the worst cop I ever knew."

So she'd guessed correctly. Kozlowski didn't care for Black. "I'd still like to ask him a few questions. Can you tell me where I might find him?"

He cast another glance over his shoulder, seemed content with what he saw and continued, "Last I heard he was working as a security guard for a shopping center in a pretty rough part of town."

"So he's fallen on hard times."

"You could say that." His lips twisted as if Black's misfortune pleased him. "Are you familiar with the city?"

"Not really."

"Then you won't truly appreciate how far he's fallen until you see for yourself. I'll draw you a map."

Just that quickly, Kozlowski had become an ally. Interesting what a little fame could do. "What didn't you like about Black?" she asked while he sketched.

"He was…odd."

"In what way?"

"Like me, you've seen some pretty sick stuff, right?" He

slid the map through the portal as she nodded. "It's not something we enjoy, but it's part of the job and we handle it the best we can."

"I'll go along with that."

"Well, Black was different. He didn't just tolerate the violence and depravity, he *thrived* on it. The sicker the situation, the more excited he got. He was one demented son of a—" he caught himself "—gun," he finished. "I don't know how his wife stands him and I can't help wondering how his little boys will turn out."

"So…you're telling me he liked murder scenes?"

"Or fight scenes. Or car accidents. Anything bloody. He took pictures and kept the grossest ones in a scrapbook. He attended every autopsy he could, then went on and on about the details. Toward the end, he even kept an online journal."

"How do you know?"

"I read it. I think we all did. It made him look worse than most of the guys we put away."

"What'd your chief think of Black?"

"Didn't like him. No one did."

Jasmine knew that some seriously twisted minds gravitated toward police work. Fortunately, most would-be criminals failed the aptitude tests and background checks necessary for the job. But no system was perfect. "How'd he get on the force to begin with?"

"He wasn't so bad when he started. He grew worse as the years went on."

Jasmine took the map and adjusted the strap of her purse. "What finally got him fired?"

The door opened behind Jasmine and a heavyset woman came in. Kozlowski called a fellow desk sergeant to the window to handle the visitor, then told Jasmine he'd take his break and meet her out front.

After weaving through the desks behind the bulletproof glass, he emerged in the lobby through a metal side door. Then he held the outer door open for her and followed her to one side. "If you tell anyone I told you this, I'll deny it," he said.

She raised her hand in the classic oath position. "I won't say a word."

"One of the detectives here caught Black trying to steal some evidence on an important case."

So this was what he'd been burning to divulge. "You're kidding."

He waited for a middle-aged man who was approaching the station to go inside before responding. "I'm not. It was a double homicide, and we definitely had the right guy. Why would Black want to fix it so the perp could get off? It's beyond me."

"A bribe?"

"Possible. It's tough to support a family on a cop's salary, and his wife was out of work at the time. But we don't really know."

"Was he a detective by then?"

Kozlowski scratched his head. "No. He never made detective."

"Did he know the defendant?"

"Not that we could ascertain."

"He must've had some reason for doing what he did."

He shrugged. "Could've been a bribe, like you said."

Or he wanted to make the department look bad. Maybe it was his way of taking revenge on coworkers he didn't like and who didn't like him.

"He claimed he was just checking things out, making sure all the evidence was there," Kozlowski told her. "But he wasn't on that case, either."

"How was he caught?"

"Another officer surprised him while he was trying to switch some DNA samples."

"Was he ever drawn up on formal charges?"

"No. The chief didn't want the publicity, not with all the post-Katrina stuff. He was working too hard to get this department back in shape, rebuild the public trust."

"And without a recommendation, Black wouldn't be able to get on anywhere else either, so he couldn't do the same thing again."

"Which is why he resorted to security work. He has to make a living somehow, you know?"

Jasmine glanced at the map Sergeant Kozlowski had given her. "He works here?" She pointed to the X Kozlowski had put in the center, beside Big Louie's Supermarket.

"A friend of mine saw him in the parking lot one night, wearing a security uniform. There's a rowdy bar in the same strip mall. That's probably why he's there, not the supermarket. But I can't remember the name of the place."

"How long ago was he spotted in that location?"

"Maybe a month or two."

Jasmine hoped Black still had the same job. "What about Detective Huff?"

"What about him?"

"Was he a good cop?"

"The best," Kozlowski said without hesitation.

And yet Huff had bent the rules, too. Kozlowski had already acknowledged as much.

"Where is he now?"

"I heard he moved to Colorado."

"Denver?"

"Don't know."

"What was Huff and Black's relationship like?" Jasmine asked.

"The day Huff left, he walked into the chief's office and told him Black was a danger to society." He grinned. "Only with a few choice words thrown in."

Jasmine swallowed a sigh. Huff had cheated with the search warrant. Fornier had taken the law into his own hands. Black had tried to destroy evidence.

It was getting difficult to tell the good guys from the bad guys.

# 7

How the hell did she know?

Just three days ago, Romain had cut his leg on a nail protruding from a piece of scrap lumber he'd been using to build his screened-in porch. He probably should've gotten a tetanus shot, but that required going to town and seeing a doctor, which he wasn't particularly eager to do. Instead, he'd hoped for the best and recently he'd noticed the wound had started to heal. He'd forgotten about it until Jasmine had made that comment at the restaurant. He certainly hadn't mentioned it to anyone.

Setting the groceries he'd bought on the counter, he strode to his bedroom, dropped his jeans and peered at his upper right thigh.

Sure enough, there was still a scab. It was quite apparent—but it was also in a place no one else had seen in a long, long time.

"I'll be damned." Her abilities were uncanny, and that made him even more uneasy. He'd never been much of a believer in the supernatural. His *mamère* had repeatedly told him that one in every three women was a witch; since he'd never know which one was and which one wasn't, he'd better treat them *all* right. He'd grown up with that kind of talk, had learned to disregard it as the manipulation and superstition it was.

So what was Jasmine? Smoke and mirrors—or the real thing?

He heard a knock at the door and wondered if she'd decided to put off her return to New Orleans. Considering what *he* wanted to do, her company wouldn't be entirely unwelcome. Especially now that he knew she'd somehow seen him without his clothes on. Her revelation told him she wasn't as opposed to what he'd suggested last night as she'd implied.

On the other hand, her gift frightened him, and so did her goal. Her journey would lead back into the past—and that was someplace he never wanted to go again.

"T-Bone! You d'ere? T-Bone!"

"Speaking of witches," he mumbled and went to the door.

"You fa-get old Mem, boy?"

When he'd moved to the swamp, he'd found Mem living even more meagerly than he was. At first she'd refused to answer the door and he'd had to leave whatever he'd brought her on the porch. Now, he had the opposite problem. She kept a lookout for his truck and waited anxiously for the supplies he provided.

"Have I ever forgotten you?" he asked. He'd bought her groceries; he'd just been in too big a hurry to see what remained of that nail injury to stop anywhere, least of all Mem's. He knew she'd tie him up with some chore, fixing her roof or her window or some such thing if she could.

"No."

"Exactly. And I didn't forget today." He nodded toward his truck. "Go ahead and get in. I'll drive you and your groceries home," he told her.

"What'd you get me?" Mem wanted to know.

"Eggs, butter, flour, sugar. The usual."

She leaned heavily on a cane, her wrinkled face rapt with anticipation. "Coffee?"

"Of course." There were beignets, too, but she didn't need to know everything.

"D'at's a good boy. Your *mamère,* God rest her soul—" one arthritic hand moved in the sign of the cross "—would be proud of her T-Bone. He does not forget old Mem. No, he doesn't. And for him I cast my most powerful spells."

"It's a fair trade," he said to salvage her pride.

"D'at's right." She nodded her gray head. "I bring you d'is." Thrusting one hand into a fold of her brown, sacklike dress, she withdrew a sachet filled with her special blend of herbs. She made him a new one almost every week. "It will give you power. Power to have anyt'ing you want."

Nothing could bring Adele back. Or Pamela. But he forced himself to accept it. "I'm just happy we both have enough to eat," he grumbled.

"You always find plenty of de shrimp and de crabs," she said. "It's magic. *My* magic." He thought his shrimping and crabbing success had more to do with hard work than herbal sachets, but it didn't hurt to let her think he saw value in what she did for him.

"I can tell," he mumbled.

"D'ere was a car here last night," she said, her voice rising suspiciously.

He grinned at her abrupt change of topic. No doubt she'd been dying to know about his visitor ever since she'd spotted Jasmine's arrival. "Just another witch," he teased.

He'd expected her to chuckle at his answer. But Mem's

eyes grew dark, her pupils shrinking to mere pinpricks. "She's bad luck. Tell her to stay away." She waved her arms in an adamant motion, then started toward his truck.

Romain hesitated before following. Mem was full of dire warnings. *Don't go out on de bayou, not today, T-Bone... Beware of de storm d'at's brewing... It'll be a hard, hard hurricane season, you mark my words....* To her, something as innocent and natural as a broken tree branch served as a harbinger of bad luck. Too superstitious for her own good, she was determined to look out for him whether he welcomed it or not. But today her words matched his own concerns too closely to disregard them.

"You worry too much," he told her.

She stopped shuffling long enough to tap her temple with one crooked finger. "Mem knows."

And this time Romain wondered if she was right.

While waiting until it was late enough to visit Big Louie's, Jasmine called every sheriff's office and police department in Colorado, searching for Detective Huff. By the time she finished with those and started on the short list of marshals' offices, she was beginning to realize that even if Huff had relocated to Colorado after leaving Louisiana, there was no guarantee he'd still be in the state.

At least focusing on these calls helped keep her mind off Romain Fornier, who'd become a recurrent theme. She wouldn't have been so concerned if her preoccupation with him was limited to what he'd told her about Adele's name on that bathroom wall—the strange capitals, the funny *e*—but it wasn't just that. More often than not, she found herself staring at the bed in the corner of her hotel room, picturing him there, which said a lot about what he'd managed to do to her in the short time she'd known him.

"What's gotten into me?" she asked herself, and was more than a little startled when she heard a response.

"Excuse me?"

Jasmine had forgotten she'd already dialed—and she certainly hadn't realized that someone had picked up. "Is this the Bayfield marshals' office?"

"Yes, it is."

"Is there an Alvin Huff working there?"

"Alvin Huff, did you say?"

"Yes. H-u-f-f."

"I'm sorry, I've never heard of anyone by that name."

"Thank you." With a sigh, Jasmine hung up and moved her finger down to the next office on the list. Most marshals' offices served small communities of about 1600 people. She couldn't see Detective Huff going from the Big Easy to a small Western town in the Rockies and figured she was probably wasting her time. But she had a few more minutes before she planned to leave and decided to call another one or two.

The Crystal Butte marshals' office was next. Clearing her throat, she dialed and, once again, asked for Huff.

"Just a minute, please."

"He's there?" she nearly shouted, jumping out of her seat.

"I'm about to check," the woman responded, obviously startled.

"Thank you. Thank you very much."

Jasmine paced the floor in her small room while she waited. "Be there," she whispered. "Be there."

The woman's voice came back on the line. "I'm sorry,

Deputy Marshal Huff's left for the day. Can I give him a message when he returns tomorrow?"

"Yes. Please tell him Jasmine Stratford from The Last Stand, a victims' nonprofit organization in California, needs to speak with him. It's urgent."

"Would you like me to call his cell to deliver this message, Ms. Stratford?"

"If you wouldn't mind."

"No problem."

"I appreciate your help." Jasmine gave the woman her own cell number and disconnected, then paced some more. But when Huff called her back, he wasn't particularly forthcoming.

"I was told you needed to speak with me."

"Yes. I'm Jasmine Strat—"

"I know who you are."

She stopped moving. "You do?"

"I looked you up online when I got your message. You run a victims' charity in California. You sometimes work as a consultant for the FBI and other police agencies and have helped solved a few high-profile cases. You were on *America's Most Wanted* November twenty-fourth, which led to the capture of a pedophile. Am I leaving anything out?"

*Friendliness, for one…* "The fact that my sister was kidnapped sixteen years ago, and I'm committed to finding out what happened to her. That's why I'm calling you."

"If I remember right, your sister was taken from your family's home in Cleveland."

Remembered right? Jasmine was fairly sure he was sitting in front of his computer, reading all the information he'd pulled up about her. "That's true. But the box I just received with my sister's bracelet in it was mailed from New Orleans. And the note that came with the bracelet was written in blood—using the same strange mix of capital letters and the odd *e* that you attributed to Moreau when he wrote Adele Fornier's name on the wall of the public bathroom."

*"Attributed?"* he echoed.

"That's what I said."

"Moreau murdered that little girl. I'm sure of it."

There was no mistaking the passion in his voice. "If that's true, Moreau must still be alive. Because whoever sent me that package did so only a week ago. And I can't imagine two men with such a unique signature, can you?"

"Moreau's dead."

"Then how do you explain the coincidence?"

"I'm not explaining anything. I'm simply telling you there was far too much evidence in Moreau's house for it to have been anyone else. There was a pair of pants with her blood on it, a video of him sexually torturing her, and one of her barrettes."

"There *has* to be an explanation."

"If there is, I don't have it. That case nearly ruined my career. And it cost Romain Fornier, a man I greatly respect, far more than it cost me. I don't want anything to do with what happened in New Orleans."

Jasmine had thought he'd be more intrigued by current developments. Obviously, she was wrong. He'd been too badly burned. "What about Pearson Black?" she asked.

There was a moment's pause, as if the change of subject took him aback. "What about him?"

"Fornier said he kept inserting himself into the investigation, that he had more than a passing interest."

"Black was dirty. He'd sell his soul for a couple hundred bucks."

"You think someone bribed him to blow your case?"

"That's exactly what I think."

"Who would've put up the money?"

"Moreau's mother or brother. When a cop's willing to sell his integrity that cheaply, almost anyone can buy him. It's even possible Moreau himself promised to pay. Black visited him in jail plenty of times, claiming he was doing research on the criminal mind, that he was planning to write a book."

"I don't think he's gotten around to the book, but I hear he wrote a blog for a while."

"I wouldn't recommend reading it—unless you have a cast-iron stomach."

Her second warning. Jasmine could barely imagine what kind of stuff she'd find there… "I don't have a cast-iron stomach, Deputy Huff." Pretty much the opposite, in fact. "But I *am* determined to find out why this case appears to be so closely related to my sister's. Do you know how I can access his blog?"

"I'm telling you, it's not related. It can't be."

"It has to be."

It was his turn to sigh. "Thanks to Black's twisted sense of humor, it's easy enough to remember. Go to www.CopsBedtimeStoriesByBlack.com."

She jotted the URL on the page of police departments she'd printed out in the lobby downstairs. "How do you like working for the marshals' office?"

"I love it. Can't you tell?" he said and hung up.

Jasmine frowned as she put down the phone. Huff hadn't given her as much as she'd hoped. She wished the lab would get back to her on what the evidence revealed. But the technicians had said it'd be at least three weeks.

With everyone she knew far away from Louisiana, and Christmas on the horizon, three weeks seemed like an eternity. It'd be the middle of January by the time she heard from the lab.

Briefly, she thought of Romain—again. Would he spend Christmas out on the bayou? How did he survive in such isolation day after day?

*Forget Fornier.* She had things to do.

Taking her room key from the desktop, Jasmine went down to the lobby. It was 9:30 p.m., late enough to make it likely she'd find a security guard at Big Louie's. But first she wanted to take a look at Black's online journal. She thought it might be smart to know a bit more about the ex-cop before confronting him in a dark parking lot on the seedy side of town.

It wasn't the amount of violence in the blog that surprised Jasmine. She'd been prepared for that. It was the contemptuous tone. Black's comments, even on an average traffic stop, painted him as the only rational, "normal" individual involved. He claimed he was growing jaded. Bemoaned it again and again. But Jasmine got the impression that he *loved* the power that went with the uniform. His complaints about what he encountered every day were merely an excuse to speak freely and express more disrespect and cynicism toward the average citizen than she could endure.

She wondered if he realized that those "stupid assholes" he belittled for infractions as minor as a tardy car registration were the very people who paid his salary. If so, he didn't understand the term "civil servant." Especially the "civil" part…

"You're a piece of work, Mr. Black," she muttered as she skimmed the grim details he'd recorded about a serial killer in Colombia. As with the previous entries, he focused most heavily on the perpetrator's sicker obsessions, relishing everything that was disgusting and inhumane, and offering his own hypotheses. But Jasmine was already familiar with Pedro Alonso Lopez's crimes and didn't respect Black enough to concern herself with his verbose and self-important analysis, so she skipped most of it. She was more interested in Black's handling of the everyday than his fascination with a psychopath who had over three hundred deaths to his credit.

Jumping a little farther down, she read an entry titled "Dumb Blonde" dated fourteen months ago. According to Kozlowski, that would've been shortly before Black was fired.

Never fails. If a woman thinks she's got a chance of avoiding a ticket, she'll do just about anything.

So I pull this woman over today, right? We'll call her Lola since I can't use her real name. I walk up, she rolls down her window and I find myself staring in at a woman with every beauty aid—Botox lips, silicon cleavage down to her knees, long blond hair, probably from a bottle, fake red nails, lots of makeup. She looks like some kind of porn star, you know? The kind of woman who makes you roll your eyes—and adjust yourself at the same time. She also had a lead foot, which is why I wanted to have a chat with her.

"What did I do, Officer?" she says to me, all wide-eyed—the very picture of innocence.

I tell her she was speeding, ask to see her driver's

license and, of course, the tears start. She doesn't have it. It's not in her purse, at any rate. She blubbers through the usual excuses, telling me she recently lost her purse. I smile but keep writing the ticket. So she switches tactics and asks me, in a sultry voice, "Is there anything I can do to get you off, Officer? I mean, to get you to let me off? I don't have the money for a ticket. And my boyfriend will absolutely kill me if my insurance goes up again."

Her boyfriend is paying her insurance bill? At this point I have to ask myself if he's even dumber than she is. What some guys will do for a good lay, huh?

That was it—the end of the account.

Why had he chosen to write about a fairly routine traffic stop?

Jasmine checked the date of his other entries. He'd posted this out of the blue, after he hadn't written for three weeks, and he didn't follow it up with anything else for another ten days. It was the only entry that didn't deal with blood and guts and a Sherlock Holmes style of unraveling the mysterious. The next blog referred to the Blond Bimbo, too, as if his meeting up with her had been really out of the ordinary.

Surely, there had to be more interesting incidents in the life of a cop than getting propositioned by a woman with no morals. That had to happen occasionally, didn't it? Especially if a cop seemed susceptible—by staring at cleavage down to a woman's *knees,* for instance? After all, contact with desperate women of low character pretty much came with the job.

Jasmine read the entry again. *What some guys will do for a good lay...* How did he know the blonde was a good lay?

Suddenly, Jasmine rocked back. Could he have taken her up on her offer? *Something* had happened, something more than he'd spelled out.

*She looks like some kind of porn star, you know? The kind of woman who makes you roll your eyes and adjust yourself at the same time.* He liked what he'd gotten that night. Liked the perks that sometimes went with being a cop.

"Is anything wrong?"

Jasmine glanced over her shoulder to see Mr. Cabanis's daughter watching her from the front desk. "No, why?"

"You have this…sort of disgusted expression on your face."

With good reason. She was sickened that a man like Black had ever been allowed to wear a badge. Was he the one who'd leaked the information about the illegal search? And, if so, what did *he* get out of it? After reading Pearson Black's online journal she guessed he never did anything that didn't benefit him in some way.

Jasmine was sure it was Black, although he'd lost a few pounds since the picture on his blog was taken. He'd converted that fat into muscle. At least that was how it looked to her. As she drove by him, she couldn't see any evidence of the rounded paunch he'd had or the double chin. He was a tall, thick-necked man who wore his security jacket unzipped despite the cold and obviously took weight lifting very seriously. With his build, his face shadowed by stubble and hair rumpled enough to make Jasmine wonder if he'd bothered to run a comb through it before going to work, he looked mean in the way some pit bulls look mean. As if he should be wearing a spiked collar.

He leaned against his sedan in the dim light of the parking lot and put out one cigarette only to light another.

The lounge Kozlowski had mentioned was called Shooters. It was nestled between a liquor store and a bargain remnant store just down from Big Louie's. Jasmine frowned when she saw the name, hoping it'd been inspired by shot glasses of booze and not by the number of drive-by slayings in the area.

Finding an empty parking stall between the bar and the supermarket, she made sure she had her Mace, turned off the engine and got out. It was unlikely the ex-cop would be dangerous; he had no record of violence. But he wasn't her only concern. The lounge had iron bars on the doors and windows and graffiti on the walls, and so did the supermarket and almost every other house or retail establishment within three blocks. This wasn't the kind of neighborhood in which she really wanted to be alone. She wasn't all that confident Black would risk himself to protect her, despite those muscles and the security emblem on his car.

As she crossed the section of parking lot between them, she tried to get a feel for the safety of the situation and the man she was approaching. But she felt nothing that gave her any real guidance, except a general anxiety—what anyone else would feel, she supposed. It wasn't as if she could use her gift on demand. Occasionally, she suspected it might be possible to develop her psychic powers to that point, but there were too many drawbacks. Growing more sensitive to such input meant constantly having thoughts and feelings that were not her own, and she didn't want to live that way. It was difficult enough when she had to explore what she could pick up on the cases she worked.

Her boot heels clattered on the pavement as she walked. Noticing her coming toward him, Black straightened and blew the smoke from his cigarette off to one side. "You must be lost," he said, giving her the once-over.

She waited until his focus reached her face. "I look *that* out of place?"

"Have you *seen* the women in this part of town?"

She'd actually seen more men than women. Several were hanging around outside the door of the lounge, talking to each other and watching her. One had whistled when she got out of her car, another was currently indulging in a few catcalls that included commentary on how well she fit into her jeans. "Are those women you mentioned the type who make you roll your eyes—and adjust yourself at the same time?" she asked, cocking an eyebrow at him.

One eyetooth had grown in like a fang, and it showed as Black laughed. "No, they're whores and crack addicts. Not half as pretty as you. No temptation to me at all."

She ignored his allusion to her appearance. "The blonde was a temptation, though, right? Lola? The one you pulled over for speeding a year ago?"

"She was a temptation, all right. Until I found out that she was a he."

Jasmine didn't know how to respond. "You're kidding, right?"

He chuckled softly. "No."

"How'd you find out?"

"When I insisted I wouldn't accept the driver's license she—he eventually provided, which gave his name as Henry Hovell, he decided to show me proof."

"Why didn't you add *that* to your blog? It would've made for a great twist at the end."

"Because I found him attractive as a woman. And that's not something I wanted the other guys ribbing me about at the station." He took a long drag on his cigarette. "Anyway, last I heard I was already fired from the department, so you can't be Internal Affairs."

"No."

"Then why are you here?"

"I have a few questions for you."

His eyes raked over her again. "And those questions brought you all the way here?"

"It's about the Fornier case."

His smile disappeared—and with it that single, very unattractive fang. "I wasn't on that case."

"I heard you followed it closely."

"Who told you that?"

"Some of your buddies down at the station."

"I don't have any buddies down at the station."

"Most police officers are pretty close. Why didn't you fit in?"

"They couldn't take that I was a better cop than they could ever dream of being."

And his blog was proof? She didn't think so. "Were you out to prove it—to show them?"

"I don't remember getting your name," he said instead of answering.

She handed him her business card. "Jasmine Stratford. I'm with a victims' charity in California."

There was no sign of recognition. "You're a long way from home."

"I'm also a freelance profiler with reason to believe Fornier might've shot the wrong man when he went after Moreau. Do you think that could be true?"

Black flicked his ashes onto the ground. "Don't ask. You don't want to start poking around in the Fornier case."

"Suppose you tell me why."

"What's that old cliché? Let dead dogs lie?"

"It's 'sleeping dogs.'"

His grin slanted to one side. "Not in this case, right?"

Jasmine didn't appreciate his sense of humor. "That's not a good enough answer."

"Try this one." He leaned toward her, engulfing her in a cloud of smoke. "Because you might regret it later," he whispered. "Is that better?"

He was too close. Jasmine almost reached for her Mace. But she sensed that he was only trying to intimidate her, and she refused to let him know he'd succeeded. "Is that a veiled threat?" she asked, standing her ground.

"Not from me." His smile returned as he leaned back—and with it that fang. "Why would I want to hurt you?"

"You tell me."

"I have no personal stake in the case." He shrugged, but the action didn't seem careless as much as studied. "I'm just informing you that there are people who won't be happy to have certain details brought out into the light, people who have a lot to lose."

"Like who?"

"Like whoever really killed that little girl. Moreau was a pervert. I'll grant you that. But he wasn't the man who murdered Adele Fornier."

The men outside Shooters who'd been trying to attract her attention had given up and gone back inside. The wind was kicking up, and it was starting to rain. "What about the evidence?"

She thought she had him, but he didn't even blink. "Someone planted it. The blood on the pants, the barrettes, everything."

# 8

"How do you know?" Jasmine demanded.

Tossing away his cigarette, Black shrugged again. "Anyone who really looked at that crime scene could tell you Moreau didn't hide those things under his house."

"Why not?"

"They were put there from the *outside*. Whoever did it entered the crawl space through the cellar door."

"So?"

"So, if you'd just killed a girl in your house, you sure wouldn't gather up the evidence and take it outside and around the back to go in through the cellar door. Why risk letting someone see you when you could simply lift the trapdoor in the pantry and put it down there?"

"Why would he have to walk around? Every house I know has a back door."

"His was completely blocked off." Black pulled a new cigarette from the pack in his shirt pocket and shoved it in the corner of his mouth, unlit. "There was a big freezer in front of it, piled high with boxes full of all kinds of shit. There's no way Moreau bothered to move it and then put it back. He had too many other options. Besides, those boxes on the freezer were dusty as hell. They hadn't been touched in months, not even for cleaning. He lived alone at the time, and take it from me—he was a slob."

"Maybe the trapdoor was blocked off, too."

"Only with a sack of potatoes. It would've been easy to use—yet no one did."

"How can you be so sure?"

He thumped his chest. "Unlike Huff, I did my research. It had an old wooden floor, you know? Someone had painted the pantry, even the floor, at least a year before Adele went missing."

"And some of the paint fell into the crack along the trapdoor and created a seal," she said, picking up on where he was going with this.

"Which wasn't broken when we entered to perform the search," he finished.

"How did you see that?"

"I checked it, and I tried to tell Huff. But all he could see was Moreau's rap sheet. He'd found his pedophile. He'd found his victim's clothing. End of story." He cupped a hand around his cigarette as he struck a match and added, "Some detective *he* was."

"Was there any evidence someone had used the cellar door?" Jasmine asked.

"Plenty. The lock had rusted so it couldn't be opened. There were marks on the lintel indicating someone had recently forced it from the outside using a crowbar or something. There were also scuff marks in the dirt near the entrance. The bloody pants, along with the video and barrettes, were on the ground not two feet away from the entrance, as if someone had tossed them in and shut the door."

"You pointed that out to Huff, too?"

"I tried."

"But…"

He tossed the match away and breathed deeply, exhaling as he answered. "He said Moreau could've walked around and forced that door open as easily as anyone else."

"Unlikely though you make it sound, that's true," Jasmine said. "They were *his* pants, weren't they?"

"They were khaki work pants *like* the pants he typically wore. But how many men wear khaki work pants? Only jeans are more common."

Jasmine took a moment to process what he'd told her. He had a point. But she didn't like him. And, with what Kozlowski had shared about him, he didn't have a lot of credibility. "What about the size?" she asked.

He took another drag before responding. "Didn't match. They were one size smaller than the pants hanging in Moreau's closest."

"One size isn't enough to draw a conclusion," she argued. "It's possible to own one pair of pants that are slightly smaller than the rest. They could've been bought before Moreau gained weight. Or maybe he was on a diet and bought them because he was slimming down."

Tilting his head back, Black blew a fresh stream of smoke into the sky. "Why am I wasting my time with you?" he asked. "You're just like Huff. You see what you want to see."

Jasmine had to admit she was feeling defensive of the overzealous detective. She was defensive of Romain, too. Even more defensive of Romain. If what Black said was true, he'd been acting on erroneous information when he shot and killed Moreau.

But part of her couldn't help believing Black. Someone other than Moreau had killed Adele Fornier. It was the man who'd sent her the note. A man who was very definitely alive.

"Why couldn't Huff see what you saw?" she asked. "Wasn't he concerned about those irregularities?"

"Like I said, Huff was so convinced he had the right culprit, he was blind to everything else. And let's be honest. Solving such a high-profile crime wouldn't hurt his career. He wasn't above a little ambition. He wanted a conviction, and he did what he could to get it. I blame him and not Fornier for Moreau's death."

"So that's why you informed on him."

Throwing his cigarette on the ground, Black grabbed her arm in one lightning-quick move. "I *didn't* inform on him. I kept my mouth shut, okay?"

Obviously, she'd touched a sensitive spot. Or he was slightly deranged.

Jasmine glared at his fingers. "Let go."

"Don't try to tell me about things you don't understand."

She met his glittering gaze. "I said let go. *Now.*"

"Or what?" His warm breath fanned her cheek, smelling like tobacco. "What's a little gal like you gonna do?"

"Press charges for assault, if I have to."

Before he could say anything else, two men stepped out of the lounge. Jasmine glanced over at them, ready to cry for help, but he dropped his hand and stepped back.

"You're gonna wind up getting hurt, you know that?" he said.

"Another threat, Mr. Black?"

He hooked his thumbs in the pockets of his blue pants. "This isn't a safe place for a woman to be, especially at night. You'd better get out of here."

She *wanted* to leave. She felt a barely tethered aggression in this man, and it frightened her. But she wasn't finished yet. "Why would Huff blame you if you didn't do it?"

"He's convinced I did. Just because I didn't agree with the conclusions he drew during that search. Just because I tried to make him see there was something more going on." He spat at the ground. "It's thanks to him that I'm rotting out here doing nothing all night."

Or maybe Huff was right, and it was Black who'd enabled a child killer to walk free, causing a grieving father to snap. "If it wasn't you who snitched, who was it?" she asked.

"Moreau's mother, I guess," he said sulkily.

"Huff claims she wasn't there."

"She wasn't. At least I didn't see her. But Moreau could've told her, right? That's not too much of a stretch. Or maybe it was someone else. I wasn't the only cop on that search. Kozlowski and Brenner were both there. They could've leaked it. Maybe someone overheard them talking at the station."

Jasmine found it odd that Kozlowski hadn't mentioned his own involvement. But Black's next statement raised even more questions.

"For that matter, it could've been Fornier's brother-in-law."

"His *brother-in-law?*" she repeated.

"Yeah. He's some hotshot attorney from Boston who was nosing around. Fornier thought he was trying to help, but the guy kept getting in the way."

The rain came down harder. Shielding her face with one hand, Jasmine considered this revelation. "You're saying he might've stumbled on the information and accidentally allowed it to get out?"

"Or maybe not so accidentally. From what I heard, he wanted his niece found, but there wasn't much love lost between him and Fornier."

"What was the source of the contention between them, do you know?"

His eyebrows knitted as if he was irritated by the question. "I have no idea. I'm just telling you it was there."

"Then…with so many other possibilities, why does Huff insist it was you?"

"Because Huff doesn't know his head from his ass. He botched that case, so he pointed the finger at me. I'm the scapegoat. Don't you get it?"

Jasmine "got" that Black was jealous of Huff. He'd aspired to the position of detective but hadn't made it, although he clearly considered himself superior. Was he telling her the truth, or had he been trying to push Huff from his pedestal by derailing the investigation? "Where did Moreau live when you did the search?" Jasmine asked.

"Why do you want to know?"

A gust of wind blew her hair around her face. "Because I do."

Clicking his tongue, Black shook his head. "You have to see it for yourself, right? What I've said isn't enough."

She didn't bother responding to that. "Can you tell me how to get there?"

"Sure. But you won't find anything new. I opened the trapdoor to prove my point the night I discovered it was sealed shut."

Maybe she wouldn't find anything beyond the marks on the lintel Black had mentioned. But she might *feel* something. Her abilities sometimes worked that way. "I need to be able to get the setting straight in my mind."

"Suit yourself," he said. "Like I told you, I have no personal stake in the case." Their eyes met, but only for a brief moment before he turned his attention to getting himself another cigarette. "It's 2303 Sea Breeze Way in the Garden District."

"How come you know the exact address after so long?" she asked.

He lit up again. "I have a great memory."

"It wasn't even your case."

"I go over there occasionally," he admitted. "His brother and I are friends."

Huff had mentioned Moreau's brother. In fact, Huff thought the brother might've bribed Black to help Moreau out of trouble. "His brother lives there now?"

"Yep. So does his mother. They sold their house to pay Francis's attorney fees and then moved into his place after he was arrested because it was cheaper."

Jasmine blinked raindrops from her eyelashes. "Where's his father?"

"Died years before the move. Heart disease."

"Thanks." Figuring that was all he had to say, she turned toward her car, but he spoke again.

"Be careful."

Pivoting, she raised a hand to once again shield her face. "Of what?"

He flipped his hair out of his eyes, and his teeth—including that fang—glowed white against the heavy beard growth on his jaw. "In this case, if the bad guys don't get you the good guys will."

Jasmine couldn't unwind enough to sleep. Every time she began to drift off, she'd see Pearson Black leaning against his car, smoking—and, seconds later, that smoke would roll over her like a suffocating blanket, burning her nose and throat, making it impossible to breathe. She'd startle into wakefulness, tell herself it was just a dream, then stare at the storm raging outside the window until her eyelids began to close and the whole cycle repeated itself.

After experiencing the same nightmare for the third time, she began to worry that it was some sort of premonition. Was there more to Black than the morbid, drama-loving braggart he seemed to be? She sensed that he'd been selective in what he'd chosen to share with her, but why hold anything back? And was there any truth to what he'd said about that evidence being planted?

Hoping to ease her tension enough to finally get some rest, she was about to get up and take a hot shower, when her cell phone rang. A quick glance at the alarm clock on the bedside table told her it was after midnight, but midnight in New Orleans was only ten at home. She figured it was Skye or Sheridan checking in with her.

"What's going on at the ranch?" she said, smothering a yawn as she answered.

"The ranch?"

Jasmine blinked and sat up. It was a man's voice. With the thunder making such a racket, and her disquieting dreams about Black, she didn't immediately recognize it. "Who is this?"

"Romain Fornier."

It sort of sounded like him. But she thought he didn't have a phone. He'd moved out into the middle of a swamp because he didn't want to deal with other people. "Where are you?" she asked.

"At the Flying Squirrel."

The ramshackle tavern with the stuffed alligator beneath the overhang at its entrance. She remembered seeing the building, which was basically a lean-to adjacent to the little grocery store on the outskirts of Portsville.

"Tell me something only you'd know." She was half teasing, but after her encounter with Black there was still that trace of doubt in her mind, that uneasiness that came from being in a foreign place.

"I have a cut on my right thigh."

"Yeah, it's you."

"How'd you know?" he asked at length.

His tone indicated that he didn't like accepting what he was apparently beginning to accept. And she could understand why. *She* didn't always like accepting what she could do. "I touched it," she said.

"When?"

Jasmine reacted to his subtle, sexy change of inflection by lowering her voice. "When I was touching the rest of you."

"Damn. Where was I when you were doing that?"

She smiled. "Asleep, I guess."

"Next time you want to explore, would you mind waking me? I think it'd be a lot more fun."

"From my perspective, it wasn't bad the way it was," she said.

"Oh, yeah?"

Her smile broadened. "Yeah."

"Tell me about it."

The gruffness in his voice made Jasmine's heart pound. She was drawing too close to the flame of their attraction, but it seemed harmless enough, since he was two hours away and she was barricaded in her hotel room. His voice on the phone gave her something to hold on to in the dark. "I was on top," she murmured.

"I like it so far." His voice went even deeper. "Was I inside you?"

Jasmine knew she shouldn't let this continue, but the excitement flooding her senses goaded her on. "Yes. A perfect fit."

He groaned. "It's getting better."

Scooting lower in the bed, she covered her head with the blankets. "You were speaking to me in French. I don't know what you were saying, but—"

"What'd it sound like?"

She had no trouble recalling his words. She'd repeated them to herself at various times throughout the day, relishing the wonder she'd sensed in him at that moment. *"Tu es belle."*

"You're beautiful," he translated.

A surge of warmth seemed to lift her up and carry her over a large swell, as if she were riding an ocean wave. "Too bad you couldn't have meant it," she said wryly, trying to reach solid ground again.

"Why not?"

"You haven't seen what you were looking at when you said it."

"I've seen the rest of you. What else did I say?"

"I'm probably going to slaughter it, but it was something like *'Il est été trop long.'"*

"Wait a second…. This is beginning to sound familiar."

"Really?" she said with a laugh. "I thought you were asleep."

He hesitated, seemed to wrestle with disbelief, then succumbed to the irrefutable proof in her description. "And I thought my fantasies were my own."

"I didn't ask to be invited to your party."

"You weren't invited. You crashed it. How?"

All she knew was that they'd both wanted this strongly enough to make it happen. "I have no idea."

"Does this kind of thing occur often with you?"

"Last night was the first."

Silence. Then he said, "But you enjoyed it?"

"Every moment." That memory should've lasted her through a lot of lonely nights, but here she was, already craving more.

"Somehow it wasn't as good for me as it was for you," he complained.

She swallowed to ease a sudden dry throat. "What was wrong with it?"

"It wasn't *real*."

Jasmine's breathless excitement told her it was a very good thing they were so far away from each other. Any closer, and he'd be at her door or she'd be at his. "Real is overrated."

"How so?"

"It gets people into trouble." *With a capital T.* Throwing the covers off her head, she took a deep breath of the room's cold air and tried to work her way back to logical, to sensible, to responsible.

"What kind of trouble are you afraid of?" he asked.

The kind of trouble that came with a man like Fornier: the addiction, the craving, the risk, the heartbreak. "Losing control."

When she was young, she'd given in to the need to escape, to feel anything but what she felt when she thought of her sister. It'd been a long, hard road since then, pulling herself out of the mire of drug addiction. She was determined to make better decisions, to hang on to her self-respect and protect her future.

"You'd be safe with me."

*Yeah, right.* That was what they all said, wasn't it? "I had some interesting experiences when I was younger, enough to know what I want and what I don't," she explained.

"How does one night with me threaten that?"

"It's out of character."

He chuckled softly. "I was afraid you were going to say it's out of the question."

"It is out of the question."

"I'm not convinced." He hesitated as if contemplating the problem. "You're running scared, but you're not un-reachable. Somehow you participated in that fantasy, too."

"Maybe you're the one who's psychic."

"You already let me know how much you liked it. But you didn't have to. I can tell when a woman's inter-ested—and when she's ready to bolt. What's made you so skittish?"

"A determination to avoid past mistakes, I guess."

"You've been hurt?"

"Not by a man. Not directly, at any rate."

"Then it relates to your sister."

She was letting this conversation go on too long, but she liked the sound of his voice, the quiet intimacy she felt despite the small, lonely room. "Maybe."

"What happened to you after she went missing?"

"Everything." He was treading too close to matters she never discussed with anyone—even Sheridan and Skye—if she could help it. Kicking off the rest of the covers, she redirected the conversation. "Why'd you call?"

She could tell he wanted to press the issue, but he

allowed her to change the subject. "I was wondering if you managed to find Black."

"When you walked out of the restaurant, I got the impression I'd never hear from you again."

"I figured the same thing."

"And then…"

"And then I had a few drinks." She heard him sigh. "Probably a few too many."

Lightning flashed, brightening the room. Jasmine watched the rain roll down the outside of the window, listened to it plink against the fire escape. "I found him."

"What'd he say?"

Other than getting him to answer any questions that might come up about Moreau, Huff and Black, Jasmine was fairly sure she didn't want to draw Romain any further into her investigation. Handsome though he was, he had some deep scars, which made him unpredictable, maybe even a liability. "Nothing, really."

He laughed disbelievingly. "You're not going to tell me? You want me to trust you, but you're not willing to trust me?"

Basically. But when he put it that way, she saw the unfairness of it. She also saw that it might be worth telling him if he could refute Black's claims. "I don't want to upset you."

"You're about six years too late for that."

"Fine. Black insists it wasn't Moreau who killed your daughter."

"Of course he'd say that. He's the one who destroyed the prosecution's case."

"He says he wasn't the one who talked about the botched search. He says it could've been Kozlowski or another cop who was there that night." She thought of Romain's lawyer brother-in-law, but decided that was too big a stretch. Why mention it? She shouldn't, not until she had more to go on.

"Can he prove it?"

"No. Or he would've done so." She remembered the painful grip of his hand on her arm. "I think he's been accused one time too many for a man of his temperament."

"What does that mean?"

"He doesn't take kindly to it."

"He didn't hurt you…"

"No."

"What about the evidence? No matter how it was gathered, or whether it was admissible, it was still there, in Moreau's house."

"Black claims it was planted."

"By whom?"

"He doesn't know."

There was some rustling on the other end of the line, and Romain's voice turned sarcastic. "Of course not."

"I'm not saying he has a lot of credibility. I'm just repeating what he told me."

"But you're tempted to believe him."

She tried to choose her words carefully. "He told me a few details that had the ring of truth. I need to check them out. That's all."

"I didn't kill the wrong man, Jasmine."

It was a terrible possibility—but the note she'd received made it seem more likely than not. "You might have."

"Go to hell," he snapped and hung up.

Jasmine couldn't blame Romain for his sudden flare of temper. No doubt he'd called, hoping that what she'd found would reassure him, put his mind at rest. Instead, she'd done just the opposite.

The rapid shift of emotion, his and hers, left her more depressed and exhausted than before she'd spoken to him. She needed to keep her distance from Fornier. That was all there was to it.

So why did her fingers itch to call him back?

She couldn't breathe. Only it wasn't Black's cigarette smoke that threatened to suffocate her. It was steam. Thick, hot, heavy steam. She was in a shower. And Fornier was with her. She would've recognized the way he handled her body, the way he kissed, even if her hands hadn't immediately sought out, and found, that identifying cut on his thigh.

"It's me," he murmured, his body slippery as he purposely brushed against her. "Did you think it'd be someone else?"

No. But she'd been nervous, apprehensive. Too many dark thoughts had made her feel that way.

"Relax." He ran a bar of soap over her breasts and stomach, pausing to take advantage of her more sensitive spots. "You want this, don't you? You want me as long as it's safe."

The bitterness in his voice reminded her that their last conversation hadn't ended well. He was angry. It was apparent in his movements, which hinted at barely leashed emotion. But Jasmine didn't care. He was as masterful with her body as he'd been the first time. Sure of himself, sure of her. She'd never known a lover like him.

Bending his head, he let the water run over them both as he kissed her, nibbling her bottom lip before toying lazily with her tongue. She could taste the water, his mouth, and then his skin…

Light came from a muted source in another room. A

fire? A lantern? Whatever it was, it wasn't very bright. She didn't know any place that was so dark and quiet and private, any other place she'd rather be....

Romain lowered his head to lick the water beading on the tip of one breast. Jasmine was beginning to tingle, to want him to do more, and she let him know it by curling her fingers into his broad shoulders.

"You like that?" he whispered.

"Mmm…" She arched into him, and he laughed.

"Patience, *ma belle fille.*"

Closing her eyes, she moaned as his fingers began to work in conjunction with his tongue. Soon her pulse was pounding in her ear, so loud she couldn't hear the water anymore. But she didn't care. About anything. Especially when he knelt in front of her and used his hands to pin her against the shower wall.

His mouth was so soft, so warm…

She made fists in his thick hair, eager to take what he offered even as she was tempted to reject it. It was…intimate. Too intimate. She'd never felt so vulnerable.

But he moved her hands away, insisting she trust him, and she soon lost the will to fight. Dragging a gulp of steamy air into her lungs, she held her breath and turned her face into the spray, letting him do as he would, and it wasn't long before her legs began to shake. She gasped, ready for the climax he promised her—

And then he stopped.

"What's going on?" she whispered helplessly.

His hands slid up over her hips and around her waist, pulling her against him, his mouth at her ear. "You want more?"

She dragged in another breath. "What do you think?"

"I think you know where to find me."

Just like that, he released her and let her fall, except she didn't hit the ground. She jerked awake and found herself wrapped in her own blankets, tormented with frustration.

At first she thought she'd somehow experienced another of his fantasies. But she doubted he'd dream up a shower when he lived out in the swamp with no running water.

No, she couldn't blame this one on anyone but herself, and the conversation they'd had earlier.

She wanted to make it real. But she refused to go to him. Instead, she got up and read, paced and wrote down every piece of information she'd collected since coming to Louisiana. Then she drew a picture of Fornier, vilifying him with mean eyes, a harsh mouth and a devilish goatee.

But it changed nothing, of course. Crumpling the picture, she threw it away and occupied herself by playing Hearts on her computer until the storm dissipated and the sun began to rise.

Finally, at seven, her alarm went off. "Thank God," she said as she crossed the room to turn it off. It was time to get showered and dressed so she could visit Moreau's house. Once she left for the day, she'd be too preoccupied to think of Fornier.

She peeled off her pajamas in preparation for a shower. But she couldn't forget him as easily as she'd hoped. When she passed the mirror, she paused to study her reflection. Would he really consider her beautiful if he ever saw her?

*I've seen the rest of you....*

Damn him. How had he managed to get inside her head so quickly?

"I don't want to make love with him," she told her reflection. But the way her skin burned at the thought told her she was a liar.

# 9

Moreau's house looked deserted. Jasmine knocked at the front door, even called out, but no one answered, which felt decidedly anticlimactic.

She should've asked Black if Moreau's mother and brother worked during the day. He seemed to know them pretty well, which was odd. She could understand a cop becoming friends with a victim's family; that happened occasionally. Empathy, a desire to make things right, a sense of responsibility, frequent contact—those were the threads that connected the protector to the protected. But it was rare for a cop to form a lasting bond with the family of a *perpetrator*. Those families tended to maintain faith in the innocence of their loved one, which made the two parties natural adversaries.

Of course, if Huff was correct, Black had played a fundamental role in Moreau's release, so there was that.

Stepping off the sagging gray porch, Jasmine gazed up at the dormered windows on the second story. The place had a shut-in feeling, as if the occupants didn't like visitors even when they were home. The blinds were pulled. The garage, which was separate from the house, had a big padlock on it. Most glaring of all was the No Trespassing sign tacked to the cypress tree in the front yard.

Not the friendliest place Jasmine had ever been. There was no barking dog, no welcome mat, no Christmas wreath on the door.

"Bleak," she muttered. She could definitely see someone like Moreau living here, which made her glad no one was there. Maybe it wasn't legal, or ethical for that matter, to snoop around, but as long as she didn't break in or steal anything, she wouldn't get more than a slap on the wrist if she got caught.

She wanted to see the cellar where the video and those pants bearing Adele Fornier's blood had been found, wanted to examine the marks on the door. It made sense that a home owner wouldn't crowbar his way into his own cellar if he could get in easily via an alternate entrance.

A glance up and down the street confirmed that no one was out, which gave her the nerve to move toward the garage, skirt around the old Buick sitting in the drive and head to the backyard. As uninterested in visitors as these people seemed to be, she expected a gate, but there was only a chain-link fence, with nothing separating the front yard from the back.

Careful to muffle her footsteps—she was positive they'd announce her presence to the world—she slipped between the house and the garage, where the first thing she saw was a pile of at least thirty garbage bags full of trash. Jasmine couldn't understand why anyone would create a dump like that, but the sheer number of bags, and the dilapidated state of those at the bottom, indicated that the Moreaus hadn't taken their garbage to the curb for quite some time.

"Strange." She shook her head as she stared at the mound, but was almost instantly distracted by the cellar door. Too warped to close properly, it stood open by an inch or so. The gusty wind snapping the tops of those plastic bags and whipping at Jasmine's long hair had no effect on it.

She pushed her long bangs out of her eyes as she neared the three steps leading down to the cellar—and noticed a couple of soggy cigarette butts on the cement landing. She knew Moreau's mother and brother could be smokers, but the sight of those butts made her think of Black.

Had he come here last night after his shift was over? She couldn't imagine Moreau's brother or mother having any business that would entail waiting at the cellar entrance in the dead of winter. Especially considering the stench of all that garbage. There were no chairs, no barbecue and no garden. And these butts looked recent.

Removing her digital camera from her purse, Jasmine snapped a picture of them and of the garbage pile—she didn't know why, except she found it so weird. Then she located the Baggies she kept in her purse and carefully lifted the cigarette butts into one. Black had already admitted he was friends with Moreau's brother, which gave him a reason to come to the house. But she'd been involved in enough police investigations to be vigilant about every detail, and these gave her the impression Black had stopped by last night or earlier this morning.

Did her investigation threaten him in some way? Had he visited the Moreaus to warn them that she'd be coming?

She wished she could get more of a feel for the person she'd sensed in her mind, the one who seemed almost desperate to be normal, and yet knew he never would be. But that encounter had frightened her too much. She couldn't convince her mind to accept another contact like that, couldn't seem to get anything these days—except the brief snatch of Fornier's dream when she was in Portsville.

Moving closer to the cellar, she examined several marks on the panel and the lintel. Sure enough, someone had used a crowbar to open this door. She just didn't know when. Or why.

After taking two more pictures, she put a hand on the damp wood and shoved. The door didn't budge at first, but with continued pressure she finally got it open.

The smell of damp earth greeted her. Water dripped somewhere in the far corner; it sounded as if she was standing at the entrance to a cave. The Moreaus obviously had a drainage problem or a leak. But if they didn't mind thirty bags of garbage right outside their back door, they most likely didn't care about puddles and mold in the cellar.

So where had Huff found Moreau's blood-smeared pants, that tape and Adele's barrettes? Black had said they'd been tossed near the entrance....

She took out the flashlight she'd bought on the way over and used it to scrutinize the muddy, undulating ground. Farther away, boxes and bags sat on a wooden pallet—storage, it appeared. Jasmine was curious to see what the Moreaus were storing, but she didn't want to leave the safety of the exit. The closer she drew to the cellar, the worse she felt about this place. Bad things had happened here. She wasn't sure whether it was Adele's experiences she felt or someone else's, but there was suffering.

Her beam revealed something that struck her as odd because it was over by the dripping water, in a corner that didn't seem to have good access or any storage. What was it? A white rag?

Nervously hitching her purse higher on her shoulder, Jasmine bent to clear the low doorway so she could get a better look. She had no plans to go farther. The negative energy coming from the house and the cellar was like a hand, pressing her back. But she just needed a few seconds, a chance to change the angle of her flashlight—

Movement behind her made the hair on the back of her neck stand on end. But she didn't have even a split second to turn around. Someone yanked her purse away and pushed her hard at the same time, sending her flashlight and camera flying as she pitched forward.

She landed in the mud. Then the screech of wood scraping rocky cement echoed in the damp air, followed only by the rattle of a chain, the snap of a lock and her own cries for help.

The cellar stank of decomposition. Or maybe it was her sixth sense. She didn't know if she was actually feeling something or merely reacting to her own fear, but she kept envisioning dead bodies rotting in shallow graves around her—thanks to the work of a psychopath she'd helped catch last year—which made it difficult to keep panic at bay. She'd seen too much in her years with The Last Stand—too many crime scenes, too many grisly pictures—not to recall the worst of them now, when she was locked in a place that literally resonated with evil. No one even knew where she was.

Actually, there was one man who knew exactly where she was—the man who'd locked her in here. She was pretty sure it was a man. Only a very strong woman would be able to pull that stubborn door closed so quickly.

A crack between the door and its frame allowed Jasmine a narrow glimpse of where she'd stood a few seconds before. But she couldn't see anyone, couldn't hear anything.

Where had he gone? What did he hope to achieve by locking her in? And was he coming back?

"Hello?" She banged on the door, trying to attract attention or break the lock, or both. "Can you help me? Please! I'm down in the cellar, in the Moreaus' cellar. Help me, please! Hello? Is anybody there?"

She went on like that for what seemed forever—until both shoulders were bruised and aching, and her throat felt too hoarse to yell anymore. She would've continued banging despite her exhaustion if she'd thought it would help. But her efforts seemed futile. If the neighbors were home, they were inside and couldn't hear her. Or, more likely in this working-class neighborhood, they were away until dinnertime.

Shivering because the mud and wetness of the ground had seeped through her jeans and sweater, she pulled her coat tighter and turned to survey her prison. The cellar, more like a crawl space, was dark, except for the crack of light beside the door and the beam of her flashlight, which created a perfect yellow circle on the cinder-block wall. She was hungry, thirsty, in need of a bathroom. But it was probably the knowledge that she couldn't do anything about those needs that made her notice them.

*Fight the fear. Concentrate.* She'd learned enough from Skye's self-defense classes back in Sacramento to know that, above all, she had to remain calm and be resourceful.

It would be easier if she weren't so overwhelmed by dark images, images of violence and death.

Covering her eyes, she tried to block out where she was and counted several deep breaths. There had to be another way out of here.

Hunched over so she wouldn't hit her head on the low ceiling, she recovered her flashlight and began to search for anything that might offer an opportunity or inspire a plan.

Black had mentioned a trapdoor leading into the pantry. He'd said there'd been nothing but a sack of potatoes sitting on top of it the day he and Huff performed the search. That gave her some hope. With luck, the Moreaus hadn't added any more heavy items and she'd be able to escape through the house.

Unless it was Francis Moreau's mother or brother who'd locked her in. If they were up there, Plan B might not end too well....

No. It was Black who'd locked her in. She'd discovered those cigarette butts, hadn't she? And he was the only one who knew she'd been planning to come here.

"Pearson Black, I hope you rot in hell," she said, because talking to herself seemed to help.

Jasmine found the trapdoor easily enough, as well as a small lightbulb positioned next to it. When she pulled the dangling chain, the light went on and she felt slightly comforted. In a place like this, more light was definitely a good thing. But her feeling of relief didn't last. She couldn't get the trapdoor open. It was locked from the other side.

What now? She had to get out of here before Black—or whoever else had locked her in—came back. If he meant to harm her, this was giving him plenty of time to plan the method. Lord knew he wouldn't have to worry about getting rid of her body. He could simply bury her here. Or stuff her in a black garbage bag, seal it and drop it on top of that pile in the yard. No one would complain about the stench, because it couldn't get much worse than it already was. And no one would report her missing. Not for days. By the time Sheridan or Skye got worried enough to initiate a search, she'd be dead. The police would go to the hotel. Maybe they'd even trace her movements as far as Mamou and Portsville, but that was where her trail would grow cold.

Cursing, she picked up the flashlight she'd put down when she found the lightbulb and peered into the darker recesses of the cellar. She had to be creative.

Could she dig her way out?

Tracing the perimeter with her beam of light, she tried to assess her chances. The ground was damp, but she had nothing besides her flashlight with which to dig. Whoever had locked her in would likely return before she'd made any headway. Or the Moreaus would come home.

No, digging wouldn't get her anywhere. She had to wait for the Moreaus. They'd help her, wouldn't they? Just because Francis had been a pedophile and possibly a murderer didn't mean *they* were bad, too.

But *someone* was bad—truly evil. She sensed danger in this place. And the memory of that unequivocal No Trespassing sign in the yard loomed large in her mind, robbing her of confidence. Obviously, the Moreaus didn't want to be bothered by anyone and not only had she come onto their property without an invitation, she'd been nosing around.

She wasn't meant to come out alive.

Wiping the tears rolling down her cheeks, she sat on the edge of the pallet and rested her head on her raised knees. Too bad she hadn't gone to Romain's after that telephone call. Making love with him would've made for a much more pleasant final night on earth than the one she'd spent.

And then she heard the creak above her. Someone was home.

She just didn't know if that made things better—or worse.

\* \* \*

"Why would he make such an outlandish claim?" Romain turned his back to the entrance of the small grocery, hoping for a few minutes of privacy while he talked. Pumping the pay phone full of quarters wasn't the most convenient way to make a long-distance call, but this wasn't a conversation he wanted to have in front of Casey Lynn or any of the other people who'd let him use their phones.

"You know Black," Huff replied. "He's a troublemaker."

"It sounded as if he was pretty adamant. I think Jasmine believes him."

"He's got to justify what he did in some way, right?"

Romain stepped aside as toothless "Doc" Crawley passed him with an armful of groceries. "Hey, Romain. You orderin' up d'at bride?"

Momentarily distracted by the question, Romain scowled. "What bride?"

"Casey said you're tired of livin' alone. D'at you want a woman. It's cold d'is here winter, eh?" he said with a knowing laugh.

"Gossip," Romain said and waved as the old man got into his 1950s Cadillac.

"Romain." Huff was trying to regain his attention.

Romain plugged his left ear against the noise of Doc's engine. "What?"

"You've been through enough. Tell Jasmine Stratford to stay the hell away."

Good advice. And yet last night, when he'd called her, Romain had done everything he could to bring her back. "She's looking for her sister."

"So?"

So he couldn't help feeling some sympathy for her. He

understood what she'd suffered in a way few others could. And, for the first time in years, he wanted a woman, just like the gossip said. Maybe not a wife, but definitely a warm female body in his bed. And it couldn't be any woman. He wanted Jasmine. "She's been through a lot, too."

"I know. But her sister was kidnapped sixteen years ago. Chances are she's not going to find her. And that happened in Cleveland. It has nothing to do with you."

"Did she tell you about the note?"

"Of course."

"And?"

"It's a coincidence."

"But she wrote the words the way they appeared in her note *before* I told her how Adele's name was written on that bathroom wall," he said.

"The man who found Adele's body has been running his mouth, that's all. Someone's heard the details, and now they're using them. She's probably dealing with some kind of Moreau copycat. Or a prank."

Maybe that explained the note. But there was more. "Jasmine said Adele's killer took a necklace of hers before the actual kidnap."

No response.

"Huff?"

"I'm here." He sounded weary, but Romain plunged on. He had to put this to rest. Trying to escape, to ignore the loose ends, wasn't working.

"She's right," he said. "Adele had a necklace that went missing just days before she did. I didn't think anything about it at the time, didn't connect the two incidents."

"Until Jasmine Stratford arrived."

"That's right."

"Romain, children are always losing things. You don't know that anyone took Adele's necklace."

But Jasmine could describe the necklace even though she'd never seen it. If she could do that, why wouldn't the rest of what she said be true? "Adele didn't lose it. It was stolen," he insisted.

"Fine. Believe Ms. Stratford. I guess it's possible. Moreau had Adele's barrettes, didn't he?"

"She was wearing those the day she was kidnapped."

"What's your point?"

"Moreau was out of town the week prior to the kidnapping, remember? He was in Tennessee, delivering those warehouse lights. We had to establish that he'd been home in time to have taken her."

"And we proved that easily," Huff argued. "Moreau was spotted at the school that morning, watching her on the playground. Where are you going with this?"

"He wasn't in New Orleans when the necklace disappeared."

"How do you know exactly when that was?"

"Because it happened at the club." Jasmine had said Adele's murderer stole it from a locker. The only lockers Adele ever came into contact with were the pool lockers at the club, which was how he'd established the timing. "We went swimming there the Saturday before she disappeared."

"You think someone got into your locker and took her necklace."

"Why not?"

"Presumably because it was locked."

"We never locked it because it required a quarter to get into it again, and the only things we ever took with us, besides a couple of sodas, were an extra pair of goggles and some sunblock. She forgot to take off her necklace before we left home that day, which is why it was in our locker."

"So you're saying Moreau *didn't* take her. You're saying that whoever did it had to be a member of your club."

"Not necessarily. They were having a special promotion that day, and the place was open to the public. Free ice cream and swimming for the kids, providing Mom and Dad sat through a sales presentation."

"Oh, that narrows it down." Huff sighed. "Don't you realize that you have nothing to connect these two incidents except Jasmine Stratford's claim that Adele's abductor also took her necklace? Maybe someone else took it. Another kid who admired it or…whatever. Anyway, how would Jasmine know anything about it?"

Romain didn't want to get into that. "She just does."

"I've read up on her, Romain. She's not psychic. She's a fraud."

"I found nothing online to suggest that."

"Because no one wants to risk a slander suit. But I called the Sacramento PD and talked to some of the cops there. One guy told me he brought her in on a case where she insisted the victim was still alive, and they found her dead a week later. She'd been dead for three months. Don't fall for the act."

Jasmine had already admitted that it wasn't an exact science. And no one could've told her about that cut on his thigh. He sure as hell knew she'd never really touched it— or him. *That* he would've remembered. "She knows things about me no one else does."

"She's trying to use you. She thinks you might be able to help find her sister. But you can't. So leave the past alone. Trust me, you'll be better off."

"I can't leave it alone," he snapped.

"Yes, you can. If what she says is true, you killed the wrong man. Do you really want to live with that knowledge?" he nearly shouted.

No, but he couldn't care more about himself than the children who might be harmed, probably *had* been harmed, if Adele's killer was still out there. "You don't understand."

"No, I don't," Huff agreed. "Because if you did kill the wrong man, I'm equally responsible. I told you it was him. I still believe it was him."

"We have to face the possibility that we were wrong. We can't let any more children be hurt!"

"We weren't wrong, damn it! We couldn't be wrong. I saw that tape. I *know* what Moreau did!"

Romain clenched his jaw against the image that flashed through his mind—his daughter crying for him while Moreau forced her to do unspeakable things. "You're right," he finally said. "I don't know what the hell I'm thinking."

"You have more guts than anybody I've ever met. I admire you for that. But I'm done with the case, Romain. I don't want anything more to do with it. What happened is behind us. We've both moved on, right?"

Romain glanced around at the two-bit town that provided the basic necessities he hauled to his shack in the swamp. "Yeah, we've moved on," he said.

Jasmine held her breath as she listened to someone cross the floor above her. Who was it? Were those footsteps heavy or light? She wanted to at least ascertain whether it was a man or woman. But she had no idea. Not really. She hoped it was Moreau's mom. If it came to a physical confrontation, she'd have a better chance against a woman.

So…should she yell? Jasmine couldn't decide. She felt as much negative energy coming from above as she did everywhere else. It seemed as if the whole place was overrun with evil intent. She'd been trying to convince Romain that Moreau couldn't have killed his daughter, that the child's murderer must still be alive. She couldn't figure out any other explanation for the note she'd received. But she sensed that *someone* had been killed here. She was getting odd, violent impressions. A struggle. A gun. Blood.

She was about to bang on the trapdoor when she remembered the white fabric she'd noticed before she was imprisoned. She'd never figured out what it was, hadn't thought of it since her focus had changed to escape. But she remembered it now. And she wondered whether it had something to do with the level of foreboding and despair that hung so thickly in the air.

Swallowing hard, she pointed the beam of her flashlight toward the far corner. At first she couldn't see anything except muddy earth but, against the dark backdrop, it didn't take long to locate that snatch of white. It was over by the puddle.

*Plop…plop…*

As Jasmine inched closer, her chest grew tight with tension. She loathed this corner of the cellar even more than the rest. Cobwebs caught in her hair and on her hands, and the scratching of small rodents, scrambling to stay out of the spotlight, made her muscles ache with tension. No doubt the trash stacked on the other side of the wall attracted more rats than a normal cellar would, but now she was beginning to see a purpose behind all the garbage. Was someone trying to cover up the sickly-sweet stench that was becoming increasingly apparent?

The scent of wet wood, wet earth and garbage combined to help camouflage what she thought she detected, but she was sure that something or some*one* was buried down here. And if it was murder, the police needed to know. There was probably a family somewhere, searching for a loved one, just as she'd been searching.

Heart hammering erratically, she stopped a few inches from the white cloth, which stuck out of the ground as if attached to something bigger.

Brushing away a clingy web, she steeled her nerves to grab hold of the fabric. It was wet and slimy to the touch, which made her shiver in disgust. She almost pulled back her hand. But she could see a button along the edge. It was a shirt.

The footsteps above fell silent. In some corner of her brain, Jasmine acknowledged and recorded that information, but she was so intent on what she was doing, she didn't react to it. Her arms felt weak as she yanked on the fabric and, when it wouldn't give way, even weaker as she began to dig.

But it took only minutes to discover what her heart already knew: it was a corpse.

# 10

The body had been there for a while. Long enough to decompose completely. Jasmine wasn't going to dig the skeleton all the way out to make sure, but the cranium she'd exposed had only a small bit of leathery skin still attached to the scalp and a patch of sandy-colored hair. There were teeth in the skull but of course no eyes.

This wasn't a child. But it was repulsive enough despite that. Shaking, more from shock and fear than cold, Jasmine scrambled away. What'd happened before this poor person was buried in the Moreaus' cellar?

Her mind created a picture of a desperate struggle, but nothing more.

She had to get out. Before someone realized what she'd discovered. Before the man who'd locked her in here returned. Before she wound up rotting in a shallow grave like the corpse staring sightlessly back at her.

Once again cognizant of movement above her, she hurried toward the trapdoor, planning to beg for help, if need be. But halfway there, she stopped. She couldn't leave the body exposed. If the person inside the house was the one who'd taken that life, and he or she knew Jasmine had found the remains, she'd be even less likely to survive the day.

She had to cover it up.

Struggling to collect her breath as well as her strength, she fought the dry heaves that made her body spasm and went back to the disturbed mud. She shook and shivered and gagged uncontrollably, but she managed to use her flashlight and her hands to begin the reburial. When she finished, no one would be able to tell she'd been digging. At least from the trapdoor. It was too dark.

*Almost there... Nearly done... Keep at it....*

Squeezing her eyes closed so she wouldn't have to watch, she shoved the muddy earth over that white shirt and odd-looking torso, working her way toward the head. It was slow progress. She could barely make her arms obey the commands of her mind. She was too afraid her fingers might touch that flesh or bone or hair, didn't want to think that this had once been a human being.

A slight swell remained in the earth when she was done. She patted it down the best she could and crawled to the trapdoor. She was getting muddier by the minute, but she couldn't stand, couldn't walk. Her legs wouldn't support her weight. It felt as if every bone in her body had turned to jelly. She'd seen some gruesome spectacles in her life, but generally in a designated "crime scene" setting with police officers in attendance. In those situations, she could maintain a certain detachment. Evaluate on a cognitive level. Analyze. Hypothesize.

Now, it was *her* life in danger.

"Hello?" Her fists felt like twenty-pound weights as she lifted them to bang against the trapdoor. "H-help me! Please! I'm locked in. Will you help me?" She began to knock with the butt of her flashlight and, eventually, she heard the creak of footsteps drawing closer.

She wasn't sure what she'd expected, but it wasn't the gentle face of the person who peered down at her.

"Where'd *you* come from?" she asked, blue eyes behind a pair of glasses widening in shock.

Jasmine nearly burst into tears. This woman wasn't dangerous. With her soft white hair and the chain attached to her glasses, she reminded Jasmine of the average American grandmother.

"S-someone l-locked me in here," Jasmine stammered.

"Who?" A second woman came into view, much younger than her counterpart and quite attractive.

"I d-don't know." It was difficult to quell the chattering of her teeth. "I d-didn't see him."

"I *told* you I heard something, Beverly!" the younger woman exclaimed.

So this was Mrs. Moreau. Jasmine had read her name in the papers as the witness that'd caused the case to be dropped.

"It's fortunate you called me," Beverly said, but there was a hint of resentment in her voice that made Jasmine pay particular attention. Especially since the second woman seemed so oblivious to the older woman's true feelings.

"I hated to disturb you. I know you work at night and need your sleep during the day. But I didn't want to intrude on your privacy by searching for the source of that noise without you."

"No one likes a nosy neighbor," she agreed. "Now, where's that little ladder of mine?"

Jasmine hoped she could find it, and wasn't disappointed. A moment later, both women handed the ladder down to her and, resisting a final glance at the grave in the corner, Jasmine climbed out.

"Look at you. You're covered in mud!" Mrs. Moreau said. "What have you been doing down there?"

Jasmine had been about to sob out every gory detail and suggest they call the police. Surely these women had nothing to do with what lay buried in that cellar. Surely they didn't even know it existed, would be as shocked as she was. But Mrs. Moreau's question gave her pause. Wouldn't the average person be more concerned with how Jasmine had come to be in the cellar in the first place?

"I've been trying to get out." She curled her fingers into her palms so they couldn't see the dirt beneath her nails.

"You poor thing!" It was the younger woman again. "What happened?"

"I c-came to the house to speak with Mrs. Moreau and—"

"Why would you want to talk to me?" Beverly demanded. "I've never even met you."

"We've never met. I'm Jasmine Stratford. I work for a victims' charity. I wanted to ask if your son—"

"Phillip's out of town."

"He is?" The younger woman seemed surprised by this information. "I'm Tattie, by the way," she said to Jasmine. "I live next door."

"Nice to meet you," Jasmine mumbled, but Tattie wasn't listening. "Where's Phillip?" she asked Mrs. Moreau again.

"He went to Lafayette to see that woman he met online." She gave Jasmine a glass of water.

Jasmine accepted the water, but she was too uneasy to drink, even though the house was neat as a pin. Scrubbed and polished—if a little cluttered—it was an extreme contrast to the pile of garbage sitting right outside the back door and the general sense of neglect in the yard. The kitchen smelled mildly of cats, which was no wonder because there were three in the kitchen alone, but everything was in its place. There wasn't a dirty dish on the counter, a magazine or newspaper cast aside on the table, or a cupboard left standing open. "I was talking about Francis."

A slight tensing around the mouth contradicted Mrs. Moreau's otherwise genial appearance. "Francis is dead."

Jasmine wondered if Mrs. Moreau blamed her son, society, herself or Fornier for that harsh reality. She definitely blamed someone. "I read about that." Jasmine couldn't bring herself to say she was sorry. Not after what she'd found in the cellar. "I was hoping you could tell me if he ever traveled to Cleveland."

"He traveled all over the place," Tattie interrupted. "He was a truck driver and made deliveries for a lighting company. Didn't he, Bev?"

"Yes, just like his father used to." A second later "Bev" turned back to close the cellar door and replace the things that'd been disarranged in the pantry.

"How long ago did he start doing that?" Jasmine asked the neighbor.

"Why do you care about the details of a man's life when you didn't even know him, a man who's already dead?" Joining them again, Bev spoke before Tattie could answer. "Not after what you've just been through."

It was a smart dodge, if it was a dodge, because it got Tattie pressing Jasmine for details. "Why would anyone lock you in the cellar?"

"I have no idea."

"Should we call the police? Are you hurt? How do we find the person who did this to you?"

These questions came from the neighbor and not Mrs. Moreau. Francis's mother didn't seem too concerned, which added to Jasmine's discomfort. But she decided to untangle all of that later. For now, she wanted to get out of the house. "The police won't be able to do anything." They wouldn't even be able to enter the cellar without a warrant, not unless Mrs. Moreau allowed them to search and, as cagey as she was, Jasmine knew she wasn't likely to do that.

"Are you sure?" Tattie asked.

"I'm sure. It happened too fast. I didn't even see his face." Just his cigarette butts.

Tattie shook her head. "That had to be terrifying."

"At least you weren't hurt," Mrs. Moreau inserted.

Jasmine put her glass of water on the table as a way of breaking eye contact. Maybe Mrs. Moreau hadn't been the one to lock Jasmine in—Jasmine already knew the older woman didn't have the strength for it—but Francis's mother had known about it. She hadn't answered the front door when Jasmine had initially knocked, although she was apparently home at the time. And she hadn't responded to Jasmine's pleas for help from the cellar, although she must've heard them.

It was the neighbor's intervention that had, possibly, saved Jasmine's life. "Yes, at least I'm not hurt," she repeated. "But he got away with my purse."

"So it was a purse-snatching," Tattie said. "Are you *sure* you don't want to call the police? I know chances are slim that you'll get your stuff back, but it's worth reporting."

"I'll do that later. The only thing I need right now is a ride to the car rental place so I can get a second set of keys."

"I'll drive you wherever you need to go." Mrs. Moreau patted her hand and it was all Jasmine could do not to flinch away from those hardworking, callused fingers. She was about to say she'd rather walk when Tattie came up with an alternate plan.

"No, Bev. You stay here with Dustin."

Who was Dustin? Fortunately, Jasmine didn't need to ask. Tattie barely took a breath before volunteering the information. "Beverly's other son has special needs," she explained. "I'll take you."

Jasmine hadn't heard about a third Moreau son. She wanted to ask what was wrong with him, but that was far too indelicate a question. "I hate to trouble you," she told Tattie. "If you'd rather lend me forty dollars for a cab, I promise I'll get it back to you as soon as I have access to my own money."

Tattie consulted her watch. "It's no trouble. My youngest doesn't have to be picked up from preschool for another hour. I've got time." She stood. "Why don't you call the car rental company and tell them what happened while I go grab my purse?"

Jasmine was directly behind her. No way was she letting the neighbor leave without her. "I'll talk to them when I get there."

Tattie shrugged. "If that's how you want to do it."

It was exactly how Jasmine wanted to do it. "Thank you."

"I can't believe someone stole your purse and locked you in a *cellar,*" Tattie said as they walked to the front door. "It's broad daylight. You'd think you'd be safe. For the most part, this is a good neighborhood."

And yet, a man who was, at the very least, a child molester had once called this "good neighborhood" home. Jasmine wondered how long Tattie had lived next door, and if she knew about Francis Moreau. But she didn't comment. Tattie's questions were mostly rhetorical, anyway.

"It's just as well I had to run to the library and happened to hear you," she went on. "You could've been down there for hours! Maybe all night. Beverly couldn't hear a thing above the TV. Isn't it lucky I came out when I did, Bev?"

Mrs. Moreau, who was following them to the door, said it was lucky indeed. But Jasmine doubted she truly felt that way. She was lying about the TV. Jasmine had knocked, gone around the house and spent the past hour or more in the cellar. If the TV was so loud, why hadn't she heard it?

What had this elderly woman planned for her? Was it Mrs. Moreau who'd killed the man buried in that muddy corner? Or was she covering up for the person who did?

"Thank you for coming to my rescue," Jasmine said to Beverly as she stepped outside. She knew Mrs. Moreau wouldn't have done anything without Tattie's interference, but she wanted to spark a reaction.

"I'm glad you're safe," she said, her smile unwavering. "It could've ended so differently."

Like it had for the poor man wearing the white button-down shirt. "If not for Tattie," Jasmine murmured.

"If not for Tattie." She nodded and held the door open for them. "You might want to be more careful in the future. I don't think it's safe to go poking around other people's houses, do you?"

Jasmine froze where she was. "I thought you didn't know I was here."

"I didn't," she said. "That's just general advice."

Tempted to pursue it, Jasmine hesitated. But someone shouted from upstairs, distracting everyone. "Mom? Are you coming? Mom? What's going on?"

Beverly's eyebrows knotted in concern. "I'd better go," she said abruptly and pulled the door shut.

"That family's gone through so much," Tattie confided as they walked to the blue house next door.

Jasmine was anxious to lead the police to the body in that cellar, to see what Mrs. Moreau had to say then. She could scarcely think of anything else. But she was also interested in what Tattie could tell her, so she forced herself to listen.

"What's wrong with Dustin?" she asked.

"He has some neurological disorder. The doctors can't figure out what it is. They thought it was multiple sclerosis, but he doesn't have the telltale lesions on his brain. Then they thought it was lupus. Now I don't know what they're calling it."

"So he's an invalid?"

"Basically."

"And Phillip?"

They passed two wire reindeer in the yard. "He's fine, thank goodness. He's actually the only normal boy of the three."

"Then you know about Francis."

"Of course. Thanks to the media, everyone does."

They'd reached Tattie's porch. Jasmine held the screen while the other woman unlocked the front door. "Did you know him?"

"Not very well."

"Do you think he killed Adele Fornier?"

"Probably. On the surface, he was as mild-mannered as they come. But he wasn't right in the head. You didn't have to be around him very long to realize that." Tattie motioned for Jasmine to precede her inside. "Can you imagine what it'd be like for a mother to have a child murderer for a son? That's got to be harder than anything."

Under other circumstances, Jasmine would agree. But Beverly Moreau wasn't an ordinary mother.

Beverly Moreau stood near the recently disturbed earth under her house and used her cell phone to call a man she'd been taught to call Peccavi. She knew the word was Latin, knew from past church attendance that it had something to do with sin, but she didn't know the exact meaning. She'd asked him once and received no answer—just the barest hint of a smile.

"I'm coming," he snapped without a greeting. "Do you know how hard it was for me to get away this time of year? I'll be there as soon as I can."

Beverly examined the camera she'd discovered near the door. It was covered in mud but it still worked. "We're in trouble," she said as she went through the pictures Jasmine Stratford had taken.

"Don't panic. Everything will be fine."

As usual, impatience rang through his voice. "It's not going to be fine!" she snapped, responding aggressively for a change. "She found Jack while she was here." Beverly almost used Peccavi's real name but caught herself at the last second. He'd decided it was safer if he went by a nickname. It wouldn't have pleased him had she slipped up, especially on the phone. But it was difficult to remember such an odd name when she was this upset.

His voice turned to a threatening growl. "What do you mean, 'while she was here'? She'd better *still* be there."

Bev wiped some of the mud off the camera. "She's not."

The foulness of the curses that streamed from his mouth made her wince. "What happened?"

Anxiety gnawed at the ulcer she treated with handfuls

of antacids every day. "My next-door neighbor heard the screams. With her standing in my kitchen, I couldn't pretend I didn't hear them, too."

More cursing. "That bitch neighbor is too nosy for her own good."

Beverly liked Tattie. She was a busybody, but she meant well. She was the only one in the neighborhood who'd shown any sympathy for her when Francis was shot. "So what are you going to do? Kill her?"

"Shut up! We're on the phone, for God's sake. I'm just saying Phillip should've taken care of the problem before the neighbor got involved."

"He locked her in the cellar. That was the best he could do."

"The *best* he could do?"

"*Taking care* of that kind of problem is your forte, not ours."

"It doesn't require anything special. Only a club and the guts to use it."

"Phillip had other things to do."

"I bet he did."

She didn't bother to argue. They both knew her son had left to escape the situation. He didn't like the screaming, the knowledge that he was the reason Jasmine Stratford was trapped—and what might happen because of it. Bev was angry that he'd abandon her when she needed him so badly. But at least he possessed a conscience. If only Francis had been more like Phillip, maybe she'd still have him, too.

"He'll be back soon," she said. At least she hoped he would. Phillip was becoming more and more unpredictable. Sometimes she feared he'd succumb to the depression that plagued him and kill himself—or turn them all in. But she wasn't about to share her concerns with Peccavi. She knew what he'd do. *No weak links.* That was his motto. Jack had become a weak link, and Peccavi had shot him, just like that. Then he hadn't wanted to risk anyone seeing them remove the body, so he'd buried him in her cellar.

"Phillip's a pussy! It's his fault we're in this mess!"

"He'll be back," she said again.

"So where's the Stratford woman now?"

After slipping the strap of the camera around her wrist, Beverly climbed the ladder she'd passed down to Jasmine. "She just drove off with my neighbor."

"Get hold of Phillip, and tell him to stay away from the house until after the police arrive."

"Stay *away?*" She closed the trapdoor. "Why?"

"I want whoever shows up to be dealing with you."

Because no one would believe she could be dangerous. Beverly understood that. But she couldn't understand Peccavi allowing the police to discover Jack's body. "You don't want to move…you know what?"

"No. Don't touch it. It happened before Francis got himself in trouble. We'll make sure he gets stuck with the blame. Everyone knows what a sick bastard he was. And the police will be hoping for an easy answer. It's Christmas Eve. No one wants to take on a cold case they're unlikely to solve, especially on the biggest holiday of the year."

Her youngest son was already immortalized as a monster. Beverly hated to add to that legacy. But she saw the brilliance of Peccavi's plan. "What reason would Francis have had to…you know?" As much as it pained her to acknowledge it, Jack wasn't Francis's usual kind of victim.

"There could be a million reasons. Jack and Francis both worked for the same delivery company, right? They were friends. Maybe he got too close, got suspicious of Francis's activities. Or they had a disagreement over money. Just play dumb. Cry and mention Francis's name. 'How could he have done this? Not another innocent person…' That sort of thing. There won't be much of an investigation if the culprit is obvious—and he's already dead."

Beverly was a little surprised by the risks Peccavi had taken in speaking so plainly, but she knew he had no choice. They had to get their story straight or they'd be sunk; the police could arrive at any moment. "Will Ms. Stratford buy that, too?" she asked as she shoved a sack of flour over the trapdoor.

"No. She'll keep poking around, searching for answers."

"How do you know?" Beverly removed her shoes, washed the mud off the rubber bottoms, then put them by the back door to dry. It'd be best if the police didn't know she'd gone down to the cellar.

"Because she's stubborn. I've seen her on TV, heard the way she talks."

Definitely not what Beverly wanted to hear. "But she knows she got lucky today. I saw it in her eyes. Maybe this scared her enough that she'll go back to wherever she came from and mind her own business."

"That isn't gonna happen."

"Why not?"

"She's been looking for her sister for years. If she was going to give up, she would've done it by now."

Beverly felt a trickle of guilt for all the innocent people who'd been hurt. But there was nothing she could do about it. She knew too much to change anything now. And she couldn't pay Dustin's staggering medical expenses any other way. "So what do we do?" she asked.

"I'll take care of Jasmine Stratford."

After cleaning the camera and hiding it in a drawer, Beverly went to the front of the house and peeked through the blinds. Jasmine's rental car was still sitting at the curb, where she'd parked it. But the street remained as quiet as ever. No police yet. "Be careful."

"Mom? Where are you? The pain's coming back! Mom?"

Dustin… Beverly's heart sank. He was so miserable. And there was so little she could do to help him.

"I'll be right with you, honey," she called, but at the top of the stairs, she went into the room she used as an office, where she'd dumped the contents of Jasmine Stratford's purse.

"Hang on," she told Peccavi. "I might be able to help…."

Shoving one of her cats off the chair—another stray she'd picked up at the transfer house a few months ago— she sat at her desk and shuffled through the wallet, address book, gum, candy and papers she'd examined earlier. She'd found a confirmation notice from a hotel in the French Quarter just as Tattie showed up at the door….

There it was. Plucking it from the pile, she held it up to the sunlight streaming through the window so she could read what it said. She hated to pass this information along to Peccavi. She was so tired of the violence, the secrets, the fear of discovery. But the police would soon be at her door. Again. If she didn't take preemptive measures, the situation could escalate, could get even worse than it had with Francis.

"She's staying at *La Maison du Soleil* in the French Quarter," she said. "And I've got her room key."

"You do?"

"It was in her purse."

"They'll rekey it," he said.

"Not if you get there before she does." Then she hung up and swallowed some more antacids.

It was one of the worst days of Jasmine's life. Not only had she been locked in a cellar and discovered a corpse, she'd lost her purse and everything in it—her cell phone, her wallet, the address book she relied on so heavily, her camera. Being stripped of those things made being away from home on Christmas Eve that much worse. She felt like a turtle that'd been turned on its back and couldn't right itself.

She sat in her rental car, watching the police officers going in and out of the Moreau residence across the street. They'd been working the crime scene for quite a while. She didn't know how long. It'd taken her three hours to get a new set of keys and to have someone from the car rental company drive her out here. By the time she'd arrived, the police were engrossed in their work, and no one wanted to tell her anything.

She'd stopped one young officer, asking him to look for her camera while he was in the cellar. He'd agreed but hadn't come out for over an hour, and when he did he told her he hadn't seen it—in a voice that indicated it definitely wasn't a priority. Before he walked away, however, he mentioned that she should check with the home owner. Evidently, Mrs. Moreau was cooperating with the search, which surprised Jasmine almost as much as it relieved the police. They were in a hurry. Some were due to get off soon and wanted to go home to their families.

Spotting another man in uniform heading to one of the

vehicles in front of Tattie's place, Jasmine got out of her car. "Have you identified the body?" she asked.

The officer gave her a blank expression. "We don't know anything yet."

"When might that change?"

"I can't say."

Of course not. In his mind, she wasn't anyone who needed to know. And she doubted it'd be different with any of the other cops. She was a civilian from a different state. She had no power here.

With a sigh, Jasmine got back into her car. Kozlowski had been off today, so there was no one she could ask for more information. The desk sergeant she'd spoken to when she'd called to report her discovery had said a detective would want her to come in to make a statement. She could talk to someone then. But, thanks to the holidays, it'd be Monday or Tuesday before anyone got around to her. This was obviously a very old killing and nothing would likely change over the course of three or four days.

Regardless of what the police would or wouldn't do, she was wasting her time here. Even Tattie wasn't out and about. Jasmine guessed she was inside the house with Mrs. Moreau; she hadn't seen the neighbor since her return.

After putting on her seat belt, Jasmine started the engine. Earlier, she'd cleaned up as best she could in Tattie's bathroom, but she was hungry and tired and wanted to get back to the hotel. Without cash or credit cards, she didn't have any way to purchase a meal, but she figured she might be able to order from the bar downstairs and put it on her room bill. Even if she couldn't, she'd have a hot shower and then a comfortable bed to sleep in until Skye could wire some money to the closest Western Union. While she waited at the car rental place, she'd canceled her credit cards and called her friends. But she hadn't told them the whole truth about the reason she needed help. She saw no reason to ruin their Christmas by telling them she'd run into trouble. It was easier to say she'd simply lost her purse.

She was just pulling away when she noticed an old Camaro coming from the opposite direction. With all the police vehicles clogging the street, the driver had to angle to the side to make room for her to pass, but his eye held hers a little too long—long enough to let her know he recognized her.

Stomping on the brakes, she quickly shoved the transmission into Park and got out. A red flush to his cheeks gave him a flustered air, as if he was tempted to drive away, but she had him cornered.

She knocked on his window and he finally cracked it open a few inches.

"What do you want?" he demanded, wearing a dark scowl.

"Who are you?" she asked.

"None of your business."

But Jasmine could guess. He looked almost identical to the picture of Francis Moreau she'd seen on the microfilm in the library: short and stocky with dark wavy hair, small dark eyes and a Roman nose. This had to be a close relative—most likely his brother.

"You're Phillip," she said.

The furrow between his eyebrows deepened, but he didn't contradict her. He waved at his house. "What's going on?"

She noticed a pack of cigarettes on his dashboard. "You can't guess?"

"If I could, I wouldn't have asked."

Right. Was this the man who'd locked her in the cellar? Who'd left those butts? Or had the spark of recognition she'd witnessed come from having seen her on TV? "There was a body in your cellar."

He didn't react. "Who told you that?"

"I'm the one who found it."

"You're kidding."

Jasmine didn't read much surprise in that comment, or in his expression. "Did you know it was there?"

"No."

*A lie.* She could tell by the whitening of his knuckles on the steering wheel. "Who was he?" she pressed. "What happened?"

He opened his mouth to respond, but before he could, his mother called his name. Jasmine glanced up to find Mrs. Moreau standing out on the front lawn, watching them with her hands propped on her hips.

"Phillip! There you are. Get in here. The nightmare we went through with Francis isn't over yet."

He didn't move right away. He looked at Jasmine almost as if he was pleading for something. Then the line of his mouth turned grim and his attention shifted resolutely toward his mother. "It doesn't exactly come as a shock. My brother was a murderer," he told her. Then he nearly drove over her toes as he forced her out of his path, squeezing between her car and a cruiser.

Gruber Coen flicked his TV remote to replay the *America's Most Wanted* episode he'd recorded on his satellite system's hard drive. He'd just spoken to Peccavi. Peccavi had called to tell him Jasmine Stratford had come to New

Orleans, but that wasn't unexpected. Gruber had invited her here.

What did astonish him was the fact that she'd already connected the note he'd sent her with what he'd written on the wall when he dumped Adele's body.

He whistled as he watched the way she used her hands when she talked and the emotion flitting across her face. He was especially interested in the sadness she exhibited when she talked about her little sister. He wished it roused some pity in him, some vestige of conscience. But it didn't. His head told him he should feel sorry for her, be ashamed, stop his behavior, but the only thing he really felt was a stirring of the desire that made him do what he did—and a trace of admiration. He'd assumed Jasmine would connect her sister's disappearance to Adele's murder at some point—but not so fast. She was quick, much quicker than he'd expected.

The thought both excited and terrified him. Would *she* be able to stop him? Had he finally met his match?

God, she looked like her sister. Except she was missing that fearful expression he'd liked so well in Kimberly. Jasmine wasn't scared of anyone. She was shrewd, determined, strong.

Turning up the volume, Gruber listened once again as she described the personality characteristics of a recent sex offender who'd been victimizing little boys.

*Fucking pervert.* What kind of man wanted to have sex with a boy?

He pressed the volume button on the remote. This was the part where Jasmine talked about her sister, and he didn't want to miss it. He didn't have to worry about the neighbors. No one was going to hear anything in the cement bunker he'd built. That was the beauty of it. He could do anything down here.

"I was twelve years old when my sister went missing. A bearded stranger came to the door and asked for my father."

Gruber smiled. He no longer wore a beard. According to his sister, who constantly pointed out his every flaw, he had a weak chin and needed the facial hair to camouflage the defect. But he knew it was important to periodically change his appearance. Maybe Jasmine was smart, but he was smarter. Even vanity couldn't get in the way of survival.

"After he left, I realized my sister was gone, too," she was saying.

He remembered that day as if it was yesterday. Peccavi had sent him to Cleveland to pick up another kid Jack had scouted the previous week, and he'd bumped into Peter Stratford in line at a fast-food joint. They'd struck up a conversation, and Peter had offered him a temporary job.

Gruber still wasn't sure why he'd ever gone to the address Peter had given him. Except that he'd been bored and looking for something to interest him. Then there she was. So easy. A gift. He'd promised her an ice cream cone for showing him such a nice cartwheel, told her they'd bring one for her sister, too, and she'd climbed right into his truck.

The phone rang. With a curse, he stopped the program and returned it to the beginning, planning to watch it all over again as soon as he was off the phone. He enjoyed studying Jasmine, enjoyed fantasizing about finally meeting her, looking into her eyes and telling her he was the one she'd been searching for these past sixteen years.

"Hello?"

It was Roger, or someone he called Roger. Gruber had no idea what his real name was. He only knew that he wasn't as good a scout as Jack had been.

"What is it?"

"I have one for you."

"Where?" he asked.

"Right here in the city."

"Are you crazy? That's too close."

"This is a contract baby."

Meaning Roger had found a prostitute or some other woman desperate enough to give up her baby for money or drugs. They acquired the children who went through their little company in a variety of ways. Buying them from crack addicts and prostitutes was the least dangerous—at least for him as the pickup man—because they paid for what they took.

"It doesn't matter," Gruber insisted. Because of a close call years ago, and because they based their entire enterprise out of New Orleans, they didn't usually take children, via any method, from their home area. Peccavi constantly stressed how important it was to keep all illegal activity as far away from the transfer house as possible.

"Peccavi's making an exception," Roger said. "He's not happy with the money we've got coming in right now."

And because babies were hard to come by and always sold for a premium, Peccavi occasionally relented on this rule. "Then why can't you pick it up?"

"I'm in Detroit, looking for something a little more specific."

Gruber frowned and rubbed his bare chin as he stared at the frozen picture of John Walsh on his TV screen. "She's giving it up on *Christmas?*" he said. Apparently she was even more hard-hearted than his bitch of a mother had been.

"She wants to be able to buy herself a few things. Do you mind?"

"Some kids don't have a chance," he grumbled.

"That's our business, isn't it? Giving them a chance."

Gruber had to laugh. Roger's self-delusions sometimes boggled his mind. "You really believe that shit? That we're angels in disguise?"

Defensiveness infiltrated Roger's response. Obviously, he didn't want to face reality today. "I believe that Peccavi's got his hands full right now, and he wants you to take care of this. Do you need *him* to call you?"

Gruber almost said yes. Without some intervention, some distraction, he feared Peccavi would kill Jasmine before Gruber had the chance to confront her. But if Peccavi could stop Jasmine that easily, she wasn't a worthy adversary. And Gruber couldn't threaten his own livelihood—possibly his life—by doing anything to make Peccavi suspicious. Like her sister before her, Jasmine was an indulgence, a risk. He had to play it smart or the man he worked for would turn on him the way he'd turned on Jack….

"You gonna answer me? You there?" Roger asked.

"I'm here. Go ahead and give me the details."

Roger spouted off a set of directions, which Gruber copied on the back cover of *Sports Illustrated,* a magazine he sometimes read to make himself feel like an everyday guy. He bought *SI* or even *Playboy* occasionally, although he knew it wouldn't really work. He *wanted* to be an everyday guy. But he'd never been like other men. "Got it," he said when he was finished.

"At least you don't have to travel for this one, eh?" Roger said.

Gruber tossed the pen aside. "I guess." The mother was home from the hospital and staying in a motel room courtesy of Peccavi. All he had to do was pick up the baby and take it to Beverly Moreau at the bungalow that served as their transfer house.

But leaving his bunker took him away from the pleasure of watching Kimberly's sister talk about *him* on national television, and he hated Peccavi and Roger for that.

# 11

Returning to her hotel for a meal and a shower sounded better in theory than it actually turned out to be. By the time Jasmine reached *Maison du Soleil,* it was nearly six o'clock and dark. The businesses along St. Philip Street—and everywhere else—were already closed for Christmas Eve.

Jasmine pulled to the curb and stared up at the building. With its festive lights glowing eerily through the fog, she felt as if she'd entered a Christmas ghost town. The fact that the French Quarter was normally so lively and boisterous made the loneliness seem more intense. And the weather didn't help. Even the high-powered streetlights cast only a dim glow on wet, shiny streets.

"Some Christmas this is," she grumbled. Even The Moody Blues was closed, leaving her with little hope of a meal. And the person who'd stolen her purse had the key to her room. He didn't have her room number, but that didn't reassure her. It was such a small hotel he could easily have gone door to door until the key worked.

Was he in her room, waiting for her?

The letdown after the adrenaline rush of the afternoon had left her exhausted but not relieved. She still felt apprehensive, although she couldn't say why. If the person who'd

pushed her into the cellar had wanted to harm her, he'd
already had the chance. At this point, she was pretty convinced that was Phillip, who didn't strike her as all that dangerous. Besides, even bad guys celebrated Christmas. If
she'd learned anything in profiling, it was how normal—at
least on the surface—criminals could be.

Hopefully, the man who'd taken her purse had a family
and all the usual Christmas obligations. She'd simply get
her room rekeyed and hole up until morning, when the
money would arrive and she'd be able to move to a different hotel.

Her decision made, she drove a few blocks to the public
lot, where she'd already paid for a week in advance. She
parked the sedan and got out.

Her footsteps echoed on the pavement as she walked
through the fog. She felt strangely bereft without the
security offered by the contents of her purse and wished
she had her Mace. But maybe she was being paranoid. She
could buy another can tomorrow, after the money showed
up.

As she reached the entrance to the alley, she glanced up
at her hotel—and froze. The fog was so thick she couldn't
be sure, but she thought she saw a light shining in her room.
Had she left it on herself?

The fears and doubts she'd battled only moments before
descended again as she wondered what to do. She couldn't
return to her room alone, not without a weapon. She could
call the police or ask Mr. Cabanis or his wife or daughter to
accompany her. But chances were she was jumping at
shadows. And even if one of the Cabanises walked her to her
room, there was no guarantee someone wouldn't be hurt.

Then she remembered the fire escape. She could use it to take a quick peek, see whether it was safe to go back.

Grazing her fingertips along the gritty brick surface of the building, Jasmine walked slowly. She didn't want to twist an ankle or fall over a pile of garbage or worse. She might be risking more by coming into this dark alley than by returning to her room, but her curiosity about that light coaxed her on.

A rock skittered across the ground, and she halted abruptly. She was pretty sure she'd dislodged it with her own feet, but the noise heightened the foreboding that'd settled over her when the wind died down and the fog rolled in. It took her a few minutes to recover the nerve to press forward, but the closer she got the more certain she was that the light was coming from her room.

The metal of the fire escape felt cold and clammy beneath her hand. It shook as she stepped on it, and she wondered if it'd bear her weight without pulling away from the building. The metal squeaked loudly as she gave it a strong jerk, but when it held fast, she managed to summon the confidence to climb it. If everything was okay, she'd be able to enter her room, at which point she'd pack up her belongings and ask to switch rooms.

But everything wasn't okay. Her room wasn't as she'd left it.

Although the light actually came from the bathroom, she could see that the bed had been torn apart, the drawers of the nightstand pulled open, her computer thrown to the floor....

Someone had come here, just as she'd feared.

Pressing a hand to her chest, she stood with her mouth agape, scanning the interior—until something moved. Then she blinked and refocused. A man, dressed in a long black trench coat and wearing a black ski mask stared back at her, just on the other side of the glass.

With a scream, Jasmine scrambled down the fire escape. She thought the locked door would give her a good lead but the fire alarm sounded briefly, and she knew he was coming after her. She could feel the fire escape shimmy as he jumped down a few steps with every stride.

She slipped and fell on the wet metal and had to get up again, which cost her valuable time. Still, she hit the ground before he reached her. But it was so dark she tripped on a pothole and nearly fell into a puddle.

He jumped to the ground only a few feet from her. She felt the air stir and briefly wondered if she'd be able to hide. She couldn't outrun him. Whoever he was, he was in good shape. But her hope of hiding didn't last more than a second. He had a flashlight, which he snapped on—and the beam found her immediately.

Croc, who owned the Flying Squirrel, was a widower. He'd grown up in Portsville and had one of the best shrimping boats in the area, but these days it was his son who used it. Croc went out on the bayou every once in a while, but he was getting old and seemed happier pouring beer for other fishermen, listening to their stories and retelling a few of his own.

Romain had always liked Croc, but he was never more grateful to have him in the community than during the holidays. Most other places were closed, especially for Christmas. But not the Flying Squirrel. Croc opened from four until midnight 365 days a year.

"You gotta love a dependable Cajun," Romain said, as he tossed a few peanuts into his mouth.

"Who you talkin' to down there?" Croc demanded.

Romain swiveled to face him. "You. I said I'm ready for another beer."

"'Course you are."

As Croc pulled the tap, Romain rested his elbows on the wooden bar and glanced around at the handful of people who were smoking, drinking and playing darts. It wasn't the best Christmas Eve he could imagine—nothing could equal those he'd shared with Pam and Adele—but drinking made the holidays bearable. The Flying Squirrel beat his other offer, anyway. His parents had invited him to Mamou for the night, but his sister, Susan, and her family had already arrived from Boston. They'd be staying for most of a week, so he intended to make himself scarce—except for dinner tomorrow, of course. He'd join them for a couple of hours, but only because his parents would be disappointed if he didn't.

"You were here last Christmas, too," Croc commented, placing Romain's beer in front of him.

"I didn't know anyone was keeping track." Romain had been sitting at the bar long enough to be drunk, but he wasn't. He hoped that would soon change. Until Jasmine's unexpected arrival, he'd been doing fine. If it wasn't for the questions she'd stirred—and the holidays—he'd *still* be fine.

"I'm gonna have to drive you home again, aren't I?" Croc said with a fatalistic frown.

Romain knew the old guy didn't really object. "Maybe."

"Once or twice a year isn't bad, I guess." Croc straightened the basket of peanuts and wiped the counter, although it was clean. Then he cleared his throat.

"You got something more to say to me?" Romain asked. It wasn't like Croc to hover.

"I was hoping—wait a second." He stalked off to handle an argument that'd broken out between the Gatlin twins over a game of darts. Although they were both in their mid-twenties, only ten years younger than Romain, they still lived at home. They settled down when Croc threatened to call their parents, and he returned to the bar. "I hear you're gonna order a bride," he said to Romain.

Romain made an impatient motion. "One little joke, and now the whole town's planning my wedding? I'm afraid you received unreliable information."

"It's a good idea. It's not like you're gonna meet anyone hiding out on the bayou. And you don't wanna spend every Christmas with me, do ya?"

"I wouldn't mind," Romain said. "I like it here." He did mind, but he didn't see how his life was going to change and figured he'd be better off accepting reality.

"I can tell you like it here." Croc waved as someone else came in, then shifted his attention back to Romain. "Sometimes you like it so well you drink enough to risk alcohol poisoning. Then you stumble out to my truck, I drive you home, and you don't show up for more than a beer or two until your daughter's birthday or your wedding anniversary or the anniversary of your daughter's death, and it's time to drive you home again."

"Thanks for reminding me. But in case you can't tell, the point is to *forget*." Romain tossed another handful of peanuts into his mouth in a casual motion meant to disguise the fact that, thanks to Jasmine Stratford, this Christmas was even more difficult than the last.

It *had* to be Moreau who killed Adele. Romain had stared into the man's flat, empty eyes, witnessed that taunting half smile and known on a bone-deep level. Hadn't he? Yes! So the rest didn't matter. And yet, the questions Jasmine had raised continued to haunt him….

Croc wiped the counter again. "Why not create some new memories?"

"Why not mind your own business?"

The old man wrote something on a napkin and shoved it at him.

"What's this?" Romain growled.

"A Web site where you'll find lots of beautiful Russian women."

"You've been online?" Romain would've been amused if he wasn't so annoyed by the unwelcome interference. Croc wasn't the type to familiarize himself with a computer.

The old man shrugged. "Casey and I checked out a few places."

Meddlesome Casey again. Romain needed to be more careful about what he said to her. "Sorry, I'm not interested." He pushed the napkin back.

"Why not?"

"It was a joke, okay? I don't plan on ordering a bride."

"You should. Think of what you're missing."

"A prostitute can take care of what I'm missing."

With a scowl, Croc leaned close. "You know it wouldn't be the same, my friend."

Romain held up a hand. He'd heard enough. "This is all pretty ironic coming from you."

"Why's that?" Croc asked.

"You lost Marie what…twenty years ago?"

"Twenty-two. But that's exactly my point."

Romain met his meaningful stare.

"I don't want you to turn out a lonely old man like me," Croc said.

"Everyone has problems, Croc. There's nothing wrong with the life you're living."

"But you could have something better. You're still young. Why not start another family?"

It wasn't like they were talking about growing vegetables. *Your tomatoes died? Maybe you should try a different variety....* He'd had the only family he ever wanted. He couldn't love another woman or have more children because he couldn't bear the possibility of losing them, too. "Enough already."

Croc lowered his voice. "Someone has to say it, T-Bone. It's time to put the past behind you and move on. Let Pam and Adele go, let them rest in peace knowing you'll be okay."

Romain clenched his fists. Suddenly, he felt like fighting. He knew he was being rash even as he shoved away from the bar and faced the room, but the need for release goaded him on in spite of that. "A hundred bucks to anyone who can beat me in a freestyle boxing match," he announced and pulled the bill from his wallet.

"Damn, T-Bone, you want to get busted up on Christmas Eve?" someone called out.

But the Gatlin boys exchanged a look of silent communication and smiled eagerly. They'd been angling for a match for months. "I'll do it if you'll let my brother help me out," Terry said.

Romain weighed the odds. Two on one was a little more than he'd bargained for. The Gatlins were lean and mean and had a reputation for not fighting fair. But a fight was a fight. At least it would give him a chance to release the anger charging through him.

"Deal," he said and threw the first punch.

\* \* \*

The man's hand closed over Jasmine's ankle, dragging her back, scraping her cheek, hands and knees on the rough blacktop. She broke several fingernails clawing at the ground, searching for purchase, but it was no use. He had a sure grip. The only thing she could do was wait for a better opportunity, which came when he released her ankle to reach for her arm or her hair. Then she rolled over and kicked him in the groin, just as Skye had taught her.

With a gasp of pain, he crumpled to his knees, giving her the split second she needed to get to her feet.

Only problem was—her mind screamed "Run!" but her legs wouldn't fully cooperate. It felt like she was moving in slow motion. She could hear him following her, could make out the tap…tap…tap…tap…tap-tap-tap of his footsteps gaining on her from behind. He seemed a little unsteady at first but was soon running at full speed.

She couldn't outdistance him for long. She had to get out of the alley, find someone who'd be able to help. But there wasn't anyone around.

Her decision had to be a split-second one. Should she dart toward a major street and try to stop traffic? Or attempt to reach her own car?

Her car was closer, and she wouldn't risk getting run over. But neither would she have much chance of being rescued if he caught her.

When she rounded the corner, she glanced off a Dumpster that seemed to materialize out of nowhere. Hoping her pursuer would do the same, only hit it squarely, she managed to keep running. But he must've made a wider arc because he missed it entirely. She could hear him catching up with her. She could also feel his absolute determination.

*I'll kill you for this, bitch!* echoed through her brain as if he screamed it at her.

By the time she made it to the parking lot, Jasmine's throat burned and her lungs felt like bursting. She had only a few yards to go, but she wasn't sure she'd be able to unlock the car before he was upon her. If he caught her while she was trying to get in, it'd be all too easy to drag her out and—

She couldn't let herself think of what came after "and." It weakened her, allowed fear to confuse her judgment.

*Block out the impressions. Think!* She had to do something to slow him down, to buy the few seconds she needed to get away. But what? She was out of options, out of energy, out of breath—

And then she saw it. A sharp stick, lying in the dim yellow circle provided by the floodlight that illuminated the Parking $2.75/hour or $35/day sign. Bending to grab it, she whirled and threw it in his face.

She wouldn't have hurt him very badly if he'd been farther away. But he was close, and he hadn't expected the blow.

He cried out when she hit him, and staggered back as she pressed the button on her key ring that unlocked the driver's side door. She thought she might've blinded him because he shook his head as if he couldn't clear his vision. But she didn't wait around to find out. She got in her car and nearly slammed his hand in the door when he tried to stop her.

"Oh, God." She was shaking so badly she could barely insert the key in the ignition.

He pounded on the window—hard enough to break it. He was *trying* to break it. But she managed to start the engine. Then she popped the transmission into Reverse and squealed out of the parking space, leaving him in a cloud of exhaust.

Jasmine sped west on I-10. She told herself she was getting out of town where she could regroup and decide what to do next, but she didn't have enough gas to drive anywhere without a specific purpose. She was going to the bayou, to Romain Fornier. Her father was another option, but he lived in the opposite direction, and she wasn't about to show up at his place battered and bruised on Christmas Eve. Especially since she'd been investigating Kimberly's disappearance….

Strange, perhaps, but Romain's felt safer. And yet going to him was a gamble, as well. She had only enough fuel to get to Portsville and no way to fill her tank for the return trip. If he refused to help her, she didn't know what she'd do.

He'd help her, she told herself. Or someone else would. Forty dollars for gas would do it. That wasn't a lot. She'd deal with returning to New Orleans tomorrow. Right now she couldn't concentrate on anything except finding somewhere safe, taking a bath, closing her eyes.

But Romain's house was dark when Jasmine reached it— at barely nine o'clock. Had he gone to Mamou to spend Christmas with his folks? She hadn't seen his motorcycle as she came through town, but she knew he had another car or truck.

She sat in his drive, chewing her lip as she let her engine idle. She supposed she could go back to town and try to find him, but if he wasn't there it wouldn't do her any good to have invested the time—and the gas. And she was already so tired.

She had to go in the house—to get in somehow, even if the door was locked. She couldn't stay out in the car without so much as a blanket. She'd freeze to death. But going inside meant braving the bayou, and she was still leery of the creatures that inhabited the swamp. She was accustomed to wide-open spaces, dry land, domesticated animals....

Leaving her headlights on to discourage anything from eating her before she could clamber onto the porch, she scoured the ground for signs of movement while she ran to the door.

"Romain?" she called as she knocked. "Romain? Are you home?"

A cacophony of noise surrounded her—chirping, clicking, splashing and rustling—but there was no answer from the house. *Please come to the door. Let me in. I need food, sleep, money, reassurance....*

"Romain?"

Again, no response. But the door was unlocked, and a flashlight sat on a ledge to her right.

With a final frightened glance at the dark trees that seemed to hold the swamp at bay, she crossed the threshold and locked the door behind her. Then she breathed deeply, taking in the reassuring scent of the man whose voice had created such desire on the phone last night, a scent she found oddly comforting. He didn't have electric lights and she didn't know how to deal with any other kind, so she used the flashlight to locate his bedroom, which was as neat as she'd expected and not completely devoid of personal mementos. On his dresser, she saw a framed photograph of him, his wife and his daughter. They were at the beach, running from a large wave. Romain had Adele on his shoulders and was laughing as he held Pam's hand and pulled her along.

"God, they look happy." Jasmine moved the flashlight closer. The tiny inset photograph she'd seen of Pam in the papers didn't do the woman justice. Romain's wife had been beautiful, tall with long blond hair and the same golden skin he possessed.

Envying the relationship they seemed to have had, she lowered the light. At least he'd once loved someone with his whole heart. Jasmine had never met anyone who'd stirred that kind of passion or commitment in her. "So what's the truth? Is it better to have loved and lost or never to have loved at all?" she murmured to herself.

She wondered what Romain would say about that as she stripped off her filthy clothes and did the best she could to wash up. The only water was freezing and came out of a big metal can in the bathroom, but she felt calmer when she'd wiped away the dirt and mud and cleaned her cuts and abrasions.

She'd made it. She'd gotten out of the cellar and out of the alley. She was fine; she was safe.

Now all she had to do was appropriate something to wear and get warm.

After a quick search of Romain's drawers, she came up with a thick cotton T-shirt and a pair of boxers, both of which smelled as fresh as any laundry she'd ever done. Teeth chattering, she pulled them on, then piled her own clothes in a sack and put them by the back door. She wasn't sure she'd ever be able to get them clean and doubted she'd want to wear them again even if she could. They'd always remind her of the cellar and what she'd found there.

Putting on a heavy coat of Romain's that'd been hanging on a hook by the front door and a pair of his boots, she clomped out to turn off her headlights and decided to move her car. His house was about as remote as a house could get, but people might come by to wish him a merry Christmas and she didn't want her car to be spotted. She'd rather go unnoticed until she felt strong enough to venture out again.

After she returned to the house, she put Romain's coat and boots where they belonged and nearly climbed into his bed. Lord knew she was tempted. That was where she'd feel safest. But even if he was out of town for Christmas, moving into his private space felt a little forward—like Goldilocks in *The Three Bears*.

After dragging some bedding from a closet at the end of the hall, she curled up on the couch instead and, as soon as she grew warm, fell asleep.

The Gatlin boys had done a damn fine job. They'd bloodied his right cheek, probably bruised a few ribs, and caused him to bust up his knuckles worse than he'd wanted to. But the patrons of the Flying Squirrel had taken a vote and called it a draw so he still had his money.

Groaning as he got out of Croc's truck, Romain squinted through a skull-splitting headache as he looked back at the old man. "Thanks for the ride." At least he'd get a good night's sleep. According to his watch, it was barely ten-thirty.

"What the hell were you trying to do, kill yourself?" he snapped.

"Maybe," Romain muttered, and shuffled toward the porch.

Croc waited, giving Romain the benefit of his headlights, and Romain managed to cross the uneven ground without falling. It wasn't until he reached the front steps that he realized something was different. Someone had been at the house. The flashlight he left out for after-dark returns was gone.

He tried the door. Locked.

But he rarely bothered to lock the door....

Straightening, he gazed back at Croc, wondering if all the booze he'd consumed was playing tricks on him. But then he spotted something else. A car sat off to the side of his drive, parked back in the trees.

Croc rolled down his window and stuck out his head. "Everything okay?"

Romain held up a hand. "Fine," he said. But things weren't fine at all. He was pretty sure that car was the rental Jasmine had been driving—and she was the one who'd ruined his Christmas to begin with.

Reluctant to let Croc know he had company, especially *female* company, he waited until the bar owner had gone before taking his hide-a-key from under the porch and opening the door. He didn't want to see Jasmine, and he didn't want her to see him. At least, not like this. His behavior didn't always make sense, even when a therapist tried to explain it. He knew because the judge at his trial had ordered him to have weekly sessions with a psychologist to "help him deal with his anger." She said he suppressed his feelings until they couldn't be suppressed anymore, and then he acted on them in counterproductive ways. But, as far as Romain was concerned, all that talk had been a waste of time. He already knew he wasn't coping with his feelings well, didn't need anyone to tell him that. And he still felt better after five minutes with his fists than hours of trying to explain why he wanted to use them.

The shrink didn't seem to understand that talking wouldn't make him the man he once was: the proud soldier, the doting father, the loving husband. She kept pointing to what he could give the world, claimed he could still have everything he ever wanted. But it wasn't just the fact that he'd lost his wife and daughter that ate at him. It was the *way* he'd lost them, especially Adele. Moreau's actions had stripped him of the confidence he'd always possessed that he could protect his own. Now the pursuit of happiness seemed more like a crapshoot. What good was anything that fragile?

It was pitch-black inside, and he was slightly unsteady on his feet, but he had no trouble navigating the furniture. Where was Jasmine? If she had to be here, she'd better be in his bed. Even if he was too banged up to make love to her at the moment, her warmth and softness pressed up against him might ease his aches and pains, help him relax. And there was always the possibility that he'd feel okay later on….

But she wasn't in his bedroom. Once he lit a lantern, he found her on the couch. "What are you doing in my house?"

"Romain?" She stirred, squinting against the light.

"Does someone else own this place?"

"Can you turn that off?"

He was about to blow out the flame. But what he saw made him hesitate: she had almost as many injuries as he did. "What the hell?"

"The light!" She put up her hands to block it, but he ignored the complaint. Lifting her chin, he shoved her hair out of the way so he could get a look at her.

"What happened to you?"

She gazed up at him, now fully awake, her eyes focused on his own injuries. "I could ask you the same thing."

"I had a little trouble at the Flying Squirrel."

"Someone jumped you?"

"It was more like two someones. And I asked for it. Your turn."

Shivering, she drew the blanket higher. "It's so cold in here."

"Does that surprise you? It's winter, and you came to a house with no utilities."

"I'm already regretting it." She tried to pull away, to get up, but he pressed her to the couch with one hand on her shoulder.

"I asked you a question."

"I fell, okay?"

He set the lamp on the table and took her hands, studying the scrapes and gouges and broken fingernails he'd glimpsed when she'd tried to swat the light away. They looked as if she'd clawed her way out of a coffin. "*This* happened when you fell?"

"That and more." She folded back the blanket to show him, but the first thing he noticed was that she was wearing his clothes. His body reacted with a significant rise in hormones. But he was too concerned about the injuries on her knees and feet to mention the fact that she must've gone through his drawers.

"Where were you when this happened?" he asked. "Not here in Portsville—"

"No, in New Orleans. In the alley by my hotel."

"What were you doing in an alley?" He wasn't sure why, but finding her this way was sobering him up fast.

"Someone was chasing me."

This didn't sound like anything he wanted to hear. "Who?"

"I think it was Pearson Black. Or Phillip Moreau. Whoever it was wanted to kill me."

That didn't make sense. The danger was over. Moreau was dead; life was supposed to be normal again. "Why would anyone want to kill you?"

She wilted as she considered the question. "I don't know. Can we talk about it in the morning?"

He wanted to talk about it now. But there was no point in making things worse than they already were. She was here, where he could look out for her; she'd be fine until daylight. "Are you planning to stay on the couch?"

He'd meant to be nice, knowing he'd have a better chance of getting her to accompany him to the bedroom if he could manage a little charm. But the words came out far too clipped for charming. They sounded more like a challenge.

He held his breath as he awaited her answer. *I blew it. What the hell's wrong with me?*

"Do you have another suggestion?" she asked hesitantly.

His heart began to pound harder. Fighting the conflicting emotions inside him—the pull of desire against the reluctance to feel any kind of need—he forced himself to respond with some heartfelt honesty. "I could keep you warm."

He hadn't meant to sound *that* vulnerable, but it worked. "Warm would be good," she said.

Relieved, he ignored his pain and carried her into the bedroom. And just the scent of her as she curled around him was enough.

# 12

$G$ruber hesitated, cordless telephone in hand. He knew Peccavi didn't like to be bothered unless there was a good reason. But he was dying to know what'd happened to Jasmine. Was she alligator bait? Was the sister of his beloved Kimberly now dead?

Pivoting at the end of his bunker, he headed toward the couch and table, where he preferred to watch TV. A small closetlike room to one side held a cheap port-a-potty designed for RVs, but Gruber didn't like emptying it. Unless he had a prisoner that made it necessary, he simply went upstairs.

He glanced at the clock. It was after midnight, but Peccavi would be up. He could phone, couldn't he? What would it hurt?

He knew what Peccavi would say, that it was a risk. But they weren't in any danger. There'd only been one close call—when Adele had tried to escape and Gruber had had to kill her to stop her from screaming. He should've done something other than dumping her body in that restroom; he should've hidden it in the bayou or driven it out of state. Instead, he'd made a public statement to punish her father for being so damn tenacious. If Adele hadn't seen that news clip of Fornier talking to her, telling her how much he missed her and wanted her home, she wouldn't have tried what she did.

He'd never forgive Romain for that.

Gruber set down the phone, then picked it up again. He had to know if Peccavi had killed Jasmine.

Preparing an excuse for the phone call, he dialed before the uncertainty returned.

"Hello?"

Gruber had his number blocked, so he identified himself. "It's me. Gruber."

Peccavi immediately lowered his voice, and Gruber had the impression he didn't want to be overheard. "This had better be good."

"It is good. I wanted to tell you I got the baby to Beverly."

"She already notified me. That's part of her job, not yours."

"But I thought you might like to know that the mother has a friend who might be a prime candidate for our…program," Gruber lied.

"We don't pee in our own pool."

"You took this one," Gruber said.

Peccavi hesitated. "The circumstances were right."

"Don't you want to at least hear what I found?"

"Fine. How far along is she?"

Gruber chose what he thought would be a tempting figure. "Seven months."

"Did you talk price?"

"I told her we'd make sure she and the baby are happy. She's so strung out she can't take care of a child, anyway. We'd be doing the kid a favor."

"And?"

"She said she'd think about it."

"Did you get a number?"

"She doesn't have a phone right now. But she knows how to contact you via the Web site."

"Then I'll get her the way I do all the others. This can wait—"

"Don't go!" Gruber cried before Peccavi could hang up. When he didn't hear a click, he assumed his employer was still on the line. "Did you take care of our little...problem?"

"What problem?"

"You know what problem. Our visitor from California."

There was a long pause, so long Gruber felt sure Peccavi had hung up. "Hello?"

"No."

*"No?"*

"She got away. And nearly killed me in the process."

Gruber couldn't believe it.

"But don't worry. I'll take care of her," Peccavi added, obviously determined not to let her get the upper hand a second time.

What had gone wrong? Gruber wondered but was afraid to ask. Peccavi was normally as efficient as he was greedy. He claimed they were successful because of *his* work ethic and self-discipline, but Gruber was the one on the front lines who actually did the kidnapping. Peccavi just managed the business and arranged for the false documents. He had his truck driver scouts find children throughout the country, kids who matched the "wants" of potential parents gathered through a network of adoption attorneys. Then Peccavi paid a premium for each referral and sent Gruber out to pick up the kids. After that, he ordered the forged adoption papers and birth certificate. How hard could the coordination of that be?

Trying not to think about how often he'd been slighted

by Peccavi through the years, Gruber focused instead on the strange elation he felt knowing Jasmine was still alive. And that she'd bested Peccavi, of all people. If she'd managed to outsmart Gruber's boss, she was worthy; she was everything he'd thought she'd be. *Stop me...*

"Where's she staying?" he asked.

"She was at a small hotel in the Quarter, but I doubt she'll go back there."

"So we've lost her?" Gruber filled those words with an appropriate amount of concern, but he was smiling to himself. He hadn't meant for Jasmine to attract Peccavi's attention. Stupid Beverly should've called him instead. Jasmine had been locked in the cellar, for crying out loud. Gruber could've taken her home with him that night and told Peccavi she was dead.

The missed opportunity rankled. But ever since he'd framed Francis for Adele's murder, Beverly didn't trust him. Even after he'd planted that evidence and told her and Peccavi about Francis's past indiscretions, she was tempted to believe her son's protestations of innocence.

"We haven't lost her, not entirely," Peccavi was saying. "Beverly found a napkin in Stratford's purse that has some directions written on it."

"Directions?"

"To Portsville."

Gruber put on the same episode of *America's Most Wanted* so he could see Jasmine again. There she was...beautiful, just like Kimberly. "Portsville's a pretty small town."

"Exactly. She can't hide there for long."

*I won't give up until I find my sister...* Jasmine was saying on the television.

The thrill of the hunt, perhaps the most fulfilling part of

the killing ritual, swept through Gruber. Picking a new victim was almost as much fun as torturing her. "Why not let me handle it?"

"You want this one?"

"I don't mind helping out. It's easier for me because I don't have a family to worry about."

"It's outside your ordinary duties. What I have in mind is permanent."

Gruber nearly laughed aloud. Peccavi thought he was the only one who knew how to kill just because he'd taken care of Jack when Jack tried to get out of the business. "Consider it a Christmas present."

There was a protracted silence.

"Well?" Gruber prompted.

"Make sure you take…the remains far out into the swamps."

They certainly couldn't bury this one in the Moreaus' cellar.

"No one will ever find it," he promised. But he was in no hurry to dispose of her. He'd never broken a spirit as strong as Jasmine Stratford's.

He wondered what it would take….

When Jasmine woke up, Romain's hand was on her breast, but she was still wearing last night's clothes.

Slipping out from under his arm, she turned toward him. She thought he might wake at the movement, but he didn't. His chest rose and fell evenly beneath the blankets, and his eyelashes rested against his cheeks.

She frowned as she studied the damage to his face. He'd taken some hard hits last night, but he was still handsome. Especially in repose. Probably because it was the only time he ever let down his guard.

She wondered what he'd been like before the loss, the bitterness, the life-altering decisions. A few laugh lines bracketed his mouth….

He opened his eyes and gazed back at her, but he didn't move. She wondered what he was thinking. Had he expected to find her in his bed? She'd smelled alcohol on him last night. Maybe he didn't remember carrying her in here.

"Surprise!" she said softly.

He cocked one eyebrow. "I wasn't that drunk."

She laughed at how quickly he'd picked up on her thoughts. "I'm guessing you were drunk enough to give yourself a raging hangover. How's the headache?"

He winced as he touched his bruised cheek. "Nothing compared to the rest of it."

"What happened?"

"Too much testosterone."

Mixed with too much recklessness, no doubt. Romain had too much of a lot of things, especially sex appeal. "You want to tell me about it?"

"Not really."

"Why not?"

"I'm sure your story's more interesting than mine. Why don't we start there?"

She combed her fingers through her tousled hair as she propped herself up against the headboard. The room was cold and uninviting compared to the space she'd occupied curled up beside him. She wished she hadn't awakened quite so soon. "Let's see…. Yesterday I had my purse stolen, got locked in a cellar, discovered a corpse and stumbled on a man wearing a ski mask who tried to kill me."

"Tough day at the office," he said, but she could tell he

wasn't taking her experiences lightly. "Maybe you should give me a few more details."

Inhaling a deep breath, she told him everything, from visiting the police station to finding Black and learning about those marks on the cellar door, to returning to her hotel. He stiffened as he listened. She knew she was bringing a situation he preferred to leave in the past into the present, but he didn't complain.

"So Black's the only one who knew you were going to Moreau's place?" he asked when she finished.

"Yes."

"But like you said, it could've been Phillip."

She nodded.

"It's possible he saw me from the house and came around to the backyard."

"What about the cigarette butts you collected? There was more than one, right? As if someone had hung out there for some time?"

"True. I was sure Black had left them. But Phillip smokes, too, and I couldn't smell any evidence of it in the house. I'm thinking his mother makes him go outside. And he's not social enough to want to be seen by the neighbors. He probably stands under the overhang near the cellar door, where he has some privacy and solitude."

His expression revealed surprise. "How do you know he's not social? Have you met him?"

"I saw him in his car, briefly."

He seemed to consider her response. "What did the man who came after you look like?"

"He was wearing a mask and a long trench coat. With the fog and the dark, it could've been *Mrs.* Moreau and I wouldn't have been able to tell."

"What about height?"

"Not too tall, not too short. I know I should be able to give you more, but details aren't exactly a priority when you're running for your life. All I cared about was getting away."

Romain's hair was sticking up and his eyes still retained some of their sleepiness, but he was sexy in a delightfully rumpled way. "And now that it could've been Phillip and not Black, you're beginning to believe what Black had to say."

"I'm just telling you the marks were there, on the door."

"But anybody could've broken in, and for a variety of reasons."

"It's just something Huff should've considered."

He rolled onto his back, and the muscles in his arms bulged beneath the sleeves of his T-shirt as he linked his hands behind his head. "He did consider what he found— it was my daughter's blood. What are the chances of being framed for a crime like that?"

Jasmine tried not to notice the appealing spectacle he made—powerful and warm as he watched her from beneath those dark lashes. "Unlikely, but not impossible."

"Huff doesn't trust Black."

"That doesn't mean Black's lying about this."

"It means he's *probably* lying." The bed creaked as he shifted again, this time punching up his pillows. "You said the body was in Moreau's cellar."

"That's right."

Romain didn't say anything for a moment. When he did, his words sounded like they'd been forced through his teeth. "Was it a child?"

Jasmine nearly reached out to touch him, to console

him if she could, but she felt too helpless in the face of his grief, a grief she read in every line of his body. "No. A man. He died violently—I could sense that a struggle had taken place."

"A recent struggle?"

"It wasn't a fresh kill. I'm guessing it happened five, six years ago."

That was better somehow, better for him. But it still wasn't *good* news for anyone. "So what does that tell you?" he said, and sat up. He couldn't seem to get comfortable. Maybe it was his injuries, but Jasmine suspected it had more to do with her presence in his bed. They were too aware of each other on a sexual level.

"That there's more to this than we originally thought," she said. "Who called in the tip about Moreau carrying a large bundle into the house the night Adele was taken?"

"The neighbor across the street. A woman by the name of Tracy Cooper."

Jasmine hadn't seen any activity at that house. "Do you know if she still lives in the same place?"

"I have no idea. Until you showed up, I was trying to put this behind me. I hadn't even talked to Huff, until yesterday."

"You called him?"

"I wanted to ask about you."

"What'd he say?"

"That you're desperate enough to do or say anything if it'll help you find your sister."

"That was nice of him," she said.

"He thinks you're faking the psychic thing, that you're a fraud," he added.

She confronted that kind of skepticism almost every day

of her life, and not just from strangers, either. It went with the territory. But it was never easy, and hearing it from Romain bothered her more than usual. "What do *you* think?" she asked, bristling.

"I think you aren't going to find your sister by reinvestigating Adele's case," he said. "Regardless of the details, Moreau was a murderer. The body you found should tell you that much. He's gone. Whether you agree with what I did or not, I've done my time. It's over. Let it go before you get yourself into more trouble."

He was still "doing his time." But she saw no need to say that. "If it was really over, there'd be no danger to me or anyone else," she said instead.

He pressed a finger and thumb to his closed eyes. "Why won't this go away?"

He was talking to himself, but she answered. "Because, like I said, there's more."

"More what?" he demanded, dropping his hand.

She pulled her knees close to her body, hugging them to her chest—and his eyes immediately fell to the wide legs of her boxers and the bare thigh they revealed. "More secrets. More lies. More guilt," she said, trying to keep her mind on the discussion. "Why else would someone try to kill me simply for looking around a cellar?"

He blew out a sigh. "What about the dead guy?"

She was losing her focus, concentrating on the shape of Romain's lips. He had nice lips, lips that made her think of what he'd done to her in that shower fantasy…. "What about him?"

"Do you have any idea who he might be?"

"No clue. The police might, but—" she frowned "—my name hasn't been added to their phone tree. Even if someone tried to call, they wouldn't be able to reach me. Whoever stole my purse has my cell phone, too."

"You can't get service down here, anyway." His gaze flicked over her bare legs once again. "Why'd you come to me?"

"This was the only place I could think of that felt safe." She tried to discreetly lower her legs, but she wasn't wearing a bra, and that soon became as much of a distraction as her legs had been. "You're staring," she finally pointed out.

"Do you mind?"

Jasmine recognized his arousal, but she sensed negative emotion, too. It was *her* emotional history that bothered him—and the fact that he wanted her but wished he didn't. "I'd like it better if you weren't angry."

His eyebrows drew together. "I'm not angry."

He'd lived with that emotion for so long, he probably wasn't even aware of it anymore. "Would you rather I left?" she asked.

"No. You know what I'd rather you did." His voice grew rough. "The question is whether or not you're as interested as I am."

"That depends."

"On what?"

Coming to her knees, she inched closer to him. The wariness that entered his face told her how hesitant he was to trust her. He reminded her of a wild animal, watching the advance of a human. When she smoothed the hair off his forehead, she almost expected him to flinch or knock her hand away. He was so ready to close himself off, protect himself. But he didn't. He let her touch him, let her kiss his temple, his cheek, his lips. Was he remembering what such tenderness felt like?

"Be careful," he warned as her fingers delved into his hair.

"I won't touch your injuries."

"I'm not worried about my injuries." He spoke so close to her mouth their lips actually touched. "I'm warning you not to start this unless you're willing to finish. It's been too long for me. I'm not playing games."

"I'm not playing games, either." As she pressed her lips to the strong pulse at his throat, his hand moved to her thigh. He let it rest there, testing her to see if she'd object. When she didn't, he slid his hand up the leg of her boxers to cup her bare bottom. Then his eyes fluttered shut and he dropped his head back as if he'd just sampled heaven. "God, that's good," he breathed.

Jasmine's heart was racing so fast she could hardly speak. "I should tell you I'm not on the Pill or...or anything." Generally speaking, she had no reason to use birth control. She hadn't even kissed a man in two years.

His eyelashes lifted, revealing fresh intent. "I have a couple of condoms. They were given to me by a friend when I left prison, so they're pretty old, but they should work."

Prison. That word hit her like a blast of cold air, and she instinctively pulled back.

He didn't reach for her, didn't try to convince her not to worry about his past. He froze as though he expected the encounter to be over. Maybe that was why he'd brought up the subject—to make sure she knew what she was doing. But it didn't matter. She wanted him too badly to stop. He was a stranger, and yet she felt as if she knew him, as if they'd already made love. "A condom is better than nothing."

His hand slid back up her leg, seeking what he'd found earlier. "I'm glad you see it my way."

"You're right," she said when she'd recovered enough breath to speak.

"About what?" He watched her closely, reading her responses, feeding off her excitement.

"I much prefer this to a dream."

He smiled as he pulled her against him. But when he touched her lips with his, it was very light. He was merely growing familiar before coaxing her to open her mouth to him and let him take the kiss deeper.

He smelled like the outdoors, which was intoxicating in itself, but the security she felt in his arms was even better. She felt as though he could protect her from anything.

She let him kiss her, kissed him back—and clung to him as the hand in her boxers grew bolder and more possessive.

He broke away first, breathing heavily as he looked down at her. *"Je suis ivre sur le seul goût de toi."*

"What does that mean?" she asked.

"In summary, wow," he said while yanking off his T-shirt. He'd done it as a practical matter, not to show off, but the sight of his bare torso sent a fresh charge of hormones through Jasmine.

"Wow indeed," she breathed.

"What?"

She tugged at her bottom lip. "Nice chest."

He was too focused on her to respond to the compliment. "Your turn."

She struggled to gain some control over her galloping heart rate, but it felt as if she'd stepped off solid ground. She couldn't remember ever being so completely enthralled. "I hope you weren't making false promises on the phone," she teased. Suddenly self-conscious, she'd resorted to talking as a way to put off removing her clothes.

"I don't make promises I can't keep," he said and placed her on her back.

Jasmine's hands curled into fists. "That's good news. I *think*."

His gaze swept over her. "I only see one problem."

That she was suddenly terrified to go past the point of no return? "What's that?"

He ran a finger beneath the elastic waist of her boxers, raising gooseflesh on her belly. "Access."

He began to remedy that, but she quickly stopped him. "I'm a little nervous," she explained. "Maybe I can make you…uh…happy another way."

His eyebrows went up. "You're serious?"

"I think so."

"Sorry, I'm not remotely interested in a consolation prize." He slipped his hands under her shirt, brushing his thumbs over her breasts. "But we don't have to do anything until you're ready."

She didn't remember giving the go-ahead on the clothing removal, but her shirt was gone a minute later. She didn't object. Catching his whisker-roughened chin, she forced him to look her in the eye. "This is crazy. Are we sure we want to do this?"

"You're kidding, aren't you?" He was obviously too far gone to even consider bailing out.

"I'm not kidding."

"Trust me." He trailed kisses down her neck, moving lower until he touched the tip of one breast with his tongue. She gasped and tried to pull away, but there was nowhere to go. Her escape attempt was halfhearted to begin with.

"Something wrong?" he murmured.

She didn't answer him. Her boxers were already on their way to her ankles, and from then on he made sure the only thing she uttered was a moan.

Romain's injuries hurt, but not nearly as much as he'd expected. He made love to Jasmine twice before he even remembered he'd been in a fight.

"I've finally made up my mind." Her shyness gone, she lay next to him covered only in a fine sheet of sweat, one arm over her face.

He rolled onto his side so he could admire the view. She was even more beautiful than he'd imagined. But very different from Pam—smaller, darker-skinned, bigger-breasted, with stunning, almond-shaped eyes that'd been so unguarded they'd held him mesmerized as he moved on top of her.

He hated that Pam had already entered his thoughts, but he supposed it was inevitable. "About what?"

Smiling, she lifted her arm to peer at him. "I don't think we should make love."

"Okay," he said. "I won't touch you." But he ran a finger from her collarbone to her belly button, and she didn't stop him. "We're out of condoms, anyway."

"Then my timing's good."

Personally, he wished they had one more. "You ready for breakfast?"

"Definitely."

"Do you like *pain perdu?*"

"What is it?"

"French toast."

"As long as it comes with coffee," she said and yawned as she stretched.

He resisted the urge to cup her breast again. "I can arrange that. Would you like cream?"

"And sugar."

He got up to put on his boxers, jeans and a sweatshirt. It was a crisp morning. Now that they were no longer sharing body heat, he was beginning to feel the cold. He needed to start the stove. "Would you like a pair of sweats until I can get a fire going?"

"That'd be great."

He tossed her the clothes, then told himself to get busy. But he couldn't help lingering to watch her dress.

"What?" she asked, smiling.

His clothes almost swallowed her. They would've fit Pam a lot better. She'd been nearly six feet tall, only three inches shorter than he was. But he actually preferred the look of Jasmine in his sweats—which made him regret letting her wear them.

"I just wanted to…" the past intruded, destroying the euphoria of a moment before and overwhelming him with guilt "…thank you," he finished.

"For what?" she asked in surprise.

Now cold and empty inside, he forced a smile. "For this morning."

She eyed him, suddenly leery. "You don't have to thank me."

"I should. That was the best fuck I've had in years."

Her expression changed, grew shuttered. He'd taken what she'd given him, what amounted to the most incredible two hours of his life since Pam died, and thrown it in the dirt. He supposed that, subconsciously, he'd been trying to remind himself that she *wasn't* Pam, that she would never be Pam. And he hated her for being able to satisfy him in a way only Pam could satisfy him before.

But he instantly cursed himself for lashing out. He knew it had everything to do with him and nothing to do with her, one of those things the psychologist had told him he did to ruin his own happiness. Except this time he'd ruined someone else's, too.

An artificial smile replaced the sincere response of a moment before. "Yeah, well, that's what they all say."

She was trying to shrug it off, to pretend she didn't care that he hadn't valued what they'd shared. But he saw how quickly she folded her arms over her chest, how desperately she wanted to hide herself from his view. Until just now, she'd been completely trusting, warm—and he'd made her pay for it.

Shoving a frustrated hand through his tousled hair, he searched for the words to undo what he'd done. "I'm sorry," he said. "I didn't mean it."

She held up a hand to stop him. "No need to explain. I understand. Meaningless is meaningless, right?"

# 13

Jasmine couldn't wait to get out of Romain's house. She'd known better than to get involved with him, but she'd never expected him to make her feel so cheap. Actually, she was more embarrassed than offended—because their lovemaking had been special to her.

God, she was an idiot. She generally had a good head on her shoulders, lived a cautious life, avoided anything that might be awkward later. How had she stumbled into this?

She hadn't been herself yesterday. She'd been through too much, must not've been thinking straight. *Let it go. Forget it.*

After a mostly silent meal, Romain forked up the last of his French toast and looked at her. "Tell me about yourself."

"Why?" She added more sugar to her coffee. Thanks to the potbellied stove, the house was growing warm. Had she been less eager to escape his company, she would've enjoyed the morning. The primitive but comfortable house. The isolation. Even the surrounding bayou. For the first time, she could see the peace and beauty of this place.

"I'm curious."

She took a sip of her coffee. "What do you want to know?"

"Have you ever been married?"

She briefly considered whether or not she wanted to tell him but figured it didn't matter. After the next few minutes, she'd never see him again. "Once."

"So Stratford was your married name?"

"No, it was a short marriage. I went back to my maiden name."

"How short?"

"Two years."

"Why?"

"We were too different. It just didn't work out."

"No kids?"

She hesitated. Why was he trying to get to know her *now?* As far as she was concerned, it was a waste of time. "Does it matter?" she asked.

"That's too personal a question?"

"I have a steady boyfriend and a couple of kids waiting for me at home," she lied.

He gave her a wry glance over his coffee cup. "You wouldn't cheat on him."

"And I wouldn't be here at Christmas if I had kids. So I guess you could've answered both questions yourself."

"Not even for your sister?" he said.

She cut off another bite of French toast and pushed it around in the syrup. "Not for anyone."

"Didn't you and your husband want a child?"

"My husband was infertile. Or—" she caught herself, realizing that wasn't fair to Harvey because she didn't know for sure "—maybe it was me."

"There are tests for that sort of thing."

"We weren't together long enough to pursue it. But he was married three times before and had no children, so I'm thinking there's a good chance it's not me."

Romain had been leaning back in his chair, watching her as she attempted to finish her breakfast. When he heard this, his chair thumped as it hit the floor. "Your ex was married three times *before* you?"

Fairly certain she was getting a headache, Jasmine rubbed a finger over her left temple. "He was a bit older."

"What's a bit?"

"Thirty years."

His jaw dropped. "Holy hell! How old were you when you married him?"

"Twenty." She raised a hand to forestall his reaction. "But he wasn't wealthy by any stretch, so don't imagine I'm some kind of gold digger."

"You married for love?"

No. But it seemed unkind to simply admit it. "In ways," she finally said.

"That's hardly what I'd call an unequivocal answer."

She didn't have to give him an answer at all, but it was as pointless to refuse as it was to finish the conversation, so she remained polite. "I was completely screwed up. He turned me around." She shrugged. "I owed him a lot."

"So you decided to thank him with 'I do'?"

As famished as Jasmine had been when Romain first mentioned breakfast, she found she couldn't get through more than half of her *pain perdu*. It tasted great but kept getting stuck in her throat. Giving up on the meal, she pushed her plate away. "It happens."

He eyed her leftovers. "I thought you were hungry."

"Not anymore."

"Don't you like it?"

"It's fine. I'm just…full."

The way his lips drew into a straight line—the same lips

that had touched every part of her body this morning—indicated he wasn't pleased by her answer, but he didn't press her to eat more. "Where'd you meet this guy?"

She sighed. "Somewhere between Indiana and Illinois."

"Most people are able to come up with a more specific answer to that question."

She glanced at the battery-powered clock over by the small generator-run refrigerator. "I think I should be heading out." She knew she was going to feel stupid asking for money after everything that'd happened, but she had no choice. Clearing her throat, she broached the subject, trying to get it over with quickly. "Is there any chance you could lend me forty bucks?"

When he didn't answer right away, she hurried to explain. "I'll send it back to you, of course. You can pick it up at the motel in Portsville since you don't have mail service out here. I have a friend who's wiring me some money, but it's in New Orleans, and I need gas to make it back." She faltered as she began to realize he might not have money. "If you don't have it, maybe you'd vouch for me so I could borrow it from someone you know. I'm good for it."

"Fishing is a living," he said, obviously offended. "I've got money."

"Great." She smiled in relief. "So…"

"No problem." Getting up, he started clearing away the dishes. "But right now, we've got to get ready or we'll be late."

She frowned, her coffee cup halfway to her mouth. "Late for what?"

"Dinner at my parents'."

"I'm not going to your parents'," she said. "I have to get back to New Orleans."

"It's Christmas."

"So?"

"You can't have that much to do."

"I have a lot to do." She gave up on her coffee, too, and carried the rest of the dirty dishes to the sink. "In any case, Christmas isn't my favorite holiday. I don't mind skipping it."

"It's not mine, either. But it's important to my parents."

She threw their paper napkins in the trash. "Wonderful. I'm sure you'll have a nice visit with them."

"You're not returning to that hotel room alone," he said. "And I can't go with you until tonight."

Jasmine pulled up the sweats he'd lent her because they were puddling at her feet and probably made her look too small to take care of herself. "That's ridiculous. I don't need you to come with me. I just need forty dollars. If you'll risk the loan, I'll get out of your way." She started from the room as if to change and leave, as if it'd already been decided, but he caught her elbow and turned her toward him.

"Listen, I understand that you're finished with me, that you wouldn't let me touch you again even if I begged. I screwed up and now you can't wait to get the hell out of here. I deserve that. But regardless of what you might think of me, I don't want to see you hurt."

Funny that he'd been the only one to hurt her in years. "I appreciate the sentiment," she said. "But I'm not your problem."

He laughed softly, almost bitterly, and dropped his hand. "You came to me."

"Then we both got what we wanted and now I'm ready to leave."

Something passed through his eyes, but Jasmine

couldn't identify it. She was too busy struggling with her own emotions. "I'll give you the money when we get back," he insisted.

She couldn't spend the whole day with him. Every time she looked at him, she craved another taste, another touch. It was like being mesmerized by flames, like reaching out to them even after she'd been burned. "But your parents aren't expecting me," she said, trying a different approach.

"They'll be glad to see you. If you're there, my sister and I will have less of an opportunity to ruin the big feast."

"Your sister?"

"She's visiting, along with her family."

Jasmine remembered that Black had mentioned Romain's brother-in-law, but it was such a long shot that said brother-in-law would have any involvement in Kimberly's disappearance—or anything else of consequence to her— she wasn't willing to take the risk of accompanying Romain just to meet him. "I don't know them. They don't know me," she argued. "And I don't have anything to wear."

"I'll figure something out."

"I'm definitely not wearing *your* clothes."

"I know a girl about your size."

"A *girl?* Don't bother her."

"She won't mind."

He was being far more stubborn about this than she would've expected. "Why don't I stay here and wait for you, then?" She waved at the dishes they'd stacked near the sink. "I could finish cleaning up."

"You wouldn't wait. You'd walk to Portsville and hitch-hike from there."

"So? *What do you care?*" she snapped, frustrated by his unyielding refusal.

He studied her for a moment. "I guess meaningless isn't meaningless, after all."

"Do they fit?" Romain asked, standing outside his bedroom door.

Jasmine didn't answer right away but, after a moment, he heard her voice. "Close."

When he'd handed over the clothes he'd borrowed from Casey's teenage daughter, she'd shut him out, which disturbed him almost as much as the way breakfast had gone. He wanted to watch her dress. Not because he wanted to see her body as much as he longed to regain the intimacy he'd so impetuously destroyed.

"Are you going to open the door?" he asked, growing irritated.

"I'm coming."

The door swung open and she stood in the entryway.

The jeans fit nice and tight, the way he liked them. Unfortunately, so did the sweater. It pulled in front, drawing attention to her breasts, and she kept fiddling with the fabric in an attempt to loosen it.

"It looks great," he said, trying to sound believable. It *was* great, but the kind of great a man would be more likely to appreciate than a woman.

"How old was the girl who gave you these clothes?" she asked, turning back to the mirror. She'd waited in the truck when he'd gone into Casey's house—hadn't met Casey or her daughter. But he knew Casey had peeked at Jasmine through the windows. He'd seen the curtains move as he backed out of the drive.

"Thirteen."

"No wonder."

"She's the only person in Portsville even remotely close to your size."

"She's not my size. This sweater is too tight."

He agreed, but telling her so would only make her more self-conscious. "It's fine. If we find a store that's open, I'll buy you something better along the way."

"I've got to get back to New Orleans to pick up my money," she grumbled. "I hate being so dependent."

"The money will be there waiting for you."

With a sigh, she stopped adjusting her top. "I guess this will have to work. Anyway, it beats how I looked in your T-shirt and boxers."

"I wouldn't say that." He caught her eye in the mirror and had a flashback of her staring up at him this morning, naked and on her back, their fingers and other body parts intertwined. Now *that* was a beautiful sight.

"Are we taking my car or your truck?" she asked, shifting her gaze away as if she could read his thoughts and they made her uncomfortable.

"I was thinking it might be fun to take the bike. I have an extra helmet," he offered.

Her teeth sank into her lower lip as she considered it. "I've never been on a motorcycle."

He pulled the keys from his pocket and tossed them in the air. *"Alors vous allez à comme le tour."*

"English, please."

"You're going to like the ride."

"That doesn't mean I won't regret it later," she said.

And he knew she was talking about a different kind of ride altogether.

* * *

Jasmine couldn't get comfortable on the back of Romain's motorcycle, not when she was trying so hard not to hold on to him. She kept changing the position of her hands, searching for a good grip on the bike instead, but then he'd make a turn or switch lanes, and she'd have to grab him again.

Eventually, he pulled over to the side of the road and flipped up the screen on his helmet. "What's wrong?"

"Nothing," she said.

"Why do you keep fidgeting?"

"The speed and motion of the bike makes me nervous," she said, but that wasn't true at all. *He* made her nervous.

He twisted to see her clinging to the backrest. Then he muttered a curse, lowered the screen on his helmet and they took off again. After another few miles, however, he reached back one hand at a time and brought her arms around his waist, and she didn't move after that because he went even faster and she was afraid she'd fall off if she let go.

When they reached Mamou, Jasmine was exhausted from two hours of fighting her natural inclination to let her body relax into his. But staring up at Romain's parents' neat, middle-class home she felt too tense to worry about the fatigue. His family had already started pouring out the front door—a motorcycle didn't exactly make a quiet entrance.

"Here they come," she whispered as he took her helmet.

He didn't respond. He was getting the packages he'd wrapped in ice out of his saddlebags.

Jasmine smiled politely as a tall, rather austere-looking woman, who had to be Romain's mother, drew close to shake her hand.

"Romain, you didn't tell me you were bringing a date."

His mother was obviously pleased, so pleased and acutely interested in Jasmine that Jasmine immediately felt the need to explain.

"I'm not a date," she said. "I'm just…someone who—" She glanced at Romain, seeking his help. She didn't want to mention Moreau or the investigation, didn't want to bring up a difficult subject. But he didn't fill the gap in the conversation. "I'm someone who didn't have anywhere to go for Christmas so Romain dragged me along," she finished lamely.

She'd said it with a laugh, but it didn't come off as funny, which made her feel like even more of an idiot. She'd engaged in passionate sex with this woman's son for no real reason except that she'd wanted him too much to say no. And now she was wearing the clothes of a thirteen-year-old girl while trying to explain her unexpected appearance at their house for dinner. Never in her life had she felt more out of place, even the year she'd gone to visit Sheridan's family for Christmas and they'd forgotten she was coming and given the guest room to a cousin.

"You're welcome here," his mother said. "Any friend of Romain's is a friend of ours."

Romain handed one of the packages he'd taken from his saddlebags to his mother. "Shrimp," he told her. "Merry Christmas."

"Do I want to know what happened to your face?" she asked.

"Accident. Nothing big."

"Accident," she repeated as if she'd heard it too many times. But her expression as she hugged her son suggested she'd hold him longer if he'd let her.

"Jasmine, this is my mother, Alicia," he said. "Mom, this is Jasmine Stratford."

"It's a pleasure to meet you, Mrs. Fornier," Jasmine said.

"Please, call me Alicia." She gestured toward the man with thick white hair and broad shoulders who had accompanied her down the front walk. "This is Romain's father, Romain, Sr."

"Nice to meet you, too," Jasmine said with a nod.

His large hand swallowed hers, and she sensed an inherent strength in the elder Fornier that reminded her of his son. Embittered or not, Romain gave the impression that he could hold his own in any kind of battle. Now she knew where he got it.

"Welcome to our home," his dad said.

Their smiles made Jasmine feel a bit better—until she caught sight of the woman coming up behind Romain's father. This had to be Romain's sister. With their streaked blond hair and nice even features, they looked too much alike to mistake the connection. Unfortunately, the way she pursed her lips and lifted her chin suggested Romain wasn't on good terms with her.

"A little late, aren't you, T-Bone?" she said with a taunting lilt to her voice.

Romain's face took on a look of indifference, but not before Jasmine caught a flicker of hurt. She suspected he cared as much about this member of his family as he did the rest but, for whatever reason, he wasn't about to let on. "Jasmine, this is my sister, Susan." He tilted his head to see the child trailing behind her. "And her eight-year-old son, Travis," he added.

Susan cocked an eyebrow at her brother. "And?"

"And what?" he said.

"Could we get a frame of reference here? This is the first woman you've brought home since Pam died. What is she to you? A friend, a lover, a wife?"

"None of the above," Jasmine quickly interjected. "As a matter of fact, we don't even like each other very much."

Susan clapped as she laughed. "Perfect! You and I will get along great."

Romain shot Jasmine a glance that seemed to challenge her denial of lover. Or maybe it was only a guilty conscience that made her interpret it that way. But she offered him a serene smile she didn't feel, and he turned to his sister. "Where's Tom?" he asked.

"On the phone, talking to his parents." She rolled her eyes. "They hate it when we leave Boston."

"So does he," Alicia said under her breath.

"What about the other kids?" Romain asked. "I thought they'd be running all over the place. Mason's three by now, isn't he?"

"He'll turn three next month. He and Curtis are in front of the TV. Mom and Dad gave them a new game system for Christmas, and it'd take a lot more than a visit from an uncle who never calls or writes—an uncle *they barely know*—to pull them away from it."

Jasmine held her breath as she waited for Romain's reply.

"You told me they didn't need an ex-con for a role model."

For a moment, Susan looked as if she'd retract that statement, maybe even apologize. But then she straightened her shoulders. "They don't."

"Because a philanderer father is so much better."

"T-Bone." His mother touched his arm and angled her head toward Travis, and he muttered an apology. Fortunately, little Travis didn't seem to be following the conversation; he was merely waiting for a chance to break in.

"Do all those trophies in our room belong to you, Uncle T-Bone?" he asked eagerly.

Romain mussed his hair. "For the most part."

"How'd you get them?"

"Track and basketball."

"And football," his father said. "Romain was quite a running back. I think he could've walked on to a college team if he hadn't joined the marines," he added for Jasmine's benefit.

He certainly had the build of an athlete. But Jasmine was trying not to think complimentary things about Romain.

"I'm going to play football like you," Travis announced.

A genuine smile curved Romain's lips for the first time since they'd arrived, giving Jasmine hope that this might be an enjoyable visit, after all. But his sister cut him off before he could respond. "No, you're not. Only big dummies who don't care if they blow out a knee play football."

"I never blew out a knee, Susan," Romain said with strained patience.

"But you did get a concussion. I often wonder if that's to blame for everything."

"If I remember right, you were the one who encouraged me to play my senior year."

"Yeah, well, that was before I realized what a disappointment you'd turn out to be," she snapped and went inside ahead of them.

Portsville was quiet. A truck passed, going in the other direction, but it was the only vehicle Gruber had seen for miles. The cemetery looked like it'd be more fun than the town.

He pulled into Portsville's small grocery store to buy a drink and see if he could glean any information. What business did Jasmine have here? Why did she leave New

Orleans for rural Cajun country? It had to have some connection to the reason she'd come. She was here at his invitation, after all.

His car door groaned as he forced it open. He needed to buy a new sedan. He had a truck that was barely a year old, but he mostly kept it around back, out of sight. His old Honda Civic was much more nondescript; he preferred to come and go unnoticed.

The ice machine in front of the old grocery store rattled, catching Gruber's attention. Man, what he could fit into a freezer that size! His own freezer was getting too packed, which made it difficult to save everything he wanted—

"They're closed." A ruddy, bowlegged man had just come out of the bar next door.

Gruber knew he had to look stupid, standing there with his hand on the door, gazing fondly at an ice machine. "What'd you say?"

"I said they're closed." The man motioned toward the clumsily printed sign taped to the door. Merry Christmas! it read. See you on December 26th!

"Oh." Gruber blinked at it. How had he not seen that?

"You visiting for the holidays?" the man asked.

"Just passing through."

"I'm Croc. I own the bar here. I don't open till four, but if you're hungry, I'll make you a burger."

*Croc?* The Cajuns down here were such rednecks. "Actually, I'm…um…looking for my sister."

The man's bushy eyebrows went up. "Does she live in town?"

"No, but she mentioned coming down this way to, you know, sightsee. Her name's Jasmine Stratford."

Croc chewed harder on the toothpick dangling from one

side of his mouth. "Never heard of her. What does she look like?"

"She's small, attractive. Part Indian."

His eyes were riveted on Gruber's clearly Caucasian features. "Indian?"

"East Indian. We have different fathers," he said.

"I haven't seen anyone by that description. But you might check with Henry over at the hotel. He put up a few visitors this past week."

Gruber glanced down the dock to see a sun-bleached wooden building on pilings. The words *Lil' Cajun* were painted on the side. "I'll do that," he said. "Thanks."

"No problem. Good luck finding your sister."

"By the way—" Gruber caught the man's arm. "If you happen to see her, don't tell her I was here, okay? I'm trying to surprise her. For Christmas."

Croc gave him a friendly nod. "I won't say a word."


"You're East Indian?"

Jasmine hesitated with a bite of lamb halfway to her mouth. She hadn't expected to be the focal point of the Forniers' dinner conversation. She was just tagging along with Romain until she could get back to New Orleans, where she hoped to promptly forget him. But, from their behavior, Romain's family hadn't seen him with a woman in a very long time, and they were more than a little curious about her.

"My mother's East Indian," she explained to Susan, who'd asked the question. "She came from India about five years before I was born. My father was raised in Ohio."

"You have beautiful skin," Alicia said.

"And eyes," Susan's husband, Tom, added. "They're so unusual."

Because he'd said next to nothing so far, and that comment had been made with far too much enthusiasm, all heads turned in his direction.

Rather soft but handsome in a slender "polished professional" kind of way, he spread out his hands. "What? She does!"

"Thank you," Jasmine said and tried not to notice the tightening of Susan's jaw.

"It's interesting that your parents come from such different backgrounds." It was Romain, Sr. who filled the awkward silence. "Where do they live now?"

"They're divorced. My mother lives in Ohio, where I was born. My father moved to Mobile a few years ago."

"Alabama?"

"That's right."

"Mobile's not too far from Portsville," Susan said. "Do you get to see him very often?"

No doubt Romain's sister was wondering why Jasmine was sitting at their dinner table instead of her own father's. "Not really. Not since he remarried. And I don't live in Portsville. I'm from Sacramento."

Tom's fork clinked against his plate as he put it down. "Sacramento's clear across the country. How'd you meet Romain?"

"We know it wasn't in Sacramento," Susan said under her breath. "My dear brother would've had to leave the bayou for that."

Romain's eyes narrowed as he chewed, but he didn't respond. His mother seemed relieved that he let the barb go, but Jasmine wished he'd say *something* to steer the conversation away from her. If she told them about her missing sister or her work at The Last Stand, it'd invariably bring up what'd happened to Adele, which wasn't a subject anyone would enjoy discussing, especially at Christmas dinner.

No one had recognized her from *America's Most Wanted,* so she decided to make up a reason for her and Romain to have crossed paths. She hated to lie, but she also didn't feel her personal details really mattered. After today, she'd never see these people again. "A mutual friend introduced us."

She felt Romain's attention settle on her and wondered if he was surprised, but by the time she glanced at him his focus had already shifted to his brother-in-law, who was drinking far more than he ate.

"Who?" Tom asked.

"Poppo," she said, recalling the bogus name she'd given the old Cajun at the hotel.

"I know a lot of people in Portsville," Susan said. "We had cousins down there when we were growing up and spent at least a month of every summer on the bayou. But I don't recall a Poppo." Frowning, she focused on Romain. "Do I know him?"

"I'm pretty sure you don't," Romain said. Fortunately, he didn't say that he didn't know him, either.

"So you crossed four states just to visit Romain?" Tom asked.

"I was already here on vacation when I met Poppo, and he said I could—" she searched for a credible link "—buy some fresh shrimp from Romain."

"Are you vacationing alone?" Susan asked.

Jasmine turned the stem of her wineglass because it gave her something to do with her hands. "My best friend was planning to come with me, but she recently got married and backed out of the trip."

Tom didn't bother to hide his astonishment. "What made you choose Cajun country for a Christmas vacation?"

"I've heard a lot about it."

"Have you ever been here before?" Obviously, he thought she was crazy.

"No."

"And you have no family in the immediate area."

"That's right."

"Just because *you've* never liked it down here doesn't mean other people don't," Susan muttered.

"I love coming to *Mamère's* and *Papère's!*" Travis announced. When he tried to fling a pea across the table at his younger brother, his grandfather took away his spoon.

"I realize that some people find this place sort of quaint and charming, but it isn't Hawaii," Tom retorted. "I'm amazed that someone from California, who doesn't have family in the area, would plan a trip to Portsville at Christmas. It's equally incredible she'd hook up with my brother-in-law, who's become such a recluse he barely even socializes with his own family anymore." He lifted his glass as he looked around the table. "Am I the only one who finds that strange?"

The expression on Romain's face suggested he was about to tell Tom to mind his own business. Tom was getting tipsy and starting to act brash. But Alicia reached over to squeeze Romain's hand, obviously begging his forbearance, and he managed to reel in his temper.

"No stranger than my brother going to prison in the first place," Susan said, unable to resist pushing Romain a little further.

"*Who* went to prison?" Travis asked, suddenly tuning in.

"No one you know." Alicia's pointed smile told Susan

and Tom to shut up. Susan seemed cowed because her oldest son had picked up on her words so quickly, but Tom had drunk too much to worry about subtleties.

"No one on my side of the family," he said.

"Your family has their share of secrets," Susan responded.

Romain raised his glass to Jasmine. "Isn't this a pleasant family meal?"

Jasmine smiled helplessly because she didn't know how to answer. It'd be too obvious a lie to agree. It was all Romain and Susan could do not to wind up in a shouting match; Alicia was constantly running interference by warning this person or that person with a touch or a glance; Romain, Sr. was obviously concerned with helping his wife for the sake of "company;" and Romain clearly wanted to punch Tom in the face. Besides the children, Tom seemed like the only person really enjoying himself. Of course, he'd had enough alcohol to find almost anything enjoyable, but at least *someone* was smiling.

"Peace on earth, goodwill toward men," she said and clinked her glass against Romain's.

His mouth twisted into a wry grin, then he downed his wine and went back to his meal.

Tom watched this interplay over the rim of his own wineglass. "It's good to see you with a woman again, Romain."

"Thank you, Tom," Romain said. "And I know she's pretty." He winked. "No need to mention it again."

"She *is* pretty," he agreed. "Not like Pam at all, though."

Susan didn't say anything, but Alicia cleared her throat and murmured Tom's name in a warning tone.

"What? I can't talk about Pam? I knew her, too. She was my sister-in-law," he said, but then he waved toward

Jasmine and changed the subject as if he wanted to avoid any further conflict. "So what did you do? Pick a random spot on the map and say 'I want to go there'?" Another thought seemed to occur to him. "Or…maybe you needed to get away. Are you running from a bad breakup or an abusive husband?"

Jasmine choked down the bread she'd just bitten off. "No. I'd heard a lot about the beauty of the bayous and decided to see them for myself."

"And what do you think?" It was Romain, Sr. He had a firm grip on his knife and fork as if tempted to use them for more than cutting meat, but his voice remained as calm as ever.

"I like it here." And that was the truth, a truth largely inspired by those few moments when she'd first opened her eyes this morning and found Romain's large, warm body wrapped around hers. She knew she'd never forget the pale winter sunlight as it streamed through his window, or the chorus of rain outside. "But the thought of alligators makes me a little nervous," she admitted.

Romain, Sr. spoke up. "Alligators won't hurt you. They're generally not aggressive."

"That's what people keep telling me, but it'd only take one bite to ruin my day," she said with a laugh.

Susan broke out of the morose silence into which she'd fallen. "How'd your parents meet, Jasmine?"

Jasmine didn't want to talk about her parents any more than her reason for coming to Louisiana, but it seemed the safest alternative at the moment. At least she wouldn't have to lie. "They went to college together."

"You said your mother was an immigrant?"

"She came from India with her parents when she was

fifteen. But her parents returned shortly after I was born so I don't know them all that well."

"She's Hindu?" Tom asked.

"Yes. Nearly eighty percent of India is Hindu."

"But only a small number of people in America are," Susan said. "Was your father religious?"

"Actually, he was. I don't think he is anymore, though."

"Hindu?"

"Christian."

Tom poured himself more wine, after which Romain, Sr. not so subtly moved the bottle away from him. "What does that make you?"

Following Kimberly's disappearance, Jasmine had gone through a period of confusion. Her mother was adamant that she'd lose her salvation if she didn't embrace Hinduism, and her father was equally adamant that she'd go to hell if she didn't remain a Christian. She was hoping there was some place reserved for people like her, who felt torn and couldn't decide if one way was any better than the other. "I guess my beliefs are sort of a blending of the two."

"So Christmas doesn't have much meaning for you." Tom probably felt as if he'd solved the riddle of her presence at their table. It was merely another day, another meal.

But that wasn't true at all. As much as she might deny it, Christmas meant a great deal to Jasmine. It always had. But she'd learned to downplay the family aspect so she wouldn't be disappointed when her holiday experience was so different from everyone else's.

She searched for a way to explain without making herself seem pathetic but couldn't find the words. More than she ever had before, she missed the unity her family had once known. It was a poignant ache in her chest. Prior to

Kimberly's disappearance, she'd been on solid ground emotionally, but had struggled to regain her footing ever since. The abduction had robbed her of a sister she loved and split her family apart more ruthlessly than a hatchet.

The tears that sprang to her eyes came suddenly. She didn't want to be here with these strangers. She wanted to have Christmas dinner with her family. But that family was dead and gone. That family would never be the same, *could* never be the same, even on Christmas.

"If you'll excuse me, I've got…something in my eye." She left the table, walking calmly until she cleared the doorway. Then, when they could no longer see her, she fled to the bathroom, locked herself in and sagged against the door.

# 14

The knock came far sooner than Jasmine expected. She'd thought the Forniers might give her a few minutes to herself. No such luck. They probably wanted to quiz her on what had caused her parents' divorce or if and when she and Romain had made love. They couldn't simply mind their business and leave her alone, could they? That was too much to ask.

She ignored the first knock. But another came right after it.

"Jasmine?"

It was Romain. She was tempted to tell him to go away. She needed to pull herself together and paste another smile on her face. But she was even more tempted to tell him off for bringing her here. With that thought in mind, she wiped her tears, unlocked the door and let him in.

"Are you okay?" he asked, closing the door behind him.

"You have a screwed-up family," she said.

He studied her for a moment. "I'm not going to disagree. But…are you sure this is about *my* family?"

She wanted to avoid that—it was too much of a direct hit. "Why didn't you stop them?" she whispered harshly.

"From what?"

"From drilling me!"

"Those are the types of questions people ask every day, Jasmine. 'Where are you from? What do you do? What do your parents do?' It's called getting to know someone."

"They don't need to know me!"

"I wanted to hear what you had to say as much as they did. Is that so terrible?"

"You wanted to hear me lie about my reason for being here?"

He shoved a hand through his hair. "Not that. The other stuff."

"What's the point?"

He stared at her without answering.

"Well?" she prompted.

"I know you practically purr when I hum in your ear, that you have a different smile when I tell you how beautiful you are—one that says you like hearing it but can't quite believe it. I know you would've enjoyed that motorcycle ride if you weren't so busy trying *not* to enjoy it. And I'll never forget the heavy-lidded look you get right before you—"

"Stop." She raised a hand. Her heart was already racing. "You don't know anything about me, Romain. Not really."

"Exactly. I know things about you almost no one else does. And yet I don't know why you left your husband, or why you don't want to see your father, or why talking about Christmas makes you cry."

"Because those aren't the kinds of subjects discussed in a superficial relationship!"

He took her hands and stroked her knuckles. "I already told you I'm sorry about what I said this morning."

Although she could tell he wasn't accustomed to offering apologies, he seemed so sincere it was hard not to forgive him. But that was the problem with people like Romain. Sometimes they were moody, even hurtful; other times they were too charming to resist.

Besides, she *couldn't* forgive him or she'd get involved with him again. "As far as I'm concerned, we can be friends. I'm not holding a grudge," she lied.

"Maybe you could say that like you mean it." The boyish smile he gave her begged her to do just that—and nearly destroyed her determination.

"I thought last night was incredible, okay? I've never experienced anything like it. The way I wanted you. The way you touched me—"

"Now we're getting somewhere," he said and she couldn't help laughing.

"I'm not finished. I liked what happened, but it scared the hell out of you, made you want to shut me out. Fine. No problem. I'm willing to let it go. I didn't come to Louisiana to get involved with you or anyone else. Just tell me, considering all that, why I'm at your parents' house for dinner!"

He caught her chin, tilting her head so she had to meet his eyes. "You're here because I knew I'd never see you again if I let you go."

She blinked, stunned by the admission. "Isn't that what you *want?*"

"No."

"But, in a way, you hate me."

"I don't hate you," he said.

"You don't like me, either."

"I don't like anyone right now, even myself." He ran a thumb over her lower lip, and every nerve in her body began to tingle, to crave his touch. "But I want you," he said, his voice dropping to barely above hoarse. "No confusion about that."

When he kissed her, she told herself to pull away, to end it immediately, but that was the last thing she wanted to do. She kept telling herself, "One more second…only one more second," until her arms were around his neck and they were plastered together, kissing as passionately as if they hadn't made love twice already.

"T-Bone?"

It was his mother's voice that finally broke them apart. Fortunately, Alicia was calling him from down the hall, not right outside the door.

"Just for the record, I don't like you, either," Jasmine whispered, breathing heavily. She could've clarified that she didn't like his *effect* on her, but she was more comfortable leaving the statement as it stood.

"I'd still take you right here in my parents' bathroom if I thought I could get away with it," he said and walked out.

Jasmine spent the rest of the meal, and the cleanup that followed, trying to avoid any contact with Romain. Conversing with Tom and Susan wasn't exactly enjoyable, but Jasmine really liked Alicia and Romain, Sr., and Susan's kids were adorable. They gave her something to focus on, something that didn't cause a tidal wave of inexplicable emotion—with raw desire at one end and fear of making a life-changing mistake at the other. She hoped Romain's family hadn't noticed the tension between them, but she knew Susan, at least, was watching them too closely to miss it.

After the dishes were done, Jasmine decided to make a few phone calls before dessert. Although she rarely spent

Christmas with either of her parents, she felt obligated to wish them a merry Christmas. And Skye and Sheridan would be wondering why they hadn't heard from her.

"Is there a phone I could use to make a few long-distance calls?" she asked Alicia as she hung up the dish towel she'd been using to dry the dinner plates. "Someone stole my purse yesterday, so I can't cover the charges up front, but I promise I'll send you a check before the bill arrives."

Alicia slipped an arm around her shoulders and gave her a gentle squeeze. "I'm not worried about the bill, honey. I'll show you to my husband's den, where you'll have more privacy."

Romain was watching a football game with his father. Jasmine stuck her head in the room and explained that she'd be on the phone, then followed his mother down the hall.

Alicia led her to an office where there was a desk, two old but comfortable-looking chairs with a small table between them, and row upon row of books lining one wall.

"You can use that phone there." Romain's mother pointed at the desk. "I'll let you know when we're having dessert."

"Thanks."

Alicia started out of the room but turned back at the door. "I'm so pleased to see my son with such a nice woman."

Jasmine understood what she meant. She was tired of watching Romain suffer and was grateful to see him display some interest in regular life. She probably hoped that Jasmine's presence marked the beginning of a complete turnaround. But that only made Jasmine feel worse about the lies she'd told. The hope she was giving this woman was *false*. If anything, she was pulling Romain deeper into the past, not helping him heal. Once she returned to Sacramento, they'd all be lucky if he wasn't in worse shape than before.

"He's a strong man. He'll be fine," she said, trying to convince herself as well as his mother.

"He has a good heart, a *really* good heart. If only you can…give him a chance."

And nurture him along. She knew what his mother was suggesting: time, patience, love. But Jasmine wasn't about to offer her heart to someone as high-risk as Romain. She purposely picked safe men, men who were ploddingly steady, even-tempered, easygoing. Men who didn't have to cope with a surfeit of anger every day. After what she'd been through with her parents, she needed that kind of security. But she couldn't explain that to his mother without revealing her true purpose for being in Louisiana, so she simply smiled and nodded.

When Alicia left, Jasmine released a deep sigh and sank into the seat behind the desk as she picked up the phone. She planned to give herself a small break by making the friendly calls first.

Skye answered on the third ring. "Hello?"

"It's me."

"Jasmine! I've been trying to reach you all day."

"Merry Christmas to you, too," she said.

"Merry Christmas. But you had me worried. Where are you?"

Jasmine could hear David in the background. It sounded as if he was standing right beside Skye, mumbling endearments as he kissed her neck. "In Mamou."

"I really hope you're not spending Christmas alone in a hotel room."

"No, I'm at a…friend's."

The soft giggle that came across the phone had nothing to do with the conversation. "Dave, stop," Skye said. He murmured something that sounded sexy and loving—intimate enough to make Jasmine envious of their relationship.

"You've already made a friend?" Skye asked, her attention returning to Jasmine.

"Well, he's more of an acquaintance. Not really a friend." Why she'd felt the need to add that, she didn't know.

"*He?*"

"Don't jump to conclusions. He's just someone involved in my investigation."

"How old is he?"

"Thirty-five, thirty-six. Somewhere in there."

"That's close to your age."

"And your point?"

"He must be a pretty nice guy to take you home for Christmas."

He'd taken her to his bed, too. That didn't make him Mr. Wonderful. But Jasmine saw no reason to reveal her own lack of good judgment. "He's nice enough to include me in his family's celebration. That's it."

"So he's married?"

"I'm talking about his parents' family. He's a widower."

There was a pause as if Skye was trying to read Jasmine's tone. "Is there *any* spark between the two of you?" she finally asked.

"None," Jasmine said but she had to smile. She'd probably never told a bigger lie. Romain was the only man who'd ever made her wonder if spontaneous combustion was actually possible. "Why do you ask?"

"The lack of detail's a little suspicious. There's something going on or you'd be more up-front about how you met him and how he's connected to the investigation."

"There's nothing going on."

Another pause. However, in the end, Skye seemed to buy it. "Disappointing, but for the best, I suppose," she said. "Much as I'd love you to meet someone, I wouldn't want you to move halfway across the country. I'd miss you too much. And we couldn't manage The Last Stand without you."

"I'm not going to meet anyone in the short time I'll be here."

"Did you like my gift?" Skye asked, changing the subject.

"I don't know. I left it at home with Sheridan's. I thought we could get together when I return, have dinner and a belated celebration."

"Good idea. When will that be?"

Jasmine assumed David was momentarily distracted by something besides his wife, because Jasmine couldn't hear him anymore. "Don't know yet."

"I wish you were here," Skye said. "Christmas isn't the same without you. It's been just the two of us for the past five years."

That sentiment brought a lump to Jasmine's throat. "I wish I was there, too."

"Did you get the money I sent you?"

"Not yet. I'll pick it up when I'm back in New Orleans."

"I take it the police haven't found your purse."

"No. At this point, I doubt they'll recover it."

"Odds are you're right, but it'd be nice."

Jasmine was about to ask if Skye had heard from Sheridan when a crumpled piece of paper in the wastebasket caught her eye. A double take confirmed that it had bold, red writing. Writing that made Jasmine shiver.

"Jasmine?"

Leaning over to reach it, Jasmine plucked it from the garbage. "I've got to go," she mumbled.

"Already?"

Jasmine's hand shook as she smoothed out the letter. It appeared to be written in blood, just like the note she'd received. Only this one said: JoKe iS On yOu.

That was it, but Jasmine discovered the accompanying envelope by digging through the rest of the trash. Like the package that'd come to her house, it'd been mailed from New Orleans but didn't bear a return address. The addressee's name, written in blue ink, had been traced over and over, which was also familiar.

"Mr. Romain Fornier," she read.

"What'd you say?" Skye asked, but a noise made Jasmine whirl toward the entrance.

"I don't think that's addressed to you," Tom said.

"Jasmine, answer me," Skye was saying.

"I'll have to call you back." She hung up as Tom approached with his hand outstretched.

"May I?"

Jasmine wasn't about to relinquish what she'd found. "No," she said, putting it behind her back.

His eyebrows lifted toward the hair he'd gelled off his forehead. "You have a great deal of interest in my father-in-law's mail—especially for someone who's simply on vacation in Louisiana." He smiled, but there was an undercurrent in his voice that made her uneasy. "Why don't you tell me why you're *really* here?"

Considering the letter, she decided to let him know the real reason for her trip. "My sister went missing sixteen years ago. And because of a cryptic message a lot like this one, I'm here to find out what happened to her."

"So you're a cop."

"A forensic profiler."

"Fascinating line of work," he said, but he didn't seem surprised.

"Sometimes."

"And how does Romain figure into your situation? Besides the fact that he's finally met someone who's brought his libido roaring back to life."

She ignored the second part. Not only was it tacky of Tom to say so, his suggestive tone put her on edge. "I'm not sure how he figures in."

"Did he get a note, too? Is he trying to convince the police to reopen Adele's case?"

"He hasn't gotten anything." Or surely he would've told her by now. "I don't think our correspondent knows how to find him. That's the reason for this." She held up the crumpled letter. "As far as Romain's concerned, there's no connection between Adele's kidnap and my sister's. He's trying to put the past behind him."

"Poor Romain," he said with a *tsk.*

"You don't say that with much sympathy."

"He's not the type to inspire sympathy."

"Even after everything he's been through? He's your brother-in-law."

"Believe me, I know who he is. He has a very long shadow." Walking to the window, he gazed outside. "It's going to rain," he commented.

"What is it you don't like about Louisiana?" she asked.

"I don't feel comfortable here. These are Susan's people, and they're always judging me."

Jasmine didn't respond. What he had or hadn't done was none of her business. But she could tell from what Romain had said on their way in and Tom's interest in her at the table that he paid more attention to other women than he should.

"You don't think Moreau murdered Adele, do you?" he said, turning back to face her.

It wasn't a question. "Let's just say I'm open-minded about the possibility that there might be someone else," she said.

"And you're here to find the real killer."

"Obviously, you're open-minded about the possibility, too."

"These letters would certainly suggest it. There've been others, you know. I got one at my house, too. This guy is blanketing the family with them, trying to get to Romain."

*Trying to get to Romain.* But why would taunting Romain be that important to him? "When did this start?"

Tom raised a hand to signify silence as footsteps approached. It was Travis. They knew because he called back to one of his brothers.

The door wasn't quite closed. Travis didn't seem to notice them as he moved past the office to the bathroom, but once his son was gone, Tom shut the door to guarantee their privacy. "Ours came a month ago, after Thanksgiving. My in-laws received one then, too. The letter you have in your hand arrived yesterday. Really upset the old man to get another one," he added. "I think he was hoping the first one was a fluke and this would just…go away."

None of them wanted to believe that Adele's murderer

was still out there, and she understood why they'd feel that way. "Does Romain know about these letters?"

He grimaced. "Of course not. Alicia practically threatened to disown Susan if we so much as breathed a word of it."

"Maybe she's afraid he'll go after someone else."

"That's not the reason. It can't be."

"Why not?"

"Alicia doesn't believe he killed Moreau. No one in the family does, not even me."

Jasmine blinked in surprise. "But the shooting was on tape. How can you or they believe anything else?"

Tom went over to the desk and picked up a photograph of Romain as a little boy. He was holding a fishing rod and standing next to a fish that was bigger than he was. "He caught that thing at ten years old," he said, handing it to her. "Impressive, huh?"

"It's a nice catch," she said. Where was Tom going with this?

"He was always the best at everything." He sighed loudly. "Tough to compete with a guy like that."

Jasmine had sensed that Tom and Susan didn't have the perfect marriage. Now she wondered how bad it really was. "What does that mean?"

"It means I don't know where to put my support. Now that he's fallen from his pedestal I don't look so bad myself, and my wife isn't constantly throwing him up to me as the gold standard. I'm almost afraid to see him recover."

"And yet you recognize that as selfish and petty. I hope."

His grim smile indicated he recognized it all too well. "You see my dilemma."

Jasmine put the photograph back where it belonged. "Romain's your brother-in-law, not your rival."

"Still, I'd give anything to have Susan think as highly of me as she once did of her brother."

"You're not going to get her to think highly of you by cheating on her." Jasmine knew she had no business saying so, but she couldn't resist. And they'd asked *her* enough personal questions.

He straightened the collar on his polo shirt. "I know, but the damage is already done—it's not like she'll ever forgive me for my…" his smile turned sardonic "…indiscretions. And sometimes the temptation's too great to resist. I don't know if I could ever trust myself. It's nice to live the fantasy for a while, to feel like a god to someone, even if it doesn't last."

And the resulting anger and possessiveness his affairs inspired in Susan confirmed that she cared. It was a double payoff.

"Take you, for instance," he went on.

"Me?"

"You'd be too attractive to resist."

"Because you think I'm with Romain. That's the temptation. You want to convince yourself you're just as desirable as he is."

"Am I?"

Jasmine knew Tom wouldn't be saying half the things he was saying if he hadn't had too much to drink, so she edged away from his inferiority complex. He'd probably be embarrassed when he sobered up. "You're married," she stated flatly.

"It wouldn't matter even if I wasn't, would it?"

She ignored the question and asked one of her own. "Did you know about the illegal search of Moreau's house?"

"No."

"You're sure?"

"Positive."

"Pearson Black insists he's not the one who leaked that information to the defense. He thinks it might've been you."

Tom brought a hand to his chest. "Me? How could I leak something I didn't even know about? I wasn't there that night."

"There were several cops who were. One of them could've confided in you."

"No one did. And if I knew, I wouldn't have told. I loved Adele. I wanted to see her killer caught and, at the time, I thought Moreau was her killer."

"Until the letters."

"Until the letters," he repeated.

"If your wife doesn't believe Romain pulled the trigger and killed Moreau, what does she hold against him?"

"Have you slept with Romain?" he asked.

"What does that have to do with anything?"

"That's a yes."

"How about answering the question?"

He chuckled softly. "You're determined. I'll give you that."

"Are you going to tell me?"

Sighing, he shrugged. "The fact that he wouldn't fight the charges, that he went to prison when he might not have had to if only he'd tried to avoid it, that he's pulled away from her after they were always so close."

Jasmine knew the last one probably hurt the most. "Why is Susan so convinced he *didn't* kill Moreau? I understand there's got to be a denial factor at play, but when an incident's caught on tape—"

"Have you seen the tape?" Tom sat on the edge of the desk and crossed his arms.

"No, but I've talked to someone who did, and he acted

as if there was no question. It was a cut-and-dried case of a father allowing his grief to provoke him into retaliating. And Romain knew how to use a gun."

"He knows how to use a lot of weapons. But he didn't do it," Tom said.

"I've seen it happen to far less volatile men," she pointed out.

"Romain never loses control."

He'd lost control while they were making love. He'd forgotten to be angry and miserable. He'd cast all his cares aside and simply *lived*. She suspected that freedom had been so foreign to him he'd tried to destroy the happiness it brought afterward. "Grief can get the better of anyone."

"Perhaps. But my wife was walking with him as they moved out of the courthouse. She saw it happen."

Her heartbeat suddenly erratic, Jasmine stepped closer. "And?"

"She claims Detective Huff fired his own gun."

Could it be true? "If she's right, why didn't Romain say anything?"

"To be honest with you, I don't think he remembers exactly what happened. He was in an emotional tailspin. But he wouldn't risk hurting some innocent bystander in order to assuage his own pain. You don't know Romain very well if you think he could do that."

"Did Susan tell him what she saw?"

"Of course. She pleaded with him before his trial, during his trial, even afterward. I was almost invisible during that time. Saving her brother was all she cared about."

Jasmine was willing to bet that was when Tom's affairs had started. Somehow, it all made sense, terribly sad sense. "He wouldn't listen?"

"He wouldn't listen."

"What was his response to Susan?"

"He said he'd *wanted* to kill the bastard, and that in itself made him guilty."

"If Huff shot him, why wouldn't he come forward?"

Tom flicked a speck of dust off his khaki pants. "That's obvious, isn't it?"

Jasmine supposed it was, although she expected more from Huff. "And the motive?"

"That's also obvious. After the embarrassment and humiliation of the trial, he knew he'd lose his job because of that pervert, and he snapped. Once the shot was fired and everyone swarmed Romain, he was probably terrified by what he'd done."

"Terrified enough to let Romain take the blame."

"I don't think Huff had it planned that way, that he had it planned at all. Romain just made it easy for him by doing what he always does."

"Which is…?"

"Taking the heavy end."

"But why would he do that in this situation?"

"Here's what I figure. To him, it'd be the only thing that makes any sense. He was praying for justice and, thanks to Huff, he got it—along with the assurance that Moreau couldn't hurt another child. He was satisfied, relieved, even grateful. At least Moreau's death put an end to the matter. If Romain had to go to prison, it was just for two years. But if he stepped forward to say it was Huff, and they could prove it, the detective would be put away for life."

It was something else that made a sad sort of sense. "I want to see that tape," she said. "Do you know anyone who has a copy?"

"Romain does. Susan must've made fifty copies. She sent him one every week for a year."

Jasmine wondered if he'd kept any of them. "Are you telling me all this because you love your brother-in-law—or because you hate him?" she asked.

"A little bit of both, I suppose." Tom rubbed his perfectly smooth chin. "Are you going to tell the others why you're really here?"

"I don't see the need to upset everyone on Christmas Day, do you?"

"No. I don't see the need."

Maybe he wasn't as drunk as she'd thought. With a smile, she reached out to touch his arm. "Forget the past and be the husband and father you could be," she said.

A knock at the door interrupted before he could respond. "Tom?"

It was Susan. Dropping her hand, Jasmine turned just in time to see Romain's sister open the door.

"Looking for me?" Tom asked.

Jasmine could tell he expected the worst—he'd set himself up for it—but if Romain's sister was upset at finding them together, she didn't reveal it. "We're about to have dessert."

Tom shot Jasmine a cryptic smile. "When Romain's around, it takes her longer to come running."

"For God's sake, it's Christmas," Susan hissed.

Jasmine had planned to consider the information Tom had given her and leave it at that—for today. Although she knew she'd have to tell Romain about the notes, it seemed preferable to let his family enjoy the holiday in peace. But she couldn't miss the opportunity to hear what Susan had to say about the shooting. Or to let Susan know it was what she and Tom had been discussing in private. "What did you see that day on the court steps?" she asked.

Susan's eyes cut to her husband.

"She's a forensic profiler researching her sister's disappearance," he explained.

"Does Romain know?" she asked.

"Yes."

"Then he wouldn't want me to tell you what I saw."

"Why not?"

"Because it's pointless *now*. He already paid the price. Why get Huff into trouble? That's what he'd say."

"And I'd say it's important because you and I both know he might've killed the wrong man."

A dark shadow passed over her face. "That's what troubles me," she said. "But Romain made me promise not to discuss it with anyone."

Jasmine found it odd but admirable that she'd remain loyal to Romain despite their estrangement. "Just tell me where I can get a copy of the tape."

Susan stared at her. Then she disappeared and returned a few minutes later with a disk in her hand. "Here you go," she said and walked out, taking her husband with her.

When their footsteps had receded down the hall, Jasmine circled the desk and perched on the edge of the chair. "What a Christmas," she muttered and since everything was already sliding downhill, she called her father.

# 15

"Romain Fornier lives in Portsville?" Gruber asked.

The gruff old Cajun at the motel gave a single nod. "Yes, sir. Like I said, he's out on de bayou. Your sister was here just a day or two ago, lookin' for him."

Of course. That made sense. Jasmine had already connected the note she'd received with the way he'd written Adele's name on that wall, or she wouldn't have gone snooping around the Moreaus. But how had she found Romain when he couldn't?

She was good. He had to hand her that.

"How long has he been here?"

"Coupla years, I guess."

"Does he have an address?" Gruber had sent several messages to his family, who'd been much easier to locate. He enjoyed the torment he knew it would cause Romain to realize Adele's killer had gotten away, after all.

"No."

"He doesn't have an address?"

"Nope. D'ere's no mail service out d'ere."

No wonder Gruber hadn't been able to find him. Romain had been living out on the bayou without services.

Suddenly, Gruber felt very powerful. He'd done that to

Fornier. He'd leveled a Reconnaissance Marine, stripped him of everything….

"You know Romain?" the man said.

"We're old acquaintances. Can you tell me how to get to his house?"

The hotel manager tapped his fingers on the counter. "What'd you say your name was?"

"Mike Smith."

There was a slight hesitation, then he said, "Sorry, Mike. I've only been out d'ere once or twice myself, and it was dark at de time. I don't t'ink I could find it again. But if you'll give me your number, I'll pass it along when I see Romain."

He was lying. Gruber could tell. The brief hesitation told him that. People who didn't customarily lie were never very good at it. "What about Jasmine? Is she still in town? Is she staying here?"

"No, sir. She checked out a coupla days ago. I haven't seen her since."

He'd spoken far more stridently. But because he was lying about Fornier, Gruber couldn't believe him about Jasmine, either. "Right."

"Would you like to book a room for de night?"

"No." Now that he'd made some inquiries, he needed to disappear, lie low. But he wouldn't go far. *Someone* had to know where Romain lived. He'd figure it out eventually. Then he'd wait.

Timing was everything.

Jasmine's conversation with her father was tense but polite and lasted all of five minutes, about a minute longer than her conversation with her mother. *How are you?*…

*Fine... Are you having a nice Christmas?... Wonderful, you?... Definitely.*

Her conversation with her mother differed significantly in one regard. "Did you like the dress I sent you?" Gauri had wanted to know. Jasmine had claimed she loved it, but she hadn't even opened it. It was at home with her other presents, waiting for her return—whenever that would be.

"Did you receive the basket I sent you?" Jasmine had asked.

"I did. We're eating the summer sausage and some of the French cheese today."

She could've taped herself with one parent and merely replayed it for the other, except that her father hadn't sent her a gift and didn't say anything about the basket of wine, fruit and cheese she'd shipped him. She kept quiet about her presence in Louisiana and, of course, no one mentioned Kimberly. It was as if Kimberly had never existed—except that she was standing between them.

Slipping the note she'd found into the pocket of her jeans, Jasmine started for the dining room. She could hear Romain talking about the game but didn't catch his father's response. A second later, beaters whirred in the kitchen— Alicia making the whipped cream for the pecan pie. Judging by their shrieks and laughter, the kids were wrestling in the living room, where Romain and his father were trying to watch TV, but Jasmine had no idea where Tom and Susan had gone. She hoped they'd taken a nice long walk so they could have a chat about saving their marriage.

She was about to step into the kitchen to see if she could help serve the pie when she noticed an open door—and glimpsed a room decorated in blue and cluttered with trophies. Romain's old room.

She had no reason to be so interested in the memorabilia

she noticed inside, but her steps slowed as she passed it, and she eventually turned back. The opportunity to get a glimpse of what Romain had been like before grief had made such a dramatic impact on his life was too tempting to resist.

There were sleeping bags and suitcases strewn across the floor—evidence that Susan's kids were spending their nights here, which was probably what'd piqued Travis's interest in all the trophies. There were certainly enough of them. Jasmine noted several MVP awards, a few signed baseballs, a wooden bat with *July 1984* etched on it. But she already knew he'd been successful in sports. Then there was his military service. She read a letter from his commanding officer displayed, along with a couple of medals, inside a shadow box on the nightstand. It said he'd saved the life of a helicopter pilot who'd crashed in enemy territory; he'd gone in and carried the injured man out. That letter ended by saying, "You can be proud of your son. He's a damn fine marine."

Jasmine smiled and read that part twice, but it was the pictures gracing his dresser that ultimately caught her attention. They were of Romain at various high school dances— prom, senior ball, turnabout—always with the same leggy blonde she'd seen in the family photo at his bayou shack.

"Very pretty," Jasmine murmured as she picked up one that showed them in matching T-shirts.

"You're missing dessert."

At the sound of Romain's voice, Jasmine straightened. She felt a little awkward at being found in his room but decided to act as though it wasn't a big deal. Turning, she held out the picture. "It looks like you and your wife were very young when you got together."

"We were sixteen." Hooking his thumbs into the pockets of his faded jeans, he leaned against the doorjamb.

Sixteen... Jasmine returned the picture to its place on the dresser. "You're lucky."

He seemed surprised by the comment. "Until she died and any question like it would be in extremely bad taste, most people asked me if I was sorry I'd committed myself at such a young age."

"Were you?"

"No."

"Then she was lucky, too."

His eyes lingered on the picture but he didn't comment.

"Have you ever been with anyone else?" she asked.

He gave her a boyish grin. "This morning."

"You're saying you've made love to only *two* women?"

"Pam and I were married right after high school. That didn't leave a lot of time for fooling around."

"What did she do when you went to the Gulf in 1991?"

"Worked as a secretary and lived at home. I couldn't offer her much back then. Fortunately, she hung on."

"What made you go into the military?"

"Some friends of her parents moved to town. They had a son our age. Her mom and dad didn't want her to marry the only guy she'd ever dated, so they pressured her into seeing him, and she broke up with me. My parents were nagging me, too. They wanted me to do something with my life before settling down, but I already knew I needed a more hands-on challenge than college, so I joined the marines." He lifted one shoulder in a shrug. "The breakup didn't last and we ended up getting married just after we graduated, at which point I regretted joining the military."

"Do you still regret it?"

"Not really. Those years were hard for us, but the discipline and experience I gained made me a better husband."

She nodded toward the medals. "I guess the pilot you saved is happy you chose the military, too."

"Any of us would've done it," he said, and she knew he wasn't being modest. He truly believed it.

"Well, it's still impressive."

"What about you?" he asked.

She tucked her hair behind her ears. "I've never saved anyone."

"Considering the kind of work you do, I'm sure you're wrong about that. You save all the people who'd be hurt if you weren't on the front lines, right?"

She'd never really thought of it that way. She did what she did because she could. And, indirectly, it felt like her efforts somehow made up for her inability to protect Kimberly. "Maybe."

"But that wasn't what I meant," he said.

"You've lost me."

He came into the room, grabbed a football Susan's boys must've left behind and tossed it from hand to hand. "Your surprise that I've been with only two women makes me curious about how many men you've been with."

"A lot." She grinned. "Obviously, I'll sleep with anyone."

"Which puts the number somewhere around…five hundred?" he teased.

"Closer to four hundred. I've kept close count. I have *some* morals, you know."

"Getting involved with that many guys is quite a feat for a woman who's afraid to take off her clothes."

"They were all very persuasive, like you."

"You took some time off when you were married, didn't you?"

"My marriage only lasted two years, remember?"

"Two years," he repeated. "Did you love him?"

"I loved him. But I wasn't *in* love with him. I learned there's a rather meaningful difference."

He flopped onto the bed, still tossing the ball. "Have you ever been *in* love?"

"No."

*"Never?"*

"No."

He stopped throwing the ball and met her eyes. "Maybe you're too cautious."

"Maybe I haven't met the right person," she retorted.

"What came between you and your husband?" The ball was going back and forth again. It made a thumping sound as it landed in each palm.

"I realized I wasn't doing him any favors by pretending to feel something I didn't."

A wry grin curved Romain's mouth. "I'll bet he was glad to be rid of you."

If the grin hadn't been enough, the flash of straight, white teeth would've told her he was joking. It was a side of Romain she hadn't seen before. He'd been dark, brooding, passionate, intense. But not playful. Until now.

"He handled it well." Surprisingly well. His generosity in letting her go made it that much harder to leave him. But she'd grown beyond the need to have a father figure who approved of her, and Harvey wasn't what she wanted in a husband. "We're still friends," she said. She told herself that whenever she recalled the disappointment she'd caused him. "I have good relationships with all three of the men I slept with before you."

She thought he'd capitalize on the truth—that she'd been with only three men besides him. But he didn't. He chucked the ball onto the pile of sleeping bags and sat up. "You're proud of being *friends?*"

The challenge in his voice startled her. "I guess I am. Why?"

"That's pathetic."

She propped a hand on her hip. "What's pathetic about it?"

"It's easy to walk away friends if there's no passion to begin with, no real commitment, no real...*joining.*"

"Not everyone can have the kind of relationship you had with Pam, Romain."

"I realize that, but...are you really so in control of how you feel?"

Not with him. She'd already proven that. But she did what any smart girl would do and lied. "Always."

He shook his head. "No, last night wasn't a calculated decision."

"Last night didn't mean anything. We've been over that."

He studied her for a moment. "How could I forget?"

"I guess we'd better get back to the others," she said, but he didn't get up.

"What did Tom have to say?" he asked instead.

Jasmine knew he wasn't pleased that they'd had a private conversation. But she'd been hoping to wait until after they left to tell him about the messages sent to his family. She had no idea how upset he'd be and didn't want to ruin Christmas for everyone by creating a scene or causing him to become any more remote than he already was. "Tom's in love with your sister."

"Pulled you aside to say that, did he? When he's been undressing you with his eyes since he met you?"

She toyed with the yarn hair on top of a toilet plunger

dressed to resemble a blond bombshell with huge red lips—obviously some sort of gag gift. "He's got issues, I agree with that. Serious issues. I don't know if Susan and Tom will be able to save their marriage."

"Susan won't give up. Not while the boys are at home."

"I guessed that's why she's stayed with him."

"She'll soldier on for the kids' sake."

Jasmine thought of Tom's assertion that Romain hadn't fought the charges against him because he knew he'd get a much lighter sentence than Huff. "Reminds me of someone else I know."

"She's tougher than I am." Here was proof of the respect he felt for his sister. If only Susan had been there to hear it.

"If it makes you feel better, what Tom said had nothing to do with coming on to me."

"He didn't gush about your pretty eyes?"

The sarcasm in his voice revealed that he hadn't liked Tom's compliment, but she was sure it had more to do with the protectiveness he felt toward his sister than any possessiveness he felt toward her. "No."

"Then what did he want?"

Jasmine pulled the note from her pocket and walked over to give it to him. A flicker of apprehension crossed his face when he saw it, but by the time he took the paper from its envelope and read it he had his emotions in check.

"Tom gave you this?" he asked, his expression stony.

"I found it in the trash can inside your father's study. Tom walked in and caught me with it."

"Why was he following you?"

"I have no idea."

"Do you know how long ago this came?"

She hadn't given him the envelope. It wouldn't have

made any difference, anyway. The postmark was too faint to read. "According to Tom, yesterday. They didn't tell you because they don't want you thrust back into all of this."

"What's the other option? Ignore it? If Moreau wasn't Adele's killer, someone else could be out there, doing God knows what!"

"I've talked to the police in New Orleans. They don't act as if they've been facing a rash of child abductions." But she understood his fear; she shared it.

"Have you ever looked at the missing children notices inside a post office? Children go missing all the time—with little or no upheaval in everyone else's lives."

"I'm going to find him," she said stubbornly. "I have to."

Cursing under his breath, he closed his eyes and shook his head. But when he opened them again, she saw resolution staring back at her. "So do I."

Bev didn't want to work on Christmas night but, thanks to Peccavi, she didn't have a choice. He'd accepted a baby—obviously a drug user's underweight and colicky child, not fit for most of their clients. And he'd gotten into a haggling war over the only other child they had right now, so Billy, which was what she called him because they never used real names, hadn't gone to his new family as planned. Instead of no kids, she had two.

A noise in the next room told her that Billy had just knocked down the tower of blocks he'd spent the past thirty minutes building. At least she agreed with Peccavi that the boy was worth more than the sixty grand they'd initially agreed to. He was better than any of the children they'd had so far. He had the brown hair and green eyes the rich couple in Boston had ordered, as well as a perfect bill of health.

And he was bright. Bev had seen that for herself. At only three years old, he could say his ABCs.

What bothered her about this kid was the way he kept asking for his mama. He'd been in the transfer house nearly a month, but the little guy wouldn't forget, wouldn't give up, like most of them did. Bev didn't mind taking care of the younger children. They adjusted quickly. After a few weeks, they quit crying and begging for their parents, and she enjoyed babysitting them. She treated them well, gave them what they needed and chose to believe they went to a safe place—a place where they'd be just as loved and cherished as they were in the homes they'd lost.

In some cases, she knew they were actually better off than they'd been. Like the crack baby who'd finally stopped crying and fallen asleep in the nursery. Although the adoptive parents' various lawyers referred to Peccavi generally stipulated no prostitute or crack addict's child, and no family history of mental disorders, diabetes, multiple sclerosis, epilepsy, alcoholism, etc.—no imperfections at all—Peccavi cheated where he could. Children ordered to specification, like the ones they tried to provide, weren't easy to come by.

Four-year-old Mary Jane had come from a mother with an inheritable deafness trait. She could hear, but the syndrome could appear in her children—the adoptive parents' grandchildren. Still, it was a rare enough trait that the parents hadn't thought of having her tested for it, and last week she'd gone to a producer in Beverly Hills. He'd paid a hundred thousand to have a child who resembled his wife, an aspiring actress who didn't want to risk her figure by giving birth to a child of her own.

"What a way to spend Christmas." Bev sulked, flipping through channels on television.

Billy must've heard the word *Christmas* because he came out of the playroom where he also slept and pointed at the fireplace. "Santa!" he said. "Santa Quaz!"

Santa Claus was supposed to come *last* night, but Billy was still waiting. Bev would've bought him something, but she'd expected him to go to his new family today. Roger, someone Peccavi had brought in to help them when Jack decided he wanted out, was supposed to handle the transfer. But Peccavi had gotten a hot tip on a prospective buyer in Houston, who'd requested two children, and had Roger fly off to meet them. Peccavi would've had Phillip step in and take Billy to Boston. Phillip usually handled the less important deliveries and some of the pickups, as well, if they weren't too far away. But with Jack's body being discovered, Peccavi was too short-tempered and preoccupied to finish arranging the details.

Meanwhile, Bev had to take care of the kid on Christmas Day, knowing that the mother he asked for almost constantly was someone he'd never see again.

She wondered if he'd remember his mother later in life, and how those memories might surface. Would he be standing in the office of his law firm someday and suddenly remember a woman bending over his crib, a woman who looked nothing like the mother who'd raised him?

Bev felt melancholy imagining how unsettling that would be, so she tried to shrug it off. He was young enough that he'd forget, she told herself. She couldn't recall anything before the age of five. He'd be fine. Just like beautiful little Mary Jane, who was happy so long as she had a comfortable lap to climb into and a warm smile to gaze up at.

The phone rang. Muting the television, Beverly reached

over to pick up the handset and almost knocked over the rickety side table. "You'd think we could get some decent furniture after all the money he's made," she grumbled but managed to right the table and improve her tone before answering. "Hello?"

"The deal busted," Peccavi said.

Beverly's ulcer complained as her stomach tightened involuntarily. "Which deal?"

"Which deal do you think? That cheap bastard in Boston won't pay what Billy's worth."

"What about his wife? Can't you get to her?"

"I was hoping she'd soften him up, but they saw some show on black market babies and started asking too many questions. They didn't think I'd be able to deliver paperwork that could withstand close scrutiny, which is bullshit. Anyway, I had to cut them loose."

"What does that mean?"

"I have to find a new buyer," he snapped.

"But Billy matched their order. He's got the brown hair, the green eyes—"

"There're a lot of couples out there who'd be interested in a boy of his caliber and, believe me, we'll end up getting more for him than those tight bastards were willing to pay. Maybe we'll get as much as we got for the girl last week."

Bev watched Billy drive his metal car around the coffee table. "You think so?" Sometimes when they landed such a windfall there was a bonus in it for the workers. Bev could use a bonus. Phillip's car was on its last leg. And Dustin's doctor had recently informed her that his treatments were going up again.

"Why not? Roger called a few minutes ago. An infertile

doctor and his wife have ordered a baby boy and a girl toddler. Roger's going to try and talk them into switching genders and taking what we've got."

"You don't think the other couple will come back for Billy?"

"No. They don't have the guts to go through with it. They're too scared."

"But this other deal could take a while." Bev didn't want to look after Billy anymore. He reminded her of what Dustin had been like at that age, which threatened a painful parting when the time came.

"That's why we pay you the big bucks, Bev. You'll take care of him until he's placed."

*Big bucks...* Peccavi was the only one making big bucks. He paid her as much as he had to—and no more—in order to keep her doing what she did. He took her for granted, but she'd worked for him so long she probably couldn't get another job. She'd trained as a nurse, but that was years ago, when her kids were small. She'd have to retrain if she wanted to get back into the medical field, and even then the younger applicants would have a decided advantage. She'd wind up working in a nursing home somewhere, barely making enough to pay the mortgage. Wages like that wouldn't cover the experimental treatments that were Dustin's only hope.

"What about the Stratford woman?" she asked. "Have you found her?"

"Gruber's taking care of that."

Billy brought Beverly his toy car. He wanted her to play with him, so she rolled it absently around the table. "Why him?"

"Because he doesn't have anyone expecting him for Christmas."

"And if he screws up?"

"He won't. Anyone who can snatch kids as easily as he can should be able to handle a woman."

*Peccavi* hadn't been able to handle her, but Beverly bit her tongue so she wouldn't say that. She smiled every time she remembered the sight of him at her back door in the middle of last night, covered in mud and limping after trying to catch Jasmine at the hotel.

"So what do you want me to do?" she asked.

"Just stay with the kids. I've got to get home."

Fortunately, his job gave him the perfect excuse for working late hours. And that uniform even provided a nice cover for any injuries he might sustain. "What about Dustin?"

"What about him?"

"I don't like leaving him alone on Christmas."

"You've got to be able to work. What do you think I pay you for?"

She fumbled around in her purse, searching for her antacids. "I have more than this job to worry about. I have a sick boy who needs me!"

"This job is what takes care of that sick boy, who isn't a boy at all. And don't forget it. Besides, Phillip's there, isn't he?"

Phillip wouldn't look after Dustin very well. He wasn't himself these days. He'd been acting strange ever since he'd had to deliver that little redheaded girl—Bev had called her Christy—to her new family in Florida. He'd been gone for two weeks and refused to explain where he'd gone. Then there was the cellar when he'd been forced to shove the Stratford woman inside. That had upset him again....

"Yes." She found her medication and took two tablets.

"They'll survive. We do what we have to."

He was going home to spend Christmas with his family, wasn't he? "Can I take the kids home with me? Just this one time?"

"And let your nosy neighbor see you with them?"

"Billy's from Connecticut. No one's looking for him here. And we don't have to worry about the baby. She won't even be reported missing."

"No. It's a chance we can't take. Our system works because we stick to the plan, and we never make exceptions. Got it?"

Beverly rubbed her burning stomach, wanting to tell Peccavi to go to hell. But she didn't dare. She needed him too badly. "Got it," she grumbled and hung up.

"Mama?" Billy tapped the phone with his pudgy hand. "Mama?"

"No, that wasn't your mama." Beverly went to the kitchen and came back with a cookie. "But you'll meet your new mama soon," she said and felt her heart melt a bit more as he smiled and clapped at the treat she held out to him.

It was every bit as awkward saying goodbye to Romain's parents as it'd been saying hello. Maybe more so.

"I'm glad you came," his mother said, hugging Jasmine at the door.

"Thank you. Dinner was fabulous."

"I wish you hadn't brought the bike." Alicia frowned as she released Jasmine and pulled her son into her arms. "I have all these leftovers I could've sent home with you."

"You have Susan's family here. They'll help you eat them," he said.

"She's a lovely girl," Alicia told Romain in such a loud whisper that Jasmine heard every word. "Don't let her get away."

Romain didn't respond, and Jasmine didn't have a chance to check his expression before his father hugged her, too. "I hope we get to see a lot more of you."

"I'd like that," she said and was surprised to find it was true. Romain's parents were great. She could tell how much they loved each other and their children and was jealous of Pam all over again. Pam had fit in here; she'd *belonged* with Romain.

Jasmine had never really belonged anywhere. Not since Kimberly disappeared.

"It's getting colder," Romain said as he straddled the bike. "We should go."

Jasmine glanced back at the house, feeling bad that Romain and Susan had given each other only a tight-lipped goodbye. Tom had been in the den on the phone with some other member of his family; Jasmine had simply told Susan to say goodbye for her. The boys, except for Travis, who'd paused his game to run over and hug his uncle, had waved from where they sat in front of their PlayStation 2.

"Zip up that jacket," Romain warned.

She dutifully fastened the leather coat he'd lent her, and he started the engine. She expected him to drive off, but he put the kickstand down almost as soon as he'd put it up.

"What's wrong?" she asked as he got off.

"I'll be right back." He disappeared into the house, nudging past his parents, who were at the door to give them a final wave.

When he came back, his jaw was still set, but he seemed somehow relieved.

She lifted the mask on her helmet. "Where'd you go?"

"I had something to say to Tom."

"Goodbye?" she teased.

"I told him he'd better not cheat on my sister again or he'd have me to answer to."

Jasmine felt her eyebrows go up. "Did Susan hear you?"

"I don't care if she did. I won't allow him to continue treating her the way he has—or he's going to suffer a little himself."

Jasmine smiled. Romain's family was worried about him. But he was healing. He was finding his way back.

Jasmine put the disc Susan had given her into Romain's DVD player while he was out baiting and lowering crawfish traps. Evidently, the season started in winter. Because much of his food came from the swamp and not the small market where he purchased staples like flour and sugar, he had to take care of a few things before the day ended.

In any case, they'd already decided to wait until morning to head to New Orleans. There wasn't any rush, at least for today. The lab was closed, so she couldn't call and press them for information on the items she'd dropped off. Her appointment with the sketch artist wasn't until the day after tomorrow. And, with Sergeant Kozlowski off for Christmas, she doubted she'd be able to get any information out of the police about the man she'd found in the Moreaus' cellar. She had some research she wanted to do on Phillip, Dustin and Beverly Moreau and Pearson Black, but she couldn't knock on the doors of their friends and family on Christmas night. She could search the Internet for public records, but that wouldn't take long, and morning would be soon enough. Which meant they'd be staying at Romain's place another night.

Jasmine wasn't sure how she felt about that, but she knew it would be safer than returning to the hotel—and a waste of money to get another room when they already had shelter.

A newscaster's voice suddenly boomed out, and Jasmine jumped up to grab the remote and turn down the volume. Checking traps sounded like it might take a while, depending on how far away they were, but she wanted to be as quiet as possible, in case he was anywhere near the house. There was no point in letting Romain know she had this clip until she'd seen it and determined its value to her investigation.

The grainy picture had a superimposed red stripe at the bottom of the screen that read, Shocking Reversal In Moreau Trial. It showed people pouring out of a courthouse and trickling down several wide steps. Some were weeping, some were involved in heated conversations, others simply looked stunned; it was obvious that a tragedy had just occurred.

Jasmine could imagine what that moment must've felt like—the bitter disappointment of the prosecution, the elation and relief of the defense. The police had the culprit in custody. They'd recovered what appeared to be irrefutable proof. And yet it didn't matter.

Then she saw Romain, coming out of the courthouse, and froze the playback. Thinner and wirier than he was now, he seemed haggard, almost gaunt. Jasmine could see the heartache in the hard lines of his face. The shadow of beard proved that he hadn't thought about his appearance in several days. Susan was walking on his right, sporting a short, sassy haircut very different from her current long layers, looking just as upset as her brother. A trim man Jasmine took to be in his late forties walked on Romain's left, wearing a dark blue jacket.

Huff? Had to be, Jasmine decided. His salt-and-pepper hair was cut in a short, military style, and he had the seasoned air of a man who'd seen everything—yet he was *still* rocked by the D.A.'s decision to drop the case.

Pushing the play button, Jasmine leaned closer to the TV, riveted as Huff took off his jacket. She caught a brief glimpse of the gun in his hip holster before the crowd closed in. Then the picture began to bounce as the cameraman jogged behind the reporter, trying to be the first to reach Romain.

"Mr. Fornier, what do you have to say about seeing the man who allegedly killed your daughter go free?" the young woman asked.

"Nothing. He has nothing to say," Susan replied.

Everyone ignored her as another reporter, this one a man, tried to crowd between them. "Mr. Fornier! Mr. Fornier! Do you still believe Francis Moreau murdered Adele?"

"Of course he murdered Adele," Susan shouted.

Again, Romain didn't answer. He stared at the press as if he wasn't even seeing them. Then his gaze cut to Moreau, smiling and talking in front of some other cameras a few feet away. Because of the pandemonium, Jasmine could only catch bits and pieces of what he was saying, but she got the gist. "Justice would…in the end."

A shot suddenly rang out and Moreau dropped. Everything happened so fast, it was difficult to tell who had done what.

Backing up, Jasmine played the scene again, keeping her eyes on Romain's hand. He came down the steps, the reporter approached, Huff grabbed him by the elbow and tried to pull him away. There was a brief sighting of a hand with a gun, the blast, and then Huff and several others swarmed Romain and pushed him to the ground.

Replaying it again, frame by frame, Jasmine watched the hand come up a fraction of an inch at a time until she stopped it where the gun was about to go off. Was it Romain's hand? Or Huff's?

She couldn't tell. It was a tiny detail in a very large picture. She needed to take the clip to a video specialist, have it magnified to see if there were any distinguishing characteristics on that hand.

"Where'd you get this?"

Jasmine had been so absorbed in what she was doing she'd forgotten to worry about Romain. Still holding the remote, she turned to see him standing in the doorway between the kitchen and living room.

"Susan gave it to me."

A muscle flexed in his cheek as he stared at the screen. "Don't go digging around in my past," he said. "What happened on those courthouse steps has nothing to do with your sister. Stick to what might help you find her."

She wanted to find the real Romain as much as she wanted to find Kimberly. She couldn't abandon this now. It mattered. She didn't want to believe he could lose control to such a degree, regardless of circumstances. "Did you do it?" she asked.

"Leave it alone."

She put the remote aside and stood up. "Tell me."

"Of course I did it!" he snapped. "Who else would care that much?"

"Huff had access to that weapon, too."

Romain's hands were dripping. Grabbing a towel from the counter, he dried them. "I did it," he said and stomped out.

Jasmine replayed the segment once more. She told

herself what he might or might not have done was none of her business. She was trying not to get too involved with him. But she couldn't keep herself from following him out.

He sat on a stool in a small screened-in porch attached to the back of the house, taking oysters out of one bucket and tossing them into two others.

"What are you doing?" she asked.

He tapped the shell of the oyster he'd just picked up and threw it into the bucket to his right.

"Are we not speaking?"

With a glance in her direction, he scowled. "I'm separating the live ones from the dead ones."

"Knocking on the shell tells you that?"

"If they're alive, they close up. The dead ones can't be eaten."

She saw another stool near the periphery of the small lean-to and pulled it closer. The coat he'd lent her for the motorcycle ride was in the house, but she didn't want to go back for it now. "What if the shell's closed to begin with?" she asked, folding her arms against the cold.

"If it's dead, it'll be a clacker—it'll make a different sound."

They sat without further conversation, with only his tapping and the clunk of each oyster hitting its respective bucket to break the silence. Jasmine thought Romain might ignore her indefinitely, but after several minutes, he surprised her. "I don't remember actually pulling the trigger, okay?"

She watched several more shells move through his capable hands. "Will you tell me what you do remember?"

Head down, he kept working. "I remember *wanting* to do it. I remember seeing Huff's gun and realizing how easy it'd be. Then people started screaming and several men, including Huff, forced me to the ground."

"Have you seen that tape?"

He looked up at her. "Of course I have. Susan insisted I watch it a few hundred times."

"She was there. She saw it all."

"She was there, but I can't imagine she saw anything very clearly. There was so much noise and confusion, so many people. I can't even describe it to you, not the way it really was." He shook his head, the expression in his eyes troubled. "It was unreal."

"If you don't remember pulling the trigger, why did you plead guilty?"

Another shell hit the bucket. "Because I don't remember *not* pulling the trigger. That day was mostly a painful blur. And I wanted to wipe that self-satisfied smile off Moreau's face. Pam was gone so I didn't have that to stop me. Adele was gone, too—because of him. I had nothing left to lose."

"Have you taken that DVD to anyone who might be able to magnify it?"

Finished with the oysters in the original bucket, he opened the back door to dump out the remaining water. "No. I didn't see any reason to put Huff at risk. Then or now. He had a family, I didn't. And whether or not I was the one who shot Moreau is merely a technicality. I wanted him *dead*."

"Wanting to do something and actually doing it aren't the same thing, Romain," she said.

He loomed over her and his voice fell. "When the desire is that great, it's close enough."

Jasmine stood. "No, it's not."

"He's gone and the world is better off because of it," he said. "It's over."

Jasmine wished he didn't appeal to her the way he did, but it was all she could do not to touch his cheek, not to crave his kiss. Part of her didn't care what he'd done, what he might do, whether or not she'd get hurt—and that made it a frightening compulsion. "But if Moreau was framed, Huff might've killed the wrong man…or caused you to do it. He might've been responsible for the real culprit going free." She clutched his arm. "Let's find out who did what, okay? Let me take this to a specialist and see if he can determine who fired that gun."

His eyes dropped briefly to her hand. "Why?" he demanded. "So we learn it was Huff. That's not going to tell us who really killed Adele. It's not a good use of time or money."

She felt the warmth of his skin through his long-sleeved T-shirt and it seemed to burn her cold fingers—and start fires in other places, too. But she refused to succumb to that desire. "Are you sure it's time and money you're worried about?"

He jerked away. "I have no idea what you're talking about."

"I'm wondering if you're afraid to know for sure, afraid to find out what you're capable of."

He glared at her. "Send it," he said. Then he picked up one of the buckets and stalked past her. The outer door slammed shut behind him.

# 16

It was miserably cold on the couch, but Jasmine couldn't figure out why. She was still wrapped in the bedding Romain had given her, which had been warm enough when she'd fallen asleep. So why the sudden drop in temperature? Why the odd feeling that something was *terribly* wrong?

Turning onto her side, she tried to talk herself out of the foreboding that seeped beneath the blankets, chilling her to the bone. She was safe here. Few people even knew that Romain's house existed, and those people were his friends. Besides, he wasn't far away. He'd left his bedroom door open when he'd gone to bed—an obvious signal that she could join him if she wanted. As a matter of fact, she suspected he'd taken the bed hoping she *would* join him. But that was an invitation she made herself resist. She knew what would happen if she climbed in with him. They couldn't sleep together without touching, and they couldn't touch without stripping off their clothes and falling into the same frenzy they'd enjoyed this morning. Their attraction was too strong.

*Just listen to him breathe. He's right there. He's—*

Suddenly, her heart leapt into her throat. That *wasn't* Romain she could hear. It was someone else. A stranger.

Wait, not a complete stranger. *The man who'd sent Kimberly's bracelet.*

How Jasmine knew it was him, she wasn't sure, but in her mind's eye she could see a window standing open, could see the curtains on either side stirring in the freezing night air. He'd cut the screen and crawled through. Now he was walking silently through the house. Familiarizing himself with the layout. Checking the exits. Looking for someone.

*Looking for her!*

The hair on the back of Jasmine's neck rose as she sensed him coming up behind her. He hated her, wanted to destroy her. He thought he'd given too much away.

*What have you given away?* her mind screamed. But there was no answer. Just cold, hard purpose. And she couldn't even yell….

Jasmine tried to keep perfectly still. She wished she could disappear, make him believe the thick blankets on top of her had simply been tossed there the way she used to fool Kimberly when they were playing hide-and-seek.

But there was no chance of that. He knew exactly where she was. He'd spotted her, followed her here.

There was nowhere to go, nothing to do but hold her breath and pray.

"You know me," he murmured and her heart pumped with fear as she felt him rise up.

In an attempt to fend him off, Jasmine rolled over and lifted her hands to protect her upper body and face, but the knife was already on its way down. She cried out as it sank into her chest, so deep he couldn't immediately pull it out. The pain was paralyzing, shocking, *disabling.* But that wasn't the worst of it. He wasn't satisfied with one thrust.

He had to stab her again and again and again. She'd never sensed such ruthlessness, such raw savagery…*ever.*

Her blood ran warm, soaking her shirt. She curled up to block the blows and the knife glanced off the bone in her shoulder, landed in her neck and cut her windpipe, making it impossible to breathe. When she heard a gurgle and realized that the odd sound came from her own throat, she knew the struggle was over, knew her *life* was over.

And then Romain was there. "Calm down." Catching her wrists so she couldn't hit him anymore, he used his weight to press her into the couch and stop her from thrashing around. "I've got you, Jasmine. You're okay. It's me. You just had a bad dream."

Jasmine blinked and stared up at him. There was no open window. No other presence. She was in Romain's shack in the bayou, as safe as ever.

But what she'd experienced hadn't been a dream. "No!" Still terrified, she tried to push past him, to get up, but he cradled her against him and spoke to her as if he was gentling a spooked horse. "Relax. Shh…"

Shaking violently, she turned her face into the hollow beneath his collarbone and began to sob. She squeezed her eyes shut, trying to believe the words he crooned to her. But she couldn't get the images out of her mind. "He killed her," she said, hiccoughing from her tears. "He thought she…was me and he…he hacked her to pieces."

Romain didn't know what to think. It was the middle of the night, and Jasmine was sitting at his kitchen table demanding he drive her to a phone so she could report a murder. But what good would that do? She couldn't provide the identity of the person who was stabbed, where that person lived or the name of the man who'd wielded the knife.

"Jasmine, if you call in like this, you'll lose all credibility." Romain had witnessed her reaction and was still having difficulty accepting that she'd been privy to a murder while sleeping on his couch.

The shaking had subsided but her dilated pupils and clammy pallor testified to the very real terror she'd experienced. "I don't care," she said stubbornly. "I have to do what I can to help that poor woman."

*"What poor woman?"* he said for the third time. "Can you come up with a name, even a first name? Initials? They're going to need a little more to go on than 'someone was killed tonight.'"

"I've never met her. I know that."

"But the man with the knife—you think it was the guy who abducted your sister."

"Yes."

A man she hadn't been able to find for sixteen years… "Where did he see her? Why did he choose her?"

Jasmine's hand went to her chest as if she was reliving the memory of his vicious thrusts. "I don't know where he saw her. All I know is that he wanted it to be me. He was trying to appease the rage he feels toward me by taking it out on someone else. A stranger. Someone who probably looks like me."

"You've been under a lot of stress," Romain said gently. "Are you sure it wasn't a nightmare? People have nightmares all the time."

"Occasionally I make mistakes," she admitted. "Misinterpret something. Become too personally involved in a case and miss clues I should've picked up. But…" she shook her head and her voice fell to a whisper "…I'm not wrong about this."

She'd been right when she'd told him about the tattoos on his body and the cut on his thigh. She'd been right about Adele's necklace. And he knew she'd shared his fantasy that first night. He had enough experience with Jasmine to believe her, even if he didn't want to. "But it's already happened, hasn't it?"

"Yes."

"Then there's nothing we can do to help the victim. She's dead, Jaz."

He watched the fight drain out of her as she covered her face with her hands.

"We have to find him before he does it again," she said at last.

"When will that be?"

"Could be a few days, could be weeks. It'll depend on the amount of frustration in his regular life. He's hardened over the years," she added, almost as an aside, "become more calculating. He'll keep going until he finds me. Right now, I'm the one he wants and he can't think of anything else."

"Why you?"

"I'm a loose end. Someone who saw his face. I'm escalating my search for him by going on national television, talking about what he did, speculating on the kind of man he is. Chances are good he's heard me swear I won't give up, and he knows I'm amassing more resources and influence in the investigative world. Mostly, he knows I'll stop at nothing." She paused, absently combing her fingers through her hair.

"Maybe something you said on television triggered a

close call," Romain suggested, "made someone question him or suspect he was involved."

"I wouldn't doubt it. That's why he sent that note. He wanted to draw me to New Orleans."

"Wouldn't that put him at greater risk?"

Jasmine turned the cup of tea he'd made her around and around. "Not if he killed me."

The possibility of losing someone else he cared about made Romain glad he'd kept this woman at arm's length. He couldn't invest his emotions in her, couldn't let himself grow attached. "Then why didn't he track you down in Sacramento?"

She frowned, finally calm enough to act more like herself. "My guess is he has trouble getting away. Maybe he's married with kids, or he has a job that won't allow it. Maybe he doesn't have the money. Some practical reason that limits him or keeps him busy with other stuff."

Romain thought of the bayou. Even when others couldn't catch a thing, he came home laden with fish, shrimp, crabs. He understood its quirks and secrets, where to find what he was looking for, when to give up on a certain spot. "And knowing the area gives him an advantage."

Her eyes met his. "Exactly."


The bloodlust had exhausted him. Breathing hard, Gruber sneered at what was left of the woman in the bloody bed. Humans were so fragile....

Using the knife he'd removed from her kitchen drawer, he sawed off her hand and shoved it in his back pocket. He used to collect pieces of jewelry or clothing, even pictures, but this was so much more personal. Unfortunately, he didn't know this woman the way he did the others, so the memento wouldn't bring him much joy. He preferred to spend days, weeks, even months with his victims—although only one had lasted that long. Peccavi kept him so busy with the business they did together, he had little time to do his own hunting. It wasn't as if he could keep any of the children destined for the transfer house. Peccavi would kill him if he tried. True, he'd been able to keep Kimberly for a while, but only because she'd been a windfall, an unexpected gift, a child Peccavi hadn't realized he'd taken.

"Tonight didn't have to end like this," he told her. It was Jasmine's fault. He wouldn't have done this without provocation. Never before had he risked harming someone in an unsecured area. It was like those rules that Peccavi always harped on. A man had to have self-discipline in order to remain safe. But once Gruber had spotted the woman at that gas station, the frustration he felt at being unable to locate Romain's house had taken over. No one in Portsville had been willing to talk to him; he was an outsider, an unknown, and they were fiercely protective of Fornier.

But he'd find Jasmine eventually, he promised himself. She was searching for him. She wouldn't go far.

Somehow, that thought made him feel better. Wiping the knife with a dish towel to get rid of any prints, he stabbed it back into the woman's dead body and walked through the front door. She lived away from the city with at least half a mile between her and the closest neighbor. He wasn't worried that anyone had heard her screams, or that anyone would see him. Which was good, since he didn't have a lot of time. He had to get home as soon as possible. His sister had called earlier to say she was coming to see him first thing in the morning. She claimed she had some information about their mother he'd want to know.

He found that highly implausible, but planned to be there when she arrived, just in case she went in and started snooping around. The door to his bunker was in the master closet—not someplace she was likely to go, but it could be seen when he didn't cover it well, and he'd been lazy of late. No one ever came to his place; he'd had no reason to worry.

The theme song from *Gilligan's Island* came to mind. He whistled it softly as he got into his car. He'd have to do something about the blood on his hands and face and in his hair. Stabbing was a dirty business. But cleaning up wouldn't be hard. He'd burn his clothes in the fireplace. And while the fire warmed the house, he'd take a nice hot shower.

They ended up driving to New Orleans rather than going back to bed. Jasmine couldn't sleep. She didn't dare close her eyes after what she'd experienced. And she couldn't seek the comfort she craved from Romain or she'd invite even more confusion and risk. She needed to stay focused, to find Kimberly—or learn what had happened to her—and get out of New Orleans. Anything else threatened the calm she'd established, the routine, the sense of balance and control she'd so painstakingly created.

"There you are!" Mr. Cabanis's daughter exclaimed when Jasmine entered the lobby of Maison du Soleil with Romain at her elbow. "We've been worried about you."

She didn't seem to recognize Romain despite all the media coverage surrounding Adele's disappearance and Moreau's trial. She was probably too young when Adele went missing to follow the story as closely as her parents.

"Have there been any murders reported on the news?" Jasmine asked.

The girl straightened in surprise. *"Murders?"*

"Have you heard anything about a woman being stabbed to death last night?"

Her eyes widened. "Here at the hotel?"

"Anywhere in New Orleans."

"N-no," she said. "But we were afraid something had happened to *you*. When the maid went in to clean your room yesterday, she found it torn apart. My mom tried to call you at the cell phone number we have on file, but you weren't picking up and no one had seen you. We thought you might've been attacked."

"Did you call the police?" Romain asked.

She smiled at him. "We did. They tried to tell us it was too soon to report Ms. Stratford missing, that she could be sightseeing or visiting friends. We would've figured that," she said defensively. "I mean, most people don't hang out in a hotel room on Christmas Day. But the mess…" She turned back to Jasmine. "It didn't look like anything you'd done. It looked like someone ransacked the place."

"Someone *did* ransack the place," she said.

The girl's expression revealed a measure of vindication. "I thought so! Should I call the police again?"

"I'll do it," Jasmine told her. "But first, tell me the maid didn't clean my room."

"No. The police told my mother to leave it, just in case."

Jasmine breathed a sigh of relief. She wanted to determine if there was any evidence that might lead to the intruder's identity. As much as she tried to tell herself it had to be the same man who'd abducted Kimberly and haunted her dreams last night, something didn't feel right about that supposition. The man with the mask had a different kind of motivation. She could tell by the utility of his actions, and the intent she'd sensed as he chased her. He'd wanted to stop her, to end her life, but it was for *practical* reasons, not to appease a grudge or feed some impulse he couldn't control.

"I'm going to need a new key," she said.

"No problem." The girl created the replacement and passed it over the counter. "We'll be happy to move you to a different room, if you want."

"There's no need. She'll be checking out today," Romain said.

Jasmine looked up at him. She was finished with Maison du Soleil, but she hadn't mentioned it yet. "Excuse me?"

"You're leaving us?" the girl burst out before Romain could respond.

"She's moving to Portsville," he said firmly.

"Not Portsville," she corrected. "Just another location here in New Orleans." She couldn't go back to the little motel hanging over the bayou or she'd end up spending all her nights with Romain. "Have there been any messages for me?"

"I almost forgot. You have quite a few. That's another reason we were so concerned." She reached beneath the desk and handed Jasmine a small stack of papers.

Jasmine flipped through them. Three were from Skye. "Call me… Where the heck are you?… The money should be there. Did you get it?" Four were from Sheridan. "Why aren't you answering your cell?… Aren't you even going to wish me a Merry Christmas?… Are you okay?… I should never have let you go down there alone!" And the last was from her father. "A woman named Sheridan called here, asking for you. Why didn't you tell me you were in the South?"

"Shit," she muttered, staring at it.

"What is it?" Romain asked.

She shoved the messages into the pocket of the jeans he'd borrowed for her yesterday and moved toward the elevator. "Nothing."

"Was one of those from the guy who broke into your room?"

"No. It's not that. It's…nothing."

He pressed the call button for the elevator. "Tell me."

"My best friend just informed my father that I'm in town, that's all."

"And that's bad news?"

The antique elevator doors cranked open, two people got off and she stepped inside. "If I wanted to see him, I would've spent Christmas with him instead of making a fool of myself at your parents' place."

"They liked you."

She pushed the button for the third floor and the doors closed. "Because they thought we had something going. They want you to get married again, have babies, be happy. They wouldn't have been too thrilled to know we've been fooling around for the sake of fooling around."

"Is that what we've been doing?" he asked dryly.

The way he set his jaw indicated a stronger emotional response than the one he gave, but Jasmine ignored it. "Basically."

"Thank God you didn't say that."

"I should've at least told them there's nothing between us."

"You did. You said we didn't even like each other."

"I don't think anyone believed me."

He arched an eyebrow. "I'm sure they could tell it wasn't

quite like that. As a matter of fact, we need to find a store. We're out of condoms, remember?"

She raised a hand. "We *don't* need more. It happened. It's over. We're forgetting it."

The elevator stopped and the old doors opened again. "What if I don't want to forget it?" he challenged.

She rubbed a weary hand over her face. "I already have."

With a slightly cocky expression, he watched her from beneath his lashes as they found her door. "Am I supposed to believe you after the way you kissed me in that bathroom?"

"You had me at a disadvantage."

He moved up close behind her, spoke into her ear. "Your only disadvantage is that you liked it as much as I did."

Jasmine's stomach lifted as if she was still on the elevator, so she stepped away. "Do we have to talk about it?"

He leaned one shoulder against the wall, blocking her door. "Does it make you uncomfortable?"

"Doesn't it make *you* uncomfortable?" she retorted.

"Not a bit. I like talking about it. I could talk about it all day. But if you don't, we could discuss your father instead."

She rolled her eyes. "How many times did we make love again? What did you like best about it? What was that little French thing you said?"

"That I was drunk with the taste of you."

That he answered at all took Jasmine by surprise. She hesitated, key in hand, then shook her head. "Stop it. Don't confuse me."

"For whatever reason, we've been thrown together. We might as well enjoy it while it lasts."

"It doesn't work that way. Please step aside."

With a frustrated sigh, he changed the subject but didn't move. "What's up with you and your dad?"

"Nothing. He's not a subject I wish to address. Ever."

"Why?"

"That's addressing it. And right now, we have other things to worry about." Like what she might find in her room.

"I'm not as bad as you think, Jaz."

Jaz? That was the second time he'd used her nickname. Only her close friends called her Jaz.

She took in his lean, powerful build, the hair that was beginning to curl over his ears, the golden skin—and let her imagination add the giant chip on his shoulder. "I'm afraid you're worse."

When he scowled but didn't argue, Jasmine felt a twinge of regret. But she had to take a stand, or she'd leave herself too vulnerable. And she'd learned from a young age that vulnerable was never good.

"Can we go in now?" she asked.

Romain took the key from her, insisting she wait in the hall while he entered.

A moment later, he called back to her. "It's safe."

The room was as she'd seen it from the fire escape, except that the bathroom was in a similar state of disarray. The shower curtain had been ripped from the rod and her makeup had been dumped in the toilet. In the bedroom, her clothes had been strewn all over the floor, and her computer—which was, fortunately, password protected and still working—had been thrown from the desk. The vicious way the intruder had handled her stuff let her know he didn't like her very much. She was pretty sure he'd ejaculated onto a pair of her underwear, which he'd placed on her pillow like a gift.

"This guy's sick," Romain said, clearly not pleased when he noticed it.

Jasmine grimaced at the sight, but there was a bit of hope mingled with her repugnance. "Semen is actually a good thing. He's left plenty of genetic material with which to develop a DNA profile."

"A profile isn't any good without a suspect to match it against."

"It's a step in the right direction."

Romain cocked an eyebrow at her. "Wouldn't most women be retching about now?"

"I'm not like most women." The viscous fluid made Jasmine nauseous; she wasn't any different there. But the thought of using that disgusting memento to catch whoever had left it gave her some objectivity, some way to deal with the creepy sense of violation that had brought on her nausea.

A deep scowl etched lines in Romain's face. "This guy is really starting to piss me off."

"We need to find a paper sack. We can't put those panties in plastic."

"I'll get one from the girl downstairs."

Romain began to leave the room, but Jasmine stopped him. She'd just spotted something that made her very happy: her cell phone was sitting on the desk.

"He can't be all bad," she joked. "He brought back my phone." She grabbed it to see if, by sheer chance or stupidity, he'd made a call or two. But she didn't get as far as pushing any buttons. The picture on the screen made her drop it.

"What is it?" Romain asked.

Unwilling to come into contact with the sheets on the bed, or even the furniture, Jasmine sank onto the floor. The queasiness was taking over. Whoever had chased her in the alley hadn't been content with ransacking the room. He'd returned—to leave her a few surprises.

Romain picked up her cell to see for himself and swore under his breath. "Is this what I think it is?"

She nodded. The picture on her screen had been changed. Instead of her and Sheridan on vacation in Mexico, there was a picture of an erect penis.

The writing above it said, "You're dead."


"We're dealing with two very different men," Jasmine said.

She'd put her cell phone on the restaurant table beside her because she was waiting for a call from the police. Seeing the intruder's genitalia every time she glanced down wasn't pleasant, but she wasn't willing to change that picture, to change anything at all, until whoever put it there had been caught.

The panties were in a brown paper sack in her suitcase, and her suitcase was in the back of Romain's pickup. Occasionally, she checked the truck through the restaurant window to make sure it was still there. She didn't want to lose that piece of evidence—or her clothes. If anything happened to her suitcase, she'd be stuck halfway across the country with a barely working computer and the cash she'd picked up at Western Union, but nothing more.

With one hand on her chin, Romain turned her head to face him. "Eat," he prodded, pointing to her food.

He'd taken her to a fast-food joint on General DeGaulle Drive in New Orleans and bought her lunch. She felt too haggard to go anywhere nicer. Her burger was mostly untouched, but she was enjoying the French fries.

"Didn't you hear me?" she demanded, shoving another fry into her mouth.

He swallowed a bite of his own meal. "I heard you. You said we're dealing with two very different people. I'm waiting for your reasoning."

"The man who took my purse and broke into my hotel room didn't write on the wall or the mirror, didn't leave a note similar to the others, even though there was a pad of paper on the desk. Plus, he had plenty of time, since he came back."

"People don't always do the same thing, not if the circumstances are different." His voice indicated he was playing devil's advocate.

"True," she said, "but a crime scene generally reflects the personality of the perpetrator, and the core of a person's personality doesn't change. So many factors contribute to it—genetics, culture, environmental influences, common experiences we all have, unique experiences only the individual has. He is who he is and he can't change any more easily than you or I can. Which means his method of operation should remain the same, too—especially if we're talking about something he does to fulfill a specific need."

He took another bite of his burger. "He left a note. He just didn't write it by hand. I'm guessing that message on your phone fulfilled his need to communicate."

"But there was no blood anywhere."

He lowered his voice in deference to the old lady who'd sat down at the table next to them. They'd spent most of the morning going over that hotel room, inch by inch, searching for evidence. Now it was noon, and the restaurant was getting noisy and crowded. "There were other bodily fluids."

"Not blood," she said, matching his low tone. "And I think the blood is important to him. The blood reminds him that he's in control, that he's the one in charge. He's killed before. He can kill again. He's telling me I'm no challenge, I'm nothing to him. That sort of thing. Remember what he put on my note? *Stop me…*"

"Believe me, semen makes a man feel in charge, too." He took another packet of ketchup from the pile she'd placed in the center of the table and squeezed it into the cardboard container that held his fries. "That's what rape's all about, isn't it?" he went on. "Whoever broke in was trying to intimidate you."

"I know. The panties, the phone—that's all proof. But… it's different from the impressions I've been getting from the man who took my sister." Jasmine frowned as she stared out the window, watching a dark cloud roll closer. It was going to start drizzling again. "The man who trashed my hotel room isn't a lust offender as the panties and the picture on my phone might suggest," she went on, trying to puzzle it out. "He's not in it for the sexual high that violence and domination give him. The fact that I got away that night made him mad, so he went back to my hotel room and did those disgusting things to tell me that he'll win in the end, that he'll stop me."

Romain drank some of his shake. "Stop you from what? *Breathing?*"

"From investigating. From finding out whatever he's trying to hide."

He ate a few fries. "I agree that going to the Moreau house threatened him in some way. But if he's responsible for the body you found there, why bother chasing you down now that you've called the police? If he's afraid of being caught, he should be getting his ass out of town."

"He doesn't feel threatened enough to leave, which tells

me he's not afraid of the police. Not yet. He's still focused on me."

"So you think there's something you've already found— or might find—that worries him."

"That's what I'm thinking." Jasmine wished she knew what that could be. "I'm also thinking that Mrs. Moreau is in on the secret, whatever it is."

"I don't understand how the trashing of your hotel room and the cellar incident ties in to Moreau. Certainly his whole family wasn't involved in what he did. And there's no need to cover for him anymore. He's dead."

"It's unusual for family members to be involved and supportive of that type of crime," she agreed. "Beyond covering it up, of course."

Finished with his own food, Romain eyed her hamburger, and she pushed it toward him. "His mother lied about being there when Huff returned with the judge's signature on that search warrant."

"But there are a lot of mothers who refuse to see what their children really are, who try to protect them. I'm guessing Moreau was a disorganized asocial personality," she mused.

"And that means…"

"There's a whole list of profile characteristics. But this type of offender is socially inadequate and usually doesn't have the leadership ability to get others to join him in his crimes—"

"You're talking about misfits? The kind of people who were shunned and made fun of at school?"

"Made fun of or simply ignored. According to Ray Hazelwood, a legendary FBI profiler, a disorganized asocial is statistically a nonathletic white male with a low IQ. He kills close to home because he feels uncomfortable leaving familiar territory, and he more often than not lives alone. Or, if he doesn't live alone, he's got his own secret places." She helped herself to some of Romain's shake. "They're typically nocturnal and sloppy, with poor hygiene."

"Almost a perfect description of Moreau."

"That's why I don't see him involving others in his crimes, especially his mother," Jasmine said. "I can't imagine a woman of Beverly's age going along with such immoral behavior, either. She has an invalid son to care for, so she's pretty stressed. I witnessed the worry on her face when Dustin called out to her."

Romain's hand halted halfway to his mouth. "No one said anything about an invalid son during the investigation."

"Why would they? Moreau was living alone when the crime occurred."

"The entire family should've been interviewed by police."

"Maybe Dustin wasn't up to it. That's probably the reason he didn't attend the trial, either."

"We need to talk to him if we can."

"I doubt Mrs. Moreau will let us anywhere close."

"We could check it out."

"First, we're going to find someone with the technology to tell us more about Moreau's shooting. I want to know whether Huff fired that gun."

If Romain felt threatened by what they might discover, only a slight tightening around his mouth revealed it. "Don't you know someone who works for the FBI who can do that?"

"It'd take longer than I'm willing to wait. It's Sunday.

We can't even ship anything today." She still had the letter from Romain's parents' house that she wanted to send to the lab.

"You could upload the video to your computer and e-mail it."

"*If* they have an expert who's available and willing to work on Sunday. Not to mention that it's the day after Christmas and a lot of people are out of town."

"It's worth a try, isn't it?"

"It's worth a try," she relented with a shrug. "I can send it to the guy I worked with on the Polinaro case. He seemed grateful for my help. He might do me a favor."

"Are you going to eat the rest of those?" Romain motioned toward her fries, which were growing cold.

"Where are you putting all this food?" she asked. He didn't have an ounce of fat on him, but it certainly wasn't because he counted calories.

"I burn it," he said.

"That's not fair," she grumbled, intent on adding more ketchup to his little pool so he could finish her lunch. She didn't immediately notice that the old lady sitting next to them had gotten up to leave—and was now standing beside their table, gaping at the picture on Jasmine's cell phone.

When Jasmine glanced up, she expected a stern scolding, or at least a disgusted huff. But the old lady didn't seem very scandalized. She merely looked from the phone to Romain and back again. "Somehow I thought you'd be more impressive," she said, and shuffled out.

Romain's jaw dropped. "Hey, that's not me. I *am* more impressive," he called after her. "*A lot* more impressive. That's true, right?" The look on his face—half-teasing, half-wounded male pride—made Jasmine laugh until her sides ached.

# 17

Gruber's sister was late. He sat on his couch, waiting for her, his eyes gritty. He hadn't been to bed yet. By the time he'd gotten home last night and washed off the blood, he'd had to start on the house. Once he viewed it as his sister would, he realized it required cleaning. Valerie was all about being "functional." She wouldn't like what she saw, and he couldn't help cringing at the disgust he'd hear in her voice if it wasn't at least *passable.*

Now he was finished but tired and angry. After all these years he was still bowing and scraping and giving her most of the power in their relationship. But she'd been more of a mother to him than his real mother, so it wasn't surprising that he'd feel *some* desire to please her, was it?

"Wasted effort," he grumbled, mad at himself for reacting to those old feelings of inadequacy. He couldn't please Valerie. She'd *never* approved of him. The derogatory comments she'd made about him while he was growing up came to mind at the most inappropriate moments: *If he wasn't so lazy, maybe he'd be more of a help to me. As it is, he's as much of a burden as my mother…. He's a little pervert. I just caught him playing with himself again…. He can't ask anyone to the dance. There isn't a girl in that school who'd go out with him….*

The humiliation and embarrassment she'd caused him with her constant ridicule created a blinding rage. Even now. He hated her, wished her dead. And yet…she'd put food on the table and made sure he had a roof over his head. She'd come home after work at night. That was something, wasn't it? That was more than his real mother had done.

A noise at the door alerted him that she'd finally arrived and, all of a sudden, he was loath to answer her knock. The woman he'd attacked last night had been so terrified. The memory of her fear made him feel invincible, like *God.* If he let Valerie into his home, he'd feel like a worthless piece of shit again.

"Gruber? Are you in there?"

At the irritation in her voice, he got up, moving as though she could control his body—like a puppeteer jerking the strings of a marionette. He stood, cast a lingering glance at the fridge where he'd put his trophy from last night, then walked slowly, inexorably, toward the door. Maybe she'd look in the freezer. Maybe he'd *show* her—

"Gruber? I'm tired. I've been working all night, and I have to get home. Give me a break here."

He should've changed his shirt. Why hadn't he thought of that? This one was wrinkled and dirty from the scrubbing. He hesitated, wondering if it was too late, but she banged on the door, and that *tone* was entering her voice. The tone that made him want to curl up and cover his ears.

"Gruber!" *You idiot.* "I need to talk to you." *I knew you'd screw this up. You are such a loser!*

And yet he continued to walk calmly to the door, opening it just as her temper flared. "There you are!"

Why did he wait? Why hadn't he staved off her displeasure by answering when she first arrived?

He didn't know. He'd cleaned all night for her. And now he'd ruined it. He'd ruined it with the dirty shirt she was already sneering at and his tardy answer.

"It's after noon," she snapped, standing there in her perfectly white nurse's uniform. "Don't tell me you were still in bed!"

She hated laziness more than anything. And he, of course, was lazy. He heard it in her voice.

"I've been working."

"At what? Every time I ask, you give me some evasive answer, which probably means you're sitting here on your ass, collecting unemployment. I know you're not working for the lighting company anymore. They wouldn't take you back if you begged them."

There it was again. The blaring message: *You're not good enough. You'll never be good enough.*

"I haven't asked you for money in ages," he pointed out.

"A year is 'ages'?" she scoffed.

It'd never be long enough for her. "How's Steve?"

"The same."

He didn't need to ask about any kids. His sister had decided, since he'd been so hard to raise, she wouldn't have children. *I've been there, done that. Noooo, thank you,* she'd say if she was ever asked.

"So, are you going to invite me in?"

He stepped aside and her antiseptic smell came in with her. No doubt she'd gotten involved in some task at work. She wouldn't have been late for any other reason. Being late was inconsiderate to others. How many times had he heard *that* growing up?

"Couldn't you clean this place up?" she said, prowling around.

Gruber halfway hoped she'd open the freezer. The thought of her resulting shock and dismay—the thought of having the upper hand with his sister—made him smile slyly.

"What's that sneaky little smirk for?" she asked.

"I was thinking of having you over for dinner."

"You? Cook?"

"I'm sure I can find *something* in the freezer," he said and chortled at his own joke.

Her eyes narrowed. "Yeah, right. What? TV dinners?"

"Not exactly."

She looked at him as if she knew he didn't mean it in a nice way but didn't want to bother ferreting out what was really behind his invitation. "Yeah, well, that's great. But Mom's dying. You know that, don't you?"

The pleasant image of his sister's horrified expression as she opened his freezer dissipated. "I know she's sick."

"And you don't give a damn."

Was he supposed to care? "She used to beat me within an inch of my life." She deserved whatever she got.

"She was none too nice to me, either. But I guess you don't remember that."

He remembered she hadn't been half as mean to Valerie. She'd needed Valerie. Valerie had taken care of her. Valerie had taken care of him, too, so his mother wouldn't have to. Valerie could do anything; she knew how to survive.

"I'm not here to argue with you about the past. What happened happened and there's no changing it."

"Such sympathy," he murmured.

"Feeling sorry for yourself will get you nowhere." She brushed at an imaginary speck of dust on her uniform. "She said you haven't been to see her once."

"I don't want to see her."

"She wasn't a perfect mother, but she's still your mother."

"And you're still my sister and I don't like you any better." He'd been dying to say those words but, once they were out, he was as shocked as she seemed to be. He was also encouraged. Maybe it was the memory of his recent kill, the memory of wielding that *power.* It was so intoxicating it made him reckless.

"What'd you say?" Her mouth hung open. It was almost as good as having her look in his freezer.

Almost. But not quite.

"You heard me."

"That's a fine thank-you for all I've done for you," she said. "Do you have any idea what I gave up to make sure you had what you needed?"

Gruber nearly cackled with incredulity. She'd *never* given him what he needed. No one had. But the old Gruber was suddenly hesitant to press his advantage. "I was just joking," he mumbled, trying to reel in the emotions banging around inside him.

"Very funny. You never did know how to win friends and influence people." She was back in charge, grinding her point painfully home. "If only I could've had a *normal* little brother, maybe my life wouldn't have been such hell."

How many times had he heard that? It was the reason he'd killed her cat when he was thirteen and shoved it in the backpack she'd left on the patio. She'd believed her rival at school had done the deed—a girl who used to taunt her for their poverty. Valerie had never figured out it was him. But he'd enjoyed her tears that night. She'd deserved the punishment. He only gave people what they deserved.

"Is that why you came?" he asked. "To convince me to visit Mother for a tearful send-off as she approaches the pearly gates?"

"I have no illusions that she's venturing anywhere close to heaven. A woman who slept around as much as she did has no hope of that. Sometimes I hate her as much as you do. But…I'm thinking about later, about the fact that we may never have the chance to make peace with her if we don't do it now." She studied him for a moment, then released a long sigh. "And I thought it might help you get your shit together to finally bury the hatchet."

"I don't have to. I'm happy the way I am."

*"Happy?"* she scoffed. "How can you be happy? You're forty years old, you don't have a friend in the world and you live in a dump."

Gruber couldn't have said what, exactly, provoked him. His sister was treating him the same way she always had. But he grabbed her by the wrist before he knew he was going to do it. And then that look came into her eyes. The flash of fear that whetted his appetite for dominance.

"Let go. You're hurting me!" She tried for her usual "I'm in command" tone, but her voice faltered just enough to tell him she wasn't quite sure of herself. He could do this. He could kill her like the others. She was nothing special, no big deal, no different from any other fragile human. Not now.

"That's what I want to do," he whispered vehemently.

"You're crazy. I've always known it." The fear was undisguised now. It flared her nostrils, dilated her eyes, filling him with a sense of power, and power was the antidote to the miserable helplessness that plagued him at all other times. "Let go before you do something you'll regret."

"I won't regret this," he promised. "I'm going to hurt you and hurt you and hurt you some more, until you beg me on bended knee to stop. And then I'm going to carve your heart out of your chest and put it in my freezer." He let his eagerness reveal itself in a broad smile. "I'm definitely going to want something special to remember this moment."

"My God," she whispered, and that was when he realized she knew he was completely serious.

Romain felt useless while Jasmine worked on her computer, trying to e-mail the video clip in a format most servers could handle. She'd managed to contact whoever she was sending it to, and that person seemed confident he could get someone else to help her. But Romain wasn't so sure he *wanted* to know whether or not he'd fired that gun. It was one thing when he thought Moreau had killed his little girl; it was another now that he faced some doubt. "Can I borrow this?"

Jasmine pulled her attention from the computer long enough to see what he wanted. "Sure."

Taking her cell phone, he stepped outside the Internet café and dialed Huff's number in Colorado.

"Hello?"

He assumed it was Marcie, Huff's wife. "Is Alvin home?"

"No. I'm afraid he's been called away on business. Can I take a message?"

"It's Romain, Marcie."

"I thought I recognized that voice. How are you, Romain?" She seemed genuinely interested.

"Fine," he replied. It was true. Despite everything Jasmine was stirring up, he was doing better than he had since prison. But he didn't want to consider why. Because that had something to do with Jasmine, too. "When did Alvin leave?"

"A couple of days ago. He was supposed to be back yesterday for Christmas dinner, but an urgent matter came up and he called to tell me he couldn't make it."

"Did he happen to mention where he was going?"

"He's in New Orleans. He said if you called to give you his cell number. He's been trying to reach you."

Romain gripped the phone tighter. "Did he provide any details?"

"No, but that's not unusual," she said with a weary chuckle. "He never does. Not until it's all over. And then, sometimes, he needs to talk. I'm sure he can tell you more. Do you have a pen?"

"Just a sec." Romain returned to the café to ask for a pen and a napkin to write on. Jasmine was exactly where he'd left her, but she was no longer working. She was staring at her screen with such intensity he could see lines of concentration on her forehead. She'd found something interesting; Romain could tell. But he had to get this number before he could ask her what it was.

"Go ahead," he said into the phone, still watching Jasmine. As Marcie rattled off the number, he wrote it down, then hung up as soon as possible and strode over. "What is it?" he asked. He expected her to say that the news had finally broken about a woman being murdered, as she'd dreamed last night.

But that wasn't it.

She pointed to her screen. "I got this message from Pearson Black. He sent it yesterday, to the general 'contact us' box at the Web site for The Last Stand. Skye forwarded it to my personal e-mail."

It was a short message. Did you find what you were looking for?

Coming from anyone else, Romain figured that could be a sincere question. Coming from the man he'd met during his daughter's investigation, those words could just as easily constitute a taunt. "He knows something."

"I agree."

"See if you can tempt him into telling you what it is."

Jasmine clicked on the Instant Message button. Black was online. Who was the dead man?

They waited a few minutes, during which Jasmine spoke with a private investigator named Jonathan in California. She asked him to dig up what he could on each of the Moreaus and on Pearson Black and, when she clicked back, Pearson had already responded.

"The beauty of the Internet," Romain muttered as Jasmine opened his message.

"There you are. Where've you been?" she read aloud. "I thought maybe I'd see you again."

"Where's his surprise over your reference to a dead man?" Romain asked. "Wouldn't most people say, 'What dead guy?'"

"You'd think so." Jasmine started typing again. Are you the one who locked me in that cellar?

CopBedTimeStories: My feelings are hurt. Why would you accuse *me*?

JazzStratford: You're the only one who knew I was going there.

CopBedTimeStories: You're not exactly invisible.

JazzStratford: You didn't answer my question.

CopBedTimeStories: What question?
JazzStratford: Who was the dead man?

There was a pause. Romain was afraid they'd lost him, that he wasn't going to answer. But just as he was about to suggest they pack up, Jasmine grabbed his arm. "Look at this!"

CopBedTimeStories: Jack Lewis. D.O.B. 12/8/54; Last known whereabouts: Longsford Community Center. He drove a van that shuttled kids from school to a center for after-hours care.
JazzStratford: How do you know?

Black's reply consisted of only one line and it didn't answer the question: Don't say I never did anything for you.

Who killed him? she wrote and sent off the message.

That's anyone's guess, came the reply. And that was it; he wouldn't respond again.

"What do you think?" Jasmine asked Romain, slumping against the back of her chair as if the sudden flow of adrenaline had left her drained.

Romain was dialing the number Huff's wife had given him. "I think Huff's in New Orleans, and we need to get his help with this."

She stood up so fast she almost knocked over her chair. "What's he doing here?"

"Apparently, he's on business and he's been trying to get a hold of me," Romain said.

But Huff didn't answer. After several rings, the phone transferred Romain's call to voice mail.

"This is Alvin Huff. I'm not available to take your call right now, but if you'll leave your name and number, I'll get back to you as soon as possible."

"It's Romain. Call me," he said and left Jasmine's number.

They waited until dark to drive over to the Moreaus'. The house looked no different from the pictures Romain had seen of it in court almost four years ago. Same drab appearance from the curb. Same peeling paint. Same feeling of neglect and isolation.

The fact that his daughter had been to this house under very different circumstances brought the memories flooding back. The call he'd received from the after-school babysitter, telling him Adele was no longer at her friend's house but hadn't come home, either. The surreal, frantic days that followed, when he'd slept only in short snatches and spent every waking moment sending out flyers, canvassing the neighborhood, working with police, appealing to the media. Detective Huff at his door four weeks later with the news that Adele's body had been found. The call about the neighbor who'd come forward to give them a suspect—Francis Moreau. The conversation where Huff explained all the evidence he'd uncovered in Moreau's house. Seeing Moreau for the first time in court. All of it. The emotions triggered by these memories were almost more than Romain could take. Gritting his teeth, he had to stop before they reached the front door.

He expected Jasmine to ask if he was okay, but she didn't. Instead, she put her hand on his back in a silent gesture of empathy and support. "*I* pulled the trigger," he managed to say. "I could do it again. This minute."

"That remains to be seen," she said calmly. "Would you rather wait in the truck?"

Taking a deep breath, he shook his head. "No. I want to see this place for myself."

"It doesn't look like anyone's home."

She'd already mentioned that the car she'd seen Phillip driving earlier was gone and so was the old Buick that'd been sitting in the drive when Beverly helped her out of the cellar.

"What does Francis's mother do for a living?" Romain murmured.

"I don't know," Jasmine said. "The neighbor told me she works nights, but she didn't say where. However, my investigator called while you were getting our pizza. She apparently got a nursing degree years ago, so maybe she's still in the medical profession."

They'd parked two streets over and walked so they wouldn't attract attention from the neighbors who, after all the police involvement, had to be especially interested in any activity at the Moreau residence. Romain imagined that, by now, the place had quite a reputation. Raw eggs were splattered around one window, suggesting that kids in the neighborhood had decided to use the house for target practice.

"They don't seem too well-liked," he commented.

"Whoever egged this place had better keep their distance in the future," Jasmine said. "They have no idea how dangerous it could be."

She reached the door first. Romain hung back, trying not to feel the confusion and terror his daughter must've experienced at being dragged inside such a place by a complete stranger.

"What makes them do it?" he asked softly as he joined

her on the front stoop. "What makes a man as depraved as Moreau?"

"I wish I could tell you," she whispered. "Most serial killers have had difficult childhoods, childhoods with a prevalence of inconsistent discipline and abuse. And many of them have suffered head injuries at one time or another. But those factors aren't as reliable as you might want to believe. At this point, no one knows what causes such deviant behavior. Lust killers and thrill killers are just structurally different. And because we can't understand or explain their behavior, we call them pathological."

No one answered the door. But that didn't surprise Romain. There wasn't a single light on in the house—at least none that he could see.

"I think we might be out of luck," she said.

"Dustin's here."

"How do you know?"

"Because they don't take him anywhere. Even to the courthouse when his brother was standing trial for murder." Romain knocked again.

"But where did he live back then?"

"If his mother was in town, Dustin was in town."

"I guess I'd have to agree with you there. It looked as if she'd been taking care of him for some time. But even if he's here, he either can't or won't answer the door."

"I can get in without him." Romain tried the door. Finding it locked, he stepped back to survey his other options.

"You're not breaking in," Jasmine said.

"Yes, I am."

She grabbed his arm. "Someone here, possibly *these* people, have killed one man already. Do you want to be next?"

"I'll take my chances."

"But if we get caught—"

"*We* won't get caught, because you're going back to the truck."

She clenched her fists. "No way! You're still on parole, aren't you?"

He didn't answer. He was too busy wondering if he might find a spare key somewhere, or whether he'd have to break a window.

"You are!"

He didn't correct her because she was right. "That means you could go back to prison!"

Pulling her into his arms, he gave her a long wet kiss, in case it was his last. "I think the police are the least of my worries, don't you?" He slid his lips down her neck, then let her go.

"Stop kissing me!" she hissed, following him.

"Why?"

"I don't like it!"

"You like it, you just don't trust me anymore. And you have good reason. I wouldn't trust me, either."

"Thanks for the warning."

"You're welcome. Now go wait in the truck."

She clutched his arm. "Romain, don't do this. We can come back when Phillip's at home. He's the one we really want to talk to, anyway. I got the feeling that he wanted to tell me something, as if…as if he had more to say."

"We'll talk to him. But I'm not going to miss this opportunity to lay eyes on Dustin."

"The man who came after me is somehow tied to this place," she argued. "He could be in there."

"No one's in there, except maybe Dustin."

"There was someone here last time, even though I thought there wasn't!"

He motioned for her to keep her voice down and lowered his own. "Stay with the truck. If I'm not back in ten minutes, bring a neighbor or use that cell phone of yours to get help."

She remained stubbornly on his heels. "No. If you're going in, I'm going with you."

Considering what she'd already been through, she had guts. But he wasn't about to let her take the risk. "It doesn't require two people."

She hesitated, glanced nervously at the house and bit her lip. But he knew that if he could convince her it'd be safer for both of them if he went in alone, she'd relent.

"Help me out here, okay?" he said. "I'll have less to worry about if you're not involved. Get in the truck, lock the doors and keep your head down. I'll only be a few minutes."

Mumbling a string of curses he hadn't heard from her before—which, under different circumstances, might've made him laugh because they seemed so out of character— she pivoted and started back. But a second later, she caught his hand and, when he turned to see what she wanted, pulled his face down to meet hers for another kiss, this one even longer and wetter than the last. "Don't get hurt," she said fiercely. Then she released him and was gone.

Romain stared after her. She was making him crave comforts he hadn't let himself crave since Pam died. If only wanting her didn't make him feel as though he was letting Pam and Adele down…

He turned abruptly as he heard a noise coming from the

house. A television. Someone had cranked up the volume until it was blaring.

Was it Dustin?

Probably. Why he wanted the TV so loud, Romain couldn't fathom. But it would cover the noise he was about to make, and for that he was grateful.

Breaking the screen on the back door, and then the glass, Romain used the sleeve of his leather jacket to protect his hand as he reached in and turned the lock.

# 18

The house smelled of cats. Two greeted him as he stepped inside, and the memory of how much Adele had loved animals nearly made him balk. Was he really prepared for what he might find?

He wasn't sure, but a morbid curiosity, an exploration of his own pain, propelled him forward. This was most likely the last place his daughter had known, the place where she'd been sexually molested, strangled and dumped into the trunk of a car.

Who was the man who'd killed her? What kind of person could harm an innocent ten-year-old girl? If it wasn't Moreau, what connection did the real killer have to this place and these people? And how did that connection affect Jasmine and her sister?

Romain moved silently through the kitchen. He couldn't see very well in the dark, but he wasn't in a hurry. A fierce, aching need to know had taken hold of him, causing him to slow down, to study and strive to understand.

The house *looked* just like his grandmother's used to look. It had cheap knickknacks in every corner, a flour-sack dish towel hanging from a hook near the kitchen sink, doilies on every table and gilt-edged picture frames with photographs from years earlier.

Francis's mother had lied for him in court. Didn't she care that he'd be put back into society, that he might molest, if not kill, another child? What had she been thinking when she saw those images of Adele's body shown in court? How could she not feel the poignant loss that'd made even the crustiest juror break down in tears?

He'd never understand, never fully grasp such a lack of human decency, he decided.

As he moved from the kitchen and the moonlight streaming in through the large window beside the door, the house became too dark to see. The blinds on the other windows were drawn, giving the place the feel of an underground burrow.

Refusing to fumble around, Romain found a switch and snapped on the light. A black cat that'd been sleeping on a tattered recliner got up and stretched, regarded him indifferently, then jumped to the ground. Two others, almost identical to each other with short, gray fur, roused themselves from the sagging sofa, and a fourth, this one with a Persian-like coat, brushed past his leg. All four were adults and considerably overweight. One approached its bowl as he watched.

He could see why they'd chosen the living room instead of upstairs. The noise emanating from one of the bedrooms was deafening—so deafening Romain didn't know how anyone could stand it. But, loud as it was, a voice suddenly rose above it. "Mom? Where are you? Mom?"

At first Romain thought Dustin had heard him break the window and believed his mother was home. Or that he'd spotted the light from the living room. But a second later, he realized that whoever was calling for Mrs. Moreau didn't expect a response. The words were more a wail, a lament.

The stairs creaked as Romain climbed them, but he doubted anyone could hear above that blaring TV. Whoever was in the back room was suffering. He'd heard the pain, the misery in that voice....

He walked down the hall, stopping in front of the last of three doors. "Dustin?"

The volume went off and silence reigned for several seconds. Then a voice called out, "Is someone there? Phillip, is it you?"

"It's me." Romain opened the door to find a shriveled man lying in a hospital bed. There was no light other than that coming from the muted TV, but Romain could see an IV trailing from the man's arm and a tray across his lap, which held a bottle of water and two remote controls. A radio sat on a small table against the wall; the television was affixed to the wall above the bed, close to the ceiling.

The man's sunken eyes widened as they latched onto Romain. "I know you! You're the man who shot Francis. I saw it on TV!"

Grabbing the metal rails of his bed, he tried to sit up but couldn't. He pressed a button on one of his remotes, and the gears of the bed began to grind as they brought him up to a sitting position. "How'd you get in?"

"I broke the door."

They stared at each other. Then Moreau's brother, whom Romain wanted to hate simply because of who he was, said, "Are you here to kill me?"

Romain could've hated him had there been the slightest hint of fear in his voice. But there was no fear—only hope.

Jasmine had the truck running so she could get the heater to work, but she couldn't stop shaking. She kept thinking about how quickly and easily she'd lost the most important people in her life—her sister, her mother, her father. Maybe her sister was the only one actually *gone,* but her parents had been absent since that same day, their absence even more painful because it involved rejection.

She couldn't stand the thought of losing anyone else, of losing Romain.

Grouping him in the same category as her family didn't make sense. She'd known him for less than a week. But he stirred something in her she'd never felt before, something powerful and all-consuming. Something that wouldn't allow them to be friends once she left.

She finally understood what he'd been trying to tell her about passion. About intensity. About *loving.*

"No, not loving," she muttered aloud. She couldn't be in love. Not that fast. She'd never even had a schoolgirl crush. She was too defensive, too cautious, too *practical.* She was concerned about Romain, that was all—as she'd be concerned about any man who'd broken into the home of a known murderer. She'd be worried about Harvey, or Bob, her last boyfriend, or Steve, the one before that…

But not with the same level of desperation. She couldn't sit out here anymore, wondering what was happening. Romain had just been gone a few minutes—not long enough to call the police and risk getting him sent back to prison for breaking and entering, but long enough for her to realize she'd made a mistake not going in with him. She had to make sure he was okay.

She cut the engine and started to get out when her cell phone rang. Caller ID indicated it was the police.

Surprised, she shut herself back in the truck so the sound

of her voice wouldn't bring out any of the neighbors and punched the talk button. "Hello?"

"Ms. Stratford?"

"Yes?"

"This is Sergeant Kozlowski."

The desk sergeant who'd told her about Pearson Black. The one who'd also helped with the initial search. "What can I do for you, Sergeant?"

"I'm afraid I have some bad news."

"What kind of bad news?" she said, terrified that he was talking about Romain.

"A woman was murdered last night."

Visions of that stranger coming through the window crowded Jasmine's thoughts. She'd been expecting this, hadn't she? And yet, the more hours that passed without confirmation, the more she'd managed to convince herself that it might've been a dream, after all.

"Who found the body?"

"The woman's boyfriend. He kept calling, she didn't answer. He went over to see what the hell was going on, and…"

"He found her body." The news upset Jasmine, made her apprehensive, but not as apprehensive as the fact that Kozlowski had called *her.*

"That's right."

With a quick check of her watch, she decided to drive down Moreau's street. Anxious as she was about this call, she was even more terrified for Romain. She started the engine again. "What made you think to tell me, Sergeant?"

"Are you sitting down?"

Putting the transmission in Drive, she gave the truck some gas and rounded the corner. "Yes." She told herself she was completely prepared for whatever he might say. But she wasn't.

"The killer wrote your name on the wall. In blood."

She stopped so fast she nearly hit her face on the steering wheel. She'd been right. The killer had wanted *her*. "The way he wrote Adele's name on the bathroom wall? With that odd mix of capitals, the strange *e*?"

"I can't tell you that. You understand," Kozlowski responded.

She understood that was basically a yes. But she couldn't concentrate on the implications of this right now. Romain was in Moreau's house. *Put off the impact; think about it later.*

She started driving again.

"Jasmine? Are you still there?"

A light glimmered around the edges of the blinds in the living room, a light that hadn't been on when she and Romain had driven past. Had he turned it on? If so, she feared Mrs. Moreau or Phillip would notice the moment they came home....

"Hello?" Sergeant Kozlowski prompted.

She slowed to a crawl. "Someone's getting nervous about my presence in New Orleans," she finally said.

"That's what I thought, too. And there's more."

"What?" She didn't bother going around the block again. She pulled to the curb to watch the house.

"I saw a picture of the deceased."

"Who was she?"

"A young professional, living alone. Her name was Pudja Vats."

The *was* brought a sharp pain to Jasmine's chest. Last night Pudja had been as alive as she was. "That's an Indian name."

"I know. And…"

Jasmine nervously clicked her nails together. "What is it?"

"She looked a lot like you."

Of course. This Pudja woman had been Jasmine's replacement. He'd killed her because of the resemblance. *God…*

"Do you know anyone in New Orleans who'd like to do you harm?"

"It's the man who took my sister," she said.

"How do you know?"

She wanted to say *I saw him.* She had seen him, on the stage of her mind. But she knew where that would lead and couldn't afford to arouse police skepticism. "He sent me a package. My sister's bracelet," she told him.

"When?"

"A little over a week ago. Anyway, I'm meeting with a sketch artist on Tuesday. I'll bring his likeness by the station when we're done."

"Are you staying somewhere safe?" he asked.

Her eyes fastened once again on the house, her heart pounding at how deceptively quiet it seemed. Why hadn't Romain come out? "Yes."

"Where?"

"In Portsville," she said absently.

"Good. I'm glad you're out of town. You'd better stay there until we catch this guy."

*Come on, Romain.* "Is there any chance you can talk the lead detective into letting me take a look at the crime scene?" she asked Kozlowski.

"No. He won't let anyone but the forensics team go near it."

"But I can help. I *know* this guy."

He hesitated, seemed to work through the scenario in his head. "I guess I could talk to him. If you're good enough for the FBI, you should be good enough for us, right?"

"I hope so." Jasmine checked her watch again. Romain had been gone for sixteen minutes—an eternity. "I have to go. I'll call you later," she said and shoved her cell phone into her pocket as she got out of the truck.

Jasmine could hear the murmur of voices coming from the far bedroom. As she climbed the stairs inside Beverly Moreau's house, she recognized Romain's. The other one probably belonged to Dustin, because it certainly wasn't Phillip's. They were talking about some adoption center where Beverly apparently worked.

Relieved to know Romain wasn't in immediate danger, Jasmine returned to the living room. She couldn't believe the Moreaus had lived here for only a few years; it looked as if they'd spent a lifetime in this place, acquiring worthless knickknacks.

Some photographs lined an old, broken-down piano. One was a family picture, taken when the three Moreau sons were quite young. The boy who was obviously Phillip, judging by his lighter coloring, stood behind his seated mother, his hand on her shoulder. Francis, with his black hair and black eyes, stood by Phillip's side. A much slimmer version of Beverly in a lime-green dress and cat's-eye glasses held the hand of a short, stocky man with hair and eyes as black as Francis's. And a toddler, presumably Dustin, sat on his father's lap. They could've modeled for the all-American family.

So what'd gone wrong? What made Francis turn out as he did? When had Dustin gotten sick?

The sound of a car made Jasmine freeze. She held her breath, waiting to see if that vehicle would stop in front of the house. But it didn't. The sound dimmed as the car passed by. She peeked through the blinds in time to see brake lights flash as it parked at a different house.

Close call. Breathing a sigh of relief, she decided to get Romain. They were pressing their luck by staying so long—but then she remembered her purse and her camera and wondered if she'd find them here. If so, she'd have more than her gut instinct to tell her that Mrs. Moreau was criminally involved with Phillip or whoever had stolen them. Maybe she'd even be able to verify a link to Pearson Black....

When she didn't come up with anything on the ground floor, she went upstairs to the first room on the right, which she assumed was Phillip's. It was far too utilitarian and messy to be Beverly's—and it smelled like cheap cologne. A single mattress lay on the floor. The bedding was bunched up with his dirty clothes, as if he blithely walked over it all when he wasn't sleeping.

He used a crate for a nightstand, which held a lamp with no shade and a cheap digital alarm clock. Except for the electricity, it could've been the cubbyhole of some homeless person camping out in the corner of an abandoned warehouse.

The closet stood open. Several boxes filled the shelves at the top; three shirts hung from the pole but no pants.

Jasmine pulled down a couple of the boxes and poked through them, but it was easy to tell they hadn't been opened in years. One contained a bunch of loose pictures, the other leftover fabric and sewing patterns for little girls' dresses.

Who'd made these? Mrs. Moreau had no girls, but maybe

she had nieces. Or maybe the patterns had been given to her by someone else.

After putting back the boxes, Jasmine turned off the light and crossed the hall to an office. It was overloaded with furniture—a desk, a twin bed that held a sleeping cat, a dresser with a mirror and a side table covered with more photographs.

There was only a narrow path for walking. Jasmine used it to get to the desk and went through the papers she found there, encountering insurance forms, prescriptions for medicines she'd never heard of, bills that showed the Moreaus were behind on their utilities and were paying $1400/month for the house.

An old, inexpensive computer sat to one side. Jasmine fired it up and let it work through its booting sequence while she searched the drawers. Pencils, pens, tape, loose postal stamps and an address book. Along with everything else, Jasmine almost passed over the address book, then thought better of it. Shoving it into the waistband of her jeans, she returned to the computer and checked its Internet history.

Someone, probably Phillip, frequented an Internet gaming site. There was also a Web site featuring doctors and other experts giving medical advice. The rest of the Web sites on the list dealt with craft ideas for children—how to make modeling clay, spider cupcakes, princess "glitter" shoes. Was this for Mrs. Moreau's work?

The voices in the next room remained low. Jasmine couldn't grasp much, just a few words out of every sentence, but it sounded as if Romain was asking what Francis had been like as a child, if Dustin had known he was dangerous.

Then a car door slammed outside and Jasmine's skin prickled with heightened anxiety. Someone was home.

Romain must've heard it, too. The talking stopped. Only a creak in the hall broke the sudden silence.

He was leaving, getting out.

*Good.* Jasmine wanted to say something, to let him know she was in the house, too, but she didn't dare make a sound. He'd see the truck, she told herself. She'd slip out and meet him there.

Forgetting about her search, she reached over to turn off the light, and that was when she saw it.

# 19

It was him. The man who'd taken her sister.

Jasmine couldn't breathe, couldn't move as she stared at the picture sitting with so many other pictures on Mrs. Moreau's cluttered side table. Kimberly's kidnapper was standing next to Mr. Moreau, the same man Jasmine had seen in the family photo downstairs, both of them years younger than they'd be right now and wearing fishing hats. Dark eyes, deceptively benign, stared back at her as Kimberly's kidnapper smiled for the camera—just as he'd smiled at her that day in their living room. He had a nice smile, chilling in its ability to mislead, and one arm slung around the shorter, stockier Mr. Moreau.

Were they related? Uncle and nephew? *Brothers?*

Someone entering the house finally galvanized Jasmine into action. Grabbing that photograph, she snapped off the light and pressed herself against the inside wall. But she'd waited too long to get out. The only exits were downstairs in the kitchen and the front door.

Sacks crinkled as whoever it was came through the living room and went into the kitchen.

Opening the office door barely an inch, Jasmine kept her eye on the hall. Could she reach the front door? Slip through it? She had to do something before Phillip or Mrs. Moreau noticed the damage done to the back door and came looking for her....

"Mom?" Dustin called from the next room.

"It's me."

Phillip, not Beverly.

"Where's Mom?"

"Where do you think? At work," came the reply. "She'll be home in a few hours."

"I thought they weren't going to have any kids over Christmas."

"Didn't turn out that way."

"All the kids were supposed to have a home. What about Santa Claus?"

"There's no such thing as Santa Claus, Dusty. You know that."

"But they don't. Where'd you go?"

"Out."

"Would you come up here? It's hard to yell."

"In a minute. I bought you some of that pie you like. You want it now?"

"Could I get some painkiller first?"

"I gave you a shot before I left."

"I need more."

There was a long pause and the answer, when it came, sounded hopeless, as if Phillip was thinking, *Please, God, not again.* "I'm sorry, you're going to have to wait."

"Come on, Phil..."

The pleading set Jasmine's teeth on edge. She couldn't imagine being in the position of constantly having to deny someone in terrible pain the medication he was begging for. She knew Phillip might be the one who'd locked her in the cellar, but she had to pity him. "We go through this every night, Dusty. You know what Mom said."

"Help me out, man!"

"Turn on the television. Distract yourself. I'll bring you your pie."

Jasmine wondered if Romain had seen the truck. What was his reaction to finding her gone? She had to reach him before he panicked and called the police or came to the door. She wanted to get out without alerting the Moreaus that she had the picture and the address book. The slightest threat could send Kimberly's kidnapper into a rage against another woman whose only crime was a resemblance to her.

But she couldn't do anything until Phillip left the downstairs part of the house.

"Dustin?"

Jasmine's blood curdled at the change in Phillip's voice.

"What?"

They were yelling over the sound of the television now, which Dustin had turned on as Phillip suggested.

"Was there someone here?"

Jasmine's heart, already pounding hard, seemed to reverberate all the way to her fingertips.

The television went off, but Dustin didn't answer.

"Dustin, I asked you a question."

There was movement in the kitchen, then a loud curse and something fell.

Jasmine covered her mouth to avoid a startled yelp and edged away from where she'd been peeking out of the office as Phillip came charging up the stairs. "Someone broke the back door!" he said, charging into Dustin's room. "Did you hear anything? See who it was?"

"I don't know what you're talking about."

"They broke the glass for crying out loud! You must've heard *something!*"

Dustin groaned, as if the pain was too much for him. "Right now, someone could cut off my head and I wouldn't notice."

There was a moment of silence, of confusion. "But you'd tell me if you did hear something, right? You'd tell me if someone bothered you."

No answer.

"Dustin! You could get Mom in a lot of trouble. Do you understand that?"

"Mom needs to be set free. You both do."

"Stop talking like that. You don't even know what's going on."

"I know it has something to do with me, and I don't like it. I'm tired of seeing the fatigue in her face, Phil. I'm tired of being a burden."

Jasmine was dying to hear the rest of the conversation, but she knew Romain wouldn't wait more than a minute or two before taking some kind of action, which would interrupt what she was hearing, anyway. It'd be better not to give herself away, better to escape with what she already had in her possession. With any luck, the missing address book and photo wouldn't be noticed for several days.

Stepping into the hall, she tiptoed down the stairs and made her way as quietly as possible to the front door. There was no sound as she opened it, but she nearly ran into Romain, who'd just raised his hand to knock. Making a quick gesture to indicate silence, she noted his expression of relief as she shut the door behind her. Then she grabbed his hand and they both ran for the truck.

\* \* \*

Romain wanted to go back to Portsville and, after their close call in the Moreau house, Jasmine didn't argue. He liked the idea of putting some distance between them and New Orleans. He knew they needed a safe place to recoup, to sleep. But he had little desire to speak on the ride home. Jasmine seemed eager to figure out what the items she'd taken might mean in relation to her sister's kidnapping and talked a lot about the possibilities, but all Romain could think about was returning to the truck to find her gone.

Plagued with visions of Phillip pulling her out of the truck and strangling her, then stuffing her body in the trunk of his car, he'd felt just as helpless in that moment as he had when Adele went missing. If Phillip had dragged her off, what could Romain have done about it? Almost nothing. Like Adele, Jasmine would've been dead before he could even try to save her. And dead was forever.

Romain had been planning to force his way into the house to search. But if he hadn't found her, he couldn't have counted on the police for help. They believed he'd shot Francis. The authorities would be so busy protecting the Moreaus' civil rights they'd do nothing until there was actual proof of Jasmine's disappearance, giving Phillip all the time he needed to dispose of her body. And then it'd be too late.

It hadn't turned out that way. But it could have. And that was enough to remind Romain that he didn't want to care. About anyone. Least of all a woman who was asking for trouble.

"What's wrong?" Jasmine finally broke into his thoughts.

Romain wasn't in the mood for confrontation. Slinging one arm over the steering wheel, he shot her a forbidding look.

"That's not an answer," she said.

"What do you *think* is wrong?" he asked. "You had no business going into that house. You were supposed to wait in the truck."

"You're still upset about that?"

*That* was no small thing. It'd scared the hell out of him. He almost said, "I can't take care of you if you won't let me!" And then he realized she didn't expect him to take care of her. *He* was the one who wanted to protect her, regardless the loyalty he felt to Pam. "I'm not upset," he lied.

"Yes, you are. You haven't said more than two words since we left."

"What do you want me to say?"

"You could tell me what you and Dustin were talking about."

He knew he should tell her and be done with it, but that moment of sheer panic still rankled. "Or maybe you could tell me why you didn't stay put."

She glared at him. "Why do *you* think?"

"Because you're reckless? Because, for some strange reason, you can't appreciate danger and stay the hell away from it? Because you think you're bulletproof, that it can't happen to you, only to other people? Well, I'm here to tell you it *can* happen, damn it! It happened to me, didn't it?"

He thought she was going to shout back at him. But her chest lifted as if she'd just taken a deep breath, and she reached out to touch his forearm. "I'm fine, okay? I'm right here, alive and well."

Embarrassed that she'd read through his tirade so easily, he shook her off. "Stop it. You don't mean anything to me. I don't care about anyone. Not anymore."

She turned to stare through the front window, but she

didn't raise her voice. "I scared you, and for that I'm sorry. I didn't mean to, okay? I did it because you scared me first."

He didn't want understanding or even explanations. He wanted a target.

Spotting a motel off to one side of the road, Romain slammed on his brakes and pulled into the parking lot.

Jasmine braced herself with a hand on the dashboard and one on her seat belt, but he didn't bother to apologize. "What are you doing?" she asked, still maddeningly calm. "Where are we going?"

"*We're* not going anywhere. I'm leaving you here. I'll give you the money you need to get out of the mess you're in, and that's it. I don't want anything else to do with you."

Finally, some real anger sparked in her eyes. "Why? Because I know you care about me, even though you don't want to? Because I saw the relief on your face when you found me at the door?"

"I'd be relieved to see *anyone* at that door. Especially anyone stupid enough to go in knowing a man had been murdered there."

"*You* went in!"

"I can defend myself!"

"Like the man in the cellar defended himself? What are you going to do against a bullet?"

The tires ground in the gravel as he stopped and shoved the gearshift into Park. He opened his door, but she caught his arm. "Tell me something, Romain. How are you letting your first wife down just because you want to make love to me?"

"I don't want to make love to you."

"That's a lie. You enjoyed our time together. You want more of it. And it's eating you up. You feel guilty because you can go on living and loving and enjoying life and Pam can't. But it's not your fault that she got cancer, and it's not my fault, either!"

Life was so much easier when he didn't have anything to lose. He'd made the adjustment, knew how to deal with each day. So why was he getting involved with Jasmine? Caring, without the old assurance he'd possessed that fate would be kind to him, was new territory. And he didn't want any part of it.

Jerking away from her, he stalked to the office, where the buzzer on the front desk roused a sleepy middle-aged man who rented him a room. When Romain walked back outside, it was drizzling, but he didn't have to encourage Jasmine to get out of his truck. She was already standing in the rain, hair and clothes damp, suitcase in hand.

Although he tried to take it from her, she refused to let him carry it as they located the room. He unlocked the door but, using her suitcase to block him, she pushed past him and grabbed the key from his hands before slamming the door.

Romain stood there, feeling far too many things to sort them all out. He knew he was being unreasonable. He regretted his actions. But he couldn't deal with the emotions she brought to life, and if this was the only way to put a stop to them, so be it.

Isolation. That was what he needed. He'd known it when they let him out of prison; he knew it now.

Telling himself it was for the best, he returned to his truck, got in and drove away.

Wet and miserable, Jasmine sank onto the bed with her suitcase at her feet, blinking hard against the tears that had started to fall. She told herself Romain didn't deserve such an emotional reaction, that she barely knew him. But she didn't have the reserves to deal with the hurt any other way, so she tried to convince herself that she wasn't crying over him. She was crying because she was exhausted and confused and…lost. Always lost.

Stripping off her wet clothes, she kicked them aside and decided to take a hot shower. She had a picture of the man who'd taken Kimberly. An actual *photograph*. And she knew that someone connected to the Moreaus would be able to identify him. That was a giant leap forward. She should be happy right now, not mooning over someone she had no business wanting in the first place.

Adjusting the faucet, she waited several minutes for the hot water to kick in, then stood under the spray, trying not to think about Romain. Or the fact that she didn't care whether or not they made love, she just wanted to be with him.

Romain drove for ten minutes, but every mile was harder than the one before. He kept picturing Jasmine standing there in the rain with her suitcase—and kept wondering what the hell was wrong with him that he could be such a jerk. He'd learned to get angry when he felt threatened, learned to fight. Prison had taught him that, and so had the tough breaks that'd led him to prison. He couldn't choose what he shut out. He had to shut it all out. But he knew Jasmine didn't deserve the way he'd treated her. She'd had a few tough breaks of her own and didn't need him to make her situation any worse.

But besides that, she was right. He wanted her now more than ever. And it made him feel disloyal—because he could no longer remember the subtleties of Pam's expressions during those intimate moments, could no longer rely on the absolute dedication that'd made other women a very remote temptation. Feelings he'd thought would never change were dimming, slipping away, and he found himself yearning to let it happen, to move on despite the loss of his wife *and* the subsequent loss of his daughter.

Maybe it was normal that human survival would make a mockery of his devotion, but he couldn't help feeling shallow for being so weak, so susceptible.

He was only a half hour from home when he began to slow. *Don't turn back. You don't want to hurt her again.* It was true and, with his track record, hurting her seemed inevitable. But he kept seeing those wide trusting eyes gazing up at him as he rolled her beneath him, and it wasn't three minutes later that he stopped at an all-night liquor store to buy a box of condoms.

A knock at the door surprised Jasmine just as she was toweling off from her extended shower. She had the television on to distract her from the thoughts spinning around in her head, but the volume was low. Surely it hadn't disturbed anyone….

Standing behind the door to shield herself, she opened it the width allowed by the security chain and saw Romain there, his hands in the pockets of his coat, his collar turned up against the rain.

She pulled the towel tighter around her and stepped into view. Romain had seen a lot more than her bare legs and shoulders and, after the way he'd acted, she didn't mind taunting him with what he couldn't have. "Did you forget something?"

His eyes went briefly to the cleavage showing above the towel. "Will you let me in?"

"No. What do you want?"

He hesitated, glanced away, then met her gaze directly. "I want you," he said simply.

Jasmine started to shake her head. She couldn't take any more ups and downs. But there was something so honest in those words, so vulnerable, that she couldn't close the door on him, either.

He had to be as exhausted as she was. "You can sleep in the extra bed," she said and removed the chain. But when he came in and closed the door behind him, he reached for her and she didn't turn him away—even when her towel landed on the carpet.

Beverly sat in her home office, utterly exhausted. Once she'd gotten Billy and the baby to bed at the transfer house, she'd managed to nap a little, too, but the newborn had slept only two hours before screaming for half the night. She was so colicky and miserable Beverly hadn't known how to help her. It was dawn when she finally settled down, time for Zalinda Sputero to start her shift. Zalinda had two kids of her own, whom she brought with her. She'd been told that the children in the transfer house were foster kids waiting to be placed and seemed to believe she was doing a good deed. The fact that Peccavi paid her in cash, like he did Beverly, should've told her otherwise, but if Zalinda suspected she'd fallen in with a bad crowd she preferred the money to a clean conscience. She had to feed her family somehow.

A noise at the door told Beverly that Phillip had followed her into the room. They'd just had an argument because he'd taken off again while she was at work, had left even though she'd told him over and over how dangerous it was for Dustin to be alone. Dusty could've tried to get up and fallen; he could've had a seizure; he could've reached the pain meds he was always begging for and overdosed. All kinds of things could've gone wrong. Why wouldn't Phillip listen?

Because he was cracking up right in front of her. She didn't know how much longer she'd be able to hold what she had left of her family together.

"I'm sorry," he muttered.

The contrition was also nothing new. He understood the pressure she was under, felt guilty when he made it worse. And yet he wouldn't do what she asked. She doubted he would've told her about the door if he'd had any way of fixing it so she wouldn't notice. As it was, he'd stuck a piece of cardboard in the broken frame, but she'd spotted it the minute she'd walked into the kitchen.

"Someone was in our house," she said.

"Nothing happened," he responded, a point he'd made several times already. "And if nothing happened, there's no need to overreact."

She spun in her chair to face him. "How do you *know* nothing happened?"

"Nothing's missing, is there?"

Not that Beverly could tell. The money she'd received on payday had been moved but every dollar was there. Even Jasmine's purse and other belongings were safely tucked away in her bedroom closet. "Not that I can see, but—"

"And it's not as if anyone bothered Dusty," he interrupted. "You can ask him. Tonight was like any other night."

Ordinarily, she would've had to motion for Phillip to

keep his voice down, but at the moment they could shout and Dustin wouldn't hear a thing. The only real sleep he got these days was right after his morning shot, and she'd given it to him fifteen minutes ago. They wouldn't be hearing from him for at least two hours. It was the only respite he received; it was Bev's only respite, too.

"I'm not sure he'd even remember it," she said. "Depends on where he's at with his meds."

"He was coherent last night." Probably too coherent. She knew Phillip hated being alone with his brother when the painkiller wore off. He couldn't handle the begging. Maybe that was why he'd left. Maybe Dustin had been too difficult.

"We still have to tell Peccavi," she said.

"Why? There's no need to bother him. He has enough to worry about. It was a vandal," he said. "You know what the kids in this neighborhood are like. We've become Boo Radley."

"Who?" she said.

"Boo Radley. From *To Kill a Mockingbird*."

"That's a book?"

"Yeah, it's a book. Everyone's read *To Kill a Mockingbird*. Don't tell me you haven't."

She hated it when he made her feel stupid. "Shut up about your books. I don't have time to read, and you know it."

"I'm just saying it's the neighbor kids daring each other. Ever since the police were here, everyone knows there was a body buried in our cellar. We've become the local house of horrors." He laughed as if he almost enjoyed the thought, but she knew he felt exactly the opposite. And suddenly she remembered that she *had* read *To Kill a Mockingbird*. In eighth grade. She couldn't remember a whole lot about it, but she remembered that it was a sin to kill a mockingbird because mockingbirds never hurt anyone.

A twinge of sympathy for her middle son made Bev soften. He wasn't sick, like Dustin. Or twisted, like Francis. But if he stayed with her, he'd have no greater chance at happiness than they did. "Come here," she said.

There was a puzzled expression on his face as she reached into her drawer and took out her money. She'd gotten paid a week ago and needed it for Dustin's care. But Phillip had never had anything. He deserved this.

Taking his hand, she put the money into it.

"What's this?" He thumbed through it, obviously shocked.

"Take it and what Peccavi gave you for your own work and leave. I know it's not a lot, but go somewhere else, get a job, make a life. And never look back."

The color drained from his face. As much as he craved his freedom, he was like an animal that'd been caged too long. Now that the door had been opened, he wouldn't go anywhere. "But I can't leave you! What about Dustin? How will the two of you get by without me?"

She couldn't imagine, but this was suddenly very important to her. More important than anything else. Phillip was all she had left. She had to be able to lie down at night and believe he was happy. "I'll manage. Just don't come back. Peccavi doesn't like loose ends. He'll kill you if he finds you."

"Mom…"

Standing, she pulled him into her arms and gave him a fierce hug. "I shouldn't have leaned on you so hard, Phil. You're a good man, as good as Dusty, but with a healthy body."

Tears filled his eyes. "I don't think I could live with myself if I did this."

"You could if you did it for me," she said vehemently. "Let there be one Moreau who got out."

He blinked repeatedly. "But—"

"It's time, Phillip." She smoothed the hair off his forehead like she used to when he was a little boy, something she hadn't done for probably twenty years. "It's past time."

He slowly straightened. "You want me to go? You really want me to do it?"

The realization in that statement made her smile. "Merry Christmas."

She sat in her office as he packed and left. He came to say goodbye, but she couldn't even look at him. It would hurt too much. She was on her own now. She'd lost her husband and her oldest son. Her youngest lay in the room next door in a drug-induced stupor. Only her middle son would escape the life the rest of them had known. But one was better than none at all. Peccavi would have no hold on Phillip. Not anymore. He could live according to that sensitive conscience of his.

After the house fell silent and the echo of Phillip's car had died down, Beverly finally roused herself. She needed to get some sleep if she was going to be any use to Dusty today. Maybe he'd feel well enough to play some cards. She could tell him how Phillip had found a lovely woman and run off to be married. Dustin was an old romantic—a story like that would make him smile. As the months went by, she could even write a few letters from Phillip describing the blissful life he was leading. Imagining that would make them both happy.

Hesitating by the phone, she contemplated calling

Peccavi and decided against it. He didn't need to know about the broken door. It'd be easier to cover for Phillip if she didn't have to talk to Peccavi for a while.

But just as she was about to step out of the room, she realized something was different. The picture of her husband that normally sat right in the middle of her table was gone.

Bending, she looked under the bed. Then she searched in and around the desk. Had it been knocked off? None of the others were askew.

Where was it? She loved that picture. It'd been taken right after Milo had decided to become a volunteer with the church youth program, and it showed him with Gruber Coen, his first "project." Beverly didn't like Gruber much. She never had. He was odd, made her uncomfortable. But that didn't ruin the picture because it showed her husband at his very finest. Maybe she'd been forced to do things she didn't want to do, but Milo never had. He tried to help boys like Gruber, to make the world a better place.

The picture was nowhere to be found.

Something else occurred to her. Maybe it hadn't been knocked off or misplaced. Maybe it'd been stolen. Not only had Gruber been the one to get her a job with Peccavi after Milo died, he kidnapped the kids they sold, at least those Peccavi didn't buy from desperate women.

Her mouth dropping open, she sagged onto the bed.

Jasmine Stratford was onto them.

Gruber sat on the couch in his favorite place, with his sister positioned beside him. He liked having her close, couldn't imagine doing anything else with her, not right away. She wasn't even cold yet, he told himself, although he knew she had to be. A body didn't stay warm for long. She'd start to bloat soon, and then she'd stink too badly to keep around.

Maybe he could figure out a way to freeze *all* of her. Or maybe he'd chop off a finger and use it to write his mother a blood-smeared farewell.

He chortled at the thought of a nurse opening his mother's mail and throwing up at the sight.

"You're so gross!"

He jumped at the sound of Valerie's voice. Had she really said that? Or had he imagined it? It'd been so clear, with just the right amount of disdain….

Fear prickled his skin as he leaned closer and put his cheek next to her mouth. No breath. She was dead. But she wasn't silent. She'd *never* be silent. What would he have to do to get some peace, for God's sake?

Maybe it was time to get rid of her body. It'd been fun while she'd kept her mouth shut. His biggest trophy so far. He loved remembering her final moments—the disbelief that'd flickered in her eyes as he forced her to go down on her knees and take him in her mouth. But she seemed determined to get the last laugh.

Leave it to Valerie. He could never top her. She'd make him look bad no matter what.

The phone, ringing upstairs, made him pause just as he began to drag her off his couch. Probably Valerie's husband again. Fortunately, she hadn't mentioned to him that she was coming by. Steve's calls were merely random efforts to find her: "You haven't heard from your sister, have you? Will you call me if you do?"

Gruber had enjoyed claiming he had no idea where she was. It was believable enough. They didn't associate all that often. Especially since she'd married Steve. Gruber didn't like her husband. He thought he was better than everyone else, just because he had a degree. *Your brother's a weird dude,* Gruber had overheard his brother-in-law murmur to Valerie at their wedding.

"I'm not going to pick up for your stupid husband," he told her. But he began to fear that Steve would come over if he didn't answer the phone, so he trudged upstairs.

At least, he didn't have to worry about her car. He'd already driven it back to the hospital and taken a city bus home.

By the time he reached the phone, he'd missed the call, but caller ID indicated that it hadn't been Steve, after all. It'd been Beverly Moreau.

"What could she want?" he muttered, and returned the call.

"Gruber?"

"I'm busy," he snapped.

"I don't care. You need to hear this. Jasmine Stratford was here."

Again? Kimberly's sister was as determined as she said she was on TV. "What'd she want?"

"Her sister, right?"

He wrinkled his nose at a peculiar scent in his kitchen. Shit, he'd left the hand of the woman he'd killed last night on the kitchen counter. He'd taken it out to show Valerie and must've forgotten to put it back. "I don't know anything about that."

"Her sister wasn't one of our children?"

She shouldn't have been. He'd taken Kimberly for himself. Peccavi hadn't known about her—until, after about two weeks, when he'd been hard up for money and decided to sell her to his boss. He still regretted that decision. He'd never been able to find another girl like her. Fornier's willful brat certainly couldn't compare. But Peccavi's business came in handy when things went so wrong with Adele. Or rather, *Francis* came in handy as a scapegoat.

"I don't keep track," he told Beverly. She wasn't supposed to keep track, either. They were all safer that way. Keeping records of any kind, even mental ones, was asking for trouble. That was what Peccavi said. And Peccavi was usually right.

"Well, she's suspicious, anyway. I think she took that picture of you and Milo I had in my office."

Valerie seemed to cackle from downstairs. "See? You idiot!" she yelled. "It's only a matter of time before you're caught. You think you can do what you've done and get away with it? You think you can kill *me?*"

"I've done whatever I want for seventeen *years!*" he called back.

"What?" Beverly asked, obviously confused.

"I'm not talking to you. Did you tell Peccavi?"

"I left him a message to call me, but I couldn't reach him. That's why I'm calling you."

What a relief! But Valerie didn't seem to agree. "You'll screw it up somehow," she yelled. "You always do."

Gruber pressed his fingers to his left temple. Why wouldn't she shut up? Maybe he could silence her if he cut her up and fed her to the alligators out in the bayou. But he didn't have time for that.

"I'll take care of it," he said into the phone.

"You will?"

"Of course. Peccavi already asked me to."

"And you haven't been able to do a damn thing about it so far." Valerie again.

Gruber squeezed his eyes shut. *She isn't talking. She's not even alive. Don't listen to her.*

"Good." Beverly sounded relieved.

"Night," he said.

"Night," she responded as if surprised he'd be so polite.

After hanging up, he grabbed his keys. He'd show Valerie. Soon Jasmine and Valerie would be watching television together.

# 20

Jasmine woke midmorning. She could feel the warmth of Romain's body. He was lying so still, she expected him to be sleeping, but when she checked, she found him awake and on his back, staring at the ceiling.

"Don't start," she warned when he glanced at her.

He rolled over and began feeling her up, making her realize that they were both growing far too comfortable with their intimacy. He was acting as if he could touch her whenever and wherever he wanted. As if he had a right. "Don't start what?" he murmured as he nudged her hair aside and kissed her neck.

She ignored a shiver of excitement and managed to wriggle out of his grasp. "Closing yourself off. Letting me know last night was just a cheap thrill, telling me you don't care about me or anyone else. I get all that, okay?" She yawned lazily; she didn't want him to guess this speech was something she'd carefully practiced before ever opening her eyes. "You're safe."

A half smile curved his lips. "You made love to me three times."

"Doesn't mean anything except that you're sort of good with your hands."

"*Sort of* good?"

She pretended to think about it. "Okay, really good." She let her gaze travel down his length. "And you have a few other attributes I find appealing."

"But you're merely using me."

"Of course." She fought the urge to curl into his side and doze off for a few more minutes, to let down her guard one last time. She was tired of always pretending. Pretending she didn't mind sharing the holidays with friends instead of relatives. Pretending what she'd felt for Harvey and the others was enough. Pretending that she wouldn't miss the deeper feeling Romain somehow inspired. "I'm not interested in a serious relationship. This is just a temporary arrangement while I'm in town. My life is in Sacramento."

Some emotion showed in his eyes. She suspected it had to do with her refusal to see the difference between last night and the previous time they'd made love. He'd been extra-gentle, extra-affectionate, and he'd said some really beautiful things. But she refused to believe any of it, refused to set herself up for disappointment. The heat of passion was the heat of passion, right? And she refused to chase something she couldn't have. She knew too well the deep dissatisfaction that stemmed from craving the ideal. For some reason, it was her lot in life to hover near the flame but never quite get warm.

"I see." His smile disappeared as he released her. "Thanks for putting me on notice."

"No problem. I wouldn't want you to fall in love or anything. Then the situation could get awkward for both of us."

His lashes lowered until she could no longer read any expression in his eyes. "Right."

Getting up, she retrieved a clean bra and underwear from

her suitcase. Aware that he was watching her dress, she made sure she kept her "I can take you or leave you" attitude in place. "So…are you going to tell me what Dustin said to you last night?"

The bedding fell away as he sat up against the headboard. "He knows something's going on. Doesn't know exactly what, but has a general idea it isn't good and wants his mother and brother out of it."

"Could he provide any details? Names, dates, anything?"

"No. They obviously protect him from anything he won't like. But he said he once overheard Phillip and Beverly talking about someone named Peccavi as if Peccavi was trouble. He thought his mother was crying at the time."

Jasmine knew she would've remembered that name if she'd ever come across it before. Grabbing the address book she'd taken from the Moreaus', she flipped through it. "Is Peccavi a first name or a surname?"

"I have no idea. Unfortunately, neither did Dustin."

Peccavi wasn't listed under *P.* In case it was a first name, Jasmine started at the beginning and went page by page, but nothing showed up that way, either.

"Google it," Romain suggested.

Wearing only her panties, Jasmine fired up her laptop and plugged in the Internet cable provided by the hotel. It took her ten minutes to get online, but the hits she received when she Googled the word *Peccavi* came up with the definition first. Apparently, *peccavi* was Latin for *I have sinned.*

"That doesn't sound good," she said.

Romain rubbed his hands over his face. "No."

It must've been difficult for Romain to speak to the brother of the man he believed had killed his daughter. "Did you tell Dustin who you were?" she asked, turning toward him.

"I didn't have to. He lives moment to moment with nothing but a television to entertain him. He recognized me immediately from all the news reports he'd seen during the trial."

Jasmine got up to finish dressing. "Of course, with his brother involved, he would've been paying close attention. Did he know anything about Adele?"

His gaze fell to her bare breasts. "No. And, surprisingly enough, he wasn't defensive of Francis. He claimed he was 'horrified' by what his brother had done. He loves children."

"How do you know?"

"He said so. And he has drawings from youngsters hanging up all over his room. He told me they're the only things that cheer him up, that he loves hearing his mother talk about the children at her work and how happy they are to go to a good home."

"She works at an orphanage?"

"An adoption agency."

"Which one?"

"Better Life."

Jasmine frowned. "That didn't come up on the background search I had Jonathan run."

"That's your PI friend in California?"

"Right. He found some reference to a nursing license years ago, but no record of current employment. I assumed she was living on SSI."

"Maybe someone's paying her under the table so it won't make her ineligible for government assistance."

Turning back to her computer, she Googled *Better Life Adoption Agency* and came up empty. Then she tried *Better Life* without the *Agency*. This time, volumes of links appeared, but none of them seemed to pertain to an adoption agency, an orphanage or anything like it. "There's nothing on the Internet about this place."

Romain got up and took her phone. "She has to go somewhere at night," he said.

Jasmine tried not to admire him as he stood there, completely naked, and called information. "New Orleans," he said. "Better Life Adoption Agency."

There was a moment of silence, then he said, "What about Better Life Foster Home? Or Better Life Placement Center?" His subsequent frown indicated he wasn't having any more luck than she had. "Better Life Children's Shelter? Better Life for Kids? Better Life anything that has to do with children?"

Finally, he thanked the operator, hung up and tossed Jasmine's phone on the desk. "Nothing." He reached for his boxers, but hesitated when he caught her watching him. "I could be wrong, but…if I had to guess, I'd say you like me better than you want to admit."

They were back to their relationship—or lack of a relationship. "I find you attractive," she admitted. "But you're not the only handsome man in the world." It was a weak argument. Handsome had very little to do with it; there was something vital about Romain that made her feel she hadn't really lived until she'd met him. He was the only man who'd ever affected her in such a way.

But she wasn't about to let him in on the secret. Turning away, she finished dressing.

He was wearing his clothes from yesterday, because they were all he had, and a dark scowl by the time she'd applied some makeup and was ready to leave. "You're the one who came into my life," he said as she gathered her stuff.

"I won't be there long," she told him again and headed out to the car.

* * *

"How are we going to discover the name of the person in that photograph?" Romain asked as he drove toward Portsville. They no longer needed a refuge; the motel on the outskirts of New Orleans had provided that. It was time to go back to the city. But he wanted to pack some clothes. They couldn't work from his place in the bayou, without telephone and Internet services, which meant it might be a while before he could return home.

"We'll have to ask around," she said, covering a yawn.

Although they'd awakened only an hour ago, the motion of the truck was putting Jasmine to sleep. He knew she'd be more comfortable if she slid over and leaned on him, but she wouldn't come that close. Not in the middle of the day when she was so preoccupied with the case and determined not to let her own needs interfere. It was only in the dark of night, when she was even more exhausted than she was now, that she lowered her guard. And then she abandoned her reservations and turned to him, making love as if she'd never been with anyone else who could fulfill her needs.

Romain loved the urgency of it, the heady, raw desire. Even with Pam, he'd never had such an intense experience. But merely making the comparison brought guilt. He shouldn't enjoy being with Jasmine as much as he did. So why did the memory of her guiding his mouth to her breast or arching into him as she accepted the union of their bodies make his heart pound like a jackhammer?

She'd reintroduced him to what he'd been missing— that was why. But everything was happening so fast, he wasn't sure they knew what they were doing. They were acting on instinct, an instinct so strong they could barely keep their hands off each other.

"The people who know are also the people who won't talk to us," he pointed out.

She played with a strand of the black, silky hair that'd fallen out of her messy ponytail. "There's Dustin."

"After last night, I doubt Phillip will leave him unattended."

Lifting Mr. Moreau's picture from its place on the seat between them, she stared down at it. "Maybe Kimberly's kidnapper is a member of the family."

Romain hated to disappoint her, but he didn't see a resemblance. "I don't think so."

"Then we dig up whatever we can about Mr. Moreau and start from there."

"Your PI friend in California can help with that, can't he?"

"Jonathan's already working on it. I told him I want as much as he can find on the whole family." Closing her eyes, she leaned back and began to nod off. Romain watched her head drop to one side and then the other, and finally tugged on her hand.

"Come here," he said.

She tried to wave him off. "I'm fine."

"If you're so indifferent to me, what're you afraid of?" She gave him a dirty look but let him pull her closer. Then she settled against his shoulder and slept until they reached the house.

The minute the truck came to a stop, Jasmine knew something was wrong. She could feel the sudden alertness in Romain's body.

Blinking, she raised her head. "What is it?" she murmured.

"We're home."

In Portsville, she reminded herself. *His* home, not hers. And then she saw what he saw—the front door was standing open. "Someone's been here."

Romain drove forward a little farther before stopping. "Stay put." Giving her a severe look, he hopped out and slammed the door.

Ignoring his order, Jasmine opened it again. "I'm coming with you. Two is better than one."

He probably would've argued with her if not for the stooped figure that appeared in the doorway. The minute he saw her, the tension drained out of him. "Mem, what're you doing here?"

The old lady had to be a hundred years old if she was a day. "Watching de place," she said, glaring at Jasmine.

"What for?"

"'Causa her." The woman surprised Jasmine by pointing a bony finger at her.

Romain lifted an impatient hand. "Stop with the jealousy. Jasmine's no threat to you. I'm not going anywhere."

That bony finger waggled at Romain next. "D'at what you t'ink. But you goin' to join your wife and chile in d'at cemetery if you not careful. You mark Mem's words. I know." She tapped her forehead. "I see it."

"Who is she?" Jasmine whispered, coming up behind Romain.

"My crazy neighbor, who doesn't know what she's talking about," Romain responded, loud enough for Mem to hear.

Mem pursed her lips so tightly they disappeared among the myriad wrinkles on her face. "She bring de devil wid her!"

"That's ridiculous, Mem."

"Ridiculous?" she shrieked, drawing herself up to her full height, which had to be all of about five foot two. "Did I dream up de man who came here? No. Was I de only one to see him? No."

*"Man?"* Now Romain was interested. Jasmine noticed the immediate change in him. "What're you talking about? Who came out here?"

"De stranger with de blood on his hands, d'at's who."

Romain scaled the porch steps in one leap and brushed past Mem. Jasmine hovered on the ground in front of the porch because the old lady had lifted her cane to bar her entrance. "Not you!" she warned. Then she genuflected. *"You* bring death."

"Jasmine!" he called.

Jasmine was about to wrench the cane away from the old lady, if necessary, but Mem lowered it just as Jasmine drew close enough, and inched to one side so she could get through.

"What is it?" It took a moment for her eyes to adjust to the dim interior, but once they did, she could see what Romain was staring at—a necklace featuring the Disney character Belle. It was taped to a wall smeared with blood.

"That's it, isn't it?"

Jasmine's voice came to Romain as if through a tunnel. The sight of Adele's necklace had taken him back to the days when his little girl would rush home from school so she could spend a few hours with him at the bike shop. Even at such a young age, she knew a lot about engines and used to share that knowledge with all his clients. They'd loved her almost as much as he had. She'd been such a feminine thing, despite the engine grease on her hands and clothes and her insistence on doing everything he did. So sweet, even after she lost her mother.

Missing her powerfully enough to make his chest ache, Romain dropped his head in his hands. What he wouldn't give to feel her arms slip around his neck just one more time....

When he didn't answer, Jasmine didn't press him. She kept her distance and let him grieve, but what he really wanted was to have her hold him, to bury his face in her neck and howl his pain to the world. And that surprised him as much as anything.

"You said you saw the man who came here?" he heard her ask Mem.

Mem remained stubbornly mute.

"Why do you hate me?" Jasmine demanded. "I don't even know you."

"You're de one who's bringing it all back."

"I'm *not* the one," Jasmine whispered fiercely. "I didn't start this, but I plan to finish it. Do you understand? The man with the blood on his hands has to be caught. Before he hurts someone else. Another innocent child like Adele. Another woman like the one he'd killed Christmas night in New Orleans."

*Before he hurts someone else...* Romain squeezed his eyes shut. Regardless of the evidence Huff found in Moreau's cellar, Moreau *wasn't* the one who'd killed Adele. If so, he would've had her necklace and Romain's parents wouldn't have received that note.

After believing Francis guilty for so long, it was almost

too much to comprehend. He'd hated Francis Moreau, cursed him to hell, *killed* him....

"God," he muttered as Mem began to chant.

"You didn't fire that gun." It was Jasmine. He could feel her presence at his elbow.

"You don't know that," he said.

She slipped her hand in his. "Yes, I do."

He gazed down at her delicate fingers, the simple ring she wore. She seemed so small and fragile, and yet she was tough. He knew that. Just like Adele, in many ways.

"You'll see," she said. "And we'll catch the man who killed Adele. I promise."

Mem's chanting suddenly stopped. "The man with de blood on his hands is de devil," she cried. "He can't be caught."

Jasmine rounded on her. "He *can* be caught, and I won't let you, your superstitions or anything else get in the way!"

"Tell her to leave, T-Bone," Mem insisted. "She bring bad luck, like I tole you she would."

Romain turned away from his daughter's necklace. "Go home, Mem," he said.

The knuckles of the old lady's hands grew white as she gripped her cane. "She's de problem. Send *her* home!"

"Jasmine stays."

"She's bewitched you!"

That wasn't a term Romain heard very often, but he couldn't argue. He *was* bewitched and, God help him, at least halfway in love. "Go home."

At the resolution in his voice, Mem pounded her cane on the floor like a judge's gavel. "You'll be sorry, T-Bone.

You'll be sorry," she promised and, taking another herbal sachet from the folds of her skirt, threw it on the ground.

Romain stared at it while he listened to her shuffle away.

"What is it?" Jasmine asked once she was gone.

With a sigh, Romain picked it up and smelled the poignant aroma. "A herbal sachet."

"What's it for?"

"I'm pretty sure this one's a curse," he said and tossed it in the garbage.

Gruber stood back in the laurel oak trees, watching the old lady hobble away from Romain's house, muttering to herself as she went. Last night at the bar in town, he'd insisted on giving two twins who were stumbling drunk a ride home, and they'd thanked him for the favor by pointing out Romain's place. But the old crone had ruined it. Once she came upon him, he was afraid to do anything for fear Romain would return while he was at it, so he'd pushed past her and run.

As the woman disappeared from view, he tried to stop the bleeding from the cut he'd made on his own arm and eyed the house. It was one thing to be waiting when Romain and Jasmine got back, to catch them unawares. It was quite another to attack them when they were on the defensive....

So what was he going to do?

Wait, he decided. He'd have his opportunity.

His cell phone, which he'd silenced before parking his car in the undergrowth of the swamp about a mile away, vibrated in his pocket. But he didn't answer it. His phone indicated he didn't have good reception. And his screen read No ID, which meant it was probably Peccavi.

He didn't want to talk to Peccavi. This wasn't business as usual; this was personal. He wanted to concentrate exclusively on Jasmine and Fornier, to hover in the background until that perfect moment arrived.

A few minutes later, Peccavi sent him a text message.

Where are u? Forget her 4 now. Time to deliver Billy.

Gruber tried to send a reply: First things first. But he smeared blood all over the keys for nothing—it wouldn't go through.

He thought of Valerie sitting on his couch at home. He had to get rid of her before the police came to ask about her. But he figured he might as well dispose of three bodies as one. If not for Romain, Adele wouldn't have disappointed him and Gruber wouldn't have been forced to turn on Francis, who was the only friend he'd ever had. Because of Romain, he'd planted that tape and the other evidence. He and Peccavi had promised Francis they'd get him off if he'd keep his mouth shut, and Francis had fulfilled his end of the bargain admirably. More admirably than Gruber had expected.

Until Romain shot him, everything was going as planned.

The whole mess was Romain's fault, and now he had Jasmine working with him.

Maybe she was sleeping with him, too. They'd been together all night, hadn't they? No doubt she'd spread her legs for a Reconnaissance Marine.

But Fornier wouldn't get to enjoy her for long. Gruber would feed Adele's father to the alligators along with Valerie.

Jasmine he might want to keep alive….

It took forever to get the sheriff's department to the house. Then they had to wait until the deputies had finished writing up a report on the break-in. Romain had followed the proper procedure for notification, but he had no hope it'd do any good. No one had been killed; nothing had been stolen. Sure, there was blood on the wall, but there weren't any words this time, nothing that would link this incident with the recent murder in New Orleans. And with Moreau dead, and both Huff and Black gone from the force, no one was particularly eager to delve into the past.

Jasmine tried calling the NOPD, had even spoken to the chief of police while they were driving back to New Orleans, but her outlook was no more optimistic after she hung up. "He doesn't want anyone else to believe Moreau might've been innocent," Jasmine said. "That would raise even more questions about how the case was handled, and how he could've allowed such misconduct."

Romain switched lanes. "But if we're right and Adele's real killer is still free—"

"Chances are good Chief Ryder will find out eventually," she said. "A man like the one who killed Adele doesn't stop on his own. That type of killing is a compulsion, a hunger. It only grows stronger."

"So you think your sister's dead." To Romain, it seemed pretty obvious that Kimberly Stratford had been killed long before Adele's kidnapping. But he was curious to see if Jasmine was still holding out hope.

She avoided his gaze. "Probably."

Romain had refused to let himself dwell on Jasmine's pain. He'd been too consumed by his own, searching for any way to avoid more of the same helplessness and regret. If he refused to care about Jasmine, he wouldn't have to share her suffering. He could sidestep the whole issue, go on living an existence numbed by solitude and anger. That'd been his plan—until now. It'd only been a few days and already he couldn't avoid her pain any more than he could avoid his own. Because he did care about her, far more than he wanted to. "It's got to be tough not knowing," he said.

"I want to bring her home, even if it's only her body."

At least he had the satisfaction of knowing that Adele was laid to rest next to Pam. That knowledge came with a price, but being left to wonder and question, to keep searching, would be worse. Jasmine had been clinging to nothing but hope for sixteen years. "If this guy is really *the* guy—" he motioned to the photograph in the seat between them "—he killed Adele within a few weeks and dumped her body in a very public place. Why do you think he didn't do the same with Kimberly?"

"He took Kimberly a long time ago. Maybe it was still early in his career and he was being cautious. Or he didn't feel the need to make such a public statement."

"But he didn't send you anything written in blood, either. Not until recently."

"No," she said. "For some reason, he suddenly wants to let us know what he's been able to get away with."

"Why do you think he's taunting us instead of the police?"

"Too many years have passed. There isn't anyone on the police force anymore who's really invested in these cases, at least no one he feels is competent enough to catch him. Who'll give him more attention than we will? He's all about getting a reaction, and these notes make us sit up and take notice."

"So he's baiting us because we're the most likely to care, most likely to try and stop him."

"That would be my guess."

"But he's still being careful. Other than Adele's necklace, he didn't leave much for us at the house. That deputy made a mess dusting for prints, but I'm willing to bet he'll soon find out that they all belong to me, you or Mem."

"Part of our killer wants to be caught, at least subconsciously. The other part doesn't. Self-preservation is a strong instinct. He's got what he knows is 'normal behavior' warring with his unacceptable desires, and we're seeing proof of that conflict."

Jasmine's cell phone interrupted them. Romain fell silent as she answered it, mildly surprised when she handed it over to him. "It's Huff."

A lot had changed since he'd worked so closely with Huff, but Romain still had a difficult time believing such a dedicated cop would purposely ignore clues and evidence he should've investigated. But maybe Romain hadn't seen the situation clearly. He'd been so shocked by everything that was happening, he'd had to rely on someone, and Huff had been the obvious choice, one of the good guys. Now Romain realized he should've kept an eye on even the cops. "Hello?"

"There you are." Huff sounded impatient, almost irritated. "You're a difficult man to get hold of."

"What's going on? Why are you in New Orleans?"

There was a long pause, then he said, "Why do you think?"

Something was different; something significant had changed.

"You know it wasn't him, don't you?" Romain said.

Huff muttered a curse, all the agreement Romain needed.

"What changed your mind?"

At the bitterness in his voice, Jasmine reached over, and Romain took her hand. It was becoming easier to accept her comfort. But he wouldn't think about that, either; wouldn't question it. Not now, anyway. What she gave him simply *was*. And somehow it made life better, especially when her arms went around him and, for a time, he could lose himself in the sensations she evoked.

"I received a note like the one you called me about. It was written in blood, using that odd mix of capitals and lowercase letters," Huff explained.

"You didn't seem to care about the note Jasmine received when I talked to you before," Romain said. "You told me it had to be some sort of coincidence."

"I would've ignored this, too. Believe me, resurrecting this case is the last thing on earth I want to do."

"But…"

"I'm a cop."

So his conscience had finally prompted him to face what he'd been trying so hard to avoid. "You were a cop when I called you about Jasmine's."

Huff blew out an audible sigh. "The note I got said something no one but the killer would know."

Romain shot a glance at Jasmine, who was watching him carefully. "What's that?"

"He told me where the fiber evidence came from."

"The fibers found in Adele's hair?"

"Yes. We couldn't find a blanket near the dump site, remember?"

"And there wasn't one remotely similar inside the Moreau residence. You assumed Moreau had gotten rid of it somewhere else."

"A plausible assumption." Huff was still on the defensive. "But this note said it was a baby blanket. He didn't wrap her in it, Romain. He gave it to her to sleep with."

The image that rose in Romain's mind made him cling that much tighter to Jasmine. He trusted her to stop the pain, and her desire to do so seemed to help. "That's what the note said?"

"The note told me where I could find a fuzzy red baby blanket."

Romain clenched his jaw. "And?"

"It's the one. It was buried in a plastic bag not far from the Old Gentilly Landfill."

"Francis's attorney went after the lack of fibers as a possible defense," he said. He'd gone after everything imaginable, eventually landing on the method through which the evidence had been collected. And he'd won. Until Romain had taken the law into his own hands....

Unable to keep driving, he pulled over to the side of the road. "I shot an innocent man." As if the notes weren't enough, the fibers confirmed it. "I killed a man because *you* said you found my daughter's blood on his clothes. Because you said you saw him doing unspeakable things to my child on tape!"

"I never said it was Moreau on that tape!" Huff insisted. "I said it was a man who fit his description, who wore similar clothes. It never showed his face, and I didn't lie about that."

"Did you lie about any of the rest of it?"

"No! I found his pants in the cellar, like I said. And he had priors. You know his history."

"Murder wasn't included in those priors!"

"I believed he got carried away, finally went too far. Whoever was on that tape *definitely* went too far."

The tape. Romain couldn't even let himself imagine it. *Don't think about it. Don't picture it.* Instead, he focused on one key word. "Believed," he repeated.

"Moreau was a pedophile," Huff said. "He wasn't an innocent—"

Romain cut him off. "Just answer one question."

"What?"

"Did you purposely overlook certain details in order to get a conviction?"

"No! What kind of man do you think I am?"

Romain didn't know how to respond. He didn't even know what kind of man *he* was. "If Moreau didn't do it, that evidence must've been planted," he said. "Who did it?"

"That's what I'm here to find out. Do you think I'd leave my family at Christmas if this wasn't important to me? If I didn't feel terrible about it?"

"Tell him we have a picture of the guy," Jasmine said. "Maybe he can help us identify him."

Apparently, Huff overheard her. "Who's that?"

"Jasmine Stratford. She has a picture of the man who killed her sister and Adele."

"Then we should meet—go over what she's got, what I've got, what you've got. Put all the pieces on the table and see if we can't come up with some leads. Can you drop by my hotel?"

Just the sound of Huff's voice, the intensity of his personality, carried Romain back—back where he didn't want to go. But he had no choice. "When?"

"As soon as possible."

"Where is it?"

Huff gave him the name and address.

"We can be there in an hour."

"I'll be waiting in the lobby," he said and hung up, but Jasmine had another suggestion.

"Let's make a copy of this. Then you can meet Huff while I go to the Moreaus' old neighborhood and start asking questions," she told him. "We need to put a name to this face."

# 21

Gruber thought it'd be easy to follow Romain and Jasmine anywhere they went. He watched it happen over and over in the movies. He'd gotten behind the wheel of his car and angled it so he could see when they passed him on the road, and he'd pulled out just at the right moment. Not fast enough to draw attention, not slow enough to make the effort pointless. But pointless it turned out to be. He lost Romain's pickup long before he ever reached New Orleans. Probably because Peccavi kept calling him, distracting him as the traffic on the road increased.

Frustrated that the old woman had interrupted him this morning and Romain had somehow outdistanced him on the road, Gruber finally answered. "What is it?"

Silence. Suddenly aware of the impatient tone he'd used, he tried to back off. "I had her," he said. "She and Romain Fornier were *right* in front of me."

"Leave Fornier out of it," Peccavi said.

"Why?"

"The more people you involve, the bigger the backlash."

That wasn't what Gruber wanted to hear. He was tired of Peccavi's dire warnings, his pearls of wisdom. Peccavi thought Fornier might be too much for Gruber. But Gruber didn't care if Fornier used to be Reconnaissance Marine or a janitor. A bullet did the same damage to one as the other. And Gruber had a bullet with Fornier's name on it. The gun he'd stolen from one of his mother's lovers years ago waited in his trunk. "We can't," he told Peccavi. "Anything happens to her, he'll be all over it. They both have to go."

Peccavi paused, then sighed. "It's not that easy to dispose of the...*trash.*"

Gruber nearly rolled his eyes. For all of Peccavi's business acumen, he had no idea who he was dealing with, no idea that Gruber had ever done more than snatch a few kids for the sake of a living. "It won't be hard for me." No one had discovered the three bodies he'd dumped in the bayou over the past two decades. There was no reason to believe he'd be discovered now. But he couldn't say that. Peccavi believed Francis was responsible for Adele, like almost everyone else did.

"You're confident, I have to give you that. Where are you?"

"On the road from Portsville to New Orleans, following Fornier and Jasmine, until I lost them."

"Forget about them for a minute, then. We have to transfer Billy."

"Why? He's fine where he is."

"No, he's not! This is our lifeblood, this is our business. I have a skittish pair of buyers, and I don't want to queer the deal by dragging this out."

Basically, he wanted the money. Peccavi was putting his share of the proceeds in an offshore account. He claimed he'd retire soon and leave the country, get him an island girl and spend the rest of his life in some tropical paradise, and Gruber believed he would. No doubt he'd stashed away quite a sum.

"Can't you ask Phillip to deliver Billy?" Gruber said. "I have things to do."

"Beverly doesn't know where Phillip went. He disappeared again last night."

"He'll be back, though, right? He always comes back."

"I don't care if he does. I'm done with him. He's not doing his job."

Which meant Peccavi would have his own body to dispose of when Phillip returned. Peccavi had certainly dealt with Jack.

It was going to be a big week for both of them. And it all hinged on doing what had to be done without leaving any trace.

"How far do I have to travel to get Billy where he has to go?"

"Utah."

There was no way. Valerie was rotting at his house. "I can't," Gruber said, more adamant than ever. "You're going to have to ask Roger. Jasmine Stratford has my picture. She knows I'm mixed up in her sister's disappearance."

Peccavi started to speak, but Gruber cut him off. "If I don't take care of this now, it'll risk the whole enterprise. If they get to me, they get to you. I'm only one step away." For the first time, he was glad he'd turned Kimberly over to Peccavi. That link strengthened his position now.

Drawing the threat back to Peccavi worked even better than Gruber had expected. "Fine," he snapped. "I'll do it myself."

As far as Gruber was concerned, it was damn time.

"Call me when you're finished," Peccavi added.

"I will." Gruber exited the freeway and stopped at a gas station to wash his hands. Then he turned right on the road that would take him to his brother-in-law's house. Showing some concern for his missing sister would buy him some much-needed time. After that he would head home. He shouldn't have gotten anxious enough to traipse all the way to Portsville trying to chase Jasmine down. Now that she had his picture, he didn't need to find her. She'd find him.

All he had to do was wait.

Because Jasmine had left her car in Portsville, splitting up meant she had to rent another one. When she mentioned it, Romain argued that meeting with Huff wouldn't take long, but they were working against the clock. The man in the picture would strike again. A vague uneasiness settled over Jasmine every time she thought of him. He was in a constant state of agitation these days, which told her something in his psyche had changed, grown more important or more immediate. She wasn't sure what that was or how she could be so certain. It was just one of those strange feelings that came over her every once in a while. The kind of gut feeling she'd learned to trust.

They had to act fast to stop him before he hurt someone else. And they could cover more ground by splitting up than by staying together.

Besides, it was becoming all too easy to trust that she and Romain had a future beyond the few passionate encounters they'd shared. At odd moments, she could imagine herself bearing his child.

"What?" he said as he dropped her off at the car rental place.

She smiled at the futility of trying to avoid the desires that flared up whenever she was with him, and shook her head. "Nothing."

"Yeah, well, this means nothing, too," he said, and then he pulled her back into the truck and kissed her soundly. She'd barely recovered before he started rattling off a set of stern instructions.

"As soon as I leave Huff's hotel, I'll buy a cell phone. Keep yours on so I can call you as soon as mine's working. I want to stay in close contact. And, whatever you do, *don't* go inside anyone's house. I don't care who it is, even if it's a child who's home alone."

"Got it," she said with a small salute.

His sober expression underscored his warning. "I mean it."

"Nothing's going to happen to me, Romain."

"I have to believe that," he said. At least, that was what she guessed he said. His voice was so low it was difficult to tell, and she was already shutting the door.

The house where the Moreaus used to live—back when Beverly's husband was still alive—was actually in a decent neighborhood. The homes were older but well-maintained. It was the sort of suburb where young families moved in and used a bit of elbow grease and creativity to dress things up. There were minivans in various driveways. Christmas decorations and lights adorned almost every house.

Jasmine parked at the curb across from the Moreaus' old address. She figured the people who'd bought the house would probably know the least about them, and planned to approach the neighbors first. With so many young families, she was worried there'd been too much turnover in the area. Quite possibly no one would remember the Moreaus, especially Milo who, according to Jonathan in California, died of a heart attack fifteen years ago.

Getting out, she pulled her coat tight against the biting wind, then walked up to the door on the left and knocked. But her first attempt was a disappointment. The aging Mexican lady who answered didn't speak English, and no one else appeared to be home. Smiling and waving to let her know it was okay, Jasmine walked to the other side of the Moreaus' former residence and rang the doorbell.

An attractive young girl with long blond hair poked her head out. "Yes?"

"Is your mother home?"

"Just a minute."

A woman with a shaggy haircut replaced the young girl. "What can I do for you?" she asked curiously.

"My name is Jasmine Stratford. I'm searching for my sister, who went missing sixteen years ago. I'm wondering if you can help me identify this young man." She held out the picture she'd taken from Beverly's office.

"Your sister was kidnapped?"

"Yes. And I'm fairly certain this man had something to do with it."

"How terrible!" She took the photograph and peered closely at it. "That's Milo Moreau on the left. He used to live next door, but he's not around anymore. He died a couple of years after I moved in."

"And the young man beside him?"

"I don't know. Once Francis Moreau did what he did— you heard about that, right? About that girl he killed?"

Jasmine nodded.

"This isn't connected, is it?"

"I think it is."

"Oh. Wow. I always thought he was weird. Mrs. Moreau was a little weird, too."

"In what way?"

"Just…super private, I guess. The last time I saw her was at a gas station right before Katrina. We were both evacuating. She'd already moved, sold the house to pay for Francis's attorneys' fees, which is why I remember running into her. It was quite a coincidence. But if you could find her, she should be able to identify the guy in your picture."

Jasmine didn't mention that she knew where the Moreaus lived or that Beverly was probably the last person who'd help her. "Were the Moreaus friendly with anyone on the street? Maybe someone else might remember this person."

The woman nibbled on her lip. "So many people have moved away. With the hurricane and the economy…" Her face suddenly brightened. "Ila Jane Reed on the corner might be able to help you. She's been here going on fifty years, I bet. She's old now, but her mind's as sharp as ever."

"I'll try her," Jasmine said. "Thank you."

"Good luck. I hope you find your sister." The woman closed the door and Jasmine made her way down the street.

Response at the Reed house was slow, but the door finally swung inward and a white-haired woman pulling an oxygen tank stepped into the opening. "Yes?"

Once again, Jasmine described the reason for her visit and held out the picture.

"He's not one of the Moreau boys, is he?" Mrs. Reed asked above the rhythmic hiss of her oxygen.

"No."

"It's my vision," she explained. "It's not what it used to be." Bending closer, she studied the photograph but ultimately shook her head. "I'm sorry. He looks familiar, but I can't place him."

Jasmine swallowed a sigh of disappointment. *Someone* had to know his name. "Thanks for trying. Can you think of anyone else who might be able to help me? Maybe someone who was particularly close to the Moreaus while they lived here?"

"There's the Blacks," she said. "Their boys ran around with the Moreau boys when they were growing up."

Jasmine's pulse leapt at the name. "The Blacks?"

"Charmaine and Doug. The Moreaus used to live across the street from them. Their kids are all grown and gone now, but Doug and Charmaine are still around."

Jasmine held the picture to her chest. "Do you happen to remember the names of their boys?"

"Dirk and…" Mrs. Reed squeezed her eyes shut as if that might jog her memory. A moment later, they popped open. "Pearson! Pearson Bailey Black. He was the youngest. What a little hellion," she added, but Jasmine scarcely heard her trailing comment.

That couldn't be a coincidence, she was thinking. Pearson was too unusual a name. "Do you know where I can find Pearson?" she asked, hoping to clarify that what her instincts told her was true.

"He was a cop. One of NOPD's finest. Until there was some mix-up down at the station and Pearson got blamed for something he didn't do. Lost his job over it. Really upset his parents. It was so unfair."

Unfair? Jasmine believed the exact opposite, but she didn't say so. "What does he do now?"

"He's a security guard. But that's temporary. He's planning to become a private investigator."

"I'm sure he'll make a good one," she said politely.

"There's Charmaine now." Mrs. Reed motioned toward a

car turning into the drive closest to Jasmine's rental car. "You should talk to her. I'll bet she can tell you who's in that picture."

With a quick thank-you, Jasmine hurried down the street. She could hear Mrs. Black getting out of her car. The telltale crackle of sacks indicated she'd been shopping.

"Hello?" she called before Mrs. Black could go in through the garage door.

The crackling grew louder as Pearson's mother came to the garage opening and peered out at her. "Hi, there. What can I do for you?"

"Looks like you've been busy."

Soft and round and dark-haired, she smiled with unabashed glee. "I love the after-Christmas sales, don't you? I've already finished most of my gift-buying for next year."

Jasmine came closer and held out the picture. "I was just talking to Mrs. Reed. She thought you might know the name of the teenager in this photograph."

"That's Milo Moreau." She pointed to the man whose identity Jasmine already knew.

"And the other one?"

"Gruber Coen."

"Coen? How do you spell that?"

"C-O-E-N."

Jasmine could scarcely breathe. At long last, she had the name of the man who'd taken her sister. The thought alone made her oddly exultant. But who was this Gruber that he could walk away with an eight-year-old girl? "Do you know where he lives now?" Her nails bit into the palm of her free hand as she silently prayed for some clue to his location.

"No. I didn't keep track of him. I never liked him, to tell you the truth. Neither did my sons. He came from an unfortunate situation, but—" she shifted her bags to her other arm and Jasmine reached out to take the heaviest one from her "—he was odd, for lack of a better word."

"In what way?"

"A loner. Always sullen. Always staring at you as if there was more going on behind those eyes than he wanted you to know. Mr. Moreau volunteered with some church group and used to bring him home. He tried to make the boys include him, but Gruber would stand off to the side with his hands in his pockets while they did normal boy things."

"Like…"

"Like playing basketball or roller hockey."

"They never got to like him?"

"Not at all. Except maybe Francis. They were both outcasts, more or less. They rode around together once in a while after they got into high school. But they caused trouble wherever they went. One time they put a dead squirrel in a girl's locker because Francis had asked her out and she'd turned him down."

Jasmine's hands were growing numb from the cold. She curled them inside the sleeves of her coat. "What about Pearson?"

Her eyebrows went up. "You know my son?"

"Mrs. Reed mentioned him to me," she said to avoid a direct answer.

Mrs. Black set her bags on the trunk of the car and took the one Jasmine was holding for her. "Pearson always preferred Phil or Dusty. But he didn't approve of what happened to Francis a few years ago, I'll tell you that much."

"You're referring to the fact that Francis was tried for the murder of Adele Fornier."

"That's exactly what I'm referring to."

"Pearson believes Francis was innocent?"

"He had some priors for sexual misconduct, and I'm not making light of that. But he didn't kill the Fornier girl. Pearson swears up and down Francis was framed."

"By whom?"

"He doesn't know. He said Francis was involved with someone named Peccavi."

"I have sinned," Jasmine murmured.

Mrs. Black tilted her head. "What?"

"That's what it means. It's Latin."

"If you say so." She began gathering up her bags.

"Do you believe there's any chance Gruber could be Peccavi?"

"I'd believe anything of Gruber."

It was cold, and Jasmine had detained her long enough.

"Thank you for your time."

"No problem," she said.

After Mrs. Black had gone inside, Jasmine stood gazing down the neat row of houses. Gruber. Francis. Pearson. Dustin. Phillip. This had been quite a street. It'd yielded two child molesters, one of whom was also a murderer.

But now she knew at least one person who could lead her to Gruber Coen. Taking out the business card Pearson had given her, she dialed his number.

Huff was waiting for him in the coffee shop at his hotel.

"Jasmine's not with you?" Huff asked as Romain slid into the seat opposite him.

"No."

"Why not?"

Huff didn't look good. He'd lost more of his hair, but it wasn't the aging process that was getting the best of him. Romain suspected he was working too many hours. Dark circles underscored his eyes, and his face was drawn and pinched. "She had other business to attend to."

"What could be more important than this?"

"Finding the man who kidnapped and probably murdered her sister."

"Aren't we after the same man?"

"Yes, but there was no need for both of us to be here."

"Did you tell her about the blanket?"

"She knows." Romain pointed to a paper sack in the seat next to Huff. "Is that it?"

Pulling out part of a fuzzy red blanket stained with mildew, Huff nodded. "I'm going to have it tested for genetic material, but that'll take a while. The fiber evidence was easier. It required only a microscope."

"You're sure it's a match?"

"Positive."

Romain sank lower and stared at it. His child had touched the blanket, maybe even comforted herself with it. "How could Adele's blood have gotten on Moreau's pants, her barrettes in his cellar?"

"He was living alone, but I'm sure his family came to visit him on occasion, so they would've been familiar with the place. Any one of them could've put those things in the cellar."

"Dustin's been bedridden for years. And Beverly is an unlikely candidate."

"What about Phillip?"

"He doesn't seem the type. Besides, it was Francis who was spotted at the school, Francis who carried in something heavy the day Adele went missing."

Huff stirred more cream into his coffee.

"He bought a new rug that day, remember? The defense brought it up in court."

"That's a convenient coincidence. I believed Francis was the murderer then. And I still believe it now."

"Me, too. I'm guessing they were in it together. But that's very rare, isn't it? For collusion on this kind of sex crime?"

Huff shrugged. "It's happened before. Some women have even helped their husbands or lovers imprison and torture sex slaves."

"We're talking about crimes against children here. It'd be a lot harder to get someone to go along with that."

"Harder, maybe. But it's conceivable."

The waitress approached and Romain ordered a cup of coffee and some scrambled eggs. "What about Black?" he asked.

"What about him?"

"He was at Francis's house the night you performed the search. He could easily have tossed that stuff into the cellar for you to find."

"But he's the one who claimed it had been planted, who tried to get Francis off, remember?"

"Are you sure it was Black?"

"Positive. I trust all the others who were there during the search."

Romain toyed with the salt and pepper shakers. "Have you ever heard of Better Life Adoption Agency?"

A strange expression appeared on Huff's sallow face. "Where'd you come up with that name?"

"It's where Mrs. Moreau works."

"She doesn't work. She lives on SSI."

"According to her son Dustin, she works nights at this adoption agency."

Frown lines etched deep grooves in Huff's forehead. "When did you talk to Dustin?"

"I paid him a visit the other night."

"Was he lucid?" he asked, turning his cup around and around in its saucer.

"More lucid than he wanted to be. I think he was in a great deal of pain."

"He must not've known what he was talking about. What he said can't be right."

The waitress brought Romain's coffee, and he stirred a spoonful of sugar into it. "Why not?"

"Because that orphanage doesn't exist. Years ago, a pregnant woman came into the station and filed a complaint saying a man offered her a large sum of money for her baby. She claimed he represented a place called Better Life Adoption Agency and promised that her child would go to a very wealthy couple." Huff took a sip of his own coffee. "So we looked into it," he went on after swallowing. "But we couldn't find any proof of such a place. And because she was a prostitute and a drug addict, and her claims were uncorroborated, we finally figured she was hallucinating or out to get someone who'd wronged her."

"Did she give the man's name?" Romain asked.

Huff's whiskers rasped as he rubbed a hand over his jaw. "It seems like she had a name, but I can't remember it. It was unusual—I recall that much."

The waitress delivered Romain's eggs, but he pushed them aside, too interested in the conversation to be bothered with breakfast. "Was it Peccavi?"

The frown lines disappeared as Huff's eyes widened. "That's it! She said a man by the name of Peccavi approached her and offered to buy her baby. She was adamant. But she was also shaking from withdrawal."

"So let's say it's true," Romain said. "Let's say the

Moreaus, at least Beverly and Phillip, and maybe Francis when he was alive, are involved in a black market adoption ring. And let's say Peccavi is the leader." It made sense, based on what Dustin had told him. It also stood to reason that the Moreaus wouldn't want Jasmine nosing around, and that they might kill someone in order to keep their secret, which could account for the body she'd found in the cellar. "Maybe Francis got out of line and started taking physical advantage of some of the children they kidnapped."

"But we now know Francis didn't kill Adele," Huff argued.

"The ring could include other people. It's possible Francis kidnapped Adele, planning to turn her over to Peccavi, but another member of the group, someone even more twisted than Francis, got hold of her."

"Twisted is right," Huff muttered into his cup, and Romain knew he was remembering what he'd seen on that tape.

Romain returned to the puzzle coming together in his head. "Say this twisted person got so carried away he killed her. Then he had to dispose of her body. He dumps her in the park restroom, she's discovered, and the hunt is on."

"At this point, the pressure's mounting and he's in a panic," Huff chimed in. "You're on television begging for clues, offering rewards. I'm doing all I can to ferret out suspects. Maybe I even question him."

"Then the neighbor calls to report that she saw Moreau carry something into the house the day Adele went missing."

Huff pushed his coffee away, too. "He's a loner, has a history of sex crimes, and he's been seen at the school. So he becomes our focus."

Something that might be problematic to their developing scenario suddenly occurred to Romain. "Wait. The members of this ring can't take the children to their own homes. It'd be too risky. There's a place off-site where the transfer happens. That's where Beverly goes each night."

"But Moreau brings Adele home *this* time. He doesn't tell any of the others because it'll get him in trouble with the ringleader—Peccavi—but he plans to have some fun before he turns her over."

Romain winced but continued to work out their scenario. "And he lives alone, so he thinks he can get away with it. But, somehow, this other guy, the guy who's even more twisted than Moreau, takes her from Francis and the situation goes from bad to worse."

"That could be it," Huff said with a decisive nod. "Once he's killed Adele, he has to make sure no one finds out it was him, especially Peccavi, because he's now endangered the whole bunch of scumbags."

Romain leaned forward, his elbows on the table. "He knows if Peccavi catches him he'll be as dead as Jack Lewis, the man Jasmine found in that cellar."

"So he frames Francis," Huff went on, "who's already the prime suspect. And Francis performed the actual abduction, so he was seen hanging around Adele's school. It's perfect."

"All he has to do is plant the evidence. The bloody chinos were close enough to Moreau's size and standard enough to be found in almost any male closet. The video and the barrettes make it even better."

Some color was finally entering Huff's cheeks. "But he throws it all in the cellar because they'll be discovered by the Moreaus if he puts them inside the house."

"Which is why the cellar door was broken before you ever got there." Romain stared at Huff, his chest rising and falling with excitement.

The waitress came by for the third time, probably to ask about the meal growing cold on the table, but Huff waved her away. "Why couldn't the man who killed Adele be Peccavi?" he asked. "Maybe Peccavi framed Moreau."

"No. Jasmine specifically said that there are two distinct personality types at work here."

"The Stratford woman?"

"She's a profiler."

"I know, but profiling isn't an exact science."

"There're two men involved." Romain had too much faith in Jasmine to disbelieve her on that point.

"Then who's Peccavi, and how do we catch him?"

"Pearson Black!" they both said at once.

"*That's* why he followed the case so closely, why he got involved and caused it to unravel," Huff added.

"I'm guessing he promised Francis he'd get him off—if Francis kept his mouth shut about the adoption business. Francis did as he was told. So Black went to work."

"And in my eagerness to solve the case and see a dangerous man behind bars, I made it easy for him because of the way I handled the search."

At the time, Romain had believed they should do whatever was necessary to obtain the evidence they needed. That made it impossible for him to fault Huff, even though Huff was a police officer and should've curbed the tendency. "A cop would be above suspicion," Romain said. "Black's job would make him privy to the case while giving him the perfect cover."

Jumping to his feet, Romain tossed some money on the table.

"Where are you going?" Huff demanded.

"We have to stop Black and whoever's working for him before someone else gets hurt."

"And how do you propose to do that? We can't confront Black. All we have is a theory, which is worthless until we can prove it."

Romain's need to act, to fight back, nearly overwhelmed him. They'd identified the enemy. "Beverly Moreau is the key. Can we offer her immunity if she turns state's evidence?"

"I can't offer her a thing. I'm not even on the force anymore!"

"Then we have to go to the chief, get him involved. He doesn't like Black. He might listen to us."

"He doesn't like me, either," Huff pointed out.

And Romain knew Chief Ryder wouldn't look any more kindly on him. By taking the law into his own hands, Romain had contributed to the department's bad publicity, since he wouldn't have shot Moreau if Huff hadn't screwed up the search.

"It'd be smarter to set Black up," Huff proposed. "Once we have him, we should be able to get the man who killed Adele. Black will give him up if he knows it's over."

"How are we going to do that?"

"We can have someone, maybe Cathy, a female officer who left the NOPD before Black was ever hired, call him up and pretend to be a potential client, a rich woman who's dying to adopt a baby. Cathy could record the call and arrange a meeting. She'd wear a wire, and once we have him on tape making the deal, he's done for."

Romain checked his watch. He'd already been at the coffee shop longer than he'd wanted to be. He hated the thought of Jasmine out there alone, asking questions that could draw the attention of someone as dangerous as the man who'd murdered Adele. But they were finally onto something that might bring an end to it all.

"What's the matter?" Huff asked.

"I'm worried about Jasmine," he said.

"Call her." Huff handed him a cell phone. "Have her meet us, and we'll bait the trap."

# 22

"What's wrong?"

Beverly pulled herself out of her thoughts and focused on the card game she was playing with Dustin. "Nothing, why?"

"It's your turn." He rested his head on his pillow while waiting for her to play.

Beverly drew two cards, made a pair with one and tossed the other into the center. She was losing; she hadn't been able to concentrate. She generally enjoyed playing canasta, but today she was doing it strictly to entertain Dusty.

"Now it's your turn," she said.

He studied what she'd thrown him, laid down a pair of aces and scooped the stack of discards toward him. "I'm taking the pile."

That certainly wouldn't help her comeback, she thought, but winning a card game was nothing that really concerned her.

"When do you think Phillip will be home?" Dustin asked as he played what he could and put the extras in his hand.

Beverly didn't have the heart to tell him the truth. Hiding behind her cards, she said, "Who knows? With Phillip, you see him when you see him, right?"

She glanced up in time to see an odd expression flit across Dustin's face. He'd been sick so long his eyes sat deep in their sockets and his skin had taken on a waxy sheen. The changes in him testified to the fact that he was sliding further and further downhill, but worrying about Dustin was an everyday occurrence. Today, Bev had something new to agonize over. Peccavi hadn't reacted the way she'd expected when he'd called for Phillip and she'd had to tell him she didn't know where he was or when he'd be back. There'd been no bitter recriminations. Peccavi had accepted the news with a cool resolve she'd found more chilling than any amount of cursing would've been—the kind of resolve he'd exhibited before he'd shot Jack in her living room.

*Help Phil disappear,* she prayed. *Help him get away for good....*

Painfully aware that she didn't deserve the blessings of heaven, she rarely appealed to God. She considered Him mostly deaf, anyway. But guilt didn't stop her from pleading for her children. She figured that was a mother's prerogative, no matter how bad a person that mother was.

"Mom?"

It was her turn. "Sorry," she mumbled.

He watched her play. "Phil's always been here when we've exchanged Christmas gifts before. That's why we waited this year, so we could all be together."

The painting Dustin had created for Phil was still standing in the corner, wrapped. She couldn't help glancing toward it. Dustin didn't have a lot of talent, but it was the best he could do, all he had to give, so his efforts meant a great deal to her. His brother liked his work even better than she did. If life hadn't been so crazy, Phillip would've remembered to take it with him.

On second thought, Bev knew he'd left it behind on purpose. Birds, flying free in the sky, were the subject of almost every one of Dustin's paintings. Keeping one would only make Phil's new life more difficult, because he'd broken away while Dustin never could. Dustin would remain trapped in a feeble body until he died.

"He's got a girlfriend," she lied. "He'll come when he's ready." In another day or two, she'd get rid of the painting and say she'd shipped it to him. "How do you like the books I brought you?"

"I love them. Especially the one on the Renaissance painters." Her gifts sat on his rolling tray, the paper he'd torn off still crumpled beside them.

"Good. I'm thrilled with the bird you painted for me, too."

"The one I did for Phil is a little different."

"But I'm sure it's just as beautiful."

"I'd like to see him open it."

She winced at the burning in her stomach. "Okay. When he gets home. It's your turn."

He didn't move.

"Dustin?"

"I think you should go to the police," he said, tossing his cards aside.

Lowering her hand, Beverly gaped at him. "About what?"

"About everything."

"You don't know what you're saying."

"Yes, I do." His words were softly spoken. "You've done

something terrible, for my sake, and you're caught in a situation from which there seems to be no escape. If you don't free yourself you may never get out."

"No." She shook her head. If she went to the police, they'd put her in prison. Then what would happen to him? He wouldn't have anyone to take care of him.

"You can't go on like this," he insisted.

His words, solemn and heartfelt, shook Beverly to the core. She was so weary inside, so sick of all she'd done and all she'd hidden. She'd burn in hell for sure. But what really plagued her were memories of the little children she'd helped Peccavi uproot and transplant. She'd tried to delude herself into thinking they'd all gone to good families. But she knew that wasn't true. Peccavi was a businessman. He used them just as he would any other kind of product—he sold them to the highest bidder.

A tear slipped down her cheek and dropped onto the table before she even realized she was crying. Milo had to be rolling over in his grave. He'd tried to do so much good in his life. But he hadn't faced Dustin's illness, hadn't experienced the desperation that'd delivered her into the hands of a man who, after the initial agreement, would hold her in his power forever.

If she let him…

"Mom." Dustin squeezed her arm. When she looked up, he continued. "I don't have much longer. I want to die knowing you're free of whatever he holds over you."

"Even if it means I'm sitting in prison?" she whispered, more honest with him in this moment than she'd been in years.

"Will it help these children?" He waved at the pictures taped on his walls.

She imagined the joy all the families who'd lost a son or daughter would feel at finding that missing child and her heart began to beat faster. "Yes."

"Then whatever price we pay will be worth it."

When he picked up the handset, Beverly almost reached out to stop him. The police had been "the enemy" for so long. But they were Peccavi's enemy, too.

"Do the right thing," Dustin whispered. "Stop what's going on—for their sake." He pulled Billy's Santa Claus off the wall behind him. "If you testify against Peccavi, I'll bet you won't serve any time. You'll get probation, but then it'll be over and no more children will be hurt."

As it happened, he'd chosen Billy's artwork, and that took Beverly aback. She'd never actually admitted to Dustin what she was doing; she was too ashamed. And yet, on some level, he *knew*.

"Mom?" he prompted when she didn't move.

It wasn't too late for Billy. When Beverly had left work this morning, Billy was still at the transfer house.

Maybe she couldn't save Dustin. As painful as it was going to be to lose her most endearing child, Dustin's disease would win in the end. They had very little time. But she could save the boy who reminded her so much of him.

Setting down her cards, she took another antacid and accepted the phone he handed her.

Pearson Black hadn't answered when Jasmine tried to reach him. She'd called him at least six times, left messages, had even tried him at the security company for which he worked. No one seemed to know where he was. Fortunately, amid her frustration, she'd thought of checking the phone book for Gruber Coen's address. It seemed too easy, but there was only one Gruber Coen listed for New Orleans. And once she actually saw the house, she knew she'd found the right place. She could *feel* it.

She slowed as she drove past Coen's address. The house appeared to be empty and even more neglected than the Moreaus' current residence. And his yard was the only one on the block without *some* sort of Christmas decoration. But it appeared safe.

Still, Jasmine wasn't about to stop, wasn't about to risk coming into contact with Gruber without some kind of help. She knew what he was capable of. She'd seen him kill a woman, watched him murder her without compunction, just because that woman looked like her.

Finally, the squad car she'd been expecting turned the corner. Breathing a sigh of relief, she parked in front and waited for the officer to get out. He left his car directly across from hers, and they met in the middle of the quiet street.

"Are you the one who called?" Young, clean-cut and not unattractive, he was probably new to the force.

"Yes, I'm Jasmine Stratford."

"Officer Ambrose." He offered his hand as he glanced at the house. "You claim the man who lives here kidnapped your sister sixteen years ago?"

"Yes. I remember his face as if it were yesterday."

He studied her for several seconds, a little too disbelieving—and inexperienced—for her comfort. Did he realize what he was getting into? She'd tried to tell them when she called, but Kozlowski hadn't been there, although he was scheduled to come in later. They'd sent her this rookie instead.

"How long have you been on the force?" she asked.

He was obviously unhappy with the doubt underlying that question. His eyebrows lowered over his clear blue eyes. "Long enough to handle this." He started toward the door, his walk brisk, cocky.

"This man is very dangerous," she warned, trailing after him. "I'm a profiler, so I've met a few criminals in my day, and he's one of the worst I've ever come across."

"In your day?" He smiled, apparently finding her statement humorous. "That makes you sound like my mother. But you can't be that much older than me."

God, he found her attractive and was flirting with her! "Listen." Jasmine stopped him. "This is serious. If your ego's going to get in the way, we're in trouble here."

"I don't have an ego." He tapped his hip. "I have a gun, and I know how to use it."

Sometimes confidence was a good thing, she told herself, as long as it was tempered by caution. And she'd certainly warned him.

When she didn't respond, he nodded at the door. "Let's talk to him. See what he has to say. With any luck he'll confess and give himself up without a fight."

The flippant statement bothered Jasmine more than anything else, but Officer Ambrose had already knocked.

Memories of the day her sister went missing, all the years of searching since, the rift with her parents, and that dream of another woman's murder—it all rushed through her mind like a river. What would Gruber say when he opened the door? Would he lie? Make a run for it? Have a weapon?

She squinted toward the largest of the front windows. He could be watching them right now. If he was, she couldn't tell. The blinds were down and everything seemed quiet, static.

"He's not here," Officer Ambrose said.

"Then we have to wait."

He stared at her as if he thought she might be crazy. "Waiting isn't the answer. We don't even know if he's coming back. Or if he's really dangerous. I'll swing by again in a few hours, keep an eye on the place."

Jasmine wasn't budging. She'd waited sixteen years for this. "No. We have to go in and take a look around. He's the one who killed Adele Fornier. It wasn't Francis Moreau."

"Who's Adele Fornier?"

"A child who was involved in a notorious kidnapping/murder that occurred about four years ago. When you were still in high school," she said dryly.

He grinned. "You have something against younger men."

"I have something against murderers."

"Me, too. But the law says I can't go in without a search warrant."

"Then you'll have to get one," she said, growing impatient.

"I'd like to help you out." He tilted his head closer. "In case you can't tell, I'm trying to win a few points here. But much as I'd love it if you'd go out with me, I still need probable cause for entering this house."

"And as much as I'd like to use your interest to my advantage, I'm already committed," Jasmine said.

His eyebrows arched hopefully. "I didn't see a ring."

"We're not married but…" She hesitated. She'd used this kind of polite untruth before, to deflect unwanted attention. It was the gentlest form of rejection. But she suddenly realized it was true. She was in love with Romain Fornier. She'd come to Louisiana to look for her sister and fallen in love.

"You're together?" he finished because she couldn't find the words to describe her current situation.

She nodded, hoping her first heartbreak wouldn't follow right behind her first love.

He motioned toward the house. "So, when did you see this guy?"

"I haven't seen him yet. I have his picture."

"How do you know it's the same guy?"

"Because I saw him at the door before my sister went missing."

A neighbor across the street came out to see what was going on; no doubt she'd spotted the cop car. "Something wrong over there?" she called.

"We'd like a word with Mr. Coen," Officer Ambrose hollered back. "Do you know where he is or when he might return?"

"No. He's a strange fellow." She threw up her hands and shook her head. "I try to stay away from him."

Officer Ambrose shrugged. "Strange isn't a punishable offense. At least not yet. I'll keep an eye on this place and get back to you."

The frustration of coming up against such a mundane obstacle was almost more than Jasmine could bear. "You can't just…leave." She wanted to add that this man had murdered a woman only two days ago, but she didn't dare undermine her credibility by blaming Gruber for too many crimes at once. *She* knew she was right, but he wouldn't. Also working against her was the fact that this young cop had probably handed out plenty of speeding tickets, but true evil wasn't something he'd likely encountered before. Therefore, he'd have little faith in its existence.

"Your phone number's on the report. I'll call you." All business now that he knew he wasn't going to get a date with her, he started toward his car, but on his way, he bent to pick up a piece of trash lying in the gutter—and then he stopped.

"What is it?" she asked.

He was frowning at the envelope he'd retrieved. "A phone bill."

"Gruber's?"

He turned to face her. "It's addressed to a woman who was reported missing this morning."

Officer Ambrose drew his weapon. After knocking again, he identified himself as a police officer and warned Coen that he was coming in. Then he used a tool from his car to jimmy the lock on the door. Jasmine doubted many cops would've handled the situation so aggressively, but Officer Ambrose had something to prove. He knew she wasn't interested in him, but that didn't stop him from wanting to impress her. He probably had visions of becoming a hero when he found the missing Valerie Stabula.

Unfortunately, if Gruber had Valerie, Jasmine was sure they wouldn't find her in good condition.

"Stay here," he said as he went in. But it was difficult to flex one's power without an audience and, once he felt comfortable that Coen was really gone, he didn't send her back out when she joined him.

"Anything?" she asked.

He put away his gun. "Nothing."

The stench was subtle but unmistakable. If there'd been any question in her mind that she had the right place, the smell alone would've convinced her. "It stinks in here."

"I can smell it."

"You know what it is, don't you?"

"It could be a lot of things," he said.

A lot of things beginning with death…

Jasmine gazed around the threadbare living room. An old green sofa that might've been dragged away from a dump sat in the middle of the floor, in front of a small television on a scratched-up coffee table. There were no pictures on the walls, just a plain clock.

A leaf blower started next door, drowning out the sound of Officer Ambrose's voice as he called the station to report where he was and what he was doing. Jasmine thought of the neighbor out cleaning his lawn. Such an ordinary, innocuous chore, in vivid contrast to her own activity—searching for evidence of murder.

Had Kimberly ever been here? she wondered as she went from room to room. Or had Gruber killed her before he came to New Orleans?

Sexual sadists were often narcissistic. They liked to talk, to brag about their exploits. But Gruber had managed to keep his dark secrets for a long time. Unless Jasmine could uncover some real evidence, chances were good she'd never know.

In the bedroom, the stench of decomposition wasn't quite

as strong, but there were other smells—dust, body odor, cheap cologne. The thought of this man coming into contact with her little sister, or Romain's daughter, turned Jasmine's stomach.

The bathroom was worse than any of the other rooms. A toothbrush lay on the counter, crusted with dried toothpaste. The toilet was disgusting. But poor housekeeping and bad hygiene wasn't incriminating. There had to be *something* here, something that would indicate Adele had once been in this place, or Kimberly, or Valerie. Jasmine knew a jury wouldn't convict a man without more evidence than a brief sighting sixteen years ago. Human memory was simply too fallible.

An antique English oak dresser was the nicest piece of furniture Gruber owned, but the mirror above it was losing its silver. It probably didn't matter, because she doubted he ever used it. He wouldn't like the image that stared back at him. She suspected it was really himself he was trying to destroy.

As Jasmine stared in that blotchy mirror, trying to figure out how to take advantage of the few minutes she had before Ambrose ushered her out, her eyes landed on the reflection of Coen's closet. There was nothing in particular to draw her attention. Except…it was closed.

Even Gruber's drawers had been left hanging open, the clothes spilling out. Why would he bother to shut his closet door?

Moving toward it, Jasmine used a finger to slide the door to one side. At first she saw nothing unusual. A few pairs of pants hanging sloppily on hangers. Some dirty clothes and several shoes on the floor. She almost headed back to the living room to see what Ambrose was doing. But then she noticed something that made the hair on the back of her neck stand up. There were drops of a dark substance, so dark it was almost black, on a pair of tennis shoes.

Holding her breath, she knelt to take a better look.

It was blood. She was sure of it.

She was about to call out to Ambrose when she saw something else. There was more blood on the floor, and the floor had a line in it, a line that…

Carefully, her heart racing, she shoved the shoes and clothes into one corner and discovered a trapdoor.

"Officer Ambrose?"

There was no response. She couldn't hear him anymore, either. Not over the noise of that leaf blower.

Determined to show him what she'd found, she started for the door. But someone blocked her path just as she stepped into the hallway.

"I'm afraid the police officer you brought here is…indisposed," Gruber Coen said. Then he laughed and the light pouring through the windows of the spare bedroom revealed the barrel of a gun pointed at her chest.

Jasmine wasn't answering. Romain had tried her at least ten times. So he left Huff at the coffee shop to go out and search for her. But when he took a quick drive through the neighborhood she'd been planning to visit, he saw no sign of her car. And when he canvassed the neighbors, one lady sent him down to the corner to another woman, who directed him across the street from where the Moreaus had once lived. But the owner of that house, someone named Charmaine, wasn't home.

Where had Jasmine disappeared? Had she learned the name she'd been looking for and gone searching for the man who'd taken her sister?

Surely, she wouldn't do that on her own! But the feeling in the pit of Romain's stomach told him otherwise. She was so obsessed with tracking down her sister he wasn't convinced she'd be as cautious as she should be.

He remembered coming out of the Moreau house to find the truck empty....

"Son of a bitch!" His hands curled into fists, but there was nothing he could do to fight the fear slamming into him. He should never have allowed her to come here alone. Like letting Adele ride her bike around the block, it hadn't seemed dangerous at the time. The Moreaus weren't even living here anymore! But the sense of déjà vu that crept over him was terrifying.

Climbing into his truck, Romain called Huff. The ex-detective had lent Romain a cell phone paid for by the marshals' office in Colorado, since he had a personal one, as well.

"You got her?" Huff said.

"No. She's gone."

Silence. Then Huff barked, "What do you mean?"

"I mean a few people saw her here earlier, but they don't know where she went."

"Have you notified the police?"

"Not yet."

"I'll do it. I have some friends down there who'll get on it right away."

But if Romain couldn't tell them where to look, how were they going to find her? When Adele went missing, they'd chased one lead after another—leads generated by Romain's own media appeals—but found nothing until that picnicker stumbled upon her body at the park. Too late. *Far* too late.

"You don't think she'd contact Black, do you?" Huff asked.

Romain kicked a pebble off the drive and into the street. "She might've gone to him with that picture."

"A dangerous idea."

"We don't *know* he's Peccavi," Romain said, trying to bolster his flagging hope.

"Yes, we do."

Romain's hand tightened on the phone. "What? How—"

"Like I said, I have friends down at the station. Beverly Moreau just called in. She fingered Black. She has proof, and she's ready to talk."

"You're kidding! So…we were right?"

"About everything. Black used to live across the street from the Moreaus. He grew up with Francis, Dustin and Phillip. Makes sense that they'd go into business together, doesn't it?"

It did. It also made sense that Jasmine would go to Black to help her determine the identity of the youth in that picture. She'd probably figured out that he used to live in the neighborhood—but she didn't know he was Peccavi.

"I can't lose another one," Romain muttered.

"What was that?" Huff asked.

"Nothing." Romain walked to the mailbox, then reached in and pulled out a stack of bills that had been delivered that day. Sure enough, they were addressed to a Mr. Doug Black. This was the home of Pearson Black's parents. This was where Jasmine had last been seen. "Where does Pearson live now?"

"Don't go there, Romain. Don't risk it. You know what happened last time, what you did to Moreau. Let me do the job I should've done in the first place," he said. Then he hung up and he wouldn't answer again.

The six-foot-by-nine-foot cement cell was freezing. Jasmine couldn't stop her teeth from chattering. But the low temperature was actually a good thing, or the dead woman on the couch beside her would be in a more advanced stage of decomposition. As it was, she made a gruesome sight. Stiff with rigor mortis, she didn't sag onto the couch as Hollywood might've depicted. Her face was contorted, her hands curled in on themselves and her arms were bent like a Barbie doll's. Her red blood cells had already settled at maximum lividity, which meant she'd been dead for eight to twelve hours, and the putrefaction of her internal organs gave off the worst odor Jasmine had ever smelled. She would've scrambled to the far reaches of her dungeon— anything to get away from her couch partner—except that Gruber Coen had chained one of her feet to a metal ring in the floor and tied her hand to the corpse's so tightly Jasmine's fingers were tingling for want of blood. "Meet my sister," he'd said with a laugh.

If this woman, who had to be Valerie Stabula, was really his sister, Jasmine saw no family resemblance. But it wasn't easy to imagine what she'd once looked like.

After making sure Jasmine couldn't get free, Gruber had turned on the television resting on a small table, pointed to a closet with a portable toilet and told her to make herself at home while he went to take care of "a few details." But even if she needed to use the bathroom, Jasmine couldn't reach it. The chain on her leg was long enough, but she'd have to drag Valerie with her, and she had no intention of even trying.

A clock on the wall ticked more loudly than the TV. Or maybe that was Jasmine's imagination. She was hyper-aware of the passing minutes, which seemed to keep time with the thoughts that ran in one continuous circle: *He'll be back soon. He'll be back and kill me. Or do unspeakable things. He'll be back soon. He'll be back and kill me. Or do unspeakable things...*

Waiting for his return was even more unnerving than knowing she was tied to a corpse and would probably rot here. She couldn't get loose. She'd already worn her ankle raw trying.

"What am I going to do?" she muttered as one program turned into another and another. Since Gruber had taken her keys, she knew he planned to move her rental car. He had to get rid of the police cruiser, too, before someone came searching for it. And he had to dispose of young Officer Ambrose's body. She'd caught a brief glimpse of Ambrose as Gruber had dragged her by the hair to see what she'd "caused." Ambrose had been stabbed in the back of the neck. He hadn't even seen it coming. And the gun that'd made him so confident was now in Gruber's hands.

Although Gruber clearly had a fascination with dead bodies, he didn't try to take Ambrose to his cement dungeon as he had Jasmine. His attitude toward Ambrose's corpse made it clear that he considered it mere garbage, something that would have to be removed. She and Valerie, on the other hand, were somehow more important to him.

Jasmine stared at the walls, wondering how thick they were. Was there any chance someone would hear her if she screamed? She'd been afraid to try until she was sure Gruber had left the house, but it'd been an hour since he'd closed the trapdoor above her. Long enough to get Ambrose out of the house. Long enough to clean up the blood.

If she didn't get help, she was going to die, anyway.

Jasmine's throat grew hoarse as she screamed. Then she listened carefully, hoping to hear a reply. But there was nothing. Just the monotonous voices coming from the TV and the disturbing sound of air escaping Valerie's body as her tissues broke down.

Turning her face from the worsening smell, Jasmine fought the tears that began to roll down her cheeks. She couldn't give up hope. Yet her situation seemed hopeless. Even if Romain came to the house looking for her, he'd never suspect a hidey-hole as elaborate and horrible as this.

Romain couldn't believe it when someone finally answered Jasmine's phone. He'd been pacing the porch of the Blacks' house, waiting for them to come home so they could provide him with some way of reaching Pearson, because Pearson was his only link to Jasmine. All he'd been able to do in the meantime was call her cell. Again and again and again.

"Obviously, you're not going to give up," said a male voice on the other end.

Romain didn't recognize the person he was talking to. "Where's Jasmine?"

"Maybe you'd like to identify yourself before you start making demands."

"Romain Fornier."

"Romain. I guessed as much." The man had stated his name with the familiarity of a friend. "You've caused me more trouble…."

"I've caused *you* trouble?" Romain echoed.

"You're a stubborn man, a fighter. I have to respect that, even if it does make you a pain in the ass. Nice work, what you did to Francis, by the way. Made it so much more convenient for me."

He'd said "Francis," not "Moreau." Whoever it was knew Moreau well. But it wasn't Black. Romain felt certain he would've recognized Black's voice. "I can't take credit for that," he said. "You're the one who set him up, right?"

He was fishing, but it paid off with an immediate confirmation. "That part wasn't so hard."

"Because Peccavi helped you?"

The jovial spirit seemed to drain out of him. "Who told you about Peccavi?"

"I've never been one to reveal my sources."

"You're a dead man, you know that?" he cried. "You don't have twenty-four hours!"

"Then why don't you come and get me?" Romain said, trying to draw his attention away from Jasmine.

A knowing snicker met his response. "Nice try. I have what I want. I have what you want, too. I'll leave you to Peccavi."

"Come on," Romain said. "This is between you and me, right? This is about Adele." And Jasmine. Payment for the past, hope for the future. "I'll give you an address. We'll meet. It'll just be you and me. You have my word."

"And let you do your Rambo bullshit? I know you were a Reconnaissance Marine, Romain. I'm not stupid."

"Feel free to bring a weapon."

There was no answer—but Romain could tell he was tempted. "Come on," he said softly. "Show me what you got."

"I've got Jasmine," the other man said and the phone went dead.

"Shit." Romain's hand shook as he called again, but the effort was pointless. Whoever had answered Jasmine's phone wouldn't pick up a second time. And another call was coming in.

"Hello?"

"Black doesn't have Jasmine," Huff said.

"You found him?"

"Yes. I've got a couple of detectives questioning him right now. Thanks to Beverly Moreau's testimony, I think we can crack the adoption ring."

"What about Jasmine?" Images of the blood on his wall at home floated through Romain's consciousness, adding to the fear and tension already coursing through him.

"He says he hasn't seen her, doesn't know anything about her."

"That's a lie! Make him tell you more."

"Come on down and you can talk to him yourself."

"Where are you?"

Huff rattled off an address that surprised him. "What are you doing in the warehouse district?"

"Black has a second job down by the docks. That's where we finally located him."

No wonder he hadn't been answering. Romain jogged toward his truck. "Do whatever you can to get him to talk. If we don't find her soon, I'm afraid it'll be too late."

*You little chickenshit. I knew you'd back down.*

Valerie wasn't anywhere close, yet Gruber still heard her voice—and chafed at the way he envisioned her looking at him after that conversation with Fornier. She thought he was weak, but he was man enough to kill Romain. He just didn't need to. Peccavi would take care of it.

*You're nothing compared to Romain.*

"That isn't true," he spat. He'd gone to Romain's place, intending to kill him, hadn't he?

*That was when you thought you could surprise him. And stab him in the back, like you did that poor bastard cop.*

"Shut up!"

He'd raised his voice so loudly a solitary woman wearing a yellow rain slicker shortened the leash on her poodle in order to give him a wide berth. He had the impulse to push her and her dog in the river, where he'd dumped the cop's body an hour ago. With the cold, drizzly weather and the late hour, there was no one else around to stop him. But he had too much riding on tonight to take any further risks. He'd abandoned the cruiser across town, caught a bus home and driven Jasmine's rental car here, with the cop's body in the trunk. Now that he'd dragged the corpse to the water and shoved it beneath the pilings of the wharf, all he had to do was ditch Jasmine's car and get another bus home. He was nearly done; there was no need to jeopardize all his hard work.

Curbing his impulse to follow the dog owner and make

her pay for her haughty attitude, he tossed Jasmine's cell phone in the water. He didn't want to hear it ring again, didn't want to be bothered. Especially by Romain Fornier.

But that didn't prevent other calls. His own phone jingled a moment later.

The screen indicated No Caller ID.

"Hello?"

"Do you have her?"

It was Peccavi. Gruber hesitated. If he said yes, Peccavi would get involved, and Gruber wanted to avoid that. He wanted Peccavi to punish Romain for belittling him, for making him feel the lesser man. And he wanted Jasmine to himself. "Not anymore. She's history."

*"Permanently?"* Peccavi clarified. "You're sure?"

"That's not easy to mistake." The last time he'd lied to Peccavi, he'd gone too far with Adele, done some things even he couldn't believe. But she'd been so defiant, so much like her father. It'd be different with Jasmine. Kimberly had been docile and sweet. He'd spent two weeks with her, hadn't even touched her, not in the way he'd wanted to, and yet he'd fallen in love. He'd often regretted that he hadn't found some way to keep her for himself. The older sister wasn't half as sweet.

"What'd you do with the…remains?" Peccavi asked.

Finally able to forget the woman with the dog, Gruber headed up the embankment, away from the path that wound close to the river. "Alligator bait."

He expected Peccavi to be grateful but, if he was, he didn't show it. Where was his gratitude? God, he was getting tired of Peccavi, tired of his demands and conceit.

"We have another problem," Peccavi said.

Gruber's mood darkened. "What is it?"

"Beverly Moreau is talking."

He froze as he reached Jasmine's car. "How do you know?"

"She called the police."

The magnitude of this hit Gruber like a punch to the gut. If Beverly had informed on him, the cops would beat him to his house. They'd probably been there already, trying to figure out what had happened to Officer Ambrose. But without any sign of their missing officer, they'd have no reason to enter. They'd wait until he got home and try to talk to him. Unless someone had sent them there, unless someone gave them reason. "Do we need to get out of town?"

"No, we're okay for now. A friend of mine took the call—a friend who's been hoping to buy a boat," he said.

"Kozlowski?"

"No need to name names."

Gruber let go of the breath he'd been holding. Of course it was Kozlowski. They'd bribed him before. "But do you think she's told anyone else?"

"No one. He promised he'd be in touch, told her not to breathe a word to anyone else or it could get back to me."

"Do you want me to pay her a visit and shut her up?" Gruber realized this would require considerable time, but providing they were safe from the police, Jasmine wasn't going anywhere. He'd never liked Beverly, anyway. He'd always known she'd sell him out in a heartbeat if she had the chance. She cared only about Phil and Dusty, had never really included him the way her husband had tried to.

"That's exactly what I want you to do. As soon as possible. Then I have something I want to give you."

"What is it?"

"A bonus," he said. "Something you really deserve."

Finally, he was getting the recognition he should've had years ago. With a smile, Gruber started the engine and switched on his windshield wipers. "I'm leaving now."

"Let me know when it's done."

"What about Fornier?"

"What about him?"

The windshield wipers moved rhythmically as Gruber pulled into the street. "He'll come after the Stratford woman. We have to get rid of him."

"You don't have to worry about Romain. I'll take care of him and call you later."

# 23

When Romain arrived at the address Huff had given him, he parked in an alley beneath the narrow eaves of a tin building. He was about to climb out when the phone Huff had lent him rang.

Anxious for any word from Jasmine, he stayed where he was to avoid the rain and answered it immediately. "Hello?"

"Mr. Fornier?"

It was a woman, the voice unfamiliar to him. "Yes?"

"This is Mrs. Black. You left your number wedged in the crack of my screen door and asked me to call you about the young lady who came by earlier."

Pearson Black's mother. "Yes. Thank you for calling. That young lady's gone missing, Mrs. Black. It's very important that I find her as soon as possible. Do you have any idea where she might've gone after speaking with you?"

"She was asking about a childhood friend of Pearson's—a Gruber Coen."

Gruber Coen. It was a name Romain had never heard before. "He was the teenager in that picture with Milo Moreau?"

"That's right."

Rain beaded on the windshield, making it difficult to see

the warehouse that was his destination. "Can you tell me where this Gruber lives?"

"I'm afraid not. But Pearson can. We just talked about it at dinner."

Romain rocked back in surprise. "Tonight?"

"Yes. I left the restaurant maybe fifteen minutes ago. That's where I've been."

But she couldn't have been with Pearson *that* recently. Pearson was with Huff. Huff had said so.

Or Huff was lying....

An uneasy foreboding prickled Romain's skin. "Can I reach your son by phone right now?" he asked.

"You should be able to. He's probably getting ready for work—he works nights—but I have his cell number."

Romain thanked her and dialed the number she gave him. "Pearson?" he said as soon as he heard the other man pick up.

"Who's this?" came the response.

It was Black, all right. Romain would've recognized that voice anywhere. "It's Romain Fornier."

"What do you want with me?"

They were enemies. Romain had blamed Black for sabotaging the prosecution of his daughter's killer, but he was no longer sure Black's motivation had been so reprehensible. "Where are you?"

"On my way to work."

"Have you heard from Alvin Huff?"

"Why would I ever hear from Alvin Huff?"

Why, indeed. Romain's heart was now lodged in his throat. "Can you tell me where to find Jasmine Stratford?"

*"Me?"* The question seemed to take Pearson aback. "I

missed several of her calls earlier, while I was sleeping. And I tried to call her back before I met my mom. But I kept getting her voice mail. Is something wrong?"

Something was definitely wrong.

In his mind's eye, Romain kept seeing that blanket Huff had brought to the restaurant. *I'm going to have it tested for genetic material, but that will take a while. The fiber evidence was easier. It required only a microscope... You're sure it's a match?... Positive.*

Romain no longer believed it. That blanket had been used to manipulate him, to convince him. That was all. There was no guarantee Adele had ever come into contact with it. Huff could've gotten it anywhere.

A deep sense of betrayal throbbed through his blood as he started his truck. He'd trusted Huff. Through the darkest sorrow of his life, he'd looked to Huff for resolution. He'd been a detective, the one person who was supposed to make sure Romain received justice. And Huff had misled him and manipulated the situation instead.

"She was asking about Gruber Coen," he told Black.

"Gruber's a pathetic bastard. What does she want with him?"

Light spilled into the alley as a door opened in the warehouse and Huff poked his head out. He must've heard Romain pull up and was wondering why he hadn't come in. Romain knew he should get the hell out—now. This was a setup. Huff had brought him here, and it wasn't difficult to figure out why.

But Romain didn't move. He stared at the man he finally knew to be his enemy, desperately wanting to obtain the justice he'd been denied. If not for Huff—or Peccavi or whatever he called himself—it was possible Adele would never have been kidnapped.

But there was one thing more important to him than revenge. And that was Jasmine. Throwing the transmission into Reverse, Romain floored the gas pedal. He rocketed back until he reached the road that would lead him out of the maze of buildings, then shifted into Drive and peeled out as he rounded the corner.

"Romain?" Black prompted when Romain didn't respond. "What does she want with Gruber?"

This section of town was deserted. The dark, empty warehouses flew past him as he sped toward the freeway. "He kidnapped her sister sixteen years ago."

Silence. Then Black said, "Not Gruber. He doesn't have the guts to do something like that."

"She saw his face. She knows it was him. And I'm afraid she went looking for him. Can you tell me where he lives?"

"I don't know the address. But I stopped by last summer to invite him to a Fourth-of-July block party my mother was sponsoring on our old street. I can tell you how to get there."

Romain memorized the directions and was about to hang up when his call-waiting beeped. Huff was trying to get hold of him.

Tempted to answer, to let the man he'd once considered a friend know the game was up, Romain's finger moved to the flash button. But he didn't push it. He couldn't allow himself even that much satisfaction. Until Jasmine was safe, he'd be smarter to keep Huff guessing.

When Huff's call went to voice mail, he contacted the police and told them everything he knew. He had no idea what they'd do with it. The man who took down the information treated it like he probably treated every other unsubstantiated report. "We'll look into it," he said and hung up.

That unimpassioned response made Romain even more aware of the fact that he could be Jasmine's only chance.

If it wasn't already too late.

When the trapdoor at the top of the stairs popped open, Jasmine came instantly awake. Knowing that she needed to conserve her strength so she could think clearly, plan well and be ready for any opportunity to escape, she'd been trying to rest and, after several hours of Gruber's absence, had managed to fall sleep. But it'd been a restless sleep, filled with nightmares of stinking, rotting cadavers.

Now her eye sockets felt like they were full of sand and her body was tense and sore. She was careful not to move the leg shackled to the floor. She'd bloodied her ankle trying to get free and the slightest touch of that iron cuff against her skin caused the most excruciating pain.

"Hurry. We've got to hurry," Gruber muttered to himself as he descended the stairs.

Jasmine had expected him to come back tired and requiring sleep. It was no small job to dispose of a body and two cars. According to the clock, it was after midnight. But if he was exhausted, he was far too agitated to show it. Something had happened.

"What is it?" she asked. As much as she'd dreaded his return, she'd actually been more frightened that he wouldn't come back. He was her only ticket out of the cement box. Even if Romain or the police came searching for her, she couldn't imagine they'd look closely enough to find the trapdoor beneath all the dirty clothes in the bedroom. Who'd ever dream such a room existed here? It was more plausible that they'd rush through the house, find it empty and move on. Without Gruber, she'd die an agonizingly slow death of dehydration and starvation tied to a corpse that was decomposing by the minute.

Jasmine wasn't sure her other alternatives were any better, but she had a greater chance of getting free if he took her out of the cement room.

"Gruber?"

He didn't respond. He carried a carving knife, which made her nauseous with fear—until he used it to begin sawing through the ropes attaching her to his sister's lifeless form.

Closing her eyes, Jasmine turned her face away. He was in too much of a hurry to be careful with that blade. She was afraid he might get frustrated and simply hack off her arm.

"Come on," he said. "Beverly's gone. Beverly and Phil and Dustin. They're *all* gone. Even the kids are gone. We gotta go before it's too late."

He was still talking to himself and struggling with the thick rope. "The Moreaus have left town?" she asked.

Straightening, he blinked at her as if he'd forgotten she was alive. "How do you know? Did you put Beverly up to this? Are you responsible?" he demanded.

The ropes were looser, but Jasmine's hand wasn't quite free. He loomed over her, his grip tight on the handle of that knife, which was large and jagged and threatening—as if the wild gleam in his eyes wasn't threatening enough. She couldn't help remembering the woman he'd slashed to death only a few days ago. She'd experienced that as though it had happened to her, and the prospect of a repeat performance caused a tremor of fear she couldn't control. She had to be careful. He was in a volatile state, unpredictable and dangerous. "I don't know what you're talking about," she said as innocently as possible.

He muttered some complaint to himself, but he finished with the rope and set the knife on top of the TV.

Once her hand was free, she rubbed it, hoping to bring back some feeling, and considered trying to reach that weapon. Could she get hold of it in time? Did she have the strength to wield it against him? The longer she remained in Gruber's control, the less chance she had of survival. But one attempt might be all she had. She had to choose her moment wisely.

Pulling a key from his pocket, he bent over her ankle. But when he saw the torn flesh and the dried blood, such hatred and contempt came over his face that Jasmine couldn't breathe. "Look at this," he ground out. "You're as foolish and stubborn as I thought. Much more like Adele than your sister."

*Your sister...* Gooseflesh rose on Jasmine's arms. What must Kimberly and Adele have suffered at this man's hands? Had they been kept in a cement cell like this one? If so, for how long? And what'd happened to Kimberly in the end?

The sight of Valerie didn't leave Jasmine much hope, but she'd waited sixteen years for the opportunity to ask. And she knew she needed to keep him occupied. "Where is Kimberly? Can you tell me that?"

"I would've told you if not for this." He waved at the damage to her ankle, the key still in his hand. "Resistance brings punishment. You'll have to learn. You and Beverly will both have to learn. When I find her she's dead. Dead, dead, dead. She needs to be punished." His eyes went to the knife. "*You* need to be punished."

"I'm new to this, remember?" she said, trying to forestall him. It'd be easier for him to travel without her, and she knew it. The knife was right there, and she was still chained by her foot. It'd take only one well-aimed thrust. "I haven't been notified of the rules yet. How can you get mad at me for doing something you don't like if you didn't tell me not to do it?"

His cell phone rang, but he ignored it. "My service sucks down in this hole," he said, distracted from whatever he'd been considering a moment before. "What does he expect? That I should be at his beck and call forever?" he asked her. "He knows to run. He knows to leave. I warned him. That's all he can ask of me."

"That's all anyone can ask," she agreed, hoping to convince him that she was on his side. She had to develop a rapport with Gruber, get him to relax and lower his guard. No matter what, she couldn't show the fear that charged every cell in her body. Fear would relegate her to a victim's position, would provoke the same kind of behavior he'd shown to other victims. Sexual sadists didn't necessarily like the act of inflicting pain—it was the *suffering* that satisfied them. And fear was part of that suffering. She had to convince him she was different, do something to change the natural course of this encounter.

"Women can't be trusted," he said.

"*Some* women can't be trusted." She shrugged. "But some men can't be trusted, either."

He tilted his head as if weighing her response.

"What?" she said. "You disagree?"

Picking up the knife, he laid it against her throat. Instinctively, she wanted to grab his arm or try to protect herself. But she knew that would be the worst thing she could do. She'd experienced it with that woman he'd attacked after coming through the window. Her feeble attempts to preserve her own life had enraged him more than anything.

Forcing herself to let the tension drain out of her body, Jasmine remained as pliable and unconcerned as possible as she gazed up at him.

"I could kill you right here. I could cut your throat and watch you bleed to death right in front of me!" he shouted when he didn't get the reaction he'd expected.

The muscles in her arms twitched. But she didn't move. If she gave in to what came most naturally, she'd be signing her own death warrant. "We all gotta go someday, don't we?" She met his eyes, refusing to flinch or glance away.

Confusion darkened his face. "You don't care?"

*Submission. Total submission.* "Of course I care. But what's the point of fighting?" Especially when it was his ability to subdue her that fed his desire to kill her in the first place.

He pulled the knife away and waved it toward the moldering Valerie. "I did that. I killed her. *My own sister.*"

Despite her best efforts to control it, Jasmine's body was beginning to tremble. She prayed he wouldn't notice. "She must've deserved it. But you have no reason to kill me. Anyway, you're in such a hurry you wouldn't even have time to enjoy it."

Obviously surprised by her reaction, he backed up, lowered the hand with the knife and ultimately nodded. "That's right. We have to go."

Jasmine wasn't sure she could force her legs to carry her. But once he finally removed that cuff, she was eager to get out of the cement room and leave the smell and constant reminder of Valerie behind her. When he hauled her up by the shirtfront, she somehow kept her feet beneath her and walked. But she was constantly aware of the knife he still held and the fact that he was within striking distance should she try to make a break for it.

He forced her to wait until he ascended the stairs, poked his head through the hole and listened. Then he waved her toward him and climbed out ahead.

The air in the bedroom was as stale as before, but it was so much better than the stench of Valerie's body, Jasmine couldn't help taking a deep breath. "Where are we going?" she asked.

"Somewhere you can give me what I want," he said. "Any way I want it."

He watched her closely to see if she'd protest, but she managed another shrug. "Whatever," she said and forced herself to touch his arm. Her skin crawled at the contact, her stomach revolted, but it was important that he believe she wasn't frightened or repulsed. That she thought he was no different than anyone else. "If I do, and you're happy with how I've performed, will you tell me about Kimberly?"

Her question didn't seem to register, but her touch did. "What are you doing?" he asked, sounding panicked.

"Nothing. I'm just asking if you'll tell me about Kimberly if I behave. That's all."

"Maybe." Softening, he covered her hand almost lovingly with his. Then, in an abrupt change of mood, he grabbed her, twisting her arm cruelly as he held her halfway out of the trapdoor and pointed the knife at her chest. "You think you're so smart. You think you know me, but you don't. If you make *one* wrong move, I'll butcher you. I'll cut your heart out and keep it in my freezer. Do you understand?"

The knife pierced Jasmine's left breast. *Pretend it's not there. Don't get rattled.* "I understand," she said.

He got out and dragged her the last two steps, lifting her easily to her feet with one hand. He was strong, stronger than she'd expected for such a frumpy middle-aged man, and he didn't release her. He kept firm hold of her and the knife.

"Can I help you pack?" Jasmine asked. "If we'll be gone for a while, you might want to take some of your things."

"Shut up and get a move on. We're out of here."

Jasmine searched desperately for other ways to detain him. There had to be a reason he was in such a hurry. Were the cops coming? "We'd only need a few minutes to collect some clothes and stuff. Or are we coming back?"

"If you don't shut up, you won't be going anywhere. You'll die right here!" He dragged her into the living room—and then he froze. He was staring at the front door, which was standing open.

"Someone's here," he whispered. He brought the knife forward. In a moment that seemed to progress in slow motion, Jasmine knew this was it. Gruber was calling it quits. He was going to kill her and run.

Then the floor creaked behind them and just when she thought that knife would slit her throat, Gruber's hand dropped.

She screamed and turned in time to see the point of a long

knife go through *his* chest instead of her own and nearly crumpled to her knees. She would have, if not for the strong arms that went around her.

"It's okay. I've got you," Romain murmured in her ear. "Thank God, I've got you."

She was crying and kissing him and telling him she loved him when the blast of a gun momentarily deafened her. She felt the bullet whiz past her shoulder, felt Romain jerk as it made impact with his body. The chest that had sheltered her, that had seemed so indestructible only a moment before was suddenly all too vulnerable as the motion threw him back. He stumbled into a wall, gasped and fell.

"No!" Jasmine screamed and turned in time to see Detective Huff aim his gun at her. His expression revealed no emotion beyond determination. He was detached, doing a job, cleaning up details.

She dove for the bedroom as the blast went off. She fully expected to be hit. But she felt no pain. She could think only of Romain, bleeding from the chest. Had the bullet entered his heart? Was he already dead?

Huff's next shot hit Jasmine in the leg. Her foot felt as if it were on fire, but she managed to grab the knife Gruber had dropped as she rolled to the side, out of the doorway and out of sight.

She heard Huff curse and walk purposefully toward her. She also heard Romain trying to distract him. "Over… here…you…son of a bitch," he groaned, and Jasmine knew she had about three seconds before he shot Romain again.

Jumping to her feet, she ignored the tremendous pain that seared her leg and used the door frame to slingshot herself forward. The sudden movement took Huff by surprise. She saw it in his eyes. He'd expected her to scramble for cover; he hadn't expected a bold frontal attack.

He turned the gun at the last second, but it was too late. She was already hacking at him—striking him, too, but she didn't know where. Desperation and adrenaline and white-hot anger sustained her. She would not lose Romain, would not allow Peccavi to cost them any more.

It wasn't until Huff fell that she realized she'd stabbed him in the neck. Blood poured from the wound like a waterfall. Several other cuts bled, too, but they were superficial. She'd gotten lucky. If one of her wild blows hadn't landed where it did, *she* would've been the one lying on the floor.

"You *have* sinned," she said vehemently, shaking from reaction. And then Pearson Black arrived with the police.

A late-morning sun slanted through the crack in the drapes as Jasmine sat by Romain's hospital bed, listening to the rhythmic beep of his heart monitor. A large white bandage encircled his chest, tubes ran all over his body, and his usually tanned and healthy-looking skin was pale beneath the fluorescent lights of the hospital room. The emergency doctor had given him six pints of blood and spent three hours in surgery, removing the bullet, which had lodged beneath his shoulder blade. Now it was a waiting game to see if he'd recover. Huff had missed Romain's heart by a fraction of a centimeter, and Romain had nearly bled to death in the ambulance.

"Hey, how're you doing?"

Jasmine turned to see Pearson in the doorway, holding two coffees in foam cups.

"I'm okay," she murmured. The bullet she'd taken had

only grazed her leg. She had a nice bandage to show for it. But she'd lied about being okay. She'd never been more terrified or worried in her life than she was right now, waiting to see whether Romain would live.

"He'll be fine. The doctors are hopeful, aren't they?"

"They aren't making any promises."

"They never make promises. They're a cagey lot. But your man's strong. He'll pull through."

*Her man.* She didn't know if Romain felt the same way about her that she did about him, but it was a lost cause to pretend he wasn't the most important thing in the world to her. "I hope so."

"Huff's dead."

Jasmine nodded. She'd already heard. "Has anyone located Mrs. Moreau?"

"She called me."

"Wasn't she afraid you might turn her in?"

"That's why she called. She wants to turn herself in. And she needed my help to make sure that a boy in her keeping made it back to his parents."

"She had a child with her?"

"She took him before Huff could get him to adoptive parents and collect yet another paycheck."

"How'd she get involved with Huff in the first place?" Jasmine asked. "She just…doesn't seem the type."

"Huff busted Gruber Coen for 'performing lewd acts' at a porn theater ten years ago, found out he was a truck driver for a lighting company and recruited him for his little sideline business. Gruber got Francis involved, and when Dustin's medical bills began to mount up, Francis got his mother a job working for Huff. Soon Phillip was part of the ring, too. As long as they didn't ask too many questions, it probably didn't seem like a big deal to look after a few kids every night. And as the truth of what was really happening became more obvious, Beverly was in too deep to back out." He shoved his hands into his pockets. "That guy you found in the basement, Jack Lewis?"

"Yeah."

"He used to work for Huff. He tried to get out and Huff shot him right there in Francis's house. That taught them all a very powerful lesson."

"That Huff wouldn't be crossed."

"Exactly."

"How could Huff keep that many people busy?"

"It was a pretty big operation. Jack and a man named Roger were scouts. Huff paid for them to travel around and troll for kids. Other guys, like Gruber, Francis and Phillip, he sent to nab them once they'd been located. Bev and another woman—I can't remember her name—helped out at the transfer house, taking care of the kids until they could be placed. He even had some prostitutes in his employ and they put out the word that he'd pay big bucks for a baby."

"And he could afford all these people?"

"Some of them had outside jobs, like Francis, who was a delivery man, and Jack, who shuttled kids back and forth to after-school care. Others were strictly at his disposal, like Gruber—who quit his job driving a truck—and Phillip."

"What got Huff involved in the first place?" she asked, trying to grasp the extent of Huff's activities.

"His uncle's an attorney. Bev thinks he gave Huff the idea, even threw him a few leads."

"That's how Huff came by his prospective clients? From leads?"

"Bev said Huff mentioned various attorneys who referred clients to him—people who didn't qualify to adopt through legitimate agencies or wanted something very specific. Or didn't want to wait the usual length of time it takes to get a child."

"He had people putting in orders for certain types of children?" she asked in astonishment.

"That's where he made the big bucks."

Jasmine shook her head. "What'd he do with all his money?"

"His wife isn't sure, but she thinks he was putting it in offshore accounts for when he retired."

"Was his wife aware of what her husband was doing?"

"Not at all. She's devastated. She found out he was planning to dump her, which makes it even worse."

Jasmine couldn't even imagine what that kind of betrayal would feel like. "What's she going to do?"

"What can she do? She'll muddle through the best she can and see where her finances are when this is all over. She taught school for years. Maybe she'll have to go back to it."

Jasmine fiddled with the edge of the sheet on Romain's bed. "What gets me is that Huff had children of his own, didn't he?"

"Two grown boys."

"How sad. They must be in total shock."

"I'm sure they are. But you need to get some sleep," Pearson said.

"I owe you an apology," she told him. "I thought *you* were the bad guy."

"Huff had the money to buy a lot of loyalty down at the station. It was easy for them to make me look like the bad guy. It was also easy for them to get rid of me."

"Kozlowski wasn't one of them, was he?"

"Yes. That's the only man I know for sure, because he took Beverly's call, yet he never filed a report."

Jasmine wondered what Kozlowski would've done if he'd been on duty when she'd tried to contact him after finding Gruber Coen's address. Had she phoned in just a few hours later, she probably would've spoken to the sergeant; she'd asked for him. Then he would have alerted Huff, and she would've died instead of the poor rookie. "Are you going to try and get back on the force?"

"I'd like to. After this, there'll certainly be enough openings. And I've been humbled, grown up a lot. I hope they'll take me."

"It'd beat working nights in a parking lot," she said with a smile.

"The chief is really trying to clean up the place. I think he'll be willing to give me a second chance. He knows I didn't tamper with the evidence on that case like Huff's cronies said I did. That was just Huff's way of getting me out of the picture."

The hand holding the coffee he'd brought her was beginning to feel warm, which began to ease the terrible tension inside her. "I'm sorry that happened."

"I take some responsibility for it. I shouldn't have written that blog. Showing off like that allowed Huff to make me look like some kind of freak, so the whole evidence thing was easier to believe."

Jasmine agreed that he'd helped them by writing what he had. "Why'd you do it?"

"I'm fascinated by the criminal mind, by deviant behavior." He took a sip of his coffee. "I want to write a book someday."

"You should do that."

"We'll see how it goes." He pulled an envelope from his pocket. "I have something for you."

Surprised, Jasmine shifted her chair away from the bed. "What is it?"

"Something Bev asked me to give you." He handed it to her, and she saw her name written in a small flowing script. Inside, she found a letter.

Kimberly Lauren Stratford was adopted by Mr. and Mrs. Joseph William Glen of Charlottesville, Virginia, fifteen years ago, after six months in the transfer house. I cared for her myself. She was a good girl, a mild-mannered child who was told she'd been brought to an orphanage because her original family had been killed in a car accident. She asked about you often, insisted you couldn't have been in the car, but with repetition, she began to believe it was true. At such a young age, she knew nothing but what adults told her, and we remained consistent in this regard so she'd be happy in her new situation. I don't pretend to be proud of my actions. I don't excuse them, either. It's time you knew. As far as I'm aware, she's still very much alive.

*Alive!* Tears filled Jasmine's eyes at this last line. Gruber hadn't killed her sister as he had Adele. Kimberly had been adopted into another family, a family in Virginia. She'd be twenty-four years old now. Had she graduated from college? Married and started a family?

Would she want to know that her old family still existed?

A movement in the bed drew Jasmine's attention, and she watched, breathless, as Romain opened his eyes. "There you are," he whispered, his voice weak but clear.

Jasmine set the letter aside. "How are you feeling?"

"Like I've been shot." A half smile curved his lips.

"You'll be okay," she told him and squeezed his hand.

"I will be now that I know you're safe."

His eyelids drifted closed again, and Jasmine turned to Pearson Black, who stood at the foot of the bed. "Thank you for bringing me this," she said, gesturing to the letter.

"Are you going to look her up? Your sister, I mean?"

"I don't know. I'd like to—but I don't want to bother her if she'd be happier as she is."

"A lot's happened. A lot of time has gone by. I don't envy you the decision." He patted her shoulder. "Good luck," he said and left.

As the door closed behind him, Jasmine glanced at the television hanging over Romain's bed. The volume was on low, but now that Pearson was gone, it was so quiet in the room she could hear a news announcer giving the top stories of the day. Gruber Coen's picture flashed across the screen, and Jasmine listened more intently.

"...house contained a freezer, in which police discovered frozen body parts from at least four different victims. Not all of these victims have been identified, but Valerie Stabula, the suspect's sister, was found dead in a concrete room beneath the master bedroom. This cell contained a television and a portable toilet. Although the police don't yet know how many victims Gruber Coen tortured and murdered, it's clear that he wasn't the man his neighbors knew as quiet and harmless…"

"Quiet and harmless," Jasmine murmured and suddenly felt an irrational urge to laugh.

# Epilogue

"Are you going up?" Romain parked the truck and gave Jasmine's shoulders a reassuring squeeze. In the three weeks he'd been out of the hospital, the color had returned to his face. The doctors said he should suffer no lasting effects from the shooting. They credited a strong constitution, but Jasmine knew his recovery had more to do with the fact that he was finally at peace with himself. The man who'd murdered Adele was dead; Romain had killed him in order to save Jasmine. But he hadn't killed Moreau. On the basis of the news footage, Jasmine's contact at the FBI had confirmed what Romain's sister had always believed. Huff was the one who'd shot Moreau. Jasmine didn't know for sure—no one did since Huff wasn't around to explain— but she thought he'd done it to put an end to the questions and probing that Moreau's shocking release would generate. The attention threatened his adoption ring. Getting rid of Moreau also satisfied Romain, who wasn't likely to give up until he'd obtained justice. Huff had put closure—false closure—on something that was far from over, and Romain had taken the blame. It was perfect and it would've worked, if not for that package Gruber Coen had sent Jasmine.

"Jaz?" Romain prompted when she didn't reach for the door handle. "Aren't you going to the door?"

"I don't know." According to Beverly Moreau, Kimberly's new name was Lisa Marie Glen. Armed with this information, Jasmine had been able to locate Lisa in Virginia, where her adoptive parents lived in a five-million-dollar mansion. Kimberly no longer lived there, but her own place was pretty impressive, Jasmine thought as she took in the Bostonian flavor of her sister's small cottage. Ralph Lauren could've designed this house. Blue and white and nautical, it peeked out from behind an arched trellis flanked by rose bushes.

"This is the moment you've been waiting for," Romain said.

But now that she'd found Kimberly, she couldn't decide whether or not to ring the bell. She was plagued by too many questions, the most disturbing of which always began with *why*. Why had her sister apparently accepted the story she'd been told? Why had she let go and never looked back? She'd *known* Jasmine was home when Gruber Coen came to the house. How could she have allowed Peccavi and the others to convince her that her real family was dead, to create a whole new identity for her?

"Come on," Romain coaxed. "At least say hello. You tossed and turned all night. I know you won't be satisfied until you see her."

A flagstone path bisected a garden that was beautiful even in February and led to the arched wooden door of the house—tempting and yet, in its own way, daunting. "Maybe she'd rather not hear from me."

"Or maybe you're hurt and angry because she's been living what appears to be a relatively normal life and never made any effort to contact you."

He'd said what Jasmine had been trying not to face, but it was true. She knew it was small-minded, that she had no right to feel rejected. But she'd always imagined this meeting as some kind of rescue. She'd prayed and worked tirelessly, held on to hope even after most people would've given up. All because she was sure Kimberly needed someone to help her escape a man like Gruber Coen. Never did she consider that her sister could be happy. Or better off without her original family. That was a completely foreign concept.

"People adapt, Jaz. You know that."

Of course she knew. They'd discussed the psychological explanation for such behavior. It wasn't unusual for kidnap victims to feel some loyalty to their captors. But the personal side of the situation still tripped her up. Even if Kimberly, as a child, had accepted that her family was dead, hadn't she grown curious in later years, remembered snatches of her early childhood and wondered? Maybe she hadn't seen the episode of *America's Most Wanted,* in which Jasmine had asked for information related to her disappearance. Then again, it was possible she'd seen it and chosen not to respond.

"It's just so hard to believe she's alive and well."

"Everyone can use another friend," he said. "You're not here to take away what she's already got. You're here to let her know you never stopped loving her. How can that hurt?"

There were all kinds of answers to that question. Her sudden appearance in Kimberly's life could cause problems between Kimberly and her adoptive family. It could stir up bad memories. It could create confusion and hurt where there was none. "Relationships are very complex things," she murmured.

Tucking her hair behind her ear, Romain waited until she met his steady gaze. "Maybe that would be true with anyone else. But you're special, Jaz. You're someone she's going to want to know."

The lump that rose in Jasmine's throat made it difficult to respond. Romain smiled as he ran a thumb down the line of her jaw. "Come on. We want her to be in our wedding, don't we?"

Jasmine wanted that more than anything. As much as she loved Romain, it'd been a difficult decision to leave Sacramento and The Last Stand and move to Louisiana. Especially when she wasn't sure if her plan to do private consulting would work. She could use another friend, even if that friend lived as far away as Skye and Sheridan. Better yet if that friend was a sister. *Her* sister.

"But it's not just me. It's my mom and dad and…"

"And there's time for that. You haven't even told them yet."

She had to know, first of all, if Kimberly *wanted* to be found. But, if so, she believed the wedding could be the beginning of many wonderful things—healing for Romain's family, resolution for her own, future children.

"Should I go up to the door with you?" he asked.

He'd been planning to wait in the car. He'd told her he wanted to give her privacy to deal with all the emotions, and she still felt she needed that.

"No, I'll go," she said and climbed out.

The distance from the car to Kimberly's front door felt like miles. Jasmine's heart pounded the entire way, and only grew louder as she reached the stoop. There, she could see beautiful urns and vases filled with greenery and flowers. Wind chimes tinkled in the chill air, sounding beautiful but slightly melancholy.

Whatever happened now, this was the end of her quest. She'd found the sister she'd lost.

Queasy with nerves, she raised her hand to knock. She halfway hoped Kimberly wouldn't be home. Then she could put this moment off a little longer. But she'd seen the BMW convertible in the drive and knew that Kimberly would open the door.

Sure enough it swung wide almost immediately and Jasmine faced her baby sister—at twenty-four years old. Where Jasmine had taken after their mother, except for her eyes, Kimberly resembled their father. At least five-eight, she had dark hair, but it wasn't nearly as dark as Jasmine's. Her eyes were brown instead of blue.

Several seconds passed as they stared at each other, and the tears Jasmine had been fighting since she drove up began to stream down her cheeks.

"Do I know you from somewhere?" Kimberly asked in a confused voice.

Jasmine wasn't sure how to answer. She still wasn't convinced Kimberly would want any connection to her past. But she had to give her little sister the opportunity to make that decision. Their mother and father had a stake in this, too. It wasn't something Jasmine could decide on her own.

"Yes," she said. "You know me. But it's been a very long time and you might've forgotten. My name's Jasmine Stratford. I was once your big sister."

Kimberly's mouth sagged open, and she began to blink rapidly as tears filled her eyes, too.

"How'd you find me?" she whispered.

"It wasn't easy," Jasmine replied with a shaky smile. "I've been searching for sixteen years."

Now was the moment of truth. Swallowing hard, Jasmine

waited for her younger sister to come to grips with the surprise—and was surprised herself when Kimberly pulled her into a tight embrace.

It was several seconds before either of them could speak. Finally, Kimberly stepped back and looked at Jasmine. "I thought I'd never see you again," she said. "They told me you were dead."

"And you believed them?" Jasmine hoped she didn't sound too accusatory, but it was difficult to hide her pain.

"Not completely," her sister admitted. "But I knew that my mother, my *new* mother," she clarified, "wouldn't like it. I'm their only child. It...it would've left them with nothing. And I meant so much to them."

"Were you happy, then?"

"For the most part. I knew I was lucky to have the parents I did. When you've already lost one family, you're pretty terrified of losing another. And by the time I was older and could do something about what had happened, I wasn't convinced I could incorporate the past into my present life, even if I could reconnect with it." She hesitated. "Do you understand?" she asked tentatively.

"I do." Jasmine battled her disappointment with a forced smile. "I'm not here to make your life harder, Kimberly."

"Kimberly..." she said softly. "That isn't even my name anymore."

Jasmine couldn't imagine how confusing and difficult this had to be for her sister, and decided to back off and give her a chance to get used to the shock. "It must be really odd to hear it again."

Her sister's eyes grew troubled. "My old parents, are they still alive?"

"Alive, but not entirely the same." Jasmine couldn't help

the somber note that crept into her voice. "Like the rest of us."

"Where are they now?"

"Mom still lives in Ohio, where we were born. Dad lives in Alabama."

She winced as if Jasmine had just jabbed her with something sharp. "They're not together anymore?"

"No. Losing you…it was hard on them."

"I—I don't know how to react." She ran her hands up and down her thighs, obviously agitated. "I…I never thought I'd see you—or them—again."

"I know." She paused. "I just… I wanted to make sure you don't need us. And to tell you—" the lump in her throat swelled again, nearly choking her "—how sorry I am that I wasn't a better babysitter."

Tears slipped down Kimberly's cheeks as she reached out and squeezed Jasmine's hand. "I'm okay. Now. The man who took me frightened me, but he didn't…you know, molest me. I think he couldn't decide whether to turn me over to his boss, which he eventually did. Then there was a nice older boy, and things got easier when I arrived in my new home."

"I'm glad." There was so much more Jasmine wanted to know, so much to say. But Kimberly was still too shocked to invite her in.

Deciding to give her a chance to absorb everything, Jasmine handed her a business card with her new cell number written on the back. "In case you decide you can combine your past with your present, after all."

Kimberly glanced down at it. "The Last Stand, Victims' Support and Assistance Nonprofit Organization," she read. "You work at this place? In California?"

"I did until I got engaged a couple of weeks ago. I'm moving to New Orleans, where my fiancé lives." Unable to resist, Jasmine gave her sister another quick hug. "Be happy," she said and started back to the car.

"Jasmine?"

At the sound of Kimberly's voice, Jasmine paused beneath the trellis and turned back. "Yes?" she said hopefully.

"When's the wedding?"

"March twenty-sixth."

"I'll give you a call." She smiled. "I'd like to be there."

"It'll be okay for you to do that?"

"I'd like to get to know you, and to see Mom and Dad again. Maybe my other parents can adjust. Maybe we all can," she said. "With time."

Jasmine returned to the car to find Romain leaning against it, arms folded. "So…how'd it go?" he asked, tilting his head to study her expression.

A smile rose up from somewhere deep within. "She's coming to the wedding. It's not a guarantee that we'll be the kind of sisters we would've been. But she's not opposed to a relationship. And I know she's healthy and doing well."

"That's enough?" He searched her face.

"It's a beginning—and that's all I can ask," she said, and he wiped away her tears.

\* \* \* \* \*

*Turn the page for an intriguing excerpt
from WATCH ME, the third book in
Brenda Novak's stunning new series about
the women of The Last Stand.
In WATCH ME, Sheridan Kohl returns
to her hometown—and her past.
She still blames herself for a death that
happened there when she was a teenager.
A death at the hands of an unknown assailant...
But as you'll discover, Sheridan finds more than
a mystery waiting for her in Tennessee.
WATCH ME is available from MIRA Books
in August 2008.*

# 1

Was he gone?

Sheridan Kohl lay in a heap on the ground, her clothes, her cheek, the entire left side of her body, wet from the moist earth. The taste of her own blood sat bitter on her tongue, but the fecund smell of the thick vegetation growing all around reminded her of her childhood. She'd grown up in eastern Tennessee, in the small town of Whiterock.

Not that this was the kind of homecoming she'd expected.

The scrape of a shovel let her know the man who'd attacked her was still close. So close she dared not move or even whimper.

After a few turns of his spade, his breathing grew labored, and she heard him grunt every so often.

*Scrape...plop. Scrape...plop.* The digging obviously wasn't easy, but it was rhythmic enough to tell her it was progressing. Although he wasn't particularly tall, he was strong; she knew that already. Even after she'd managed to get free of the rope that had bound her wrists, she hadn't been able to fend him off. Her determination to fight had only made him angrier, more violent. She was sure he would've killed her if she hadn't gone limp.

She gingerly explored her top lip. It was split, but that

was probably the least of her injuries. Unless she angled her head just right, blood rolled down her throat, choking her. She could barely open one of her eyes. And his fierce blows to her head had left her dazed, unable to think coherently. On some level, she knew she needed to get up and run now that he'd turned his attention elsewhere. But she couldn't stand, let alone make a dash for freedom. It was painful just to *breathe.*

The promise of complete darkness and total silence hovered at the edge of her consciousness. She longed to embrace it, to drift away and leave her broken body behind. But her best friend seemed to be standing at her shoulder, shouting: *Get up, damn you! Don't allow this, Sher. Gain the upper hand no matter what you have to do. Fight for your life!* For a moment, Sheridan even wondered if she was sitting in one of Skye's self-defense classes back at the victims' charity they'd started five years ago.

But then she felt the rain, lightly sprinkling her parted lips, forehead, eyelashes. She was in the forest in the middle of the night, alone with a man wearing a ski mask.

And he was digging her grave.

## SAVE $1.00

# A riveting trilogy from
# BRENDA NOVAK

# SAVE $1.00

## on the purchase price of one book in The Last Stand trilogy from Brenda Novak.

Offer valid from May 27, 2008, to August 30, 2008.
Redeemable at participating retail outlets. Limit one coupon per purchase.

52608328

5 65373 00076 2  (8100) 0 11499

® and TM are trademarks owned and used by the trademark owner and/or its licensee.
© 2008 Harlequin Enterprises Limited

MBNTRI08CPN

# REQUEST YOUR FREE BOOKS!

## 2 FREE NOVELS FROM THE ROMANCE/SUSPENSE COLLECTION PLUS 2 FREE GIFTS!

BOB08R

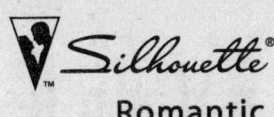

## Romantic SUSPENSE

**Sparked by Danger, Fueled by Passion.**

### Conard County: The Next Generation

When he learns the truth about his father, military man Ethan Parish is determined to reunite with his long-lost family in Wyoming. On his way into town, he clashes with policewoman Connie Halloran, whose captivating beauty entices him. When Connie's daughter is threatened, Ethan must use his military skills to keep her safe. Together they race against time to find the little girl and confront the dangers inherent in family secrets.

### Look for

# A Soldier's Homecoming

by *New York Times* bestselling author

# Rachel Lee

*Available in July wherever you buy books.*

# brenda novak

| | | |
|---|---|---|
| 32439 DEAD RIGHT | ___ $6.99 U.S. | ___ $8.50 CAN. |
| 34279 DEAD GIVEAWAY | ___ $6.99 U.S. | ___ $8.50 CAN. |
| 32328 DEAD SILENCE | ___ $6.99 U.S. | ___ $8.50 CAN. |

*(limited quantities available)*

| | |
|---|---|
| TOTAL AMOUNT | $ _____ |
| POSTAGE & HANDLING | $ _____ |
| ($1.00 FOR 1 BOOK, 50¢ for each additional) | |
| APPLICABLE TAXES* | $ _____ |
| TOTAL PAYABLE | $ _____ |

*(check or money order—please do not send cash)*

To order, complete this form and send it, along with a check or money order for the total above, payable to MIRA Books, to: **In the U.S.:** 3010 Walden Avenue, P.O. Box 9077, Buffalo, NY 14269-9077; **In Canada:** P.O. Box 636, Fort Erie, Ontario, L2A 5X3.

Name: _____
Address: _____ City: _____
State/Prov.: _____ Zip/Postal Code: _____
Account Number (if applicable): _____

075 CSAS

*New York residents remit applicable sales taxes.
*Canadian residents remit applicable GST and provincial taxes.